Leaving the Dead

A Collection of Eighteen Stories

Books by Dennis Danvers

Circuit of Heaven *series*
Circuit of Heaven
End of Days

Novels
Leaving the Dead
The Fourth World
Time and Time Again
The Perfect Stranger
The Soothsayer & The Changeling
The Watch
Wilderness
Bad Angels
The Bright Spot (writing as Robert Sydney)

For more information
visit: www.SpeakingVolumes.us

Leaving the Dead

A Collection of Eighteen Stories

Dennis Danvers

SPEAKING VOLUMES, LLC
NAPLES, FLORIDA
2023

Leaving the Dead
A Collection of Eighteen Stories

ISBN 978-1-64540-943-4

For John and Rick

Acknowledgments

I have been blessed with wonderful editors. I would like to thank Shawna McCarthy, John Joseph Adams, Jason Sizemore, Gavin Grant, John Klima, Ellen Datlow, Melanie Lemaga, and Martha Erwin who helped make these stories better.

If it be now, ’tis not to come. If it be not to come, it will be now.
If it be not now, yet it will come—the readiness is all.
—Shakespeare, *Hamlet*

Table of Contents

Here's What I Know

Here's what I know: When Mom discovered she was pregnant with me, my parents had been separated for some time. Dad had left her for another woman in another town, and Mom had filed for divorce. I was conceived during a short-lived Christmas reunion. Dad wanted her to get an abortion. She refused. On the eve of the date when the divorce would've become final, Dad caught a train back to New York where Mom was living with my brother (four at the time) and begged her to take him back. She did. I was born September 2nd. Dad was at the hospital, 5:30 in the morning. They were married for the rest of their lives, both dying at seventy-two, a year apart. Dad first.

You have to understand this story wasn't handed to me as a coherent narrative early in life like the time they met as kids or their first date with Aunt Eleanor in tow. I learned about the abortion thing when I was thirteen because they'd argue about it when they got nasty drunk and into dredging up old fights. Since I obviously survived this abortion, lying in bed hearing them argue about it, I could only get but so upset. It was never clear why I might've been aborted. I didn't know the story until years later.

The other woman, separation-while-pregnant, and near-divorce details came from Mom over pie and coffee at Denny's while Dad underwent a series of tests at the hospital next door. Dad had just been diagnosed with Alzheimer's at sixty-two, and I was separated from my second wife, so Mom thought this was a good time to bring me up to speed. I already knew Dad cheated on her, had known for years, and Mom knew I knew, but that's another story. I always thought of this as Mom's Story: Pregnant with me, waiting on a divorce, that son of a bitch knocking at the door again, wondering "Is this going to be like Christmas?"

Once my parents were gone, all this information didn't have to matter anymore. I'd narrated it for two or three counselors over the years—processed it or whatever you call it now. I figure any adult who merely had their abortion discussed in their fetal presence probably has more important things to worry about, since the decision went their way, and they've had years to get over it. I don't feel scarred. Or maybe, at fifty-nine, scarred is what I know.

But then Dad starts showing up, and suddenly it's all supposed to matter again.

He's gotten his memory back, ever since his life flashed before his eyes, and he's been sorting through the pieces, putting things together, and feeling pretty ashamed. He's had time to think, he says.

"Dad, you died twenty-three years ago."

"Has it been that long? Hmmm. It's taken me a while to find you. I wanted to tell you I'm sorry." We're standing in the musty mystery aisle in a used book store where I have more credit than I'll ever use in my lifetime. I was trying to remember the name of an author I'd been on a panel with only a few months before and coming up with nothing, not even an initial, when there's Dad, saying he's sorry.

"For what? You've got nothing to be sorry to me about. You were great. No complaints. Life's hard, and you did the best you could."

"You really believe that?"

"Heck yeah."

He looks stunned. Otherwise, he looks like I remember him before the Alzheimer's. He looks a lot like me, only shorter, a scragglier beard. We could be brothers. He laughs. He's got a nice, warm laugh. "Well, thanks. I didn't think that was gonna go this good. You want to have some coffee or something?"

"Dad, you're dead."

"I know. I like going through the motions. This place around the corner has the cutest waitresses you ever saw."

Here's the weirdest thing. When we're together, other people can see him, talk to him, whatever. They just don't remember him the next day, the next minute, far as I can tell. He orders pie and coffee, flirts with the waitress who keeps filling both our cups. When the check comes, it's for one pie, one coffee, and it's like he was never there. He shows up while I'm walking my dog, and my neighbor shows up with her dog, and we talk, my Dad charming as usual. If Dad had asked her out, she would've gone. As far as she's concerned, it never happened. "I enjoyed our talk yesterday," she says when I see her again. All I did was say, "Judy this is Bob; Bob this is Judy."

This makes it easy at first. We can say anything we want, and nobody cares because nobody remembers. But now he's showing up all the time. Dad never went to a counselor, never processed all this stuff he's been thinking about since he died—events he couldn't have made heads or tails of when he was alive. Before he died he couldn't remember the days of the week, much less the story of his life. Now he remembers it all and has only me to talk to. It's not like I can refer him to a professional counselor. He says he can only really talk to someone he had a close connection with in life. Otherwise they won't remember. I could make an appointment for myself and bring him along, but the counselor wouldn't remember him from one session to the next. Besides, I can't afford it, and Dad doesn't have any money. He can't *do* anything—make a phone call, drive a car. He can only listen in, ride along. And talk, and talk, and talk.

It doesn't take him long to get to his buried life. "There's something I've never told you," he says and proceeds to tell the story Mom told me years ago in Denny's. I let him tell the whole thing. I'm impressed their versions don't depart from each other in any significant detail except it's a little more obvious he was crazy in love with this other woman.

"Mom told me."

"You're fucking kidding me. She told me she wouldn't."

"She thought it might help me sort out things with Rachel. We were split up at the time."

"Well did it?"

"It didn't hurt. Mom was trying anyway."

"Yeah. I guess so. Was she still mad about it?"

"You mean back then? No. You were in the hospital. You'd been married most of your lives. To her that was the whole point of the story—not to give up on a marriage. She was glad she forgave you."

"You believe her?"

"Dad. Course I believe her."

"There's a part of the story she doesn't know."

"Still?"

"I haven't talked to her. I can't find her. The dead don't talk. But I read something in the library—in Dallas, when I thought you might still be there. It was Kitty's obituary. She was the woman I left your mother for. She was an actress, a singer. We worked together in advertising doing serial script shows, *Backstage Wife* and *John's Other Wife* mostly. Some Stella Dallas. She spoke the lines I wrote, sang the jingles for the products."

"I thought you wrote advertising."

"There was no difference back then. I was part of a stable who ghosted for the agency shows."

Ghosted. "All of this was in the obituary?"

"No. I'm just telling you."

"Maybe you're telling me more than I want to know."

"Maybe I'm not. The obituary said she's survived by a daughter, Maureen Powell, living in Philadelphia."

"So?"

"Kitty was pregnant too. Maureen's the right age—your age. I think she's your half-sister."

"Jesus, Dad. You got two women pregnant? What the hell were you thinking?"

"I wasn't thinking, obviously. I told you I was a fuckup."

"I knew that already. I just didn't know the extent of the damage. So why are you telling me this now?"

"I want you to help me find her."

"Her. Maureen Powell?"

"That's right."

"That's all you've got? Maureen Powell in Philadelphia? When did this Kitty die?"

"1991."

"Dad, that's fifteen years ago. What's Kitty's last name?"

"Beaumont."

"You're kidding. That was really her name? Kitty Beaumont?"

"She had it legally changed. I told you. She was an actress."

"I know. A jingle singer. Why in hell do you want to find Maureen Powell?"

"I want to introduce myself. She has a right to meet her father."

"Dad, death has made you stupid. She's come this far not knowing. Trust me. She doesn't want this information at fifty-nine."

He sulks. It's funny to think of my dad as a big boy, but that's what he was. Now he's a big dead boy. "Maybe you can understand that I'd like to make things up to her, for never once being there for her."

"How are you going to do that, Dad? You're dead." I hate to keep reminding him, but obviously somebody has to.

He looks off in the distance, a gesture I remember, like he was looking down a long, lonesome road where he kept some secret knowledge hidden. In the space of that look, he'd go down that road and back—then tell you the incredible thing he found. "Maybe I shouldn't tell you this, but I know where some stuff is that could make her some real money."

"Like what, Dad?" I don't hide my skepticism. Mom and Dad had been broke for years before they died. Surely, if they'd had anything of value, they would've cashed it in long before the Alzheimer's set in.

"Like some old records her mother and I cut with friends after-hours playing around. Dirty versions of popular jingles, stuff like that. There were some big stars there that night. Don Ameche for one. I saw on eBay something like that sold for thousands of dollars, and that's not even the most valuable stuff."

"eBay? You get on eBay?"

"I spend a lot of time in libraries. It's up there on the screens. You have to be patient. That's how I found you. I saw your books on the shelf, waited until someone took one down and looked at the back flap. It said you lived in Richmond, Virginia. I went to the airport and caught a flight. When I came across that old book store, I knew you'd come in there sooner or later. Anyway. I know where those records are and a bunch of other stuff, and I can tell Maureen, and she can sell it. Her mother's on the records. It's only right. She might want to keep them, I guess. Sentimental value. C'mon, Den, just help me do this one thing."

He used to call me Den when I was a kid. "No. I'm not doing it. It's crazy."

"I'll do all the talking."

"She won't even remember it when it's over."

"Maybe she will. Maybe she's thought long and hard about who I am her whole life long."

"Maybe she hasn't. Maybe she won't."

"Then what's the harm?"

Have I mentioned that after his advertising days Dad was a salesman most of his life? Pharmaceuticals. He'll wear me down if I let him. I change the subject. There's something I've been wanting to ask him. "Remember that time in New Orleans when Mom went shopping with Jeanette, and you were supposed to be looking after me, but you stuck me in a movie downtown? I was about ten. What were you doing?"

He doesn't hesitate. "Screwing a woman."

"Jesus, Dad. What was her name? We going to look her up next? Maybe her grandkids?"

"I don't remember her name. She didn't mean anything to me."

"Enough to dump me downtown."

"Yeah. She was something. She was a nurse. She reminded me of Kitty. Diane. Her name was Diane. Look, I'm sorry. I was a terrible father. I said. You're the one saying I've got nothing to be sorry for."

"Would you stop with that? It worked out. You shouldn't have done it, but that was a big day for me. I knew something was up, that you were doing something wrong—no idea what—and you needed me to play along. It gave me a thrill, made me feel like I'd reached some new level of adulthood. Then when I came out of the theatre, and you were late, and I was on the streets of downtown New Orleans by myself, ten years old, it did something for me, made me stronger somehow. Braver. By the time you finally showed up, I'd figured out in my head how to walk back to the hotel if I had to. I never forgot that, growing up a weird loner kid. No matter where I was, what I got myself into, I figured I could always find my way back to the hotel."

"So will you help me find Maureen?"

"We'll see," I say knowing in my family "we'll see" meant yes, because I could always wear Dad down. "We'll see" was the first sign of surrender. Mom might say absolutely not, but Dad never could say no for long, and neither can I.

When I give in we're arguing in the basement, and we get pretty loud, until I finally agree to go to Philadelphia, and he leaves out the barred back door. Sally comes down the stairs. "Who were you talking to?"

"Just trying out some dialogue." I don't want to go into it. I'm afraid she'll worry. I try out dialogue all the time—two stories above our heads in my office on the second floor, behind not one, but two closed doors.

She glances around the chaos of our basement. She doesn't ask what kind of story I'm working on that has me talking to boxes of videos rescued from the Gastón flood. "Have— Have you been feeling okay lately? You've been acting kind of strange, distant."

There's nothing for it. She's worried already. I don't like to keep anything from her. "My father's been haunting me," I say. Then I tell her the whole story.

"So you're going to Philadelphia to find your half-sister?" she asks when I'm done. By this time we're out in the daylight and have walked twice around the track.

"That's the plan. There's a convention there coming up. I can write it off."

She smiles. "It will do you good to get away."

"You always say that."

"It's always true. Can I meet him sometime?"

"Dad? Sure. Next time he shows up."

Sure enough, he shows up that night for dinner. Fortunately I've made plenty. I've never seen the woman who didn't enjoy meeting my dad. They might not think so much of him later on, but meeting him always goes well, and Sally is no exception. He gets her to telling travel stories from her days trekking though Africa in her twenties, and we go through every bottle of wine in the house. Dad's in a great mood. He can't get enough of the gorillas. He praises my cooking, which pleases me no end. He was the one who first taught me to cook. After he leaves, Sally and I make love on the sofa and sleep there.

"What got into us last night?" she asks over our morning oatmeal.

"Dad came for dinner, stayed all evening."

"I don't remember a thing. Except.... Did I tell all my Africa stories?"

"That's right."

"That wasn't just to you?"

"I've heard them all before."

She smiles. "Well tell him he's welcome anytime."

As I'm washing the crusty plates left sitting out all night, I find myself wishing there was one for him. I piled a plate high. I watched him eating, watched him slip a couple of bites to the dog who stuck by him all evening. But there are only two plates to wash.

Dad prefers to take the train to Philadelphia instead of the plane even though he used to love to fly. "I still like meeting all the stewardesses," he says. "But lots of times there's no place to sit except the toilet, and since this 9/11 thing nobody wants some dead guy standing around who's not on their little list. They keep forgetting about me, but that just makes them even more nervous. There are always seats on the train."

"They're called flight attendants these days, Dad. Not stewardesses."

"Is that right? Okay. They always have their names pinned to their chest. I usually call them by their first names. They don't seem to mind. Interesting women, stewardesses. Some of them are small town girls who've been all over the world. I remember this one—"

"Dad, we're taking the train."

We take the train, but that doesn't stop him from talking about stewardesses—excuse me, flight attendants—all the way to Philadelphia, navigating the station, waiting for a cab. When we get to the hotel—so Dad can finish the story of a Delta flight attendant named Juanita—the cabbie waits with the meter off while other cabs stack up behind us. Too bad he's going to forget the unforgettable tale as soon as he drives away.

"Do you remember Braniff Airlines?" Dad asks me as we're waiting in front of the elevator. By the time we get off on twelve everybody in that elevator must be thinking they'll never forget them. Unfortunately, I'm the only one in that boat—in that pressurized cabin at 30,000 feet with Dad and a Braniff stewardess in the galley with a bottle of champagne unzipping her pink boots. Once in the room, I jump into the shower before he can remember another airline, another route, another town, another stewardess, another woman.

When I get out of the shower, Dad's looking out the window. "What do you do when I'm not around?" I ask him.

"Nothing. I was just thinking. You remember that tape we made of jokes the first summer in Houston before I got fired?"

When Dad was transferred as part of a merger reshuffle he came into brief possession of a reel-to-reel tape recorder he was supposed to record weekly reports on. As far as I know, he never used it for that. Though over the space of a couple of weeks, night after night, we recorded all the jokes we knew on it, taking turns back and forth. I soon ran out. Dad knew tons of them, so he taught some to me and let me record them. He thought I did voices and characters well, so he taught me every character joke he knew—Chinese, Mexican, Italian—but I never could do Russians or Germans. I found them too intimidating. When Mark Russell came to a local nightclub, Mom and Dad took me, and I stole a

Chinaman joke from him that got me five star reviews even from Mom who usually just laughed and said, "You two are just awful." I don't think Mark Russell does Chinaman jokes anymore. Neither do I.

"Yeah, I remember it. How'd that get started anyway?"

He smiles to himself. "I'd just gotten off the phone with Bill, and the rumors were flying. They were going to can me for sure. They were just looking for an excuse. I knew I wasn't going to have that fucking tape recorder for very long. So I decided to have some fun with it."

"It was a good time, Dad."

"When I returned the recorder, I left that tape on it. Said it was my final report."

I laugh out loud, imagining all those farmer's daughters and bears who walked into bars telling Dad's old boss to fuck himself, and Dad beams. I've surprised him again. Am I really so different from who I used to be?

Jeez. Look at the time, and I haven't even registered yet. I have to get going. I fill him in as I'm getting dressed. "I've got a couple of panels this afternoon, then a reading later. I'll pop into the dealers' room some time in there, and come back up here around six. We can go out to eat, work out a plan for finding Maureen Powell. I'm not scheduled for anything tomorrow."

"Can I come along?" He stands up, looking pathetic, like my dog angling for a walk. *What do you do when I'm not around? Nothing.*

I start to tell him he doesn't have a badge, but I know that's not going to make any difference. The conductor didn't care if he had a ticket. He goes to the movies with me without one. Anywhere I go, he can come along, apparently, if I want him to. I'm not so sure I want him along for this sort of thing. I'm nervous enough anyway. "You'll be bored. It's just a bunch of writers and fans talking about fantasy and science fiction. You never read that stuff, did you?"

"*Topper*. *Lost Horizon*. Edgar Rice Burroughs. *1001 Arabian Nights*. H. G. Wells."

"Okay." I hold up my hands in surrender, just like Dad used to do to me.

"Besides, I've never heard you read one of your stories." He gives me a crooked smile. Of course he wants to go. He's my dad.

I was unpublished when Dad died, though he read everything I wrote when I was thirteen, not much since then, since I'd sought out what I thought were more discriminating readers. The story I plan to read is all about him. It isn't altogether flattering. I look out the window too. It's a long way down. "Sure, why not?"

I like conventions, though I'm too shy to ever feel completely at ease with the social side of them. Having an alcoholic father has made me a fairly moderate drinker, and my typical schedule is to rise at four in the morning and sleep at ten or eleven at night. Not a partier's hours.

Dad, however, takes to the convention like a duck to the flock. Wherever we go, he strikes up a conversation with someone who, charmed by his innocent enthusiasm, explains what a "mundane" is, cautions him not to say "sci-fi," or places the whole trekkie thing in its broader science-fictional context for him. This last proves no easy task and leads us into the bar. Dad's *Star Trek*—seen in syndication and processed by the Cuisinart of his Alzheimer's—isn't the same as everyone else's. The way he remembers it, the tribbles were in every single episode. Whenever the bridge would tilt back and forth, he claims, tribbles would roll this way and that with the rest of the lurching crew. In his *Star Trek*, Dr. McCoy—prone to paranoid Luddite rants and emotional outbursts—was clearly into the drug cabinet bigtime. As a representative of a pharmaceutical company, he'd seen it happen to lots of doctors over the years. By the time Dad's spinning his theory of Dr. McCoy, Space Junkie, there's a donut of people around us five deep, and someone buys us another drink.

I don't remember the panels that well except I talk more than usual, and when someone asks if I would call my work "interstitial," I say I prefer to think of it as intestinal. Dad laughs, and then everybody does, though it turns out Dad didn't get the joke. "I thought you needed some help back there," he says. "Was I right?"

He was right.

In the dealer's room, I turn my back on him for a second to talk to a reader nice enough to introduce himself, and when I turn back around Dad's admiring a woman's boots, the woman as well, of course, and they turn out to be Elizabeth Hand's boots, and I feel like a tribble caught in the headlights. She's flanked by science fiction and fantasy luminaries whose names suddenly escape me, but who've all been on the cover of *Locus*. "Liz says there's a party later, Den, a couple of parties. What do you say?"

Inarticulate strangling noises? I'm not sure. Everyone seems to accept it as yes. Dad goes on to pitch my reading, quoting and misquoting from some of the book jackets he had a chance to study for so long in the Dallas Public Library.

We stumble in a herd to the bar where I have another drink I don't need and Dad works the crowd, enlisting more recruits for my reading. We ooze into the tiny corner room where my reading is scheduled, packed to overflowing. Dad's sitting up front with Liz and Jeff Ford and Robert Louis Stevenson and Marie de France. There are tribbles spilling out of the podium. McCoy's in an aisle seat, rolling up his sleeve, mainlining di-lithium crystal meth. My hands are trembling.

"Here's what I know," I begin, and then it goes pretty well. When it's over, I shake a few hands Dad's rounded up for me to shake, and we're planning to stay in the room to hear Jeff Ford read next, when I step out for a moment to catch my breath and notice a woman sitting off in a corner of the bar. The semicircular chair surrounds her like a shell. A suspended light, a flat black cone, hovers above her. I can just make out her name tag. Maureen Powell.

She looks a lot like me. She looks a lot like Dad. Her hair's white like mine. I slip through the crowd. It's significantly quieter standing in front of Maureen's chair. She looks up from her program, and I introduce myself and take the chair across from her. Most of the crowd heads into the reading room, and it grows quieter still. We can hear the clink of glassware as the waitress cleans up after.

"I'm not familiar with your work," Maureen says.

"Nor I yours," I say. "You live in Philadelphia?"

"I used to. I moved out west almost fifteen years ago now, after my mother died. I was ready for a change."

"Was your mother's name Kitty Beaumont?"

She starts. "How do you know that?"

"My father told me."

"Did he know her?"

"Yes. They were once lovers. He thinks he might've been your father. Is that possible?"

She holds out a hand, and at first I think she means to cover my mouth to silence me, but she sights along her arm, trying to block out the distraction of my white beard, trying to get past the Santa thing to study my nose and my eyes. "You could be my brother," she says.

I can hear Jeff Ford reading in the corner room, saying, "Back in the Autumn of '57…" then someone inside pulls the door shut with a thud, and it's so quiet you can hear the piped in soft jazz lurking overhead. "Listen. Would you like to meet him?"

"Your father?"

"Our father."

"Is he here?"

"He's in the reading that just started. Can I buy you a drink? You can meet him when he comes out."

"All right. Scotch and water."

I order two Scotch and waters. "Tell me about your mother," I say. "Tell me about Kitty Beaumont."

She tells her mother's story with the first sentence she speaks. The rest is just details. "She told me my father was the love of her life, that he swept her off her feet and ran away with her, only to go back to his wife, and she never got over it." Maureen laughs. I imagine it's how Kitty might've laughed, a childlike cynical laugh. "I always thought it was a convenient story to justify never settling down, never being satisfied."

Kitty was a chronically struggling radio actress whose career peaked with a brief stint as a contentious in-law on a short-lived TV soap. She was married five times. Maureen was her only child. She shows me pictures of her stepfathers the way some women show pictures of their kids. "This one's Tom, Mom's second husband. He adopted me. That's where I get the name Powell." She herself has never married.

"I started writing science fiction," she says, sipping at her second Scotch, "because I thought we might be aliens. What about you?"

I glance at my watch. The reading's almost over. "There's something I have to tell you about Dad before he comes out. He's been dead for twenty-three years. It's his ghost you'll be talking to."

"You do horror?"

"No. Not really. I'm just trying to tell you. Before you meet him. He's dead." I sip my Scotch.

"Hmm." Her eyes meet mine. We're holding our glasses the same way, looking over our Scotches the same way, probably both of us quit smoking ten years ago, but a cigarette sounds awful good right about now.

The door in the corner flies open, and the room begins to empty out. Dad finds me right away. "That was terrific," he says.

But already his eyes are on Maureen, and hers on him.

"So you're my father," she says, and any introduction I had in mind becomes irrelevant.

"Yes. I'm so sorry—"

"Not here," she says. "Can we go someplace else?"

"Do you have a car?" he asks.

Before you know it, we're driving out of Philly into the New Jersey countryside. I'm at the wheel, following Dad's directions, so he and Maureen can talk in the backseat. She knows a lot more about the radio world than I ever did, and they talk about people I never heard of from the shows Dad and Kitty worked on together. Kitty, apparently, kept all the radio friends.

"Okay," I finally say. "Where are we going?" The sprawl has given way to countryside dotted with abandoned farms, every other one for sale. The moon is high and bright.

"It's not much farther," Dad says. He tells Maureen what he told me before about the bootleg after-hour recordings and other stuff, and how he wants her to have it. "That's where we're going now," he says. "I found it."

"What other stuff?" Maureen asks.

"There's a box of premiums, practically every one we ever offered. Mint condition."

"Holy shit," Maureen says.

"What are premiums?" I ask.

"Little toys and things for kids mostly," Dad says. "When a character's about to go on a big trek, you offer the Hike-o-Meter, a jazzed up compass for a boxtop and a dime. Membership cards. Magic rings. Kids loved it. Advertisers loved it."

"Highly collectible," Maureen adds. "Where is this stuff?"

Dad points down the long, lonesome road. "There's a driveway a couple miles on the right. Big red mailbox. Can't miss it."

"Wait a minute. What is this place?" I ask.

"You remember Jake?"

Jake helped Mom and Dad move out of the house when they lost it a few years after Dad lost his job and before he got Alzheimer's, offering the loan of his big truck, loading it up to the top, then driving off with two-thirds of their possessions never to be seen again. *That* Jake, Dad? "Yeah, I remember him."

Dad tells Maureen the story. "This is his place. He's laid up in a home in Newark about to kick off. When he goes, his heirs will get all this stuff. Till then this is an abandoned farm full of stolen property."

"How do you know this?" I ask.

"I spotted him, still working the same scam, rode out here with him with a load. Sure enough. He steals more than he can get rid of, never throws anything away. He didn't know what he had. He never thought twice about a bunch of whistles and plastic rings that glow in the dark."

I pull into the driveway, roll a hundred yards and stop. The place is completely dead.

"And you're giving all this stuff to me?" Maureen asks.

"All except one thing. I want to keep that back. Everything else."

"What?" She's the one who says it, but we're both asking.

"Doesn't matter. It's just one thing."

"All right," she says. Let the old ghost have his secrets. "There's a flashlight in the glove box."

"Wait a minute," I say.

"You want a cut?" she asks.

"No. Should we even be doing this?"

"I don't see the problem. The stuff was stolen. He's asking us to get it back so he can give it to me. You don't think he owes me? He abandoned my mother. You had a father, and I didn't. You going to help or not?"

Dad doesn't say anything, but it's obvious he sees things pretty much the same way Maureen does. "Okay. What do we have to do?"

"There's an old shed where the stuff is," Dad says. "We just have to pry a few rotten boards loose. You two can do it with your bare hands I bet." And that's what we do, loading the stuff into Maureen's trunk, except for the one thing. It's in a little flat box. "Give it to Den," he says. "I can't keep anything."

"I don't want it," I say.

"You don't even know what it is."

Maureen opens the box. Inside is a diary like they used to sell in dime stores. Only this one says *Pearl's Diary* across the front in fancy script. "Give me that," I say.

Maureen is fiddling with the lock and key. "Hold on."

"Pearl was my mother's name."

She freezes. "Oh," she says and hands it over.

"What the hell is this, Dad?" I ask.

"It was going to be part of a new show. The premiums worked so great with the kids, somebody thought, why not their moms? The show was this woman's diary, you know? A good-hearted woman married to a faithless man. The idea was we'd get the thing started, then you'd send in and get one of these diaries and write in it like you were the character in the show, and then we'd pick the best ones to put on the air. I think the idea was to try to do a show without writers. They already didn't pay us much of anything or give us a credit."

"Who was going to play Pearl?"

"Kitty."

"When was it on?"

"It never got on the air. That's the diary I pitched it with. Wrote the first couple of episodes in it and passed it around."

"You mean?"

"Yeah."

I open it up, and read out loud: Dear Diary, I got the news today from Dr. B. My worst fears are confirmed. I'm going to have another child five months after my divorce is final. Isn't that a kick in the head? How can I tell Robert? How can I not?...

Dad's not looking at me. He's staring at the ground. It's his handwriting, but it's Mom's voice. Her life.

"Didn't they go for it?"

"What are you talking about? They loved it. They went crazy for it. I couldn't do it. After I wrote it all down..." He gestures at the diary. "I just couldn't do it."

"What do you want me to do with it?"

"Keep it. Throw it away. I just couldn't see it being sold on eBay. It's yours."

Maureen's looking off, brushing tears from her eyes. She snuffles and blows her nose. "It's probably not worth anything anyway. If there was never a show."

By the time we get back to the hotel, most of the parties are winding down, but Dad finds the one where everyone still partying has ended up. We have to squeeze through a stand of tall well-watered men planted just inside the door angrily discussing the stupidity of recent award decisions and the judges who made them. There's not so much as a sofa arm to sit on, and my back is aching from the drive. My mind is in my coat pocket, in the pages of *Pearl's Diary*. I want to beg off, but Dad's determined we make an appearance.

Maureen heads toward the remains of a cake. The liquor is decimated, but it's late enough that pretending to be drunk will get me by. We hang in the kitchen where Dad gets into a discussion of faster than light travel that's going nowhere fast. I lean on the counter only to lean on *Pearl's Diary*. I take it out of my pocket to make sure I haven't damaged it. The thing's older than I am. I look inside. Every page is filled. He kept writing her life as a serial. *Dear Diary*, the last entry begins, *Robert's life is slipping away from him, slipping away from me, and I'm afraid...*

A young woman on the edge of the FLT discussion spots me reading. "What's that?"

I start to tell her. My characters are always telling all to each other. It makes sense to me. I've lived with too many secrets. But not this time. "It's just a notebook," I say and slip it back into my pocket.

"Hey, aren't you Dennis Danvers?" she says. "I was at your reading earlier about your dead father? How did it end anyway?"

"It didn't. He's still dead."

She laughs, thinking I'm joking.

I tap Dad on the shoulder. "Dad, you about ready to go?"

"Sure, son. I guess you've had quite a day."

We say good-bye to Maureen at the cake, push our way through the still-angry men now spinning elaborate theories of collusion and corruption and inside deals. "Those guys all writers?" Dad asks me.

"Definitely. Big names."

"Helluva business." He looks me in the eye, his face serious. I remember this look too, when he was handing out advice, much rarer than secrets, visions, and schemes. "Don't sell yourself," he says. At first I think he means sell yourself short, but that's not what he said. The elevator opens, and we step inside. "I got a new one for you," he says.

I bite.

"There's this dead guy see, hanging out in this old bookstore, when who should walk in but his very own son." He laughs. "Gotcha."

"You sure did."

I hold him, a frail, dead old man until the elevator doors open on our floor, and he says, "I guess I'll be going now."

"Where?" I panic. I don't want him to leave me again. I know I was just complaining about him showing up all the time, but that doesn't mean I want him gone.

"I'm going to look for your mother."

"I thought you already tried that. I thought the dead don't talk."

He looks down that long, lonesome road and nods his head—true, all true. Everything's true down that road. "Maybe I didn't try hard enough. I couldn't really face her before."

"Because of *Pearl's Diary*?"

He nods again. There are tears in his eyes.

"Good luck, Dad. I hope you find her. Will I forget you now?"

"No." He points to the book in my hands. "I'm on every page."

He watches me walk the long hall to my room. I don't look back. I go inside and wait until I hear the elevator going down, then lie with the pages of my mother's life, and read.

Leaving the Dead

Darwin thought he might be more alive than other people. Not a whole lot, but ever increasingly, until finally, in a checkout line at Target, he was the last person left alive but his checker. Gabriella, her nametag said, and she was drifting off.

Good for her he was the sort of person who reads nametags. Good for them both.

"Gabriella!" he shouted, and she opened her eyes, blinking.

"Nobody calls me that except my mother," she said.

He couldn't decide whether that was good or bad. "It says on your nametag," he said, pointing.

She took it off.

You forget you have it on, that you're labeled like everything else in the store, as if the red outfit's not enough. Team Member. That's what they called you, expected you to call yourself. She used to like wearing red. She liked that her nametag said something nobody ever really called her anymore, like some other person was on the job. "My supervisor made the nametag. She can call me whatever she wants." She said it like she might call the supervisor a thing or two, but she never would. Sweet child, her mother used to say. She scanned: Peppermint Patty. White socks. A Kindle, the cheapest. Seeds (flowers). He was a frail, pale little flower himself. Like a pot of grandma's pansies.

"Is that your supervisor over there?" Darwin detected some vague sense of rank in the woman's red garb, though the point was moot. Her hair swept up; everything else drooped. "She's dead," Darwin said, swiping his card, signing the screen with a plastic nub. Dotting the i felt particularly foolish, plastic kissing plastic, leaving a deep blue craggy dot. His illegible signature was approved and vanished, and he was thanked. Who did that? he wondered. It must be automatic. His credit was perfect. He paid everything off. Except for the student loan payments. They would never end.

Gaby (as everyone but Mom called her) squinted at Karin, her supervisor. Man was right. Still standing somehow on her tree-trunk legs, but dead as a mackerel. Gaby had never seen a mackerel to know one, but

Mom had used the expression whenever something dead came up. Mom was her authority on death. She looked around. "Everybody's dead."

"That's why I shouted at you. You were dropping off."

She didn't remember any shout. Barely audible in her family. One reason she never did. Shout. Whisper quiet was her motto. Her nickname was ironic. Her third grade teacher told her that. Like most of us, Gaby hadn't changed much since third grade. "Off. You mean dead. Dropping dead."

"Yeah, I guess. Everyone else did."

"What's going on?"

He was thoughtful. Darwin fell into thoughtful like some cats purr, just waiting for your touch. His favorite verb was *mull.* "I don't know. It just seemed to happen gradually. You know? Everyone dying a little bit every day. It kind of crept up on me. Then I looked around…" He gestured at all the dead. Some had fallen facedown into their carts. Others were still reaching out for the bottom shelf. Most had dropped where they stood. Dropped phones were dropping calls everywhere. They were dead too. Personal devices without a person.

The store kept going. The AC roared. The music played. The ads too. It was all automatic. The dead were told to expect more and pay less, then another song played. Gaby didn't mind the songs, but the happy yappy woman who did the ads totally got on her nerves. Maybe it was mass hypnosis. The wrong chirp fracked all these people's brains.

"Have you checked outside?" Gaby asked. She shut off the light showing she was open, stepped out of the stall. Normally, she could get in big trouble for that. Things obviously weren't normal.

"I'm sure it's the same out there. I was just over at Barnes & Noble, and the people weren't much more alive than the dead writers on the wall. But we should have a look-see here first, don't you think?"

Gaby figured the store was somehow her responsibility, now that everyone else was dead. That's just how she was brought up. "I'll do it," she said, thinking maybe if she left this weird little dude and walked around the store, things might be different. He could be controlling her mind. She could be insane. This could be like the Rapture, and nobody was *really* dead. She could be a spy and didn't know it. Maybe she just killed all these people and not the chirpy PA bitch after all. She'd seen all those movies and more with her brothers. She didn't know what movie this was, but anything was better than *everybody dies*. Just like that. For no reason.

Look-see. Who says look-see? That's what she was doing up and down the aisles. Look. See: Dead. Dead. Dead. Housewares. Sporting Goods. Electronics. Women's Apparel. Didn't matter. Mick Jagger was singing "Wild Horses." Still. You couldn't stop him. Somewhere, was Mick dead now? Keith? She couldn't remember whether they were still alive. There was a stroller parked in Family Shoes. Kid sitting in it seemed to be looking right at her. No. He was dead as a mackerel too. "Yeah. Let's have a look-see the fuck out of this place." She strode to the doors—*not* running—her mother's voice hollering down the long hallway to the child inside, *Gabriella! Don't you* dare *run in this house!* She burst out of that memory into daylight and stopped in her tracks.

The automatic doors whooshed closed behind her, then parted again. Darwin stood beside her. She had this weird urge to take his hand. Not a car was moving. It's not like you had to look inside each one to make sure after seeing that. Anybody stuck in this traffic jam would be screaming if they could, laying on the horn. Something. Six lanes of traffic up and down Broad Street for as far as you could see. Stopped dead. Dead inside. You could see them. The engines had all died too. No point going on, the drivers slumped, their hands slipped from the wheel—destination nowhere. It was quiet.

Darwin didn't own a car. Couldn't afford it. He'd come on the bus. He could see his return bus from here, dead at the top of the hill. There was a lovely woman's voice that told you where you were. You could hear her still singing but not quite make out the words. It was automatic. GPS, digital recordings. That sort of thing used to interest Darwin. Not so much anymore now that everyone was dead.

The traffic lights kept going through their automatic cycles. Safety first. Sure as they stopped, some of these cars would start up again, and the city would be on the hook for a major lawsuit. Darwin found the clunk of their relays reassuring. Darwin had temped in the city's Risk Management Department for a time, known among the workers as Trip and Fall. They were nice people.

"What did you mean. this *crept up on you*?" Gaby demanded.

She expressed the intensity of her feelings as quietly as ever—more quietly—whispering the last, most intense part. He found himself leaning closer to listen. She fixed him with her dark eyes. However close to death she may have been, she was fiercely alive now. In her quiet way. "It wasn't that way for you?" he asked.

She looked around. A pair of 180s. "No. This shit just happened."

"Then we have differing perspectives," Darwin said, like that was definitely a good thing, like it cheered him up somehow, like between the two of them they had this dead thing totally surrounded.

"Did you do this?" she asked.

"*Me*? Are you kidding? No. Do you think someone did it?"

"How should I know? What about the dead people? What should we do?"

Darwin was surprisingly quick with his answer. "Leave them. It won't be very pleasant around here in a few days. We can't possibly bury them all. My name's Darwin. What should I call you?" He stuck out his hand.

She knew his name. It came up on her screen when he swiped his card. Darwin Berang. What kind of name was Berang? Who names their kid Darwin? "Gabriella," Gaby said. She took his hand.

"I thought only your mother called you that."

"My mother's dead." As a mackerel. She let go of his hand.

"It's a pretty name," he said.

She wished she could say the same about his. Grandma took her to church. They pronounced it *evil-lution.* Even her biology teacher in high school got nervous when Darwin's name came up, like maybe he was a registered sex offender. Once you tell people they're nothing but animals, especially a sweaty class of 10th graders, anything might happen, right?

Even though everybody else was dead, they still had their needs, and it wasn't like anyone was going to stop them, and they'd both missed lunch. They walked across the street to the Olive Garden, trying not to look through the windshields at the dead. The glare hurt their eyes. Having needs was what set them apart from the dead under glass, piled up at the bus stop, scattered around the parking lots. At least there weren't any in the street. You'd have to be crazy to walk across this street.

They cooked themselves a nice meal in the Olive Garden kitchen after they dragged all the dead into the walk-in. There weren't that many—more employees than customers. It had been slow, mid-afternoon. The Specials didn't look very interesting. All the breadsticks were burned, the pasta gummy. There was a nice fire in the grill. They cooked steaks even though neither one of them usually ate red meat. They didn't see the harm in an occasional indulgence. They opened a bottle of Chianti. Neither one of them usually drank. Alcohol was contraindicated for someone taking Darwin's prescribed medications. Fortunately, he hadn't taken them in years, and not just because he couldn't afford them. Gaby had no prescriptions but lived with Grandma for whom anything fun was contraindicated. They clinked their glasses together, chewing and swallowing, and felt like they were in a TV ad.

"What if they turn into zombies?" Gaby asked.

"Why would they do that?" Darwin asked like maybe she had a theory about the life cycle of the dead. Darwin always liked to learn new things. He knew nothing of zombies, and his vampires were out of date.

She shrugged like she was just making conversation. She didn't like zombies. It was her brothers who were into zombies, who made her watch them on TV, then hid under her bed and reached up and grabbed her, making zombie noises in the middle of the night when Mom was at work, making her scream and giggle and wet her bed, and they had to change the sheets and wash and dry them before Mom got home. She never told.

She and Darwin were watching the TV in the dining room, making the rounds of the channels to see what they could find out about the dead. Darwin had found the remote beside the hostess. It must all be automatic, the shows and the commercials: *Two-and-a Half Men, Jeopardy, Rick Steve's Europe*. Alex Trebek wasn't dead, but he was making Christmas jokes in April. Finally, they found a live broadcast. Dead guy sat on a sofa, his new book on a table in front of him, while a dead woman was supposed to interview him. They were slumped together like they were in a huddle over the next question. Darwin thought he'd seen the book in a stack at B & N. The weather was next. It was blue. Everybody LIVE! was dead at CNN too. Darwin handed the remote over to Gaby and turned on his Kindle. It welcomed him. He was registered automatically. He shopped for the dead guy's book.

Gaby found a soccer stadium full of dead people and turned off the TV. There was music playing in the dining room, some classical music you've heard a million times she didn't know the name of. Darwin probably knew. He looked like the type who knew things. They hadn't found where to turn the music off, though they hadn't looked too hard. She thought about looking again. She wished she knew the name of this piece. She'd never know now. The first time she remembered hearing it she was watching old cartoons. Daffy Duck. She liked Daffy because he was black. He was in Italy. He had a boat. Venice. She always wanted to go there. Was it under water yet? Was everybody dead in Venice? Or had they already left and were dead somewhere else? That would suck. "Too bad about the breadsticks," she said. "I really like those. Do you have anyone?"

He hesitated. He knew what she meant. He just didn't like to admit it. It was remarkable, really. No siblings, both parents dead for some years. Largely friendless since grad school, a serial temp worker who didn't like to drink and couldn't afford to eat out, he didn't have to think long on the answer, or why it was so. He secretly never took any of the medications ever prescribed for him. He developed an interest in side effects early in life. He wondered if that's why he hadn't died—never properly socialized, he missed the moment when we were all supposed to let go. He glanced up from the Kindle. He'd just found New Releases in Literature. He supposed literature lived on no matter what—that that's what made it Literature. Something had to, besides Amazon saying it was. He pictured the New Releases like little fishes the trout hatchery dumped into the streams every year. They didn't live on. They said catch and release, but sooner or later somebody ate them. Darwin would. He loved trout. Cooked any way. Except raw. He didn't like sushi. Another reason he didn't have any friends. "No. No one," he said.

Her eyes were bright. Was that her returning life or her approaching tears or both? He didn't know. He looked away. Every time Darwin had ever encountered a crying woman, from his mother onward, it hadn't turned out well. She didn't want him getting involved. He wouldn't know what to say, what to do. He would only make it worse. Sometimes he used to look up from whatever he was doing as a kid into the glistening eyes of his parents and not know what to do. They didn't either. They found help. Lots of it.

He found the dead man's book, and though it didn't look like his sort of thing—kind of weird and offbeat and twisted—he bought it anyway.

Local author. Saw him on TV. Dead. He'd never seen a living author dead before. While he was in the Kindle Store, he downloaded all of Mrs. Gaskell for free, delivered automatically to his Kindle. That's how he justified the expenditure, all the free content. It was cheaper than a new TV. "What about you?" he asked. "Do you have anyone?"

"Me neither." Both brothers dead, Mom gone, father unknown. That left Grandma, and it was her time to go anyway after all she'd been through. Gaby couldn't feel too bad. The woman talked about Heaven her whole life long. Business must be booming there. Everybody seemed to be dead but her and Darwin. How weird was that?

Weirder? Nothing else was. Darwin was the first to notice. She thought he was just reading his Kindle, short stories he said. "Surreal," he said. She wasn't sure she remembered exactly what that meant, didn't want to look stupid asking. Then he asked her, "Have you noticed the birds?" He shut off the Kindle, pointed out the window.

She hadn't noticed, but once he mentioned it, she saw they were everywhere, not like thousands or anything, like in Hitchcock, but plenty, like usual she guessed. There weren't that many trees around here, and that made it look like more. Plenty of poles, lights, wires, and signs though. Birds looked fine. So did the squirrels. Something was making a noise in the trashcan where they'd thrown out the burnt bread sticks. She bet if she went outside and looked, there would be ants crawling around on the soda cups, or maybe with all the bodies around, they'd be crawling around on them.

She saw this movie once. Ants all over everything. Everybody. Except some beautiful redhead and a big sweaty guy who was into her somewhere in South America. After seeing that movie, Gaby and her brothers buried her Barbi with the twisted leg from the flamethrower incident in an anthill after smearing it with pancake syrup. She screamed stuff, and they laughed and laughed. That was a good time. She missed her brothers. They were twins. They had a different father than she did, but that didn't matter. They were angels to her.

A dog walked into the dining room where Gaby and Darwin had the nice big booth in the corner and looked at them peculiarly. He was a big beautiful Golden. Then they noticed his harness. He was a guide dog. So somewhere out there in the parking lot was a dead blind person who'd been headed for the Olive Garden when everybody died. Somebody must've driven them. No way they could've walked here safely from the bus. Darwin wouldn't dream of crossing Broad Street, dog or no dog. Some guy texting on his phone, steering with his knees in three lanes of traffic with a burger hanging out of his mouth doesn't care if you're blind. He's got his own navigational problems.

"Here boy," Gaby said and offered the dog a hunk of her steak. Gaby liked dogs a lot, had never lived anywhere you could have one. Especially one like this. Big as a pony. *Big as a pony* was like *dead as a mackerel*, almost. Something Mom said. Gaby had seen ponies though, sat on one. At a school fair when she was little. Her brothers were still alive then. Ty on one side of the pony, Jay on the other. This dog wasn't that big, but he was big enough, and he looked like he'd just had his hair done at the beauty shop like Grandma used to. A real pretty boy. She adored him.

"Are you sure that's a good idea?" Darwin asked when she fed the dog, but it obviously was. The dog, whose name was Elvis his collar said, camped out beside them, having decided they were his next blind responsibility. The last humans. Gaby petted and hugged his big head and told Darwin she had always wanted a dog. Elvis wagged his big tail and smiled.

He enjoys the petting, but pays close attention to everything going on around them. You think it's easy leading the blind? Harder still, people who think they can see. Elvis lets them finish their meal. He's a good boy. But they should really think about leaving. To them, they're just dead people everywhere. To others, they're food. Carrion. Not to Elvis. He's horrified at the idea. But he's a good boy. Nobody knows better than a good boy that not everybody is. You can't screw up leading a blind guy around. Eye-level with the meat counter or a dead squirrel in the road—not your concern. There's no room for error. He misses the blind man, but he can't worry about that now. He wonders if the woman will give him the bone. No begging. Elvis doesn't beg. You know why. Good boy. *Yes!* The bone. Good boys get the bone.

More wine. Coffee. Cheesecake. A little bit of lemon liqueur. Brandy. Darwin and Gabriella didn't get out much. They knew they should be moving on, but who knew when they might have the chance to go to a nice restaurant again? This one wasn't so nice when you thought about what was in the walk-in. On the other hand, they didn't want to face what was outside either. They returned to the bar, away from the windows, so they wouldn't have to look at all the dead people in the parking lot, and Elvis followed them. What was that liqueur in the tall skinny bottle? Darwin remembered his mother used to like that. He didn't usually talk about his family, meaning never, but Gabriella was a good listener. Lovely name. They'd talked so much about the dead, he hadn't found out that much about her.

Finally, Elvis stands up and barks at them. A little yip. A gentle reminder. Can't they hear what's going on outside? Smell it? Even a good boy has his limits, and the bone's already gone. Puppy bones lasted days.

They decided Elvis was right, skipped the Galliano, and went out in the parking lot. This time she did take his hand. Somehow Darwin managed to end up with his arms wrapped around her, and her face buried in his chest, which kind of forced him to take in the scene, since the top of her head was under his chin. He tried not to throw up on her head. He liked the feel of her head under his chin though. It steadied him. He didn't have much experience in the comforting department, so he rubbed his chin on the top of her head sort of like she'd done when she hugged Elvis's head. It seemed to work. Darwin felt proud.

Elvis never knew there were so many bad dogs in the world. The buzzards started it, of course, but now the dogs—you know the sort—are showing up and getting into it with the buzzards and each other. Fighting over… You don't need to know what they're fighting over. Disgusting. What's next? Coyotes? Elvis and the blind man used to live in Tucson. He was afraid to go out of the house after dark. He sits beside the man and woman and waits. This is their call.

Darwin's nice, Gaby decided in his arms, which helped her get it together. Gaby was not one to freak out for long. She grew up with zombies under her bed. They had to figure out how they were going to leave the dead and soon, as more and more dogs and buzzards kept showing up. They needed to find some wide open spaces without dead people—besides the parking lots that stretched for miles in either direction—but how to get there? Even if they could start a car, they couldn't navigate around all the rest of them. They could walk, but it would be awfully far. They were still holding onto each other as they raced through all the possibilities.

Darwin suggested bikes, and Gaby liked the idea and gave him a big hug.

They went back into the Target to pick out some bikes. Turns out they'd both had their bikes stolen just when they were getting past their sore knees and butt troubles and had started to enjoy them. They wouldn't have to worry about that anymore. The stolen part. Dead people don't steal. They were trying to look on the bright side. Listing advantages. They were both pretty drunk.

Gaby pointed out the security cameras, all automatic, and they posed and waved and decided they were looters now—something else they had in common, besides being drunk and totally surrounded by dead people. That was pretty funny, and they were both laughing by the time they picked out some extremely nice bikes for Target.

They also got some of those padded pants and gloves and baskets and panniers and food and sleeping bags and a tent and it went on and on. It was fun. They hadn't shopped much with another person, never thought of it as recreation. Gaby saw that all the time at Target. Couples showing up and just wandering up and down seeing if they felt like buying something, like they were strolling around the park. Sometimes they brought the thing they bought back still in the box, but they'd still had the afternoon shopping together, like a date, and sometimes another when they made the return. That's basically what she and Darwin were doing. She shed the red outfit and got something nice. It was easier than you might think to ignore the dead.

Gaby laughed out loud in Tents when Mick Jagger started singing "Wild Horses" *again*, and she had to explain why to Darwin so he wouldn't think she was laughing at him working up a sweat trying to put the tent on the front of his bike with bungies, and he laughed too.

Then he gave her this look like she was Barbi, and he wanted to haul her out of an anthill. Not to lick the syrup off her body—that's where her mind went—but to straighten out her twisted leg and make her forget about the ants. Gaby had soaked the Barbi's hair in Red Hots and vodka, and the ants ate her hair down to the plastic. Gaby's hair sort of looked like that, short red frizz, latest fashion mistake. Darwin didn't even seem to mind that.

They had both seen this movie.

Gaby used to sit between her twin brothers on the sofa and watch any movie that was on, and when she didn't understand it, they would both explain it to her, but they always told her two totally different things. They thought that was funny, and if she was them, older and two of them, she would've done the same thing. When she got older, they explained things they knew she understood fine just for fun, trying to outdo each other's craziness. Ty told her Helen Keller could really see and was faking it. Jay told her Captain Kirk was insane, and the Starship Enterprise never went anywhere. She missed her brothers, though Gaby felt like there was only one way to tell this story: Last man, last woman.

Darwin watched movies all day when he worked at the video store between his second degree and his third. He had a terrible crush on one of the women who worked the same shift, and she always picked out what they watched. Mostly foreign. He wasn't sure what a lot of them meant. He would forget to read the subtitles, stealing glances at her, or have to wait on a customer, but there was lots of sex in all of them. He was about to ask her to do something sometime when they weren't working, when someone figured out he lied on his application and fired him. There was this one movie. Last man, last woman. A second guy showed up who hadn't lied on his application.

Darwin kissed Gabriella before the other guy had a chance to show up.

Gaby was surprised how good a kisser he was. So was Darwin.

Elvis watches the automatic doors. Anything can set them off. A rabid coyote. Snakes. Bats. Squirrels. Smells. Dreams.

He waits.

Elvis followed them inside, of course. Gaby decided to take his harness off, let him decide what he wanted to do. She thought his harness was another version of her red shirt and nametag, an understandable mistake. He sat still while she took it off, but it made absolutely no difference in his behavior. Good dog goes deep.

Elvis only wears the harness when they go out somewhere. He doesn't wear it at home with the blind man. It's too heavy, and it rubs on his shoulder, but he doesn't complain, because he knows it's necessary. He can see. The man can't. The man's dead, and these people see, so he doesn't need the harness anymore. He gets that. He's not stupid. That doesn't mean these people don't need guidance. Elvis wonders how he ended up with the last people. Must be the good boy thing.

When he was a puppy there were lots of other dogs who weren't good enough. Some didn't even care about being good. Even when a blind man was hanging onto them.

You had to be even better if he let go, because he might need to find you.

Had to be best of all if he wasn't there and was counting on you to be good *anyway*. To wait. No matter what.

Like now.

Dead means gone, never coming back.

Good is forever, now that the blind man is gone.

Darwin and Gaby decided to spend the night in the display tent where they'd made love. They'd never done anything like that before—screw a total stranger in a display tent in the Target. It was one of the big ones, two rooms. It was fun, and they weren't *total* strangers. They had just shared a profound traumatic experience together. There was a syndrome or something wasn't there? Neither one of them could remember the name. Didn't matter now. They were both pretty happy about it.

They were too tired and drunk, and it was getting too late anyway, to leave the dead today, but they planned to get a fresh start in the morning. Their bikes were loaded up with stuff. Darwin even had a trailer hitched up to his. They both were all serious and solemn about it out of respect for the dead, but secretly they both thought it sounded fun to ride into the country and camp. Being in scouts had been like the bikes for both of them—cut short before they got to do the fun stuff. Darwin's parents took him out on a matter of principle. He wasn't sure which one. They had lots. Gaby's mom quit taking her anywhere. After Ty and Jay died. Both understood their folks' reasons at the time, but they weren't *their* reasons.

Gaby took Elvis out front, and he crapped in the bushes. He looked at her like she should pick it up, but she thought she could let it slide under the circumstances. There was howling out there. Gaby noticed Elvis didn't waste any time getting back inside.

She removed Karin's keys from around her neck and locked the front doors. She shut off most of the lights, but the PA took a key to turn off Karin didn't have. Maybe it was always going. Maybe even janitorial had to listen to it. They needed stuff that fit their lifestyle too. Gaby always thought she would like being a janitor, buffing the big empty store.

She told Elvis he could come sleep with them in the tent. There were two rooms. He followed her back to Sporting Goods but preferred to sleep outside at the crossroads of the aisles. She gave him a big bowl of dog food, the best they had, and a big dish of bottled water. What a day, she thought.

Inside the tent, Darwin had set up a camp table with a battery lantern, and he'd found pillows and pillow cases and chocolate bars and air freshener. She was touched. They made love some more. This time it was way better, and they fell asleep.

Darwin couldn't sleep. Busy brains. Too much going on since everyone died. Everything's changed. Too much to process. He decided to read. He turned on the light and started reading his Kindle. He wanted to finish the first story in the dead guy's book, then he figured he'd switch over to Mrs. Gaskell.

Gabriella, as he lovingly called her, slumbered peacefully beside him, purring like a kitten. He could've gone to another cashier, and he never would've known her. He would be alone now. He couldn't imagine he could've awakened just anybody, felt compelled to shout out her name. Gabriella was special. How could he be so lucky? What had he done to deserve this? He couldn't think about it too much. He had a tendency to do that. One of his degrees is in philosophy.

He read.

He began to worry. The first story went on and on. He paged ahead. It never seemed to stop. He skipped to the next story, and there it was, so the first one had to end some time. He tried to page back from the second story to where he'd been in the first, so he could see how much was left, but he finally gave up and went back to where he was and kept reading.

Maybe it would get better.

Anything to take his mind off the dead people. He wondered if you could smell them yet. The tent smelled like a new car. He thought of all the cars on Broad Street. Maybe he should've chosen a different air freshener. His student loan payments were automatic. He didn't want to think about it.

In the story, someone named Norwood wants to die because everyone lives forever, and he's tired of it, so he joins a Suicide Club where everyone wants to die, and they talk about it a lot in a way Darwin doesn't find particularly interesting, but even when they try to kill themselves, they come back to life like everyone else, so Norwood decides to go back to school to study paleontology because that's old dead things, and he talks a lot about that, what it all means, and about dinosaurs; then he meets a woman named Lucinda studying paleontology for pretty much the same reasons, and they talk a lot and make out a little, but all the dinosaurs are coming back to life too, so the creature they dig up devours them, and there they are, alive inside this big dinosaur headed for London to kill all the people who can't die. To be alive inside a dinosaur forges a special bond between Norwood and Lucinda…

Darwin couldn't take it anymore. He wasn't sure whether it was Norwood or Lucinda or the dinosaur, but he was getting seriously annoyed by the story. He wanted to give it a chance, but this really wasn't his kind of thing. He switched to Mrs. Gaskell. *Wives and Daughters.* He'd watched an adaptation on *Masterpiece Theatre* back when his television worked and rather liked it. It opened charmingly:

To begin with the old rigmarole of childhood. In a country there was a shire, and in that shire there was a town, and in that town there was a house, and in that house there was a room, and in that room there was a bed, and in that bed there lay a little girl, who had been swallowed by a dinosaur on its way to London to kill...

That's not right, Darwin thought. Scanned by volunteers, it said at the beginning. He paid nothing, so he had no right to complain, but still. If you were going to do something you should do it right, not tamper with a classic. There was a comfort in a story like that. You knew who it was about—this girl—who she was going to fall in love with and marry and her friends and so forth. One young man would be more interesting than the others if you bothered to look closely enough at him. This could take a while. She was still a kid, and she'll have friends and so on, some not entirely trustworthy. Parents, all of that. There were *no* dinosaurs. Not living anyway. London hadn't even been bombed yet. All the dinosaurs were still dead. Another one of Darwin's degrees is in Literature.

Darwin switched back to the dead author's story. Norwood is lying in the arms of his fellow paleontologist inside the dinosaur. They're discussing the future of their relationship. The dinosaur ate London while Darwin was with Mrs. Gaskell—then shit out the whole lot except for Lucinda and Norwood—and now they're on their way to Tokyo, telling each other why they want to die and sorting out what sort of impact this might have on their burgeoning romance. They can't decide which is more important—death or each other—without a thought of Tokyo.

The Kindle slipped from Darwin's hands, and he fell fast asleep.

After a time, the Kindle shut itself off. It's automatic. Don't worry. It saved his place.

Gaby is dreaming about her brothers. They both have holes in their heads, from temple to temple, neat little cylindrical passageways. They show her. You can line up their heads and see through to the other side. They aren't anything like the real holes, through their real heads, Ty on one side, Jay on the other in the backseat of the car. Their skulls shattered and rained down on her. Jay's. The shot came from his side. No glass. The windows were rolled down. The AC wasn't working. Mom hadn't had a chance to take it into the mechanic.

"What are you doing in Target?" Jay asks her.

They're in Electronics. All the televisions are showing the same thing as usual. This time it's real actors playing characters from an old cartoon show Gaby never watched. Mom probably did—she would watch anything when she got home from work—but Mom never went to movies. She never had time. But here she is in Electronics in her white doctor jacket she used to let Gaby play in and the stethoscope she didn't. Not after the Barbi incidents.

Mom asks her, "What are you doing in Target, Gabriella?"

Gaby's not sure what she means by that, what she's asking exactly. "Are you dead?" she asks her mother. After Ty and Jay died Mom went into a mental hospital. Maybe crazy people didn't die. Mom blamed herself. You couldn't get her not to blame herself. She'd always done everything. If it wasn't her fault, then whose fault was it? This dream Mom seems to have gotten over it. She must be dead.

"Everyone's dead, Darlin', which is why you and your new boyfriend need to leave."

"He's not my boyfriend, Mom. We just met."

"It's okay either way, but it's time to go. There's nothing for you here."

Gaby wakes up. The chirpy PA woman hasn't given it up. She wants to make your life better, not just today, but every day. For a moment, Gaby thinks maybe everyone's come back to life, and she's not sure how she feels about that, but then she's sure. She doesn't want to go back to when everyone was alive, but dying like Darwin said. Mom would say let sleeping dogs lie, even though they never had a dog, and sleeping isn't dead.

Elvis is panting at the entrance to the tent. It's a new day. Her new boyfriend's lying beside her. "Wake up, Darlin' " she says, sounding just like her mother.

Darwin opens his eyes. "Gabriella," he whispers.

They unzip the fly. Mick's singing "Wild Horses" again.

As it turns out, it's a lot easier to leave the dead than you might suppose. Elvis running alongside discourages the occasional dog inclined to give chase. They stop and have a meal at the last Applebee's on Broad Street near the mostly empty office park out past the car dealers. It isn't far beyond that before they find their pick of a dozen huge houses, each sitting on its own 10-acre lot. Most with only a couple of dead people inside. They can pitch a tent in the yard if they want or just live in one of these big houses.

They pick one of the smaller ones with a beautiful enameled wood stove in the family room and bury the owners near the gazebo in a spot with a nice view.

There are even horses at a lot of these places. Tame ones. They set them free when they go biking around the neighborhood in the afternoon, picking up a bottle of wine or bag of coffee beans, a jar of marinated artichoke hearts, chocolate bars. The trailer on Darwin's bike comes in handy. There's also a little lake and dock and boats, and they like to drift around under the stars that are burning a lot brighter these days now that the power's gone out. Not to worry. All these big places have big generators and big vehicles to siphon gas out of for as long as Darwin and Gaby are likely to live.

Unless they live forever, which doesn't sound like such a bad idea to either one of them at the moment. They tell each other their life stories.

There's never been much demand before, so they're fresh to the task and hold nothing back. Why should they?

"Mom was working in the Emergency Room and forgot to sign something and stopped off with us kids in the back and ran inside. That's when some totally random guy, who had nothing to do with us or Mom, tried to shoot someone going into the hospital, and the bullet killed my brothers, and Mom was never the same. Me neither."

Darwin holds her, kisses her wet cheeks, and they're glad to be alive. He's learned a lot, now that everyone's dead, about relating to others. He tells her the names of all the drugs he's been given and about all the different Darwins they could make him be, but what his problem was went by several names, depending on which specialist you were listening to, none of them would you want to name your kid. He was a great disappointment to his parents. He liked to learn things though. He was good at it. Still is. He's never found much use for the things he's learned before, except their own enjoyment. Now he narrates them to Gabriella who likes to hear about them while the cicadas sing and the frogs croak.

Darwin tells Gabriella about the Suicide Club story he still can't get to the end of while they're sitting on their new porch watching the horses they set free wander around in the woods, looking like they're not quite sure what to do with themselves. Moscow, Los Angeles, Rio have all fallen before the dinosaur's murderous rampage. All the content on the Kindle has been infected with dinosaurs. He's afraid it's a virus.

"Suicide Club?" Gaby says. "Definitely not interested. Dinosaurs are okay. Maybe we can find a copy of *Jurassic Park?"*

"I'll keep an eye out."

"I was just noticing our wild horses aren't very wild."

"Give them time," Darwin says. "They'll get there someday. Pinot Grigio or Sauvignon Blanc?"

"You choose," she says. "Why don't you just skip to the next story?"

"It's about zombies."

Gaby laughs. "You definitely don't want to go there."

It's not really about zombies. He just wanted to hear her laugh. Darwin loves the sound of Gabriella's laughter. It makes him laugh too. "I certainly don't." They go with the Pinot. "I think we may already have a copy of *Jurassic Park* somewhere. Elvis and I found quite a haul at the big Georgian."

"They're all big."

"The *really* big one. Elvis loved that place, racing around the tile foyer."

"I can imagine—you and that dog."

Elvis sweeps his big tail back and forth across the porch at the sound of their laughter, the mention of his name. He lies at their feet. Life is good. He hears the howling out there, way off in the distance. He just doesn't let it bother him. It took him awhile, he'll admit, to loosen up, to just have a little fun. But then, it was like a miracle. He was with the man when he found the thing. He wasn't even sure the man liked him all that much up till then, not like the woman. But it was just the two of them in a big wide field where horses used to graze. They had the whole world to themselves, and he threw it. Elvis had never had so much fun in his whole life. Frisbee. Who knew? Now they have fun every day.

There's a quiet contentment that pervades the evening, a slight chill in the air, as the moon rises in the sky, and the horses nicker in the moonlight, thinking about things horses think about.

Darwin thinks soon it will be time for a fire in the wood stove. There's a lovely enamel scene on the side. It's a snow-covered village on the other side of the world with reindeer instead of horses, and there's a dog who looks a little like Elvis, but all the people are inside, safe and warm.

Penelope Waits

Penelope waited for Odysseus. A whole house full of suitors, some of whom had to be pretty hot, and she gave none of them the time of day, weaving a shroud of all things, unweaving it at night. Meanwhile, Odysseus is boinking goddesses, having adventures, going to hell and back, bragging about it all to dinner parties packed with swooning admirers of his bullshit. That's the way the story goes. Course I'm no Penelope, and Ralph's certainly no Odysseus.

He is a cheating little rat, however. I could give you a list, but that's sort of beside the point of this story. Point is, I've learned not to believe a word he says, so when he goes camping for the weekend with a buddy, I'm thinking, *Right*, and when buddy comes back without him saying Ralph "just vanished," I'm thinking *right* again, and then when he surfaces a whole week later with totally new clothes saying he's been abducted by aliens, I say, "What's the bitch's name, Ralph?"

But he sticks to his story, even goes to the authorities and whatever, and they're about as into his bullshit as I am. One of these agent guys, kind of cute actually, asks me where I thought he was, and I tell him my theories which don't include any aliens, lotus eaters, Cyclops, or hot goddesses, only some hillbilly bar bitch with a purse full of condoms that turned into a week at a Red Carpet Inn. Once burned, twice cautious, as grandma used to say, but with Ralph I've learned to wear oven mitts. The agent laughed at that one, and gave me a sly look in case I was looking to even the score, but I'd already spotted the ring on his finger and didn't consider him suitor material.

You may be wondering about all the *Odyssey* stuff. I just did a paper on it. One of the reasons Ralph took off on his extra-long weekend was so I could work on it without him bugging me, but when he "just vanished," that proved to be a major distraction and I turned it in late anyways. Mr. Branson, the instructor, said it was so good and imaginative he didn't count any points off. Mr. Branson is definitely suitor material, but only if you're a guy. Some girls in the class tried anyway, but that's just one of many shortcuts to heartache, and I've had enough of those to last me.

I'm trying to get a little education so I can get a better job that pays more and has benefits and all that, though I like working at the dog wash, and someday, if we ever open a second location, I could, like, manage or something, especially if I pick up some bookkeeping skills and stuff, but those classes bore me to death, and the stuff I dreaded like Literature of the Western World they make you take for no good reason I can see turned out to be the best ones. I like Spanish too. *¿Qué tal, Pablo?* Consuela, one of my puppy scrubbing mates at the Waggy Washateria, helped me out, even tried to explain the subjunctive to me, which I never got, but she told me my accent is pretty good. She's illegal and should know, though she went home to visit family for Christmas and never came back. I don't think Ralph's aliens took her either.

But Ralph, who says he loves me, who says I'm the one, who says I'm all he thought about when he was in alien captivity, has begged me to give him a chance to prove it to me, to return to the scene of the crime where the beam of light came out of the sky and whisked him away, and I said okay, not because I believe him for a second, but if he's willing to go to all this trouble, he must care about me, right? Right. Besides, it's spring break, and I like camping. And Ralph won't take the meds. You think you can talk this kind of shit without getting put on serious meds?

But he believes it all, so he doesn't think he needs any meds. He has to keep his wits about him, he says: There are aliens among us.

***

Okay, I'll confess. I had hopes for the sleeping bags thing. Naked bodies snuggied up in a big warm sock might ignite a little passion. But it wasn't warm enough. The aliens left a chill that lives in Ralph's spine. Ralph's been coming here for years, he says. It's a pretty spot. Now every little noise in the night he thinks is them. He says the aliens told him there's a portal close by where they come and go to their home planet dozens of light years away.

Why can't he be afraid of bears or mountain lions like a normal person? But when something like that's real to someone, as crazy as it may seem, you have to respect their fear. You can't judge, seems to me, but what do I know?

So to say I'm not expecting to meet aliens is the understatement of the century. I don't even believe in ancient astronauts and haunted houses and all of that nonsense on the History Channel. How do they get away with calling that stuff the History Channel? So I'm trying to get a fire started, and Ralph's out gathering firewood supposedly, though he's probably just smoking a joint. I'm more worried about bears than aliens when they just show up, materialize like they do on *Star Trek*, three of them, tall and skinny and not quite right so there's no way you can think they're just some of Ralph's buddies in alien suits. Nobody that Ralph knows is 6'4" with a 24-inch waist and arms as long as my legs.

"Don't be afraid," one of them says, like that's an option, like it's not twice as scary because his little round mouth barely moves, and he's the color of a cantaloupe. "We mean you no harm."

"Holy shit!" I say, and they look at one another like they know what that means, and they're trying to figure out where to take the conversation from there since the no fear message obviously didn't take.

A different one says—you can't be sure since their mouths barely move, but he sounds different—"We just want to understand your kind."

"Did you abduct Ralph?" I ask, thinking these guys aren't very good at picking out their test subjects.

"Ralph proved inadequate," the first one says, and I can't argue with that.

"What is your name?" the third one asks me.

"Penelope," I lie because … I don't know why. Maybe I'm not such a good test subject either. "What's yours?" I ask, because that's just what you say, right?

"Serene," the first one says.

"Enlighten," the second one says—more carrot colored.

"Happy," says the third—winter squash.

"You're kidding," I say. It just comes out. Kind of rude, I suppose, but they don't seem to mind.

"We're translating," Happy says.

Makes sense. "So, what do you want to know?" I ask.

"Everything," Enlighten says.

"Oh brother," I start to say, but then I remember Mr. Branson's opening lecture where he laid it on thick about how literature opened vistas of understanding and all that, and I just happen to have the huge lit. book with me since I'm supposed to read *Oedipus* before we get back from break, so I haul it out of the tent and hand it over. "You guys read?" I ask. If they can manage English so well, I figure reading's not a problem.

"With pleasure," Serene says, with a smile? The round mouth goes oval for a second.

Then they vanish, just like they showed up, dissolving into twinkly nothing. Ralph comes stumbling into our campsite a few minutes later smelling of pot with an armload of wood and dumps it by my smoldering excuse for a fire.

I don't tell him about my aliens. I'd have to tell him he wasn't really great abductee material, and he might get his feelings hurt, and he's still acting totally afraid of them, while I thought they were kind of sweet for aliens. How can you be afraid of guys with names like Serene, Enlighten, and Happy? They took my book, so I won't be able to get the reading done, but I figure Mr. Branson likes me and will let it slide this once, since I'm the best student in the class. I'm not bragging. The competition isn't too steep.

***

Penelope's name means web-face or something like that, and I say in my paper she's like a spider who unweaves her web, the shroud she's supposedly making, to *not* catch anything, and that she and Odysseus are two peas in a pod who don't let others see who they really are in order to survive with their identities intact, so they're, like, made for each other.

I've always hoped I'd find someone made for me, but lately I've been thinking that's not happening. I'm okay-looking. Guys hit on me all the time, at least for now while I'm twenty-six and not too fat, but sooner or later I won't look so good and I will have missed my chance. Not that the guys are worth pining for. I'm with Ralph because he was so persistent it was just easier to go out with him than make up excuses not to. He works for UPS and makes deliveries at the dog wash and used to hang around while I was blow-drying some Lhasa Apso or something, saying I had a gentle touch or some bullshit. Now he just talks football with Mike, the owner who's a big Cowboys fan.

I hate football.

Lately it's been the aliens. Ralph won't let it go, which is another reason I don't say anything about mine. Mike asks him if they inserted anything into his orifices—Mike watches all that stuff on the History Channel—and Ralph says no.

"Well, what did they do?" Mike wants to know.

"They showed me pictures," Ralph says.

"Pictures of what?"

"Buildings, paintings, statues—all sorts of stuff. I don't know. They wanted to know what I could tell them about them."

"Maybe they were terrorist targets."

"They weren't terrorists; they were aliens."

"Maybe they were terrorist aliens."

When Ralph leaves, Mike suggests to me that Ralph needs to get help, and I tell him he already has. Mike's just fucking with him, since he doesn't believe any of it, which I don't think is very nice, but I don't say anything since Mike's my boss, and I don't want to piss him off. I love dogs, and I only took the job because I can't have one where I live and I can't afford a nicer place.

***

It's about a week since I met them, when Enlighten, Serene, and Happy show up at my place. I was getting worried about my book, but I was able to find everything on the internet I was supposed to read without all the annoying footnotes which are mostly useless ain't-I-smart stuff they throw in there to justify charging an arm and a leg for the book. I told Mr. Branson I lost my book, and he told me where to go online. I can't help noticing how the lies are piling up, just like Odysseus and Penelope. Oedipus was totally depressing, but kind of cool anyway. I said he was like some detective trying to find out who done it when he's the guy who did. Mr. Branson really liked that. I think the other people in the class are starting to hate me, but what can you do? You have to be yourself, right? Back in high school I never read anything I was supposed to, but I wasn't paying for the classes either. The story was guys didn't like smart girls, but the guys who did like me weren't worth being stupid over.

"How did you guys find me?" I ask the aliens.

"You wrote your address in the book," Serene says and points at it in case I forgot. There's my name, Cindy Slidell, but they don't ask why I told them I was Penelope, like they already know and don't want to embarrass me. I find this touching. A little consideration goes a long way with me. Maybe if I'd met these aliens back in high school, my life would've been a whole lot different.

"You want some tea or something?"

They like that idea, so I give them some green tea because that's supposed to be good for you, and I don't want to be responsible for making a bunch of aliens sick, and I want to make a good impression. I wonder sometimes if that isn't something started by the tea companies to sell more tea, but I have a suspicious nature, which is one of the reasons I liked Odysseus and Penelope so much.

I explain all this to the aliens while I'm making the tea and serving it. I run off at the mouth sometimes when I'm nervous. I don't do a lot of entertaining. I feel bad I don't have any good food to offer them, but I have a tube of Oreos left over from when Ralph was missing and I was stressing, and they like those just fine. I show them how you can take them apart and eat the filling first, and they really get into that. Laughing maybe? It sort of sounds like a drain backing up. It occurs to me they might be getting a sugar high. Their little round mouths are crusted with cookie crumbs, but the green tea washes most of that off.

They have lots of questions about the book, they say, and I have to confess I've only read the first part, which is kind of too bad since they have a whole lot of questions about Dante's *Inferno*. Serene says it frightened him, and Happy and Enlighten totally agree. I make a mental note to ask Mr. Branson some of their questions when I get the chance.

I tell them all about my paper for Mr. Branson, and Serene asks me why I like Penelope so much. Is it that she waited for Odysseus? I figure these guys might have somebody waiting for them back home, or wish they did.

I think about this real hard because that's not it exactly, that she just waited, until I finally say it's because she knew Odysseus was *worth* waiting for, that he could've just stayed in what most guys would regard as paradise but came back home to her because she totally got him. Happy points out that he had a lot of help from Athena who's always showing up as some random guy or even some little kid in pigtails.

"There you go," I say. "Athena's the goddess of wisdom, right, so she should know, and Odysseus is smart enough to listen to her even when she looks like nobody."

Enlighten says, "We suspect Athena might've been one of our kind."

"Do you guys watch the History Channel or something?"

This gets a big laugh from the three of them, but it was a perfectly serious question. "So are you guys going to abduct me like you did Ralph?"

Serene says, "That didn't seem to work out so well with Ralph, and you've been so willing to help us, it doesn't seem necessary."

This makes sense of course, but as I'm nodding my head in agreement, like you bet, I'm one helpful human, no abduction necessary, I can't help noticing deep inside—like some part of me just drowned—how disappointed I am.

Enlighten leans forward, the faint smell of Oreos on his breath. "Do you want us to abduct you? We could show you countless other worlds."

I panic, lose my nerve, like I've always done on the high board at the pool and say, "Of course not."

They all nod, smiling? Like they know I just lied to them a little bit, but they're aliens, in my apartment out of the blue. What do they expect?

"I have to get ready for work," I say, and they all stand up like they're going to head for the door, and vanish.

When I get to the dog wash, I have a brindle pit bull waiting to have his anal glands expressed and a bath, plus a labradoodle who needs the whole wash, cut and fluff treatment. The pit's a sweetie pie who won't quit licking my face, and the labradoodle's three kinds of frisky waiting for her turn. I suspect they're into each other. Everybody's fixed here, but you'd be surprised how little difference that seems to make.

Right when things are at their stinkiest, Ralph shows up and says he's got some news that won't wait, and for a moment I'm afraid the aliens have told him I've been seeing them behind his back, but it turns out to be the opposite. He says he can't sleep nights knowing the alien portal is right here in the county, and he has to move on like his shrink says, and so he's put in for a transfer, that he's moving to Roanoke, and he wants me to go with him.

The pit's watching us, back and forth, one to the other like he's following the conversation, wondering what I'll say. The labradoodle's yodeling for her freedom. I swear half the time it's like dogs know exactly what we're saying and there's no point lying to them or yourself either, and I tell Ralph no.

"Won't you even think about it?" he asks. "It's not like they don't have dog washes in Roanoke."

That's kind of mean, which only confirms my decision, but that's not it. It's not even that I know Ralph's not the one for me and never will be. I mean there's probably a hell of a lot more going on in Roanoke than here, where if it wasn't for Mr. Branson and the dogs I would've lost my mind a long time ago. It's that I want to stay for the very reason Ralph wants to leave: I don't want to leave the portal. Right then and there I realize I'm living for the next time I can see Happy, Serene, and Enlighten again. There's something in the look I give him, I suppose, but he doesn't try to talk me out of it really, though he gets all weepy and says he'll never forget me, which I kind of doubt is true, but I'm much too nice to say so.

***

I hang around waiting for the pit's owner to show. He's late. I don't mind. I like hanging out with Butch, the pit. I tell him my troubles, and he listens, giving me a reassuring slurp on the face. I give him a big hug. Looks like he's had troubles of his own—some scars on his muzzle, and one of his ears is pretty chewed up. I figure he's a rescue.

When the owner finally shows, he turns out to be a total asshole. He looks and smells drunk, and he's wearing a confederate flag t-shirt with a skull in the middle.

I tell him how much I like his dog.

He scowls. "Useless dog. Stinks. A total pussy. How much did he cost me this time?"

I tell him, and he starts arguing, though I know Mike must've told him up front what it would cost. He finally gives me a credit card that gets turned down, so he pulls out a roll of bills that says "dealer" to me, and peels off a few, throwing them on the counter. I make his change, and he drags Butch out to his truck, throws him in the back, and roars off. The last thing I see is poor Butch skittering around, banging into the sides. Butch wasn't a rescue. He still needed rescuing.

***

That night I stay up 'til all hours reading Dante, and I see exactly what the aliens are talking about. Dante must've been one angry guy. Gets me to thinking about who I would put in my Hell. I picture Butch's owner looking like a fireplug, dogs lined up for eternity to piss on his ugly face.

I'm waiting for Mr. Branson outside his office first thing for his office hours. It's not like there's a line or anything. I've got the aliens' questions and some of my own, and he talks to me for a long time, until he says he has to go to class, but he wants to know my future plans.

I tell him I don't know, that I've been thinking a lot about that myself.

"You should continue your studies," he says. "You are very smart and insightful," he says. "You should get a degree, go on to graduate school. You are the brightest student I've ever taught."

By the time he's done, my head's too big to fit inside his tiny office, and part of me's saying, where do I sign up, but this other part avoids the question about future plans, saying I can't afford it, that I can't just up and leave, that I don't want to leave this dumpy little town. He's got all the answers—scholarships, stipends, grants, opportunities. I tell him I'll think about it even though I know I won't.

"Don't sell yourself short, Cindy," he says.

Outside his office is a box full of books with a sign that says FREE BOOKS. On the top of the pile is the book for the second half of World Lit. "Can I have this?" I ask him as he's about to go to class.

"Of course," he says, smiling big. "It's the old edition, but they don't change much. Help yourself."

Help yourself. I've always liked that expression. "Thanks for everything," I say, picking up the thick book and hugging it to my chest, imagining a bright future.

The tent and everything Ralph and I went camping with is still at my place, and I load it in my car. On the way out of town, I swing by the address Butch's owner gave Mike, and it turns out to be right—you never know with a guy like that—and there's Butch in the yard, on a chain, naturally. I abduct him, and we head for the hills. I roll down the windows so he can smell some freedom; so we both can. Odysseus had a dog who recognized him after twenty long years when he finally made it back home, licking his hand and wagging his tail. Then the dog up and died. I cried buckets when I read that. Leastways that won't happen to Butch.

I'll miss the dog wash. I'll miss my friends. The Earth. But I keep thinking about all that must be out there, other worlds like Enlighten said. Looking through my new book I found a poem about Ulysses a few years down the road that says exactly how I already feel at twenty-six:

Yet all experience is an arch wherethro'
Gleams that untravell'd world whose margin fades
For ever and forever when I move.
How dull it is to pause, to make an end,
To rust unburnish'd, not to shine in use!

" 'T is not too late to seek a newer world," he decides. How many chances do you get?

So I'm waiting here, drinking a big mug of coffee I picked up at the 7-11—maybe my last, who knows?—waiting for Happy, Serene, and Enlighten to show up so I can answer all their questions about Hell and then some. I've got insights like Mr. Branson says. Butch is leaning up against me, his ears perked up, his eyes on the stars, waiting. He's got some insights too.

Abduct us, guys. We're ready.

Healing Benjamin

There is something in the unselfish and self-sacrificing love of a brute, which goes directly to the heart of him who has had frequent occasion to test the paltry friendship and gossamer fidelity of mere *Man*.

—Edgar Allan Poe, "The Black Cat"

I got the healing touch when I was 16 years old kneeling over my dying cat Benjamin in my bedroom. He was trying to crawl under the bed to die, but I wouldn't let him, hauling him out and wrapping my body around him, my forehead pressed against his. He was a year older than me. He'd been there my whole life. I couldn't imagine life without him. He stopped breathing, his heart stopped, and I prayed for him, though I rarely prayed then, and I never pray now, squeezing him, imprinting my will on him, picturing him raised from the dead, alive and well. I didn't know what else to do, sobbing, absolutely heartbroken, torturing myself with Joan Baez singing "Old Blue" on the stereo:

... Old Blue died and he died so hard
Shook the ground in my backyard
Dug his grave with a silver spade
Lowered him down with links of chain
Every link I did call his name
Here Blue, you good dog you
Here Blue, I'm a-coming there too!

Benjamin stirred under my hands, his heart beating hard and steady against my palm. I released him, and he rose and walked to the door, his tail erect. He wanted to go out. An hour later, he wanted back in, and he was hungry. He looked good. He looked real good.

I took him to a vet after his healing to get him checked out. I didn't take him to his regular vet, Dr. Diderada, who Ben had been going to since he was a kitten, figuring he'd never believe this was the same half-blind stiff-legged neutered tom living on borrowed time he'd basically given up on a week before. I told this new vet Ben was a stray I was adopting, and he guessed him to be about four, in perfect health. All the vets over the years guessed him to be about four, in perfect health. That's 28 in cat years, not a bad year for me. Benjamin seemingly picked an age he liked and stuck with it. I, meanwhile, kept getting older. I quit taking him to the vet years ago, having exhausted all the convenient ones. Ben was over it, and I couldn't see spending the money to be reassured semiannually that my cat was immortal. He never even had an ear mite or a flea, as if even the insect world knew he was operating under a special dispensation.

Thirty years later, I was 46, and I still had Benjamin. I'll do the math for you. He was 47. That's 329 in cat years. Even if you gave him nine lives, that made each one more than 36 years. No. Benjamin was not a normal cat.

Back when Ben was 17, my parents readily believed Dr. Diderada had resurrected him with some good vitamin supplements. They were wish-upon-a-star, somewhere-over-the-rainbow kind of people, but even they wouldn't believe a 47-year-old cat. After I left home, I didn't see them on my own turf very often, but I always lied and said Ben was a new cat. They thought I was odd for naming every cat Benjamin, but they already knew I was odd—I was their son. It helped that Ben was a fairly generic gray tabby with white boots and a nondescript meow. My ex-wife Penny knew Ben for seven years, living with him for five, but she never noticed he never aged. She wasn't a cat person. She wasn't any kind of animal person I ever discovered. She liked watching monkeys in the monkey house, but that's not the same, is it? I know it sounds weird, but that's one of the reasons we broke up. I just couldn't be with somebody who didn't like animals. When it came down to it, she didn't like people all that much. Which makes sense—people are animals, smart worrisome animals, but still animals.

Anyway, she peacefully coexisted with Ben, and he was never an issue. I never dated anyone else more than a year or so, and nobody who spent much time around Ben. Then at 46, I started going out with Shannon. That didn't last long—the just going out. Our third date started Friday at four—she took off work an hour early—and ended Tuesday at noon. I told Benjamin it was the closest to a resurrection I'd experienced in my life, and maybe it would help me understand him better. He pointed out, however, that death was a necessary precondition of resurrection. He played dead and sprang back to life, a favorite trick of his, flicking his smartass tail. I've always talked to Ben. He hasn't always answered.

For some time, Shannon and I had been practically living together, shuttling back and forth between our houses, but she preferred my place because Benjamin lived there. Benny Boy, as she called him. If he'd been a man, I would've been insanely jealous. To say they hit it off is to say Juliet was sort of into Romeo. He was equally passionate about her.

This was all good. She loved me too, Benny Boy's lifelong companion and confidante, the cleaner of the cat box, the keeper of the can opener, not to mention healer extraordinaire. But then she started asking questions. "Isn't he due for a checkup? Shots or something?"

I made the mistake of just putting her off, and then she saw a little reminder card from one of Benny Boy's many vets in my mail, this one saying he was at least eight years overdue on just about everything. So she called and made an appointment. That's kind of how Shannon was, which was one of the many things I liked about her, except insofar as it pertained to Benjamin, because I'd always figured that sooner or later reality was going to catch up with me. It was like I made a deal all those years ago that I couldn't handle my cat dying right then, but Some Day there'd be no choice, and it would hurt even worse when it finally came. But somehow, if I could just keep his death and persistent life a secret, nothing had to change.

"How old is he?" Shannon asked when they met. About four, I said, never anticipating I'd be caught in my convenient lie. So how could he be eight years behind in his shots? I feared every step I took down this road with Shannon meant Some Day was coming soon. But I couldn't stop myself. I couldn't stop her. Benjamin, closed up in his carrier, in his stoic, dignified way, neither stopped nor started, but was carried along by the tide of events—and by his carrier of course—to the vet.

Ben enjoyed crowded veterinary waiting rooms, the more crowded the better. He delighted in the spectacle. This day, there was a special treat, a harlequin Great Dane lurching about out of control, his suited keeper helpless to stop him from sticking his great nose in the random crotch, body-blocking anyone coming in the door, terrifying every animal in the place—and I'm including humans as animals—except Ben who watched from inside his carrier, purring, purring, the deep rumbling purr I know as laughter. Ben enjoyed watching foolishness. He saw a lot of it at his age.

"He's so calm," Shannon marveled, peering inside his carrier, stroking his untroubled brow with her finger, keeping a wary eye on the Dane. "Is he always this calm?"

"Oh yes," I reassured her, and then we were next, and she wanted to go in too, and how could I refuse?

After a lengthy examination, the vet, a kind, fatherly gentleman, maybe a decade older than Ben chronologically, but a mere child in cat years, broached the subject cautiously. He looked over the end of his reading glasses, up from Ben's near-empty record of perfect health. "According to our records, I last examined Benjamin 12 years ago?"

I couldn't lie, not with Shannon beside us scratching Ben's head with both hands the way he likes, waiting for my answer. "Yes."

"Which makes Ben"—he looked back at the record— "19?" He couldn't quite keep the incredulity out of his gentlemanly voice. Shannon's hands froze on Ben's noble head. All eyes were on me. Even Ben's.

Ben and I had liked this guy, so we stuck with him for three years. The math checked out. He was the last. Ben was 35, ready to do without vets—the shots and the thermometer up his ass anyway. He found the rest interesting. At least I wasn't dealing with Ben's first vet. No bluff possible there. "That's right," I said.

"Would— Would you mind leaving Ben for a few tests? An hour or so? No charge, of course."

Ben gave me an unmistakable look. *No fucking way* is a precise translation. "I'm afraid not," I said.

"Why not?" Shannon asked. She'd done a little math of her own. In her reality, Ben was six, tops, and of course, he looked four, as always.

"Nothing's wrong with him, right?" I asked the vet.

He shook his head no. "Quite the opposite. He's the healthiest cat I'll see this year. This *is* the same cat?"

I considered lying, but couldn't imagine explaining the lie to Shannon in some way that wouldn't sound sick or pathetic. "Yes. Same cat."

"He's the healthiest 19-year-old cat I've ever seen—and we don't see that many. There aren't even any tartar deposits on his teeth." He bared Ben's teeth, pointing with a ball point pen at the gleaming fangs, an indignity Ben graciously endured.

"I know. I think he's had enough for one day." Ben chimed in with a low moan, that if you know anything about cats means his patience is spent, and you're in immediate peril from the aforementioned fangs and the hooked razors that sprout from each paw on demand, the envy of every badass who ever lived. The vet got the message immediately, putting him back in the carrier with a fistful of treats.

I wasn't looking forward to the ride home. No well-timed moan was going to get me out of this one.

There was a moment, when Shannon was already in the car and I was about to put Ben in the backseat, when we were alone. I put his carrier on the roof of the car and pretended I was having trouble finding my keys, though I didn't think Shannon was paying any attention to us. She was staring out the windshield with a determined look on her face. Ben and I spoke in low tones through the bars of his carrier door, our faces inches apart. The traffic flowed by behind me, ignoring me and my cat.

"What do I do?" I asked. "She'll never believe you're 19."

"Tell her my real age," he said.

"You think?"

"I know."

"But I can't prove you're 47. She'll never believe me."

"Proof doesn't matter. You'll see. She senses I'm no ordinary cat. We have a special bond."

"Oh please. Does she sense you're a manipulative little eunuch?"

"For a cat, I'm not so little." He laughed at his own joke. Cat humor, very sly.

I put him in the middle of the backseat, so he could see out the front like he likes, got in, immediately started the car, and put it in gear.

"How can Ben be *19*?" Shannon asked.

We were parallel parked, my eyes glued to the side mirror, waiting for a break in the traffic. Following Ben's advice—I'd never known him to be wrong—I told her. "He's not," I began, "he's 47." I pulled into traffic.

There were certain advantages to telling the tale while driving. I wasn't expected to make eye contact; a brisk, even telegraphic style was perfectly acceptable; and she wasn't inclined to interrupt, argue, or question while I was waiting to make a tricky left turn across a steady torrent of oncoming traffic. The downside was I didn't have a clue how she was taking it until we were back at my place, and I turned off the engine and looked over at her. You might think she would've refused to believe me, end of story, but Shannon wasn't like that. Neither was she some wacko flake who believed any madness I spouted just because she loved me.

"Okay," she said. "I want to figure this thing out." She turned to Ben and looked at him through the bars. *Has Benny Boy been keeping secrets from his Shannon?* He looked right back. Hell. What did I know? Maybe they did have a special bond.

It was early yet, and Shannon had me dig out Ben's vet records, and while I was making breakfast, she called every vet he'd ever been to. The second one was dead and gone, the third seemed to have left town. She made appointments with the rest, booking Ben solid for the day. I wondered if he figured on this when he told me to tell her the truth. I certainly hadn't. I checked my credit card balance, and we were off.

I got pretty good at telling the story economically. I left out any mention of prayer as such—there were no priests on our itinerary, only men of science. It was amazing how many incredulous vets remembered Ben. It was the no tartar thing that seemed to impress them most. All of them, however, dismissed immediately the possibility of a 47-year-old cat and denied there was any way he could be the *same* cat despite the resemblance. One guy got pissed off, like I had something to gain by paying an exorbitant fee for ten minutes of his time to tell him a story I knew he'd never believe. Was he an idiot? Couldn't he see I was doing it for love? Most of the vets were nice, cutting looks at Shannon—*Are you crazy too? Shouldn't you be getting him help?* Shannon just wanted the facts. She examined the records of Ben's perfect checkups with care, except the pissed-off guy's; he threw us out before she got the chance.

Ben's first and favorite vet, Dr. Diderada, interestingly enough, seemed to come closest to believing my story. He was last on Shannon's itinerary. He probably should've retired years earlier. He had a distracted, dreamy quality, like an old cat. He gave us pretty much the same lecture the others had—why it was impossible for a cat to be 47—and certainly not one in Ben's condition. But this time there was something quixotic about the narrative, some sense that among all the dead and dying cats there *might* be one who lived forever and never grew old, but of course, you couldn't expect a scientific professional to speak openly of such a creature.

He bent down, looking Ben in the eye, scratching Ben's trembling chin with his index finger, in a beckoning motion, as if he hoped to lure the true cat out into the open. "Some cats are special, aren't they Benjamin? The world is their oyster." The combination of the chin scratch and the mention of oysters—one of Ben's favorites, especially fried—proved irresistibly seductive, and a resonant rumble issued forth from deep inside him so intense it made the gleaming examining table hum like a struck tuning fork, and both Diderada and Ben smiled like the Buddha. The walls behind them were plastered with lurid posters of cat anatomy, the color of rare roast beef. A plastic cat skeleton on a stand smiled too.

Shannon turned away, whispering, "I'll wait in the car," and hurried out.

"Lovely woman," Diderada said.

Last stop on Shannon's fact-finding expedition was a visit to my folks, the only witnesses to Ben's resurrection I knew how to contact. Any angels who may or may not have been in attendance had steadfastly refused to reveal themselves over the years, and my official policy toward them was blissful ignorance. I managed a cranky ignorance most of the time. I never achieved blissful, though I avoided, for the most part, totally pissed off. Still no angels, no answers. I loved living with Ben, but I didn't like living with an unfathomable enigma.

Mom and Dad loved Shannon, of course, and didn't mind at all that she'd called that morning to invite us to dinner. They were also quite delighted to see Benjamin. After their last cat Angelina died at 16—toothless, blind, and with daily IVs—they'd decided to forego cats indefinitely, but they missed having a feline presence about the house.

As I mentioned before, my parents weren't into grappling with reality. They slept under a pyramid and wanted to believe that breathing exercises and dietary supplements and the well-placed crystal would keep them forever young, though down deep they knew better. As much as they liked to flirt with the flaky, they proved immediately resistant to the notion that *this* Benjamin was the same cat who moved out almost 30 years previously. Metaphorically, spiritually, teleported, time-warped, reincarnated, alien-abducted, cloned, whatever the hell, *maybe*; but not literally the *same* cat living his life ever since, one day at a time, a few months past his 47th birthday. That would be crazy.

Ben, who'd had a half-dozen thermometers shoved up his ass already that day, was not overly invested in the proceedings until dessert. He rubbed up against Mom's legs while she was whipping cream, and when she was done, he stood on his hind legs, his forepaws extended in supplication, and "danced" (an awkward stumbling turn from the usually graceful Ben) and she gave him the beaters. I pointed out they used to go through this identical ritual when I was a kid—Ben got *both* damn beaters then too—but Mom insisted it didn't prove anything, that any cat would do the same.

Shannon maintained an aloof silence during all of this, only asking an occasional question, clarifying some detail, never venturing an opinion herself. Over dessert, Mom suggested a therapist she knew. "I went," Dad said. "I had suicidal thoughts." He popped a strawberry in his mouth. "Not anymore!"

He told us about his "crisis"—which as far as I could tell consisted of realizing that we all grow old and die. He acted like this would be news to us young people, though he was the one who said, "You're only as old as you feel, right?" Wrong. Clearly the man had forgotten Angelina. Dad now took antidepressants to make him feel good, guzzled various mood-altering teas Mom bought from websites, and he felt like a new man. I kind of missed the days Dad smoked pot in the basement and thought I didn't know, while I experimented widely. I'd often speculated that some bizarre conjunction of chemicals in my body expressed in my breath and tears might have affected Ben in some inexplicable way to resurrect him. Might as well believe in fairy dust. God's will? Divine Plan? Come *on*. He's a cat. And if he had a mission on this earth other than enjoying himself with the least possible bother, God failed to inform him of it. *Go forth and lick both beaters, my chosen one.* I didn't think so.

"Maybe you're supposed to be figuring it out for me, Jeffrey," Ben said once. "You're the one who cares about this religious crap." It was true, but I couldn't figure it out. What possible use could God have for a cat who had so little use for Him? I've always wanted to believe but never quite pulled it off except for transitory spasms of awe—what most people call agnosticism. If Ben made God more likely, he also made it more likely that He's totally batshit nuts. Give me agnosticism any day. And if I wanted something to believe in, my folks always had something new on offer. This time it was some mini-messianic therapist with a nimble prescription pad. My folks were almost becoming conventional.

Shannon was no more interested in hearing about Dad's rebirth than I was, so we didn't linger after dessert. At the door, Mom put the therapist's number in my shirt pocket and gave it a little pat. I couldn't begin to describe how swell that felt at my age.

Shannon asked one more time, holding him up as Exhibit A, snoozing in his carrier, his face and forepaws sodden from the post-whipped-cream cleaning he'd given himself, "But this does look *exactly* like the Benjamin you remember, right?"

"Yes Dear," Mom said. "But it can't be, can it?" She gave my shirt pocket another pat to let Shannon know she held her responsible for getting her crazy son to a therapist as soon as possible. I would sooner have gone to Dr. Diderada than any therapist my parents would've recommended.

Shannon was silent all the way home to my place, staring out the window at the night streets like she was a stranger in town feeling homesick. Every once in a while something would snag her vision, and she'd turn and follow it like she'd never seen it before.

I could only imagine what was going through her mind. How did you keep sleeping with a guy who thinks his cat is immortal? How did you let him rub your feet, make you breakfast, adore you, write you bad poetry, without doing something once the miraculous cat was out of the bag? Flee, fix it, lock me up, *something*. She loved me, loved my cat, even claimed to like my parents. But did she sign on for me being flat-out crazy? I couldn't imagine so.

I halfway expected her to say she was going to get in her car and drive home, sleep at her place tonight, think things over, dump me tomorrow. Not Shannon.

When we were inside with Ben, she kicked off her shoes, pulled him out of his carrier, and cradled him in her arms, nuzzling his face. She put her whole body into it. It was kind of erotic, actually. "Benny Boy, I wish you could talk," she said. He just purred like there might be something to this only-as-old-as-you-feel thing. Then she set him down and watched adoringly as he sauntered down the hall to the bed where he slept every night and half the day.

She poured herself a glass of wine. “Want one?”

“Sure.”

She poured. A lot. She drank. “I believe you,” she said. “I can’t see you having some weird serial cat fetish. Showing up at all those different vets with different cats over a twenty year period is just too strange—and for what? So you could convince me now? It has to be the same cat. It has to be Ben. It’s the only thing that makes any sense. Dr. Diderada thought so. Don’t you think?”

I couldn’t believe Ben was right again. I shook my head in wonder. “I did. He said he didn’t, but there was something… It was like no time had passed. I was five, I think, the first time I remember seeing Diderada with Ben. He gave me a lollipop when he gave Ben his treat, but Mom wouldn’t let me eat it. Sugar was poison.”

“I bet you were adorable.”

“I was afraid you’d think I was crazy. *I’d* think I was crazy if I hadn’t been there.”

She laughed, shaking her head. “It was a miracle. A blessing.” She looked me in the eye. “Have you ever tried— You know—”

“No. No way. Once was enough. Once has been more than sufficiently weird enough. I couldn’t deal with it. At first I tried to convince myself it wasn’t Ben who came back that night, but even if an identical cat who acted just like him showed up then, he’d still be 30—210 in cat years.”

She made a face, unhooked her bra, and pulled it out her sleeve. She hung it on a chair back. “I thought they changed that. That because of medical advances, it’s more like five to one.”

“150 then. Looks 20. What’s the difference? He doesn’t age. I can’t explain it.”

“So he’s just stayed exactly the same all these years?”

“Not exactly. He looks the same, but he changes, experiences new things, learns...” I almost said evolves, but I stopped myself. I’d said too much already.

“Like what?” She poured more wine for herself. I hadn’t touched mine.

“Uh. Just things in general.”

"Give me an example. One thing he does now he didn't do when he was 17."

There were dozens of simple things I could've recounted, but I couldn't think of a single one of them. They were all blotted out by the enormous eclipsing mass of what I didn't want to say: *He talks*. Would I then go on to explain he's fluent in English, speaking softly, in a half-whisper, like a breathy purr. Not really built for speech, it took him awhile to perfect his technique. He understood what I said long before he talked back.

Would I go on to explain he reads voluminously, has a passion for discussing politics, and expresses his political opinions in unique ways, like pissing and shitting on every Hummer foolish enough to park on our block.

Should I then tell her the first time he met her he told me, "She's the one for you, Jeffrey"? That would've been way too Son of Sam, don't you think? Ben suggested from the beginning, and I'd always agreed with him, that any mention of his linguistic abilities to anyone would be a very bad idea, and he'd never spoken clearly in the presence of others except for a stray word or two, easily explained away as a fluke. He was convinced if word ever got out he could talk, he'd be jailed for all eternity or until they finally carved him up to discover his secrets. He's always had a flair for the melodramatic, but I'm afraid he was right on this one. But how could I not tell her? At that moment, Ben walked back into the kitchen. He gave me the look, the same look he gave me when Dr. Whatsit who started all this with his frigging reminder card wanted to do tests.

"He tells me when his box needs changing," I offered. "He has a— a special meow."

She picked up Ben and cuddled with him. "Is that right, Benny Boy? To what do we owe the honor of your company?" She looked over his purring head at me. "I just realized. You've lived your *whole life* with him." I wasn't sure what all she meant by that, or what it might mean to her, nor did she care to elaborate. "I'm going to bed now." I followed her into the bedroom. She put Ben in his usual place, stepped out of her jeans and left them lying on the floor, pulled back the covers and crawled into bed beside him. She was asleep in moments, the two of them breathing in unison.

I got into bed on Ben's other side.

When I turned off the light, he scolded me in a soft sing-song, "You almost *told* her."

"Oh fuck yourself, Ben."

"Neutered, re-mem-berrrr?" He chuckled softly, enjoying his own humor, enjoying his endless life.

I lay awake listening to them snore together like an old married couple, wondering how these revelations were going to affect our lives, then drifted off. I dreamed Shannon was in a terrible accident, and I healed her, but when she woke up, she no longer spoke, not a word, and she blamed me. You could see it in her eyes, lonely and furious and afraid.

In the morning, Shannon came right to the point. "Jeffrey," she said. "Would you help Aubrey?"

Ben, returning from a crunching good time at the cat food bowl, jumped onto the sofa, and flicked his tail—*Careful.*

Shannon's younger brother Aubrey was in a car wreck five years earlier at the conclusion of a high-speed chase involving drugs—both in his person and in the trunk of the car—and he'd been in a persistent coma ever since. Until that moment, he was a mere fact of her existence from before I knew her, like the name of her childhood dog or where she went to high school. She never went to see him. He was as good as dead. There'd be no point. Not until now. Now there'd be a point. "You mean—"

"Heal him. Like you did Benjamin."

"I didn't *do* anything to Benjamin. It was just a weird one-time thing."

"How do you know? You've never tried to do it again. I can't *believe* you've never tried to do it again."

There was a light in her eyes that made me uncomfortable. This wasn't just about Aubrey, who everyone in her family pretty much agreed was an obnoxious little shit whose final, completely typical screw-up was not to have the good sense to die when he had the chance. "Believe it. Listen Shannon, I think this is a really bad idea."

"But this is my brother. You could save him. I know you could."

"Let me think about it, okay? I have to think about it."

"Okay. How long do you need?"

Some counselor once told impatient Shannon it was okay to ask for clear time limits—deadlines—if it would help her wait more patiently.

I'd gotten used to it. She was much more patient with a deadline than without. But this was different. I hadn't been able to figure this thing out in 30 years—how it happened, why it happened, how I felt about it, anything at all—and she wanted to know how long I *needed*? Longer than I had obviously. "Tomorrow. Tomorrow night after dinner. I'll cook. I have a Rachael Ray recipe I want to try with that chicken."

"You sure it's still okay? It's been in there a while."

"I just bought it a couple of days ago. It'll be fine."

"You don't think I'm being selfish for asking you to help Aubrey?"

"Not at all. How could asking to help somebody else be selfish?"

"If I wasn't thinking about how it might be hard for you. I don't want you to do anything you don't want to do, Jeffrey. I love you. You know that?"

"Absolutely."

"Okay then. Tomorrow after dinner." She sipped her coffee. "So you watch Rachael Ray every day?"

"She's on when I break for lunch. What can I say? She's hot. You're going to love this chicken."

To tell you the truth, I couldn't remember Rachael Ray's recipe exactly, but it involved some chopped herbs and garlic and olive oil slathered on chicken parts which were then baked. I recalled the close-up of Rachael Ray's hands slathering breasts and thighs. She was always using her hands. I loved it. I'm a whole bird man myself, but I liked the concept. I figured baked was good, so I wouldn't be standing over the stove while we were having this discussion. I didn't expect Shannon to wait until after dinner to bring it up. My tarragon plants looked like they were up to a chicken-size harvest, and I threw in a little white wine, some chopped mushrooms, a dash of nutmeg, some salt, lots of black pepper and crushed garlic, and (of course) extra virgin olive oil. It made a fine green goop.

I'd decided to say no to Shannon's request that I attempt to resurrect Aubrey. Here was my reasoning: Most important, I suppose, was my gut said no. This was no surprise. It'd been saying no loud and clear for 30 years now—no wavering. But with Shannon's petition, I'd been forced to rationally examine what I thought about it—in other words, to come up with some likely sounding reasons to validate my gut. If your mind doesn't work like that, more power to you, and hurray for rationalism and all of that, but for me reason lives to serve the gut. In this case, it was persuasive as usual.

First, I doubted I could do it. When Ben came back to life, I *really* wanted it to happen. I'd never willed anything so strongly before or since. As for Aubrey, I could *try* to want his resurrection because Shannon did—though she seemed to have gotten along fine without him in the time I'd known her—but it wasn't happening. Deep down, I felt if Aubrey were going to make a move, it should be in the other direction. So if my will and desire had anything to do with whatever process brought Ben back to life, there was little chance of success with Aubrey.

Assuming I was able to bring him back to life, the questions just began. Ben regressed from being a dying seventeen-year-old to (by all appearances) a four-year-old, and had remained unchanged for 30 years and counting. Would Aubrey, who had his accident at 26, find himself a permanent six-year-old? What effect would five years of unconsciousness have had on him? And as Ben pointed out, death is a necessary precondition of resurrection. Technically speaking, Aubrey wasn't dead. He was in that huge gray arena known as, "as good as dead." Even my silly father had casually described himself thus over dessert the previous night—but there's no such thing, is there? A prescription and some psycho-babble away from a cure isn't *dead*. Nothing's as *good* as dead. Dead is unique, no known therapy or cure.

But let's just say, everything were to go perfectly. Aubrey awakens from his deep sleep a new man of sound mental faculties who lives a long fruitful life and dies at a respectable age like the rest of us, a credit to his species, despite his previous sociopathic tendencies, having seen the light or whatever revelation the resurrected are privy to, and has been utterly transformed by the experience. Did I *really* want to be the guy who raised him from the dead? I wouldn't make it out of the hospital before they'd be doing tests on me, driving me out to the cemetery to see what I could really do. No thanks.

I didn't know why Ben came back to life and continued to live. I hadn't a clue. Until I figured that out, that's as far as it went. God might have a plan, in which case I was sure I couldn't do anything to screw it up, lacking any clear instructions otherwise, but if God had no plan, I didn't feel obliged to come up with one other than the status quo: Everyone dies. That's the way things are. Except for Ben.

Would I get a chance to say all this to Shannon after she hears no? Would it matter to her? Would I lose her? That's all I cared about: I just didn't want to lose her. I knew I should care about her brother, but to me he was an extra out of an old movie with Genevieve Bujold. I couldn't bear to lose Shannon, however. As Ben prophesied, she was the one for me. Trouble was, she had just one tiny little favor to ask, and I couldn't do it.

And there she was, coming in the kitchen door with a bottle of wine, a half hour early, as I should've known she would be, and here I was with my hands dripping garlic, olive oil, and tarragon, anointing the chicken inside and out, lost in thought, reasoning and seasoning. If I could only manage to throw the bird in the oven before Shannon rushed straight to The Issue, we could talk while it baked.

She kissed my cheek, careful to avoid my slathered hands, and opened the bottle of wine, giving a half-hearted account of her day. Traffic was lighter than usual, she claimed, to explain her early arrival. I pretended to believe her.

Ben, who'd shown up to observe the preparations the minute I took the chicken out of the fridge, didn't even glance her way. He was seated on a stool, eye level with his share of the bounty, the bag of innards I always gave him—liver, heart, gizzard—laid out on the cutting board awaiting preparation once the bird was in the oven. He liked them sautéed in butter and garlic with a splash of Worcestershire, devoured them like a lion on the veldt, if the lion had a chef. I kept the neck for making stock. I didn't treat him to such delicacies often. He liked the Chow, he claimed. "I think they put something in it," he said. "It's highly addictive. Perhaps some extract of cat nip." Ben's always had a serious nip habit, but we all must have our vices, I suppose.

Shannon poured, laughing at Ben's rapt attention to my labors. She scratched the top of his head, and he lifted it to press against her hand, arched his back to her touch, as her hand glided firmly down his back, but his eyes never left the prize. "I hope you washed your hands," Shannon said. She held my glass to my lips to give me a sip of wine, careful once again to avoid my glistening green hands and the oily bird. "I'll put your glass over here." She set it on the counter out of the way and took the stool next to Ben's. "So have you thought about Aubrey?"

Damn. "Of course. Let me get this in the oven first, okay? Then we can talk."

"Okay." She idly petted Ben a few strokes, growing pensive. She wrapped her hand around his tail, and he slowly pulled it through, like a napkin through a ring. "It must not be yes. If it was yes, you'd just go ahead and tell me."

As I recalled, the deadline was *after* dinner. I didn't count on being elbow deep in dinner when she arrived. "I'm almost done here. I just need to get this stuff off my hands and get the bird in the oven."

"Why won't you do it?"

"Can this wait *five* minutes?"

"I suppose so. I've waited five years. We all have. I just can't believe you won't…"

I body slammed the chicken on the counter and splattered oil and tarragon everywhere. "Believe it! No! The answer is no! I don't even know I can *do* anything!"

"You've never even tried!" She touched my oily hands.

It was an eerie moment, her ivory hand laid upon mine as if it weren't smeared with goop, oblivious to the globs clinging to her beige silk blouse. I felt like the Swamp Thing. Somebody loved him too, as I recall. I looked into Shannon's eyes, and there it was again. The light. She wanted me to try out my powers more than she wanted to save her brother. Let's face it. Some brothers aren't missed. But people wait their whole lives to witness a miracle. "Is that what this is all about? You just want to see me *do* it?"

"Certainly not." She almost persuaded herself. She didn't even come close to persuading me. Quite the contrary. It was too much. Years of guilt and mystery and feeling like a freak, and now the love of my life wants me to perform like a dolphin jumping through a hoop—while the saved, the eye of the storm, the miracle kitty, isn't even watching, waiting only to eat some dead bird's heart, cooked the way he likes.

"It is, isn't it? It's driving you crazy. A gen-u-ine miracle. Your boyfriend—with messianic gifts. How cool is that? Here. You want to see?" I scooped up Ben's innards waiting to be sautéed and shoved them deep inside the bird, grasped its oily breasts in both hands and waggled it in her face, then held it aloft, clamping my eyes shut, filling my mind with visions of a perfect chicken pecking celestial corn, or whatever it is they peck, cackling its head off, or maybe that was me. Shannon backed away in terror, knocking over her stool. I squeezed harder, imagined more vividly, willed more forcefully. "Come on you little fucker, live! *Live! Live!*"

And then I felt it, a squirming, writhing wriggling in my hands, and the bird broke loose, erupted from my grasp and hit the countertop, skittering wildly, huge drumsticks pumping footless oiled extremities across Formica. It was amazing how fast the fucking thing could go under the circumstances. Headless, it darted back and forth unpredictably, careening from coffee pot to toaster oven to food processor to bread machine, ricocheting off each white surface with a slimy green stripe. I lunged for it, caught a drumstick, but I couldn't hold on. It hit the floor with a sickening smack and kept running. Then out of nowhere, an airborne Ben landed on its back, digging his claws in deep. Nothing could slip from his grasp. He opened his jaws wide and sank his fangs repeatedly into the bird's thighs and chest, tearing away huge hunks of flesh and swallowing them whole, but still the bird struggled. The battle raged on, with the thing writhing to get free until Ben had consumed all but the bones. He stuck his head deep into the chest cavity, pulled out the still-beating heart, and devoured it in one bite.

There was a huge clatter behind me, and Shannon screamed again. She'd already screamed several times, as I recall. It was the stockpot lid hitting the floor. The goddamn neck was trying to leap out of the stockpot like a fish. I grabbed a long fork and harpooned it, tossing it to Ben on the floor, who polished it off in no time. No problem. I had plenty of stock in the freezer.

Ben was covered in green goop, as was I. The Swamp Thing and his Swamp Cat. The floor was a slimy, glistening extra virgin olive oil lagoon. *Dear Rachael Ray, I tried your chicken recipe and wasn't entirely pleased with the results...*

I knelt down and started washing off Ben with a wet towel. He was jazzed, purring like an outboard motor, a prizefighter who'd miraculously gone the distance and defeated the champ against all the odds. Usually he preferred to clean himself, but the prize was worth any indignity. It wasn't every day he scored an entire six-pound bird for his personal consumption. Shannon and I would have to go out for dinner, I was thinking, or there was always takeout. I was in a tiny bit of denial.

I'd been avoiding looking at her, though that must be her I heard whimpering. Finally, I looked up from my sopping, wild-eyed cat, still hyper-ventilating, his stuffed gut swelled out like he was pregnant. She was standing in the corner by the kitchen door, backed into the coat rack, still holding an umbrella cocked like a baseball bat. She'd picked it up when the reanimated chicken was headed right for her, before Ben leapt to the rescue. "Still want me to heal your brother?" I asked. In retrospect, not the best thing to say.

She looked at the umbrella as if she had no memory of how she came to be holding it. Judging from the look of terror on her face, she remembered, perhaps too vividly, what had just happened—the bizarre battle that had raged at her feet—two immortals in a battle to the death.

Ben took a step toward her. "It's okay, Shannon," he said. "It's dead now."

She threw down the umbrella and dashed out of the house. Her car started seconds later and roared off, tires squealing. I'd never known Shannon to drive like that.

"Don't worry," Ben said. "She'll be back."

"Yeah. What woman can resist us?"

The aroma of tarragon and garlic and death hung heavy in the air. I should mop it up, I thought, but I couldn't face the prospect of reliving the moment just yet. The one for me, the love of my life, was gone. Ben had wandered off and was licking the floor. Maybe he can make himself sick licking up the residue of this disaster, I thought. But that's right. He never gets sick. *Remember-r-r-r?* "I'm going out," I announced.

Ben knew not to say a word.

I walked over to the barbecue place and had chicken that tasted like vinegar and smoke, fire and brimstone. I drank cheap beer and listened to a steady stream of country and western whine, guy after guy pleading for their lovers to forgive them their sins, hanging on to enough hope to manage three chords and a catchy plea built around some outrageous conceit, but none of their desperate hope was contagious, and I remained hopeless. These guys strayed, lied, drank, whatever—typical fucked-up guy stuff. None of them had ever resurrected a six-pound roaster as a clearly hostile act in the midst of a rational discussion. No. At some point, the weirdness has to set off deeply rooted survival alarm bells to head for the hills and not look back. I didn't know how anyone could just work around something like the ride Shannon had been on ever since she was just trying to help and made Ben an appointment at the vet.

Somehow I knew this time, maybe for the only time, I was right and Ben was wrong. Shannon wasn't coming back. I started crying, and the manager came over to tell me I had to leave. I couldn't believe it. I ate his bad food, listened to his sad songs—whose composers would be out of work if they couldn't rhyme die, lie, and good-bye with cry, cry, cry—and now he wanted me to leave because of a few *tears*? I could've done a whole lot worse than tears. I had a good mind to find his walk-in and resurrect his entire inventory, set it loose in the dining room to run amok in his crappy sauce, but of course, I didn't. Wouldn't. Ever again.

Benjamin and a chicken—that's it. My healing career was over.

All attempts to locate Shannon failed. She left town that night apparently, and nobody ever heard from her. Nobody who would tell me, anyway.

A few years later, Dad died, and Mom died the year after that. I held out some hope that Shannon might show up at their funerals, but of course she didn't. Aubrey died, unplugged by his parents apparently. I read the notice in the paper. I lurked nearby in the cemetery, but only the parents and the preacher were there.

When I came home after, even Ben finally admitted we were never seeing Shannon again. "I'm sorry," he said. "I should never have surrendered to my predatory instincts."

"It's not your fault. You're a predator, for Christ's sake. It was my fault. I had no business bringing that chicken back to life."

He nodded in somber agreement. "True. True."

We missed her terribly, but we rarely spoke of her. It was too painful for us both.

My parents had left me a modest inheritance, which I invested in the stock market. After weeks fine-tuning voice recognition software so Ben could use the computer, I turned the portfolio over to him, and in no time he'd made us wealthy enough to retire and travel. We went everywhere. If Ben had read about it, he wanted to go there, and if he wanted to go, we usually went, and if we went, I never regretted it. We went to incredible places. We went to ordinary places made incredible by the wonders Ben knew we'd find there.

I soon discovered that if you have enough money, you can take your cat anywhere, especially when you get older. People put up with things from old people, probably figuring they haven't got too long. An old man denied his desires by some heartless gatekeeper may have missed his last chance. What sort of old age might such a heartless individual expect when it comes his time to travel about pathetically with some old cat in a carrier, when the sign clearly says no animals allowed? What? An empty building? Do you think homo sapiens aren't animals? What then are they, I'd like to know! Oh yes, by the time I'm 84, I can take my cat anywhere.

Trouble is I'm too sick to go anymore.

We've come to rest in Catemaco, a lovely town on a beautiful lake in Mexico, that teems with cats and *brujas*—witches—and is a favorite town of ours. We've rented a place with a balcony overlooking the lake. The fishermen still fish with hand-tossed nets from small one-man boats. I like to watch them at dusk, casting their nets into water and sky the color of burnished copper. The fish are delicious, embedded with cloves of garlic and fried whole.

They're only a memory to me now. I can't keep anything down. Everything tastes like ashes anyway. The doctor has come and gone. He's said there's nothing to be done to save me. He could admit me to the hospital, so that I might be more comfortable, but when I said I would be more comfortable here watching the fishermen with my cat, he bowed, in deference to my age I suppose, and said he understood.

Benjamin, who's befriended both cats and witches here, has returned with a woman named Hermalinda who brews teas for us both. He has broken his long silence with her, and she has agreed to come see to our needs. "Will it cure me?" I ask Ben of the tea she's brewing. I'm surprised I can smell it. I haven't smelled anything in a long while. I've had to give up cooking.

"Of old age," Ben replies, but I've forgotten what I just asked him.

"I'm afraid," I confess to my old friend.

"I know," he says. "Everything will be all right. I'll be joining you. Walk like an Egyptian." He laughs at his cat humor, very sly, but I don't get it. I wonder what Hermalinda is brewing for him. Probably nip. It's always the nip with him.

Hermalinda props me up in bed so that I might look out the balcony at the copper waters, the fishermen's nets like women's fans opening and closing, leaving behind a glistening spray of memories. She holds the cup to my lips. It tastes of cloves and juniper. She patiently gives me the whole cup, sip by sip. The last sip is sweet, like honey, like roses.

She sets a saucer on the floor for Ben and quietly slips out the door. Ben quickly laps up his tea and jumps onto the bed, spry as ever, pushing my frail hands apart and inserting himself once more in my grasp. I can feel him through my skin, thin as paper, his heart beating, hard and steady, through my fingertips. "Good night, Jeffrey." He purrs softly, and my hands tingle. I remember the tune from so long ago, centuries in cat years:

... Old Blue died and he died so hard
Shook the ground in my backyard
Dug his grave with a silver spade
Lowered him down with links of chain
Every link I did call his name
Here Blue, you good dog you
Here Blue, I'm a-coming there too!

Ben stops purring, and a moment later, his heart stops, and he's gone just like that. He's tricked me—knowing where he leads, I'll follow—fleeing the unbearable emptiness of this world without him—he's shown me the way. Some Day has finally come.

Everyone dies. Even Ben.

For me.

The Broken Dream Factory

The Broken Dream Factory was shut down. This was not entirely unexpected. I'd worked here twenty? Twenty-five? Twenty-*seven* years, and not a day went by I didn't think, *this could be my last.*

That's what I liked about it—the uncertainty, the danger even—but now this, to be shut down like some common biscuit factory because of depressed profits, labor unrest, unfair foreign competition—whatever mundane drivel it turned out to be—didn't seem right. What about a comet smacking into it? A crazed, broken-hearted psycho gunning everyone down because he couldn't take it anymore? An implosion of despair so intense that the whole place was sucked into the howling abyss? Or all of us who worked here these many years, just slipping out one night under a full moon and driving away in dark cars quieter than the cicadas? Not this. Not a sign on the door:

GOING OUT OF BUSINESS
Many thanks to our loyal customers and employees.
We will miss you.
—The mgmt

Mgmt? *What* mgmt? I never saw anybody around here answering to that description unless that stands for mean, grim, mealy-mouthed toadies. Many thanks? Twenty-seven years of heartache, and you get *many thanks*? At least they could have nailed the sign up, shown some sense of history and drama, but no, it was taped. A couple of raggedy-ass strips of duct tape held it in place. A good rain, and the mgmt would be washed away.

I lit up a smoke. We couldn't smoke outside, that was the rule, had to light up indoors in the bar, or in the bathroom laying out your rig, trying not to look in the mirror, into the cameras, into yourself. Smoking helps externalize things. Put your pain into the puff, they used to tell us. Those days were over now. No pain to puff, so they told me. A new world.

It'd been awhile since I'd seen it by the light of day. It was okay. It smelled like exhaust, but it was nice to be in the sunlight for a change. A day off. Who couldn't use a day off? I should enjoy it, I told myself.

I tried. I really did. I walked around town, but everywhere I went it was all the same. What's happened to everyone? I kept asking myself. It was like a zombie movie with smiley faces, only now the zombies drove and their children were driven, from parking lot to parking lot, then plod, plod, plod, inside, then out again. Doesn't anybody here miss their broken dreams? Don't they feel an emptiness inside now that the ache is gone? What will they sort through on long, lonely nights if not the bitter shards of what was not to be? I followed them through automatic doors, pulled along by market forces. I tossed my cigarette into the current and watched it float away upstream.

I walked up to a clerk clad in a polyester tunic, a solid bright color like a plastic toy. Would it hurt if they could wear old tweed jackets or knitted cardigans, something with some character, some life, some sense of loss, of life's unraveling? He wore a saucer-size button on his chest that read Ask Me! "Where are your broken dreams?" I asked.

"We don't carry those anymore."

"Why not?"

"People don't want 'em."

"I beg to differ."

"Sorry. We have a no begging policy. We take cash, credit cards, checks, money orders, easy terms, and hard labor. No shop-lifting, no begging."

"Do you know anyone who does carry them?"

He didn't even pretend to stop to think. "No. Why would I know such a thing? I work here. We have American Dreams on special, aisle W. You'll be much happier with one of those."

"Maybe I don't want to be happy."

"Then I can't help you, sir. We're all about happiness here."

"You can't be happy all the time."

"We have something for every minute of the day, 24/7, 365 days a year."

He talked about time as if he knew what it was. He thought it was all about numbers and motion, like lions are about whips and chairs. He didn't have a clue. He was happy all the time. "What about when there are no more years? No 24/7? No 365? The whole universe is one big broken dream. When the sun goes supernova, are you going to be happy then?"

He shrugged. "I'll be dead."

"Perhaps you already are and just haven't noticed. But what about when you *are* dead? Happy then?"

"Of course. I'll be in heaven. That's on aisle W too, at our guaranteed lowest price on the planet. Is there anything else I can help you find?"

On the planet. And what planet would that be? I wondered. "No. I'm pretty sure not." He had to be wrong. Surely not everyone was like this heaven-peddling idiot. Otherwise, I thought, it will only be a matter of time before I'm just like him. Most things, I learned in my years at the Broken Dream Factory, are a matter of time.

I approached a young couple, their cart piled high with dreams. Fresh dreams, frozen dreams, some-assembly-required dreams, do-it-yourself dream kits, sweet dreams, 100% all natural organic dreams. No broken dreams of any kind.

"I couldn't help noticing you're not getting any broken dreams. Would you like to?"

The husband said, "They don't carry them anymore. We did get an American Dream. It's the big one on the bottom there. Does that count?" He thought it was a contest. He thought I'd give him a prize if he had the right dream in his shopping cart.

"The American Dream's more like an evolving concept, isn't it?" the wife said. "You mean good old-fashioned broken dreams like old people talk about, right? Failed love, scorned art, shattered idealism—stuff like that."

"Right."

"They don't carry them anymore."

"But if they *did*, would you want some? Do you *wish* they carried them? Do you miss them?" But I knew the answer before I asked.

They traded a look to double-check they could speak with one voice as usual. "No way," the husband said. "We've got it too good. Look at all this." He pointed to the cart. Right on top was a collection of authentic replicas of dreams once entertained by exiled princes, now restored to their original opulence. Beside it was a six-pack of visionary dreams—each a unique, fully-imagined future guaranteed to evoke a sense of wonder.

Makes you wonder. If the future was that easy, how come we keep screwing it up?

"You might like some of the stuff they've got in mystic visions," the wife suggested. "My sister's into those. Snakes eating themselves, wheels of fire, many-headed beasts. Great stuff. But dark, you know? Real dark. That's why I thought you might like it." She smiled at my darkness.

"Please. I don't want to buy anything. I'm trying to understand what's happened to my life—this world I live in but don't belong in anymore. I worked at the Broken Dream Factory for twenty-seven years, and they closed it down today, taped a sign on the door."

She nodded, her smile growing thin. "Well, good luck with that."

I wondered what it would take to break her dreams, immediately scolding myself for that uncharitable thought. We didn't work that way—pressing our wares on the unwary. Each broken dream was fully adjustable for any imaginable misery the customer might desire, but the choice was *theirs*. "Thanks," I said. "Enjoy your dreams."

Outside the sun seemed too bright. I squinted in the blaze trying to decide what to do. A young man drunk on certainty offered me the dreams of Jesus, and I respectfully declined. He wanted to give me an argument like they do: Broken dreams?—if it's broken dreams you want, you can't do any better than the Lord's story: The wilderness, the temptations, the rigged trial, the torture and death—one heartbreak after another. But it doesn't stay broken, does it? Three days later, and he's not only alive again, he's at the right hand of God. What kind of mortality is that? He feels man's sufferings? I think not. He has to know how it ends before it even begins, right? A little pain, eternal paradise. Where's the suffering? This is not a broken dream. Was Lazarus a happy man when he died the second time? I doubt it. He'd understand what I'm talking about. I finally drove the believer away with my doubts. It wasn't really fair. He was an amateur, and I was a pro. At least I used to be. Now I was just unemployed.

He promised to pray for me as he fled. "You better!" I shouted after him, "God is listening! He'll hold you to it!" But I don't think he heard me. People are always saying, "I'll pray for you." I don't think they follow through, do you? It was early yet. Do you think that guy remembered every poor unfortunate soul he was going to pray for that day? Not me. He probably forgot like the rest of us. I'd pray for him if I believed in that sort of thing.

I cut across the park through a lane of evergreens. The needles made a carpet that soothed my tread. I had to calm down. I could feel myself spiraling out of control. You might think somebody who worked making broken dreams would be out of control all the time, but that wasn't true when I was working. I won't say I didn't bring my work home sometimes, but there was a calm after a hard day at work that I looked forward to, a sense of accomplishment, bittersweet, of course. What am I going to do without that? I asked myself. I'll have to learn not to do the thing I love. There, I'd said it. I loved making broken dreams. This was a revelation even to me. Enlightenment seemed to shimmer in the air before me. I was about to step into this cloud of knowing, perhaps to finally understand myself…

When out of nowhere, a pack of pounding runners rushed round me talking scores and wagers and a sudden death overtime concluded with some heroics narrated out of my hearing, beyond my interest. They think they've tamed time, I mused, even sudden death *overtime,* because they've won a wager. The gazelles think they're lions. Well, as the woman told me, good luck with that. Fools or not, the wisps of my enlightenment scattered in their wake. So what if I loved making broken dreams? The broken dreams didn't love me in return. Not enough anyway, or else this wouldn't be happening.

I bought a bottle of undying hope at the corner store and went home, sat in the kitchen and drained it dry, sat hopeless in the dark until Jane came home. "What're you doing sitting in the dark?" she asked me, turning on the lights, unloading a bag of groceries bigger than our refrigerator. What are we going to do with all that stuff? I thought. If we eat it all, we'll be too big to leave the house. There was enough meat there that if you put it all together, you could've make a pretty good-size dog. I imagined having a dog around the place to play with. I like dogs. I imagined him running out into the street, the horrible squealing sound of brakes.

"The factory closed today," I told her.

"Good," she said. "Now maybe you can get a job you like, something that makes you happy instead of miserable all the time."

"What're you talking about? A job doesn't make you happy. If you like it, it's not a job, is it? And if it's your vocation, your passion, it's never enough, so life itself is a longing unto death." Maybe I'd had my enlightenment after all, and now I was revealing it to Jane.

"Whatever. Do you want to go out? There's a new Italian/Ethiopian fusion place. You eat lasagna with your hands. They have terrific breadsticks."

"No thanks. Do you remember the time—"

She slammed a ham on the counter with a silencing smack, rattling every utensil in its hook, making the salt shaker jump and fall over, roll a quarter turn and stop. "No. Don't even start. I don't want to talk about broken dreams anymore. Not ever again. You're the only one who cares. You're the only one who's *ever* cared."

"That's not true."

"Face it, Stran. The world has changed. Nobody uses typewriters. Nobody believes in ghosts. Nobody wants broken dreams."

"Cherishes. You don't just *want* a broken dream. You cherish it."

"Screw it, I don't care. Where do you think you are? Living out on the moors? Manning the barricades? Sailing to Byzantium? Colonizing the stars? People have had it with broken dreams. More to the point, Stran. *I've* had it with broken dreams."

"You can't mean that."

"I can, and I do."

"But don't you remember the night you said—"

"I told you not to start." She turned, walked down the hall into the bedroom, and closed the door behind her, leaving me alone in the hall with the memory of the night she said forever, but never meant it now.

It's my house, I thought, but I can't stay here anymore. You devote your life to shattering idealism only to find out the one person you thought believed in you never really did. It was fitting I guess, to discover this now, now that there weren't any broken dreams anymore, just ashes in your mouth, a sick, embarrassed feeling in your gut. *Sorry about my life, everyone, I was just being stupid.*

I didn't want to drink any more, not there anyway, in my own kitchen, so I sat for a long time thinking of somewhere to go like some pitiful character in a literary novel from the 60's remembering broken dreams, until he rises, seizes the broom and sweeps out his kitchen! Not me, I decided. Let Jane sweep the kitchen or not. She can have the existential moment and the dishes. I'm leaving.

So I left. I didn't even pack. Who packs at a time like that? What would you take?

I stopped at an obscure tavern with lots of neon and drank a cognac, an absinthe, a punch of crushed lotus, and a shot of mescal with the worm. Then I took the crosstown express to the moors. They were windswept. Wild. Haunted.

The ghosts scarcely noticed me. I used to flirt with madness when I worked the night shift just starting out, so I knew a thing or two about getting an apparition's attention, but these proved elusive. Finally, I got right in the face of a beautiful wraith and said loudly, "*Who* are you haunting?"

"What?" She was listening to ghostly music, loud. She talked too loud as people do listening to their own soundtrack. The music leaked from her diaphanous earbuds like nails being pried from boards by a tinny tornado.

"Who are you haunting?" I shouted.

"Nobody haunts anymore. Leave me alone."

"If you're not haunting anyone, why don't you pass over to the other side?"

"I doubt they have anything over there we don't have over here twice as good."

"But you're dead. You don't belong here."

"You could've fooled me." She swept her ghostly arm across the landscape. The moors were criss-crossed with roads like whip lashes. Big houses like enormous tombstones lined the road. Dead people lived inside with their cars. Their mothers lived over the garage. Their mastiffs were the size of housecats. Heathcliff was a housecat. Cathy was fat. The moors were no more.

Jane was right. The world was a plain plane. But I couldn't just give up. The world needed broken dreams now more than ever. Warped visions, pointed remarks, twisted individuals.

Maybe Wanda? She was my only hope. She'd told me she never wanted to see me again, but I figured if she heard they shut down the factory, maybe she'd relent. We worked on heartaches together for ten years until we started taking our work home, calling each other up at four in the morning, listening to "Missing You" on auto-repeat through a whole shift. She wanted me to leave Jane. I said I couldn't because she'd been there for me when I needed her most, had believed in me, or so I thought. Wanda had herself reassigned to mortality. They always needed people there. I transferred to despair. Almost ruined my liver.

I called her. I'd purged the number from my phone, but I still had it in my own tortured memory. I used to recite it to myself, a mantra of temptation.

"Hi Wanda."

"Stran Fellowes. Why are you calling me?"

"Have you heard?"

"Of course I've heard. That doesn't explain why you're calling me."

"We're the only two who care."

"How do you know I care?"

"I just know."

There was a long silence. In the distance I could hear a dog barking. I wasn't sure whether it was here or there, her distance or mine. "So I care. So what?"

"We've got to stop it."

"What're you talking about?"

"We've got to break into the Broken Dream Factory and start it up again. I can't do it by myself. I need you."

"What about Jane?" She said it with a sneer, still angry, still hurt, still rehearsing it on lonely nights like it was yesterday. She cared all right.

"I've left her. You were right. She doesn't understand me."

"She's *never* understood you. Why leave her now?"

I knew it was true; there was no point denying it. "I had my broken dreams before. Now that they're gone, knowing she doesn't care… I just can't do it anymore."

A train whistle blew, drowning out the dog. Again I couldn't tell if it was my end or hers. Mine, I thought.

"Okay," she said. "I'll meet you there. Are you going to break my heart again?"

"Probably."

Her laughter was like ashes. "I guess nothing's certain, huh?"

"I still love you."

"I know. Me too. Save it for tonight. Sundown?"

"Sundown."

I hung up, and dog and train fell silent. They were at her end, her place, Cheap Motel next door to the Galaxy Drive-In. We used to make love in her bed with the curtains open watching *The Man with the X-Ray Eyes*. The memory filled me with hope, waiting to be crushed like plump grapes.

She was still driving a red '59 Kharmann Ghia convertible with a crumpled right fender and a busted headlight. The lone headlamp shone on me like a spotlight, like she was checking me out, taking aim at my heart. She got out of the tiny car in long, leggy slow motion. The years in mortality had been kind to Wanda. She was always striking, but now there was an air of inevitability about her that was irresistible.

"Not now," she said when I attempted to crush her in my arms. "We have to get inside. Did you bring tools?"

There was a chain across the door five miles long. It was wrapped around the building, across every door, window, and air shaft. "I don't need any *tools*. I have skills." It took me no time at all to find the weakest link. I took Wanda's lovely, delicate hand in mine and guided it toward the chain. "Touch it," I whispered in her ear. "Here."

At her touch, the link broke like a bubble, and she laughed. "You haven't lost your touch, Stran."

"*Your* touch," I told her. "Yours."

But we weren't so giddy once we stepped inside. The place was a mess, plunged into a deep and abiding gloom, cluttered with so much pointless crap you couldn't walk ten feet in any direction without tripping over something, damp, cold, moldy, and bitter, the huge building groaning in the wind as if it too was deciding each moment whether to go on standing or to collapse and crush everyone inside. We expected all that. What was different was that it was empty, when it used to teem with people. Now, except for us two and the rats who'd stayed, having always felt quite at home in the place, there wasn't another soul.

"It's just us," she whispered. "You weren't lying. You have any ideas?"

"I want you," I said.

"You always want me. That's not enough. There has to be more than that."

"I want you, but you don't want me."

"That's not true. Besides, where's the fun in that? We would need at least three to make it interesting. Do you think Jane…?"

"Not a chance. She's turned her back on broken dreams."

"Let's have a drink and think about this."

We went into the lounge. It didn't seem the same without the Amer-Asian junkie on the piano playing sweet jazz and the blind bartender who could get you anything you wanted, no questions asked, smoking clove cigarettes behind the bar. We made our own drinks. It was a little bit scary to be in this enormous place all by ourselves. We sat in the big booth and held each other, trying to come up with some broken dream big enough to bust out of these chains and change the world.

But nothing came to us, and we made love on the office sofa, in the back of a cab, in a choir loft (though it wasn't the same without the wedding rehearsal going on below, the sound of someone's steady tread coming up the stairs). It was just the two of us. We went to the honeymoon suite and fell asleep. Nothing broken about that.

We tried. We really did. But no matter what we did, we couldn't break the dream. Some nights we danced all night long, others we knitted and watched television. Nothing worked. Wanda planted a garden. I made a forest. We dreamed our own dreams. We shared them, swapped them, pulled them every which way, but we couldn't break them. We only managed to stretch them out, expand them. We felt comfortable in them, comfortable with each other. We wore our dreams like old pajamas.

Then one night, snuggled in bed as we were falling asleep, Wanda whispered in my ear, "I'm going to have a baby," and I was the happiest man the Broken Dream Factory had ever seen.

I delivered our son on the big bed in the honeymoon suite—Wanda's choice (and I gladly did everything my great pregnant queen commanded). And what a son came forth. I know there are those who don't love their children. That's not Wanda and me. No child was ever loved more. We named him Orph, after the two of us, Wanda and I both being orphans. We used to say that made us lucky, because we had no parents to screw us up, but then we were being bitterly ironic, wallowing in self-pity; now it was the truth in a way. We had no bad habits to fall back on, no less-than-perfect role models. We truly did our best with Orph. We taught him everything we knew, tending the garden, wandering the forest, hanging out in the lounge where he taught himself sweet jazz he'd play for us evenings, writing his own songs. He learned to read almost before he could walk and spent hours in the Broken Dreams Library reading everything, even the dead languages. He spent weeks in the balcony of the Rialto watching everything, even the never released. We all liked books and movies, but he threw himself into them like I had once dedicated myself to my work at the Broken Dream Factory, and I'd be lying if I didn't say I began to worry.

He slipped outside when he was still small enough to squeeze through the chains and came back with a tomcat. He found an old Smith & Co. typewriter in the bourbon-soaked hotel room and started writing stories for the cat he called the *Cat Gazette*. The cat, his mother, and I were his avid readers. The stories were mostly thrilling tales and unlikely adventures starring, oddly enough, the rats, who, I suspect, also read the *Gazette* when we'd all retired for the night. Their scritches and scratches were a common feature of the Broken Dream Factory's night sounds, and they seemed particularly intense whenever a new issue of the *Gazette* was published.

The tales had a profound effect upon the cat, whom Orph had named Felix Culpa. Previously, an accomplished devourer of rats, Felix promptly turned vegetarian and embraced a doctrine of non-violence. One night he slipped away to turn himself into a spay/neuter clinic and never returned.

The rats soon after held a secret counsel of their own and, for reasons not entirely clear to me, promptly departed in a horde. The Broken Dream Factory was now oddly silent at night, except for the building groaning, though even that took on a different key, as if instead of contemplating collapse, it hoped to wrench itself loose from its foundations and flee.

Orph wept, and could not be comforted. He cursed the Smith & Co. typewriter and threw it off the roof of the Broken Dream Factory. It landed on the scarecrow in his mother's garden, displacing the head. The crows were no more afraid of it than they'd been of the old head, a volley ball with a smiley face painted in blood, by Orph, of course, after watching nothing but *Castaway* for three straight days.

Orph stayed on the roof for weeks, months, sleeping up there, picking at the food his mother and I brought him, until one morning early I found him in the supply closet into the pills. He'd had an inspiration. I noticed his voice had definitely started to change. He sowed the garden with Dexedrine, and while the crows pecked it up like kernels of popcorn, he fed an enormous roll of paper into the typewriter and wired a feeder full of pills and a bottle of water to the sturdy metal frame. The crows settled on the typewriter crammed so tightly there must've been one on each key, three or four on the big spacebar, all jostling each other continuously. A circling swarm periodically smacked the return. In a week they'd written *On the Road* and flown away, to return, nevermore.

"That was interesting," Orph said.

Then he started bringing girls home. He found new ways in and out of the place Wanda and I had never known about. There were always new girls, but about the time Orph started spending more nights out than in, some of the girls started staying behind, taking up residence in the dozens of empty beds in the Broken Dream Factory. When Orph did show up for the occasional night, he'd sleep with one of them, but rarely the same one twice. They befriended Wanda and me in the mistaken notion that this might help their chances to become the one chosen for his occasional homecomings, but they couldn't have been more wrong. He seemed to choose the one whose heart was near mended, who might get some sense and go home, just about to get over him. Until he showed up again to open the wound, so she wouldn't leave. He might even write a story about her, sing her a song. Many of them were lured here by his songs. I suspected him sometimes of using the same song more than once, just changing the names, so long as it would scan. They were nice girls, every last one of them. I urged them to leave, to get a life. Wanda said I was getting soft, but she told them the same thing. "My son will only break your heart," we told them.

And each one seemed to say, "*My* heart? Do you think? I should be so lucky!"

Months now passed between his occasional visits. Girls started showing up on their own, slipping in through secret passages he'd told them about, in hopes of finding him here. Some were now grown women, so crazy in love they might as well be girls. When he came and went, we spent infinitely more time consoling the bereft afterwards than we spent with our son when he was here.

Still, he was always very sweet to us. We would see him early in the mornings before he went away. He told us things about the various places he traveled, kept us up-to-date on his accomplishments. He was writing prolifically, he said. Like the crows on the typewriter? I asked him. He liked that and laughed, "Like I swallowed them and taught them some sense."

Then he left. It was always that way. He'd spend the night somewhere in the Broken Dream Factory, and see us in the morning when he was already packed to go.

So when he came home this time and sought me out immediately because he had something important to tell me, I knew it must be serious. He came right to the point. "I'm not coming back," he said. "I'm leaving in the morning. Tonight will be my last night here. It's time I left the Broken Dream Factory for good. As much as I love you and Mom, I can't keep coming back here. I hope you understand."

What could I say? I wept, and he comforted me, weeping himself. I asked him if he was going to tell his mother, and he said that's what he was going to do next—then he was going to spend his last night here with the two of us. If only that were true.

This is an old place, no one knows how old. Some say the cellar is fashioned out of an old cavern, and if you go down deep enough there are paintings on the walls of woolly mammoth and mastodons. You hear a lot of crazy stuff around here. But it's old anyway, with secret passageways, and strange acoustics. It only took one of the girls to overhear his plans, for all of them to know soon after.

He was singing to his mother in the lounge, like he used to do when he was younger, putting off telling her he was leaving for good, working up his nerve, and maybe because he knew it pleased her so to listen to him sing and remember.

They burst into the room, all of them, all the heartbroken girls who spent their lives dreaming he would stay here with them. They begged him to stay. He said it was impossible.

"Look at Stran and Wanda!" they said. "They're proof you can live forever in the Broken Dream Factory."

"No," he said. "I created Stran and Wanda, a dream to comfort you in my absence. But now I'm going away, back to the real world, and so must all of you."

But that's not the way it was to be. They seized him, like the crows fastening onto the keys of the typewriter, five on this arm, six on that, a dozen around each leg, and a swarm around his head. "No!" they shouted, for they meant to stop him, and did, tearing him to pieces, but still his head kept singing, kept insisting it invented us all, until Wanda scooped it up and heaved it over the wall in a high arc, plummeting to earth we know not where. The girls are out looking every night. You know how the young are, ever hopeful.

We don't let on that we hear from him from time to time. He publishes stories and poems in obscure publications that are clearly his work, though he uses a variety of pseudonyms. He produced an experimental musical in West Virginia last summer that closed after a week, though it likely would've run for years on Broadway. And most weekends he plays piano and sings in a bar near a train station where the dog barks all night long. He probably does a dozen other things we don't even know about. But someone must be paying attention. He's having an effect: We've started getting orders again at the Broken Dream Factory. It looks like we might be opening back up any day now.

Once in a blue moon, Orph calls on the phone, usually when he's on the road somewhere, and the connection's nearly always bad. He says any day now he's going to catch a break.

Maybe so, I say. Maybe so. I try to encourage him anyway I can. His mother and I couldn't be more proud of him if he was the king of the world.

Desperate Love

There's nothing better than a spurned, broken-hearted lover—the persistence of the pain, the pointlessness of the desire. Your widow or widower's too easily resigned, has perhaps steeled themselves against the inevitable, may even secretly rejoice in their black garb like some giddy penguin, but a hopeless lover still hopes against hope or some such nonsense, and he is mine.

I say *he* because I prefer men, because I once was one, I suppose, or maybe it's their fondness for the grand gesture—the drunken late-night phone calls that start out pleading and wooing and end up screaming insults, crashing the wedding like Dustin Hoffman in *The Graduate* (without his success), or driving all night to Virginia and back to buy something truly lethal from a gun shop that would sell semi-automatic death to Charlie Manson if he could manage the right drawl and talk a little shit. The course of true love never did run true. A restraining order back home is just another speeding ticket on the interstate of life. Stuff it in the glove box and keep on driving because love makes the world go round just a little bit faster.

Which is what I'm doing in a suburban Applebee's at a table in front of the bar with a fellow named Matt waiting for his order to come. It seems they can't cook anything because the computer has crashed, and the man who can uncrash it has been on his way for the better part of an hour. Matt is growing increasingly surly with the young waitress, failing to understand why his burger can't be grilled. Have the flames gone out because the computer's down? I'm sure she'd find a way if she knew Matt has a loaded gun in his jacket pocket he intends to empty at the furniture store across the road once his ex-wife Melinda arrives at work for the evening shift. Matt and Melinda—isn't that too cute? I sometimes think couples hook up because of alliteration, thinking it will look good on a napkin at the reception. I've put him up to this, whispering in his ear, summoning visions of her and her new lover in his mind. Christopher, Don't-call-me-Chris. Pooh fan. The bedding manager. I swear you can't make this shit up. I also put Matt up to the burger. He's understandably not all that hungry given what he's about to do, but I like meat.

"Leave him alone, why don't you?" Selene says to me. She's sitting on the bar taking sips out of some guy's frozen margarita with a straw she dips into it, covering the straw with her index finger, holding it over her open mouth like a feeding bird, releasing it, and letting it slide on down. She makes it look sexy. Selene makes everything look sexy. I haven't seen her in an age. She looks the same. She looks good.

"Why don't you mind your own business?" I say.

"Business?" She laughs like I've made a joke, but she knows I'm not joking. She's just trying to annoy me, distract me, so that Matt here can think twice, walk out on his burger he doesn't want anyway, maybe toss the gun in a Dumpster somewhere, and get on with his life.

"What's his story?" I point to Mr. Margarita. I croon a few bars of "Are You Lonesome Tonight?" I know Selene's type. She gets off on longing.

She laughs. "Cut it out. He's a sweet guy. Kyle. He's working up his nerve to call Courtenay in accounting."

"Isn't that precious. I suppose you've been working her nerve and libido up too."

"Maybe." Her smile implies she might do just about anything. It draws you in, that smile. Even me.

I shake my head. "We're a pathetic pair, you know that? Preying on the stragglers, cut off from the herd, fucking with them for the rush of a little vicarious *life*."

"If you want to see it that way. I'm trying to help people find happiness."

It's my turn to laugh. "Bull shit. You're getting off on it. You don't seem to care that sooner or later most of your desperate lovers end up in my neighborhood with a whole other set of needs. I'm just trying to help Matt here too. He's got some serious issues to work out since his happiness ended up in the lost and found. He's looking for a little closure." I make my hand into a gun. "Bang. Bang. Bang." I touch index finger to temple. "Bang."

"*Here* Zack? Here? At an Applebee's? What is this going to do for their friendly, neighborhood appeal? Why screw a whole franchise so you can have your sick little thrill? What is it with this boyish fascination with guns anyway?"

I could listen to her talk all night, even when she's mocking me. She sounds like an oboe or a cello or something like that. It's hard to remember the subtleties. But played beautifully. "Not here. Across the street at the furniture store. Don't worry. Your guy's got time to hook up with his girl. Maybe the excitement will get them in the mood, so you can indulge your girlish fascination with fucking."

She makes a mock annoyed face, sticks out her tongue at me, and slinks into the stool beside Kyle. I never tire of watching her move, watching her work. She's fucking elemental. She leans against Kyle, one hand on his thigh, the other caressing the back of his neck, her lips at his ear, whispering something, brushing his ear. For punctuation, she runs the tip of her tongue around his ear, then sucks on his lobe. He's visibly shaken, flipping open his phone and calling Courtenay in accounting in one convulsive spasm of action. He thinks it's bravery, the poor dick. I wonder if Courtenay can hear the lustful pant in his voice. I can't listen. Selene's all smiles. Courtenay will come. Courtenay will definitely come.

"Why didn't you blow him while you were at it?" I ask.

"Men. Always in such a hurry." She lays a comforting hand on Kyle's crotch.

"I'm not a man."

"You could've fooled me. So limited in your perspective. Playing with guns."

"So what happens now? You follow them home, you're him, you're her, you're both. It's magic. They didn't know they had it in them. So what? What then?"

She shrugs one sexy shoulder. "I move on. Same as you."

"*Not* same as me. I'm at the end of the road. There's no moving on from here. I'm like that ferryman in Hell."

"Right. Just doing your job. When Matt there goes off, you'll love it, shooting innocent people. Your own action movie."

"I'm the innocents too. I'm not just the shooter."

"The difference is they die, and you don't."

"That's true. But they're alive, and we're not."

"Is that what makes you so mean?"

"It's a start."

Kyle hangs up, beaming with love and joy. This is particularly weird in the near empty restaurant, where the breakdown in food production has left a small disgruntled crowd taking turns giving shit to Anna, a nervous inexperienced waitress not up to the task. The indifferent bartender leans against the back bar reading Camus, no help at all. Maybe I'll come back for him some night.

Matt grunts, the sound of a decision being made. He's the most disgruntled of all, and while I've been sucked into Selene's little seduction, I've been neglecting him, and he slips the leash. "Waitress," he calls out, and the frightened young thing appears. "Cancel my order. How much for the tea?" He stands and takes out his wallet. I suggest he sit down, but he ignores me.

Anna says, "I'm so sorry for your inconvenience, sir. There'll be no charge for the tea, sir. Please accept—"

"I *said* how much for the fucking *tea!"* Matt's got a big, booming voice. Every eye in the place is now on my boy, even the bartender's. Camus lies face down on the bar. Anna is trembling.

This happens. The living are temperamental, impetuous. If you push them to the edge, teetering on the balance, they can be unpredictable, impulsive. A loaded gun in the pocket exaggerates this effect.

You might think Anna is too young to realize that the one thing she must not do is disagree with him, but sadly she knows this from her abusive father but nonetheless remains stupidly true to her company training. She really, really wants to do well on this job. She needs this job, so she can get her own place. "No sir, it's free. Please accept our sincerest apologies."

No? Did she say *no*? *Nothing's* free. Everything comes with a price. Matt puts his wallet away, and out it comes, the gun, sweeping across the place, people screaming, dishes crashing, quite the spectacle, just the thing our boy Matt needs to fan the flame. "I've *had*," he hollers in a near incoherent wail, "just about *enough*!"

"Nice work," Selene says to me. "I thought he was doing this in the furniture store."

"The best laid plans."

"That's mice and men."

"Us too. A computer crashed."

"I see that."

Just then, Glenn, the mid-level manager summoned to uncrash the computer, finally comes walking through the door, bored, long-suffering, clueless. Selene would definitely have to blow this guy to get a rise out of him. But the gun does the trick. He throws his hands up in the air and screams, “Don’t shoot! You can have everything!” and Matt shoots him through the heart.

The life that flashes before Glenn’s eyes is not so pathetic as you might imagine. He deserved better than he got certainly, but in the end there was something poignant about it, beautiful. In the end, they’re always beautiful. Death is life’s most intense moment.

Meanwhile, Matt’s blazing like a Roman candle, adrenalin sloshing through his veins like a flood through a storm sewer. He’s killed someone but not the right someone, so he still wants to kill someone, but there was something about the release when the bullet slammed into Glenn’s chest that filled a hollow in Matt’s chest. He’s killed a man. The hard part is over.

“Gimme your phone,” Matt says to Kyle.

Selene whispers urgently, rubbing his trembling limbs to calm him, “Do it, do it, do it,” until he does.

Matt calls Melinda. I lean in close to listen. “I’m at the Applebee’s across the street. I want you to come over here right now and bring fucking Christopher with you.”

“I will do no such thing. Must I remind you that there is a restraining order—”

Matt puts the gun to Anna’s head and hands her the phone. “Tell her if she doesn’t show up with Christopher in five minutes, I’m going to shoot you. Tell her I already killed someone I didn’t even know.”

Anna says this as best she can. Her fear is like falling into a dark pit, falling so fast she’s afraid her heart will stop. She’s been there before, she knows the territory, but this time she finds something down there like a polished stone, the size of a goose egg, and hard, impenetrable, indestructible. She hefts it. Matt’s not the only one who’s had enough. Matter of fact, I’d say Anna here has quite the head start on him. Since she was a child, before she could speak or remember. Broken heart? Big fucking deal. A calm comes over her.

That’s me.

I point out the tray full of ketchup bottles sitting on the bar beside her. She was cleaning them, something she could do without the computer’s approval. She hands Matt the phone with one hand, grabs a bottle with the other, and swings it in a vicious arc, smacking into Matt’s temple and exploding in a cloud of red glass. He falls to his knees, firing wildly, and she hits him with another and another.

Selene wraps her arms around her and pulls her away. "Enough," she whispers. "Enough, enough."

Anna kneels sobbing in the middle of the dining room. Courtenay dazedly walks through the door and sees her, dead Glenn on the floor, and Matt covered in ketchup and blood. Kyle springs from his stool and takes her in his arms, comforts her as everyone waits for the police and the ambulances. Melinda and Christopher don't show. They've called the cops instead. You can't blame them. What's Anna to them? Anna's life?

Matt's carried off to the hospital. He'll probably live, go to prison. Nobody wants to die in jail. Not even me.

"What are you still doing here?" Selene asks me. "Your boy just left."

"I don't like hospitals."

"Yeah. They keep people alive there, give them hope."

"They shoot them full of drugs and tell them lies. They die anyway. Looks like you'll have a good time tonight."

The cops are questioning Courtenay and Kyle together. He has his arm around her. She leans against him. Selene caresses one cheek, then the other. "Aren't they lovely?" she says. "They might really last."

"Nothing lasts."

"We do."

"Lucky us."

Kyle and Courtenay are told they can go, and they head for the door arm-in-arm. She's going to spend the night at his place. She wouldn't feel safe otherwise, she says.

Anna is sitting at the bar beside the tray of ketchup bottles, waiting. When the cops asked her if there was anyone they could call, she said her father. He comes through the door as Kyle and Courtenay go out. I sit down beside her.

"Leave her alone, why don't you?" Selene says to me.

"Mind your own business," I say, and she does, running out into the parking lot after her lovers. The three of them drive away, looking for happiness. Anna stays here with me. We watch them go. I put my arm around her shoulders, squeeze, a little too hard and bony, the way her father does when things get out of hand, as he likes to put it, and go too far. Here he is, standing at the bar, waiting to take us home. Things might not go so far tonight. Not far at all.

Rats, Mazes, Snakes, Magic

Back when B.F. Skinner was a BFD, I had a job working for the psych department raising rats. That's where the action was then, animal studies. If we could just figure out rats, humans were right around the corner. If you thought different, you were a throwback idiot to the stone age. The rats had the answers, and any psych department with the sense God gave a gopher, had to have their very own rat colony.

They used to buy their rats from a laboratory supply company, but that runs into some money, and they were going through serious quantities of rats. You couldn't really reuse them. Once you'd messed with them in one way, they were pretty much useless for another. If you shocked the shit out of them one week, it might affect their ability to rejoice in some paltry pellet of reward the next. This was behaviorism. The ideal test subject had no past. So when the study was over, they had no future either. Next stop: The snake house at the zoo.

I ran the colony. I was an English major, but they couldn't get a psych major to take the job. The colony had a Director, Dr. Mitchell, a faculty member who figured I was doing a great job if I didn't bother him, but I was the one who raised the rats.

They were Long-Evans rats, the black and white kind. There was a batch of gerbils once, and one guy had a roomful of rabbits that were strictly off limits—there were rumors it was a drug study—but mostly it was rats. At any one time, I was responsible for about 500 of them, give or take. No telling how many I saw come and go. There were visions of more, long-range plans. The psych faculty began their most wistful utterances with, "When we get the new wing..." A dean somewhere dreamed of a teeming Ratropolis, a recruiting tool to attract future rat runners rivaled only by the student deferment from the military draft, which had swollen the school from a sleepy state college with an uncertain future to a Major University with aspirations to become a Research Institution. That meant rats, rats, and more rats.

My job was fulfilling this need. That wasn't hard. The gestation period was 21 days, average litter size 8+, weaned at 21 days. We gave the females 21 days leisure before breeding them again. The studs, bigger, badder, tougher looking, didn't have much to do between breeding sessions, when they serviced a harem of three for a week. If a stud failed to perform, or his litter sizes were statistically below par, he got a one-way ticket to snake town.

At three, Zack, damn near the size of a miniature Chihuahua, was far and away the oldest, but his litters were consistently the largest, and he probably could have impregnated every female in the place if I'd let him, but the colony needed more genetic diversity than that. Even though he looked like a badass rodent from the dump, he was a sweetheart with people, even with other rats, unless somebody was stupid enough to mess with him. When the other males wouldn't get along, I'd put the troublemaker in with Zack. He had a fierce kick, his fat body wobbling like a kung-fu groundhog. He'd slam the other rat up against the side of the cage and just *lean*. Nobody messed with Zack twice, and his temporary cage mates returned to society, if not rehabilitated, somewhat humbled.

I also used him to demonstrate the proper handling of a rat to the sophomore Experimental Psychology students, who all had to run some pointless one-rat dance with a much less intimidating rodent than Zack, and it was my job to get them through it unbitten. 90% of achieving that goal was overcoming their fear of rats. Zack never bit even the clumsiest of them, and some of the girls wanted to take him home. He probably would've liked that if he could've taken along a female or two or three.

I also issued rats with all their records—like checking a book out of the library—to the real rat runners, mostly advanced psych students working for professors looking for publication, tenure, promotion. The rat runners, like rats in a maze, were just trying to get out of there, or at least not screw up.

I educated the rat runners in proper rat etiquette too. Some of them were more squeamish than the sophomores. They didn't want to touch the rats, but you had to pick them up to put them in a maze or take them out, when you cleaned their cages, and when you put them in a holey cardboard box for the zoo guy to pick up when the party was over. And you had to run the rats to get the grade, to pass the course, to get the degree, to have a future career. Everyone chooses their own dilemma.

I just didn't want anyone getting hurt, and the runners handled rats dozens more times than the sophomores did, with dozens more opportunities for misunderstanding. My message to the runners was simple: If the rats didn't *want* to be picked up and moved around all the time, chances are, sooner or later, the picker-upper was going to get bit. But these were young rats, dependent upon the kindness of humans since birth, bred to be friendly, sociable animals that *liked* to be handled—so there was no reason to fear them, unless you were stupid enough to give them a reason to fear you.

Some runners simply couldn't overcome their aversion to rats, and I kept an eye out for potential trouble. Gloves were a tell-tale sign of a rat-phobic runner. I strongly discouraged their use. If they were thin enough so that you could feel the rat in your hand, they offered no protection from a bite. If they were heavy enough to offer protection, you couldn't feel the little guy you were squeezing too hard—eliciting the very response you were so afraid of. Rats responded best to a friendly, naked hand, a light, responsive touch—who doesn't?—and if you had a cat at home, please remember to wash your hands first.

None of us were here for the long haul. Why not get along? All the rats kept a rendezvous with the snakes at the end of their brief run. The breeding stock joined them when they were used up, well before they were two. My hope for Zack was that he die of old age, sleeping with his harem, but I knew that wouldn't be long. Rats almost never saw four. The rat runners, too, were only passing through—four years max—on their way to Vietnam or Canada or jail, unless they were lucky or clever enough to flunk their physicals or be women—a tiny minority in the runner world at the time. Somebody had to stay home to grieve and demonstrate.

This was America, love it or leave it. Left or right. Truth or dare. Fight the Enemy here, or fight him there. There were mazes everywhere. I was reading William Blake and Phil Dick. I wanted to live in another reality. I wanted to talk to angels in my backyard. I came remarkably close.

One day I was in Rick's lab to pick up a rack of dirty cages for the cage washer, a thing like a stainless steel mini-carwash especially designed to deal with rat turds, which supposedly clogged the drains of less expensive equipment. Rick, wearing an extra-heavy-duty leather work glove, was transferring a rat from cage to maze, the rat crushed in his hand like a wad of paper. The rat was squirming, obviously in some discomfort, but Rick couldn't feel a thing through the glove. Not that he would've cared. By his own oft-repeated account, he "hated fucking rats."

"You're hurting the rat," I said, but Rick ignored me, struggling with his stopwatch. He didn't like stopwatches either. He was supposed to time how long it took the totally freaked rat to run the maze once released from the claw-of-death grip he had on her. It was all females in this study. I have no idea why. I tried not to ask too many questions. Runners were easily annoyed by my questions. "You're asking the wrong question," was their favorite answer.

Rats are agile beasts, and strong. The imprisoned rat was forcing her way through the unfeeling leather fingers, patiently pushing, pulling, kicking, using teeth and claws, until her forelegs were free. She was an exceptionally small rat, which worked to her advantage in this struggle. She seemed to stretch her body, elongating her neck and torso, until she looked more like a tiny otter than a rat. It was really quite incredible. Then she bent over, grasped the hem of the glove in her paws, pulled, and lunged, aiming her teeth at the smooth white flesh just beyond the rough leather edge of the glove.

Maybe I should've warned him, but I already *had* warned him, dozens of times. This was his party now. If Rick hadn't been wearing a glove, this never would've happened, and even if it had—rats freak out sometimes, just like humans—he would've *felt* her squirming and dropped her back in her cage long seconds ago instead of serving up his lily-white arm like a slab of cheese. How could he not notice what was going on in the palm of his own hand? Maybe he wasn't asking the right questions.

Too late.

Make no mistake. A rat bite hurts. Rick's response was quick and decisive: He drew back his great gloved hand, his fat thumb wrapped hard around the rat's hindquarters, and threw her against the wall with a sickening smack. She slid to the floor, unconscious but still breathing, leaving a thin line of blood on the painted cinderblock.

Rick bent down, scooped her up, dropped her in the maze, and hit the stopwatch. He was breathing hard, his face flushed. I didn't say anything. Usually, I would've told the bite victim to get a tetanus shot immediately, walked him over to the student health center if necessary, but I knew Rick had just had a tetanus shot a couple of weeks earlier. Some animals have a steep learning curve. And besides, I thought, would it be such a bad thing if Rick contracted tetanus, if some big dumb force picked him up and smashed him against a wall?

After a minute, he shut off the stopwatch, scooped up the Experimental Subject, dropped her back in her cage, grabbed another to drop in the maze, and hit the watch again. The fresh rat, perhaps witnessing the fate of her fallen sister, hustled through the maze with all due haste. Rick recorded the still-unconscious rat's failure with a small black X.

"You going to tell Mitchell you threw one of his test subjects against the wall?" I asked. "Is there a special symbol for that? A drop of blood? The ears and tail?" I'd been reading a lot of Hemingway for a class. I hated the macho thing, but the son of a bitch could write.

"Fucker bit me," Rick said.

"You were crushing the fucker with that fucking glove of yours. What is that, chain mail?"

"I hate fucking rats."

"So you've mentioned. Maybe you should consider another line of work."

"Yeah right. Like I'm going to find *work*. Nobody's going to hire me. I just don't want to flunk out. I *can't* flunk out. I have another year of eligibility."

"Lotsa luck with that."

I peered inside the cage of the slammed rat. She was shakily rising to her feet, her head tilted to one side. There was a tiny drop of blood on her white muzzle. She took a few steps, rocking from side to side. I looked into her eyes. She seemed to focus on mine. I judged her to be smart and friendly when she wasn't being thrown against a wall. I'd been around enough rats to form quick judgments on such matters, and since I wasn't a psych major, I didn't have to feel the least bit guilty about them. An English major who liked *Moby Dick*, the British Romantics, Vonnegut, Kesey, and Borges was free to believe any crazy shit he wanted to, as long as he took good care of the rats. None of the rat runners wanted to do it. That made sense. Do matadors raise baby bulls? Maybe they do, but I couldn't imagine such a thing. Maybe that's part of what made me lousy matador material. I moved my finger back and forth in front of the dazed rat. She was definitely focusing, tracking my movements. Then she looked me in the eyes again. I wasn't expecting that.

"When Mitchell sees this rat, he's going to know something isn't right," I said.

"What are you talking about?" He glared at his victim, but he saw immediately what I was talking about. The blood was dark now, a big ugly glob that looked a lot worse than it probably was. I'd ministered to thrown rats before, more often the victim of a panicked sophomore than a vicious senior.

"Oh shit," he wailed. "Fuck. Fuck, fuck, fuck." He ran through his entire emotional vocabulary for a while, like a burial chant. I'll spare you the rest of it. I almost felt sorry for him. The rat in the maze finished her trial, but Rick didn't notice.

"The watch?" I prompted, and he pushed it.

"What am I gonna *do*?" he wailed. "Is the fucking thing going to *die*?"

"I'll swap rats," I said. "I've got a dozen females about her age, just came back from a sound discrimination study, shouldn't affect their performance in something like this—not as much as brain damage and a broken hip anyway. Nobody has to know."

"You'd do that for me?"

I'm not doing it for *you*, asshole. "Sure thing," I said. I pulled the rat's cage out and slid it into the rack I was taking with me. "I'll bring you another rat in this cage. Leave that slot empty, so I can just slide it in and go. Leave your lab unlocked. I'll lock up when I leave, so don't forget your key. I'm only doing this once. You better treat her sisters like fairy princesses, and if I see you using a glove again, I'll rat you out."

I laughed at my own joke, but Rick didn't. I pulled the glove off his hand and waved bye-bye with it as I pushed the rack out the door. My sole passenger took an immediate interest in the journey back to her birthplace. She was moving around pretty well. I never thought her hip was broken or that she'd suffered permanent brain damage, but I wanted to get her away from Rick.

I could do things like that—swap out experimental subjects, possibly sabotaging a serious scientific experiment—because I wasn't a believer. I believed in science well enough, but not in whatever Rick was practicing. Mitchell was trying hard to be a scientist, but as long as that meant accepting Rick as part of the lab equipment, while he never touched a rat himself, it wasn't going to happen. Rick hated rats. That had to matter, that had to be, to use the lingo, an intervening variable. I would love to tell you Rick was unusual, but I won't. Mitchell either.

So I'd finally given in—ignoring the advice of Lyle, my predecessor who trained me in the ways of the colony—I'd rescued a rat, made her a pet. I couldn't pry her loose from Rick's grasp and then turn around and feed her to the snakes, could I? Lyle said if you rescued one, all the others became unbearable. Lyle had been a philosophy major, a bit intense. Like a lot of guys who tried for Conscientious Objector status, he was in prison somewhere.

But I'm not Lyle, I thought, as I treated my rescued rat's wounds and set her up in one of the nice Plexiglas cages left over from the gerbil study. Maybe rescuing one rat was exactly what I needed. She wouldn't live long under the best of circumstances. I wouldn't be raising rats much longer. Unlike Rick, I didn't have another year of eligibility. I was graduating in January, at the end of the semester. I was reading about Canada. I was studying how much a tall, skinny guy like me would have to starve himself to flunk his physical. I thought the war was wrong, based on lies and exaggerations, a civil war we had no business getting involved in. I thought the massive bombing of civilians in the north was immoral. Or I was a coward, a bad American. Take your pick.

As it turned out, I never saw Rick again. He found other ways to screw up. Mitchell caught him falsifying results, and he flunked out and went to Southeast Asia. I don't know if he died there, but he was a second lieutenant and an asshole. The probability seems high. Not as high as the zoo-bound rats, but close.

I named my pet rat Zelda. I was reading a lot of Fitzgerald then too. My first feminist professor had just told us that Scott actually stole pages out of his wife's diary to pass off as his own stuff and even published some of her stories under his name. I'm not sure why I thought Zelda Fitzgerald's story resonated with my rat's, but I did. All the runners were using others' lives to explain their own, and for a writer to have her stories stolen by someone you thought loved you would be pretty much like being slammed against a concrete wall. Besides that, she was a small, slender, sleek rat—very pretty. It was easy to imagine her as a flapper.

It was probably inevitable that I made a pet of one of my brood, if not Zelda, some other rat. I wasn't supposed to handle the future Experimental Subjects except when necessary, but my favorite job was weaning the litters, sorting them by sex, and for that you *had* to pick them up, and if I played with the cute little devils a little, what was the harm? Okay, maybe I played with them a lot. They liked to be tickled, to tussle, to play peek-a-boo. They made me laugh. There was plenty of time for Rick to throw them against the wall or Dr. Wallace to figure out new ways to shock them, or the new guy, Dr. Entwhistle, to turn them into little machines. His big project, for which he had a grant with a vague government agency, involved surgically outfitting a batch of rats with something resembling a sparkplug driven into the back of their skulls. He was waiting for a batch of males to mature of sufficient size to carry the weight, a little older than most of the experimental subjects. Usually they liked to run them young.

Zelda was surprisingly gregarious given her battered adolescence, and we hit it off immediately. I gave her the run of my desk when I was doing my paperwork, and I let her ride around on my shoulders while I fed and watered all her caged brothers and sisters. She was shy and demure at Zack's cage. Zack shouldered his way up to the front, stood on his hind legs, plastering himself against the mesh, so the front of the cage was nothing but the mighty Zack. Zelda slipped behind my neck, then peeked over my other shoulder. Zack followed us to the edge of his cage, watching her go. It was like King Kong and Faye Wray, before there were remakes. I hated to tell them, but it wasn't going to happen. It was one thing to pluck a rat from the colony (and death), but it was quite another to drop her back in for a fling. Zack was only allowed to mount properly documented females. Offspring were University Property. Zelda would never join his harem.

It was about this time Tina started running a study for Entwhistle in the lab next door to the colony. It wasn't much, a study of the correlation between reward size and performance that would give him some baseline numbers to crunch waiting for the sparkplug rats to mature sufficiently to go under the knife, some time around Christmas. Derek, one of the grad students, told me all this, claiming Entwhistle was a big catch for the department—the next wave. I bought pot from Derek. He asked me if I wanted any acid. I said no. I asked him Tina's story. He didn't have to ask why I'd noticed her.

It was drilled into the rat runners not to introduce any unnecessary stimuli into the rats' environment. Several studies had shown rats to be sensitive to smells, sounds, even different varieties of music. I usually covered all this with new rat runners, but Entwhistle had come by the colony when I wasn't around, issued his own animals, and put Tina to work. He hired Tina sight unseen, according to Derek, because she had the most work-study eligibility and his grant money would go farther. Unfortunately, she was a walking set of intervening variables.

The elevators were at one end of the long hall, next to the cage washer, and the colony was at the other. The rat runners' labs were off the hall. When the elevator doors opened, you knew immediately it was Tina. She jingled down the hall, laden with bracelets and beads, her boot heels ringing off the tile floor. Her perfume, heavy on the patchouli with something else like Chanel ladled on for good measure, was the next stimulus to precede visual contact. Her clanking keychain brought to mind Marley's ghost. It took her an age to find the right key, the one that said UNIVERSITY PROPERTY DO NOT DUPLICATE. How many could she have like that? Once inside, she propped the door open with a chair (a no-no) and turned on a cassette player she carried in and out in a huge leather shoulder bag. By this time, her rats were all going nuts in their cages—*Party! Party! Tina's here!* She played a lot of Stones. I was relatively certain Entwhistle didn't know his rats were running to a loud but tinny "Street Fighting Man" or "Sympathy For the Devil."

But she was nice to the rats, if a bit uneasy. I stopped by her lab one afternoon to pick up her dirty cages and drop off a bag of lab chow. This was a Steppenwolf day. The running rat was zipping through the complex maze to "Born to Be Wild," for what looked like a pitiful reward. I glanced over Tina's shoulder at her data. Flat as a board. Reward size had absolutely no effect whatsoever. Work ethic rats: They'd run and run no matter how small the reward. Virtue was its own reward apparently. Or maybe it was the music. *Looking for adventure...*

She recorded his time, carefully plucked the rat out of the box, showering him with comforting praise—rats like to be talked to–and gingerly put him back in his cage and slid it back into the rack. Then I realized why all her rats were so consistently eager. There was his daily ration waiting in his feeder. He started scarfing it down, a well-rewarded fellow indeed. She was taking advantage of the tenant's absence to clean and feed each cage while the rat was running. Efficient. Unfortunate.

"Are you supposed to feed them now?" I asked. "Immediately after they run?"

She made an apologetic little grimace. "I'm supposed to do it early in the morning, but I have a class. I save a *bunch* of time doing it all at once, and that way I don't have to bother them quite so much, you know?"

By *bother*, I knew she meant *handle*, but I let it go. "Did Dr. Entwhistle tell you what this study is about?"

"Reward size, and forgetting, I think—only he told me not to call it that."

"Extinction?" I suggested.

"Yeah. That's it."

I pointed at the chomping subject. "You've got these guys running for payday every time they hit the maze. The size of the reward at the end of the maze is irrelevant."

It takes a second for the coin to drop. "Oh shit. I wasn't thinking. I've had a whole lot on my mind. God. I was screwing up the whole thing, wasn't I?"

"I'm not saying that. I just raise the rats. I'm no scientist. I'm an English major."

"That's why I can trust you. None of the psych students like me. What else am I doing wrong?" She placed her hand on my forearm. I didn't think she was coming onto me or anything. I don't even think she thought about it. It came naturally, one human to another. Had a powerful effect on me, however. There it lay, a hand without a glove, touching me.

It was true, they didn't like her. She was the fool of the hour—all the runners had a dumb Tina gaff to report, even to me who didn't even know her—but I never knew her story, only her presence on the floor—a windowless, featureless environment of impeccable sterility before she showed up. Maybe every lab should have a window. "Do you want to talk?" I asked. I believed in words. Still do, I guess.

It turned out she'd transferred in from some sleepy liberal arts college where Freud and Jung weren't fools to be derided and burned in effigy, where dreams were taken seriously, and the mind not only existed, but was a subtle and complex reality; only to find herself in a colony of experimentalists, running rats, compiling data, laughing at her every time she opened her mouth and ridiculous words like *forget* or *think* or *remember* came out of it.

This was a dilemma I could sympathize with. I taught her the lingo—the runners prided themselves on a lean vocabulary—and told her a slew of unscientific words to avoid. She was nice. I wanted her to succeed. So I told her about the music, the perfume, the jingle-jangle morning she gave the Experimental Subjects every time she showed up. Not only did she not take offense, she actually got interested, asking follow-up questions, more and more about the rats and less and less about the science. She eyed her rats, her subjects. "I had no idea these guys were so *interesting*. You won't tell him, will you? Entwhistle? How I was screwing up?" She had silenced Steppenwolf and was shedding her bracelets, beads, and rings, piling them on a lab cart like pirate treasure.

"It's all the same to me. I never talk to him."

"He's not much of a talker." She looked back and forth from me to the rats. They were all looking at us, milling about in the fronts of their cages. The rustling rattle as they moved seemed to follow a rhythm like surf on the shore. Maybe they were waiting for her to put on another tape. Maybe they were thinking I'd just ruined everything with my meddling. I was afraid I'd intervened too late. Once Entwhistle saw her data, he'd figure out what happened and pull the plug, making for an early visit to the zoo for these subjects, and an early end to Tina's rat running career. She noticed me looking at her results. "Did you ever take statistics?" she asked.

"I never had the pleasure. If you're worried about the first couple of weeks' results, I'd look for similar studies and use theirs. Half the time, the guys here are just verifying somebody else's study somewhere else–have to keep the snakes fat and happy."

"The snakes?"

"Never mind. Don't worry. I won't tell him."

I told her Zelda's story. I wanted her to know what a real rat running fuck up looked like, so she wouldn't be too hard on herself. She said she'd like to meet Zelda, and I invited her to drop by any time, but she never did.

I missed the music drifting over from Tina's lab, and the hallway went back to smelling like detergent, cedar shavings, and rat piss. Now so silent that she must've been wearing slippers, she came and went all times of the day and night. Sometimes she'd be in her lab when I came in on weekend mornings to clean the racks and haul out the trash. She still talked to the rats. You could hear her murmur if you listened, but you couldn't make out the words, and sometimes, though I didn't recognize it at first, there was laughter. No matter how much work-study eligibility she qualified for, she had to be working overtime without pay to put in all those hours.

Weeks went by, and I hadn't talked to her again. Our paths hadn't crossed. I would always just miss her. I saw her once from the end of the hall as she was leaving on the elevator, the doors closing in front of her. She waved. Dressed in black—something like a leotard and black jeans—her long black hair pulled back from her white face, she looked like a giant Long-Evans rat.

I let myself into her lab. Everything looked perfectly normal. I didn't check her log, but according to my records, the rats had less than a week to run. I kept looking around, trying to find some telltale clue that *something* wasn't right, because I sensed it. Silly mammal. All I found was a doodle on a pad. At the middle was a sketch of the maze from above, dissolving at the edges, lines radiating out and looping back on themselves forming something like a pinwheel. I looked more closely at the lines converging on the center: Little eyes, little noses, little ears—little rat faces smiling. She was good. She told me she started out as an art major but switched to psychology because of a charismatic professor who had actually met Carl Jung. I wondered what her life would've been like if he'd met Picasso or Chagall instead.

I looked around one last time from the doorway. What *was* it? What was wrong? Another ordinary rectilinear emptiness, off-white and stainless steel. And the rats, of course, the essential furniture of the place. Then it hit me. The silence. All the rats, her subjects, were standing in their cages watching me, bright-eyed, alert, awake. Silent. They hadn't even started when I burst in and flipped on the lights. They hadn't scratched, they hadn't scurried, they hadn't chirped or chomped, they hadn't made a sound the whole time I was there. Or maybe they were singing "Born to Be Wild" the whole time, and I just hadn't noticed. No. I'm still certain. They were silent. How weird is that?

A few days later Entwhistle took over the lab. Mitchell, the hapless Director of the colony since its inception had somehow fallen into disfavor and Entwhistle seized the helm. I never saw Mitchell except when I went to his office to turn in my paperwork and order supplies. Entwhistle made his presence known immediately. He was waiting for me when I came into work. He was making some changes, he said. He gave me a list of new protocols for the colony. Accordingly, he said, he had already culled some of the breeding stock. My eyes went immediately to Zack's cage and saw it was empty.

"I'll call the zoo," I said, though the boxes were all flat and empty, leaning against the wall in their usual place. I always knew exactly how many there were.

"Don't bother. I incinerated them. I didn't want them underfoot. The zoo is scheduled to come tomorrow afternoon for the animals next door. See to it."

If I were a country, I would've napalmed Entwhistle. If I were the CIA, I would've dropped him into a cage of venomous vipers. Since I was a graduating senior reaching the end of what had always been a part time student job, I just quietly hated him, saving his story until now.

"And what's this?" he asked, pointing at Zelda, cowering in the corner of her Plexiglas condo. "I find no record of her."

"She's mine. She was the runt of a litter of fourteen. Her mother rejected her. I made her a pet." It was an easy lie. There *had* been such a rat, a couple of weeks before I rescued Zelda. I almost saved her. I thought about it. In the end, I fed her to the snakes.

Entwhistle grimaced. The word *pet* disgusted him. "How touching. Get rid of her."

Then he told me to set up his new rats in the lab Tina had been using. "She should be done in there by this evening."

I went to Tina's lab with the requisite zoo boxes and knocked. She wasn't there. I hated to just leave them, but I had to treat her like any other rat runner, whether I liked her or not. We'd only spoken the one time, but I thought we'd really connected. I'd obviously made too much of it in my head. One trial meant nothing, as the runners would've told me. I let myself in as before.

Only this time when I barged in and turned on the lights, the place was not only silent, it was lifeless. The rats were gone. It looked like she had already washed the cages as well—technically my responsibility. The cage washer was an expensive—occasionally temperamental—piece of equipment, and it was feared too many handlers might spook it. She didn't want me to know, to be implicated in her crime. I wondered how long she knew she was going to do this.

I don't know why I was so sure she'd taken the rats, but I went ahead and ruled out the other possibilities. Even though she didn't have a rooftop key, where the smallish incinerator was, I still checked it. We used it only for one or two animals at a time. Too many more would overwhelm it—as I verified, sifting through the evidence—the six rats Entwhistle had destroyed but not completely burned. This was due to Zack's bulk more than likely. I stirred the carcasses and finished the job.

Then I called the zoo. It took a while to work my way down to the rat detail. I recognized the guy's voice. He verified they hadn't received any rats from us since the intermittent-reward/sustained-punishment study wrapped up last week. I told him there'd been a mix-up, and there wouldn't be any rats tomorrow. He said the snakes would be disappointed. I said, "Let them eat cake."

What had Tina done with her rats? There were 25 of them. She couldn't make pets of them all, could she? I didn't know where they were, but I filled out the paperwork as if they'd gone to the zoo according to protocol, and I took Zelda home to my place and showed her around. There wasn't much to see but a bed and books.

I found Derek in his usual booth at the local coffee shop, sizing up the new waitress. He asked me if I wanted to buy some acid. I said no. I asked him if he'd heard any more about what Entwhistle was up to.

He leaned across the table conspiratorially. He was never discreet about dealing drugs, but about this he acted like a secret agent. "I'm running it for him," he said softly. "He just hired me."

"What happened to Tina?"

"I don't know, man, she just quit on him. He was kind of pissed, I think. It's hard to tell with him."

"So what is he doing?"

"The thing on the rat's head is like a little stereo broadcasting tower, emits ultrasound, something the rats *love.* The rat follows it like a carrot on a stick, this *sound*—right turn, left turn, steady-as-she-goes: remote-control rat. Is that cool or what?"

It was a sign of the times I didn't have to ask who might want to enlist remote control rats in the cause of Freedom. What embassy would be complete without one? What home or apartment? I asked if he knew anything else about Tina, and he nodded pensively. "Tina's all right," he said.

I knew that was his shorthand for saying he'd slept with her. He slept with many women, never spoke ill of them, and always spoke of them in the past tense, as if they'd all moved far away and married another man, taken vows of celibacy, or died of some unspeakable disease. No one stayed with Derek long.

"Do you remember where she lives?"

"No man, I don't remember a *thing.*" He laughed, shaking his head at the miracle of it, forgetting the unforgettable. "Do you want to buy some really good acid? Did I already ask you that?"

"No thanks."

"Department secretary—Glenda—she knows Tina's address. Tell her she took off with some keys she's not supposed to have. Glenda freaks over shit like that. She'll give the address to you. Tina was all right. You tell her I said so."

The new waitress came, filled our coffees. "You sure you don't want something to eat?" she asked me.

I shook my head. "You worried about the draft?" I asked Derek when she left. Guys of an age asked each other this question out of the blue all the time. Stupid question. It wasn't really a question at all, like old people asking each other, "Do you ever think about death?"

"Already served," Derek said. "Medical discharge. Psycho." He smiled. "Yeah. I served big time. I don't remember it. I was somewhere else. Missing in action." He held my gaze a moment. There were memories in there, behind his eyes. Maybe he didn't know they were there, but you could see them, pacing back and forth.

Derek was right, of course. I easily talked the secretary out of Tina's address, but then I didn't use it. I had a lot of other things on my mind. I quit the rat colony and turned in my keys. Entwhistle trained my successor. I graduated, I was classified I-A, I received a notice for my pre-induction physical, and I went on a diet. Derek sold me the diet pills. Normally in those days, I was 73 inches tall, 135 pounds. 127 was the minimum weight for someone my height, but the conventional wisdom from the draft counselors I spoke with was that to be safe you better be 10 pounds under. My target weight was 117.

I was waiting tables—anything more long-term was out of the question for a I-A, and English teachers were a dime a dozen anyway—and almost every night I'd grab something off a plate I was taking back to the kitchen and scarf it down—half a baked potato, a glob of cake frosting—something carbohydrate. I dreamed of ice cream and cookies. But most of the time I kept to a strict diet of six hard-boiled eggs a day and a bowl of lettuce. I drank Fresca and black coffee. I smoked cigarettes. I read about Vietnam, Zelda on my shoulder. I fed her little balls of egg yolk, and she thought I was the most wonderful creature in the world. She didn't want me to go halfway around the world and die for no good reason.

It was Sunday, the night before my physical. Derek stopped by for the occasion, and we had a drink and a smoke. He said he had a big week coming up. A team was coming for a demonstration of Entwhistle's rats next weekend, and it might work out okay for him. Entwhistle told him he would take him along if they secured funding for the next stage in their research, which he was not at liberty to discuss. He said Entwhistle was okay once you got used to him. Imagining getting used to Entwhistle and what kind of team came to see his rats only deepened my depression. I couldn't even think about what the next stage in their research might be.

After Derek left, I had another drink, another smoke. At some point, I put Zelda in her cage and took her over to Tina's. I had no idea if she still lived in the same place or if she'd be glad to see me. I told myself I was there because somebody needed to take care of Zelda just in case. Just in case what, I didn't know. There were stories of being whisked from draft board to boot camp to battlefield without a moment to make arrangements. Some arrangements. I was obviously the right guy to go get shot. I had one rat who needed looking after. The world would adjust. The other waiters had already put in for my shifts whenever I left.

If I left. I was poised to fail. I weighed 115 pounds. I was hungry. I felt like a failure. I hoped to fail. I didn't want to kill or be killed. I wasn't a complex organism, reduced to the bare minimum, ringing Tina's bell, the thought processes that had supposedly brought me there suddenly unraveling at the sound of her chimes. I had no idea what time it was.

She didn't recognize me immediately. I'd lost twenty pounds, cut my hair short, and shaved my beard. Draft counselors advised looking clean cut if you were trying to flunk your physical. There were stories of cancer-riddled diabetic long-haired freaks with ulcers passing with flying colors. "This is Zelda," I said, and she invited us in. She immediately offered to feed me, and I said I'd eaten.

"Not enough," she said, and I explained what I was up to. I was practiced at telling those who asked, but I never knew how anyone would take it. People wished me luck; people cursed me. I told myself I couldn't care what others thought, but I did care what she thought, and it came out a muddle: I'd spent weeks making myself unworthy, tomorrow was the end of it, and would she please take care of my rat? Because I trusted her.

She held me. "Stay here tonight," she said. "I'll go with you. Everything will be all right. You'll see."

This was so much more than I could have possibly imagined, I thought I might be delirious. I was lightheaded most of the time, and I hadn't had any sleep, and there was the pot and the alcohol and the nicotine and the Dexedrine. Then I heard something scratching in a cat box in the kitchen. A rat climbed out and scampered across the kitchen floor. Once I saw one, I started seeing them all. We were surrounded by rats in the bookcase, on the sofa back, on the TV. "Your rats," I said. "You did save them. When did you know you were going to do it?"

"When I knew I'd ruined the experiment, that it would all be make-believe anyway. I decided to use the time to get to know more about rats—after everything you told me about them. I thought I'd figure out what made them happy and run it *that* way, with the happiest possible rats." She laughed. "It was *really* fun. They're really quite the little characters, each one with their own personality. I gave them names, played with them. I couldn't do all that knowing I was going to kill them in the end, so I knew I'd have to take them with me. I didn't want you to know because that might've gotten you in trouble, especially when I found out what Entwhistle's up to. I researched the guy. What a creep."

She showed me her data—first from Entwhistle's work, then her own—plots of sounds emitted by rats. Entwhistle had become interested in rat ultrasounds when he was working on a possible ultrasound weapon. He zapped rats with sound of every imaginable amplitude and frequency. Snakes must've eaten a lot of deaf rats in those years. As a byproduct he found out the sounds the rats made, recording them at all frequencies under all manner of conditions. He'd been looking for aggression, something he could adapt to human purposes, but what he found was joy. Naturally he found a way to weaponize it.

"Derek said he's making remote control rats, responding to some pleasure sound?"

"*Pleasure sound.* What do you call that? He's making rats who'll spend their whole lives chasing imaginary laughter."

"Laughter?"

"He discovered rats emit high-pitched sounds when they play, when they fuck, and when they're tickled. What does that sound like to you?"

"Tickled?"

"Rats are ticklish. I'll show you." She picked up an eager volunteer from the several gathered around us.

"I know. I used to tickle the little guys when I weaned them."

"You did?"

I nodded.

She put the rat down, gave me a look that seriously deepened my delirium, and kissed me, made love to me, as if I were a soldier about to go off and die. It had been weeks since I'd cared about anything but carbohydrates. Maslow's hierarchy of needs was no joke, believe me. Sex held no interest for me. I was surprised I could perform, but perform I did, repeatedly. I wanted her more than I'd ever wanted anything or anyone.

Afterwards, we lay across her bed, still sleepless, and she said "I've built on Entwhistle's research. Want to see what they can do?" She cocked an eye-brow, tried her best to smile demonically like a mad scientist. The rats surrounded us.

"I wouldn't miss it," I laughed.

She put on Aretha. "Chain of Fools." She played with her rats on her ragged chenille bedspread, sitting cross-legged, naked, swaying to the music. They danced, or so she called it, following her ever-playful hands, this way, then that, in a spiral—little eyes, little noses, little ears—little rat faces smiling. *Chain, chain, chain...* Yes, you could call it dancing. You could call it magic. You could call it wise. They lifted me above the bed, above the whole wide world. I was so skinny gravity couldn't hold me anymore. The Earth held no reward for me any longer. I fell asleep watching them dance and dreamed I could fly.

Just before dawn, on the way to the bathroom, I was terrified by a skeletal moonlit stranger I passed in the dark. He stood in the full-length mirror on the bathroom door looking like he'd just crawled out of a mass grave.

I found a can of Coke in the refrigerator and drank it down.

Rats usually run mazes one at a time, but we shuffled through the draft physical all together. The soldiers in charge were like junior high bullies, parodies of tough boot camp sadists, the usual macho prattle, shouting instructions laced with insults and swagger. Several addressed us as *girls* and *ladies*. They could imagine nothing worse, apparently. The walls were pale piss color. There were floor drains everywhere, the floor slightly damp. Everything smelled like disinfected male sweat. There were too many men in too small a space. They must've hosed the place down every night.

They measured my height an inch short, weighed me with my clothes on—both of which I expected—but I was still underweight. The familiar height/weight chart was under the glass on the desk of the doctor whose job it was to declare me fit or not. He was the moving hand who would write my fate, the first person, all day, who didn't shout. He asked if I knew of any reason why I should fail. I pointed out that I was underweight. He peered at the chart and at my paperwork. "Why so you are," he said. If I hadn't told him, I don't think he ever would have noticed.

He seemed happy to fail me. He wasn't a military doctor. He was doing his duty, serving his country, reporting to the draft board like the rest of us. It was nothing personal. I was just trying to help him do his job.

I walked across the street from the draft board to a coffee shop where Tina was waiting for me. "I failed," I said, and she threw her arms around me and kissed me. She bought me the most expensive thing on the menu, a big pan-fried steak that spilled over the edge of the plate dripping blood and butter onto the Formica. I ate until I couldn't eat anymore, and I felt truly awful, but happy. We ordered dessert. Life was good.

I'm not sure when I first noticed the key to her lab was still on her key ring. Maybe on the way that morning, maybe the night before. I can't remember, but I knew it was there. She left her keys lying on the table when she went to the lady's room. That's when I slipped it off and put it in my pocket. I'm not sure how much of a plan I had at that moment, but I had a purpose. I had a cause.

I met up with Derek on campus in front of the library under the flag-poles. I wasn't really out of pot, though Tina and I had been through quite a bit of it, but I bought a bag anyway, and when he asked, I said yeah, I'll take some acid.

It was Spring, and we were both watching the pretty girls come and go. I was probably eating something like a Snickers or a donut. He looked at me. "You finally taking the plunge? Dropping the magic?"

"Tina and I—we're doing it together—we have the whole weekend."

"Oh man—that sounds all *right*." We did the deal, and he cautioned me. "This shit's intense. I'd start out with a half or maybe a quarter each, you know."

I told him I'd be careful. I asked how the Entwhistle gig was going.

He put the money in a fat wallet and smiled big. Life was going well for Derek. "We're showing off the goods first thing Saturday morning. Wish me luck. I can't talk about it. But this could really be big, man."

Friday at midnight, I returned to campus and slipped into the psych building. I hadn't told Tina what I was doing, employing the same logic she'd used with me. I didn't want to implicate her. I took Zelda along in my shirt pocket. She wanted to help. When we got to the fourth floor where the labs were, she stirred with excitement, sniffed the air and swiveled her ears. It occurred to me that to her the halls must echo with sounds I couldn't hear, that perhaps she remembered sounds I'd never even heard, much less understood: Rats running, laughing, fucking, being burned alive. Maybe she could smell them all beneath the disinfectant.

The startle reaction of Entwhistle's rats was accented by the metallic clatter of their headgear on the wire cages. I took Zelda out of my pocket and dropped her into the maze. She was feeling amorous. If I stroked her hindquarters, she would arch her back and wiggle her ears quite rapidly. Very cute. Definitely in heat. I scattered a few food pellets around the maze and let her scamper about while I crushed the tabs of acid into a powder and dissolved it in a little water. I counted out 18 food pellets. There had been 24 rats at the beginning. According to the log, some had died after surgery; others were eliminated when their apparatus failed. Survival of the fittest. With an eye dropper I doled out the acid in equal amounts to each pellet until it was all gone. According to their log, they should be hungry, and sure enough, despite the distraction of Zelda slinking around the place, they all ate every last crumb. All together they couldn't have weighed more than 25 or 30 pounds. If there was any correlation between weight and dosage, then I figured these rats were in for one incredibly intense trip when the laughter from nowhere started showing up and seductive Zelda smells beckoned every which way.

Maybe I shouldn't have denied them their victory. Maybe they didn't want to fail, brave gladiators every one. I collected Zelda from their maze, and together we saluted them. I'm sure Entwhistle showed them no mercy. I like to think they died laughing.

Entwhistle lost his funding and moved on. The last time I saw Derek, years later, he was telling crazy stories about remote control rats and selling his outpatient anti-psychotics to other guys in the park. Zelda died of old age in her sleep. I buried her in a window box overlooking a maze of streets and alleys. Tina moved to Alaska. She said I was welcome to join her, but we both knew that wasn't going to happen. I haven't seen her since those days.

Her rats are all dead, of course, though their descendants have flourished for several generations now, silently navigating their own mazes, following the sound of their own laughter, peeking over the shoulder of the skeletal stranger in the mirror, dancing in the corner of my eye, asking, *Can you hear the laughter yet? See all the variables? Are you ready to surrender all your secrets to the snakes?*

The Art Disease

Derek and Emily had the art disease, the both of them. Everyone they knew had it too. That's one of the symptoms: Colonies, clusters, movements, splinter groups, manifestos. Clumping, the experts call it. She had a master's in design and decorated cakes at Food One, not the one on 17th but the one near the park, open till midnight. He refused to sell out. He was determined to support himself with his art.

Selling poems in the park didn't work out. He didn't get that many buyers, and when he did, he spent way too much time discussing the poems with them—arguing actually—instead of writing new ones, but it bothered him when he was misunderstood, and it seemed he was doomed to be misunderstood—another symptom of the disease. He tried prose—carefully observed reflections on the vicissitudes of life—after taking a weekend workshop called Driveway Moments: The Eternity of Now. No demand. Light travel pieces with a profound undercurrent proved no better, partly because he hadn't done much traveling and couldn't afford to do more. He had plenty of profound undercurrent, just nowhere to put it.

He decided to go visionary. That way he could travel without going anywhere, make it *all* profound undercurrent except for a few flashy waves on the surface, and those birds—what do you call them?—cormorants, low-riders. Cool. Sufferers of the art disease saw art in everything, even waterfowl that could barely stay afloat.

There's one more thing you should know about the art disease: It's highly contagious.

"What do you mean visionary?" Emily asked suspiciously. "This isn't zombies again, is it? I'm so over zombies."

"No, no, no. Zombies are like the total opposite of visionary." His mouth was full of icing, making his words all gummy and weird, like a zombie might talk. They were finishing off a birthday cake with *Happy Birthday Shane* on it when the kid's name was actually *Shan*. Not Emily's fault, but Sofía's, who took the order and was now looking for another job, since their boss, Barb, was the one who got chewed out by the pissed-off mom who was horrified at the suggestion that all could be made right by scraping off a vowel. Sofía was a sculptor. She had a blowtorch that would cut half-inch steel plate she said, said if Emily came over she'd show her, but Emily smelled lesbian and wasn't that bored yet with the Food One and Derek. But close. Real close.

"Visionary—like William Blake," he said. "That weird prophetic stuff, but like it's real, you know, happening on the street, not just words. Blake did those great paintings, but I thought, you know, I can't paint for shit, I'll take it outside, free it from the page—from the fucking earbuds too. On the street, in your face." Podcasting was still a sore point with Derek.

"A street preacher."

"Well, sort of. I prefer to think of them as prophetic performances."

"And what do prophetic performances pay? There's an opening at Food One. You thaw stuff. There's nothing to it. I could put in a word for you."

"No thanks. This'll work. I've thought of another angle too. We need a cheaper place, right? You'd like a studio? The church on the corner's for sale."

"You sure that didn't go condo? The Townes at the Square or something like that?"

"That's the other way. The Methodist. This one's something weird. The Church of the Immaculate Epiphany. It's been for sale a while, but the condo market's tanked. We can get it cheap. Cheaper than rent."

"We?"

"The *church*. That'll be part of my vision, that there I shall found my church—the Assembly of Prophetic and Visionary Matters. Tax free."

"*Matters*?"

"Okay. Maybe not Matters, but something like that, and we raise money, tax free, buy the place, and there you go. We're set."

"By raise money you mean beg on the street?"

He counted off his points on his fingertips even though he knew she hated it: "Encourage donations at prophetic performances. Appeal to corporate and community sponsors. Apply for grants."

She burst out laughing and had to let him have the last chocolate rose to make up for it. She didn't want it anyway. She knew what was in it. She felt bad for laughing. He hadn't laughed at her Random Rags installation, which made him just about the only one. He even went along with her it's-*supposed*-to-be-funny story.

Derek, a preacher. The thought made her smile, but in a good way.

A week later, she came down on her lunch hour to see him work a crowd in the park, to see how he managed to bring in so much money. It was very scary. He was totally different, as if another person had taken him over. He wore a cape. It wasn't really a cape. Where would Derek get a cape? It was a tiny deep blue blanket stolen from the airplane ride back from his father's funeral. It didn't look as stupid as you might think.

Then he starts. Derek wouldn't even dance, but suddenly he couldn't stop moving. It was hypnotic, strangely familiar, and then she recognized it. Lately he'd be lying on the sofa with the sound off, cruising channels, mumbling, writhing like a lovesick snake. "What're you *doing*?" she'd asked. "Research," he'd said. And there it was, the artistic fruits: Anybody with moves. James Brown one minute, a movie Indian the next, Herman Munster, Britney—it was mesmerizing. The sermon made no sense at all: "The eternal moment of revelation sparks inside each and every one of you, each and every moment of your life. Let the tinder catch! Let the flames rise! Let the fire consume you! Let the smoke carry you! Signaling the universe, *I'm alive! I'm alive! I'm alive!*" He ended this outburst with the blanket off his shoulders and wafting over an imaginary fire, watching imaginary puffs of smoke drifting away over the heads of his rapt audience, and damn if the whole crowd didn't turn around and watch them too. So *that's* why he'd been watching that awful old western over and over until she thought she'd go heap big out of her mind.

"How'd I do?" he asked her after the performance.

"Unbelievable."

"I thought my timing was a little off at the beginning."

"I don't know. This is a pretty big pile of wampum."

The next night he watched *Thief of Baghdad,* and next day the little blue blanket was a magic carpet. The blanket was the only constant. He laid out loaves and fishes on it. (Loaves were $5; fish, $10. He could've asked for more). He autopsied Truth's corpse CSI fashion, covered it with the blanket, and wept, only to reveal it risen, walking among them, asking for money. He wore it like a sarong and danced around in it. He tied it up in animal shapes and talked to it. Talking Prophetic the whole time.

That's what he called it—TP—the visionary dialect. In addition to watching the obvious TV preachers, he practiced by reading aloud anything that made prophetic or visionary claims, from the Bible to L. Ron Hubbard, confiding in her that he didn't strive for coherence but sought a certain visionary unity that transcended sense. "It's all in the rhythms," he believed, and you could tap your foot to it, there was no denying. "And the silences," he added. He was the master of the dramatic pause out of nowhere, the Profound Silence, what Derek called the cornerstone of the prophetic.

And no matter what he said, and sometimes there were rivers of blood and mountains of dead and untold pain and suffering, he was deliriously, disturbingly cheerful. He practiced different smiles, tried them out on their friends, keeping only the ones that really creeped people out. And if that didn't do the trick, he gave a joyful cackle when sufficiently possessed that didn't sound entirely human. Emily knew it was the product of 40 hours of wandering in the wilderness with *Nature* and *Animal Planet.* If a heron humped an iguana, and they managed to hatch an egg, whatever came out would sound like Derek laughing.

Emily was laughing too.

Every performance ended with the blue blanket spread upon the ground, money raining down upon it, mostly bills, lots of tens and twenties. Once—a bunch of traveler's checks. Emily didn't know they still had those anymore, but the bank took them.

She studied Derek's flock, their transfigured faces, the complex looks they'd give him as their bills fluttered onto the pile. Most of them were seriously worried about the poor guy. Few doubted for a moment that Derek was spectacularly out of his mind and probably needed doctors, drugs, possibly even electroshock or surgery. There were always cards for mental health care professionals mixed in with the money. "Call her—she's really good!" someone had written on the back of one. Then added, "You're really good too!"

That's the thing. Crazy as he was, he put on an incredible show. Or in this case, the show was his craziness. He got to them even if they weren't sure how. Emily had a theory: His crazy offered a charisma uncluttered by content. He could rant, and no one felt guilty. He could rave, and no one had to worry that he just might be right.

Would they continue to be so generous, she wondered, if they discovered he wasn't a madman who preached an insane religion, but an artist inventing a religion as an art form out of channel surfing and word salad, nabbing both grant money and tax-free status while he was at it?

Emily was in no hurry to find out.

"Can you help me with these forms?" Derek would ask her, with a sweet puppy dog face, totally exhausted by his latest performance, and she couldn't say no. NEA, IRS—it didn't matter—she could do forms. She had a master's in design. She understood form. And he was a disaster at it. He'd get all verbal and metaphoric and forget whether he was being a religion or an art form and screw up an entire application. It was just easier to do it in the first place than to come along after and clean up his mess.

It was paying off, however, and not just financially. Word was getting out his stuff was definitely worth checking out. There was even a thing about the performances in *Excrement Occurs* from the guy who hates everything—he fucking loved it. Every performance was now ringed with people who got it, smiling knowingly, inviting Derek over later for drugs, and he usually went, and Emily didn't. Work started early at Food One.

And, curiously enough, at every performance, packed in close, as close as they could get, a devoted band of believers steadily grew, though it was a mystery to Emily what they believed in since Derek certainly didn't have a clue.

"Belief doesn't believe in me," he told his rapt congregation. "I don't believe in belief. Instead. Visions come. Instead. Visions come to me: Visions of the nothingness of everything! The unbelievability of belief!"

Emily was just a little weirded out by all the nodding heads. Afterwards, when a breathless believer accosted him beseeching guidance, he told her, "Go home, seize a book, any book, and read it to—You have a cat? Of course you have a cat!—read it to your cat, and a vision will come." This worked somehow, according to the woman. Everything he did seemed to work. Not only did she have a transforming vision, but her cat did too, though she preferred not to discuss details. Emily couldn't explain it. Not his knowing the woman had a cat. Anyone could see that. But the transforming part, that was something new and scary. Derek had never wanted to change the world before. He'd just wanted to make art.

Lately he'd been watching Bela Lugosi movies and Teletubbies on a split screen. Watching the happy spectrum creatures bouncing beside the swirling black-and-white living dead gave her a fierce headache. She couldn't watch the moves he was getting out of it either. She didn't know what the performance was about exactly. (Even when he explained them to her, she didn't know what *any* of them were about, because if she'd ever say, "So it's about..." The answer would always be No. Fine. Who needs meaning?)

So she'd skipped this one, though he had a big crowd, and he was telling her about it, redoing bits, talking a mile a minute. One part was the shocking tale of how Jerry Falwell discovered Tinky Winky was gay one night in a foggy London bathhouse.

"Nobody laughed," he complained. "Dead silence."

"That's because you're a religion now. Silence is good, remember? You said it last week. 'The silence of the universe means someone's listening.'"

"That doesn't make any sense. Can't religion be funny?"

"I thought it was just about the rhythms, the talk."

"*I* thought it was funny."

"I brought home some cupcakes. You want some? They're kind of blue. They're supposed to be green. Barb was pissed like it was my fault, but I'm the cake decorator. Seasonal cupcakes are not my problem. You want one? They're not bad actually."

"Sure. That'd be great."

They hung out in their big institutional kitchen. They were living in the church now. All the furnishings from the sanctuary had been sold off long ago, so it was a big empty barn of a building with bad stained glass. The main piece above the altar was Jesus as shepherd with one of the lambs' faces smashed out and replaced with weathered plywood. Jesus, who seemed to have a serious case of strabismus, took no notice.

Derek and Emily had made an okay apartment out of the church offices. They used the Reverend Buckley Duncan's former office as a bedroom. They read to each other out of the family counseling files he'd left behind. They found them inspiring: Screwed up as they were, they weren't *these* people, who, as far as they could determine, included not a single sufferer from the art disease. Buck Duncan told them to pray and forgive, pray and forgive. Nobody ever did.

There was a working bathroom in the basement with a shower, though you had to flush the toilet with a bucket until they could have it fixed. Emily had plans to turn the other end of the basement into a studio, but Food One had promoted her, so she was working a split shift and never had time to make art.

Derek held his performances in the pewless sanctuary, still with the blanket, though he made a deal with a flight attendant who was a regular to keep him in fresh ones. She brought them cradled in her arms, still wrapped in plastic, laid them reverently on the pile of money at the end of the ceremony, made smoldering eyes at Derek. Trish, her name was. Emily wanted to kick her perfect kneecaps, but you had to expect stuff like that when you were with an artist. When she did the Square Planet installation, and she got a lot of attention, Derek was really cool with it. Even after the thing with Stanley.

Derek was bringing in so much money, they not only made their church payments, they paid off their credit cards, got the car repaired, started buying wine again, fixed the toilet. They replaced the 19-inch TV, and Siena, the electronic music composer who installed cable, ripped off all the premium channels for them for free. They were even getting estimates on a working HVAC system and a new roof, the old one being the main reason they'd gotten the place so cheap. There were places in the sanctuary you could see daylight.

Derek once preached a whole sermon—though he didn't like her to call them that—to the motes of dust in a shaft of light. That was a good day. Even better was the one to the drops of rain. He knelt on the blue blanket with a stack of conical paper cups, filling them and passing them out, always somebody's hand eagerly outstretched to take one, and people actually drank the nasty-ass water full of rust and pigeon shit and God knew what-all like it was champagne and they'd just won the lottery. That night she ironed a few fifties from a laundry basket full of soggy money, and they went out and had a great time like they hadn't had in years, and Emily felt truly happy for his spectacular success, not to mention the great fuck they had on one of those little blue blankets with Jesus watching.

But then, of course, just when everything was going so well, and she was thinking about quitting Food One or at least cutting way back on her hours, Derek got tired of it. He always did. He never stayed with anything long. He might get too good at it. He might get a reputation, a following, some success. Emily tried not to judge. Some artists thrive on variety. Derek said, "Some writers just want to write about *one* thing—werewolves or sea captains or neurotic middle-aged fucks with their dicks in their hands—and that's it for them. Some only write about Canadian werewolves in the nineties who smoke too much—book after book. I'd rather drive a truck. I'd rather be *hit* by a truck!" And though she knew neither thing about the truck was true, she could respect where he was coming from as an artist even though it was bound to lead him nowhere.

So she kept working at Food One, and Derek quit doing his prophetic performances. They kept living in the church, though they quit thinking of it so much as a church and as more of a performance space, though they weren't performing either. They were waiting on a grant, several grants actually. Depending on which ones came through, Derek could decide the direction his art might next take him.

Emily was thinking she might not wait for the grants to make a move.

Derek lay on the floor of the sanctuary doing variations of Da Vinci's drawing of a man, studying Cock-Eyed Jesus and the Plywood-Faced Sheep, thinking the problem with his prophetic performances was he hadn't sufficiently adapted the vision to the move indoors, that before it was an exterior vision longing for an interior, a sanctuary, and now it was an interior emptiness longing for the exterior, the outside, the otherness… He was thinking 3-D movies…

"Reverend Merriweather?"

There was a man in a suit standing over him.

"I'm Derek Merriweather, but I'm no Reverend."

"This isn't a church, then?" the man asked.

"Nope. Not anymore." Derek got up off the little blue blanket wishing he had on more than shorts and a t-shirt, but he always had his best ideas before he showered and dressed and all of that. Some days he had to wait awhile for them to show up. The ideas. The best ones. Lately, they hadn't been showing up at all.

"I was under the impression this was an institution of religious worship. I'm Paul Throne of the Internal Revenue Service."

Derek looked to Jesus for guidance, but the Savior wouldn't look him in the eye. "Yes. Yes. Welcome. We're most definitely a religious institution. We just don't use the word 'Church' here. We've evolved *beyond* 'Church' and churchiness. Just as my flock don't address me as Reverend, for we are all equally humble on the path to enlightenment, for the way is difficult, and any one of us might find himself lost." Derek gestured to the Lamb who looked especially lost this time of day when the bright Son exaggerated the dark, wooden face, graced with mildew fleece.

"What then should I call you, if not Reverend? *Mr*. Merriweather?"

"*Captain* Merriweather," Trish called out from the back of the sanctuary, where apparently she'd been listening with a fresh bundle of blue blankets swaddled in plastic clutched to her breast. "He pilots our expedition into the unknown," she trilled.

Derek hadn't fucked her yet, and he saw in that moment that it was inevitable. She had just saved his life, his art, his freedom. What was Emily going to say about it after that thing with Stanley?

"And you are?" Paul Throne inquired of Trish, as if this were his office instead of Captain Derek's house of religious worship.

"I'm Trish Van der Waal, a member of the congregation, a *charter* member of the congregation."

"And what does your denomination believe?" Throne asked, as if it was any of his business. Derek was about to demand a lawyer.

But Trish had all the answers. "We don't believe in belief. You know those religions that believe in the literal truth of the Bible? We don't believe it exists."

"The Bible?"

"No, silly. Literal truth. Have you ever read Wallace Stevens?"

"No, not that I recall."

Trish's opinion of any man who called himself a man and yet hadn't read Wallace Stevens was writ large on her face. "Well, if you had, you'd know." Derek tried to remember if *he'd* read Wallace Stevens. He was the guy with the Mason jar, right? Or was that the blue guitar? Maybe she wouldn't ask him. He liked the way she'd taken charge. Paul Throne of the IRS was practically slinking out the door like Satan banished from the Garden. Or was that Adam? Derek hated Sunday

School. He suspected his prophetic performances were his revenge on Sunday School, not just for himself. He was nothing. But for everyone who'd ever suffered the whole dreary business.

"When are your next scheduled services?" Throne inquired on his way out. "I would like to attend."

"That's what I stopped by to ask Captain Derek," Trish said.

Captain Derek held his head up high. "Eleven, Sunday morning. We welcome everyone onboard." He moved his hand through the air like a soaring plane, and Mr. Throne smiled.

Emily was not happy. "I thought we were driving out to Willow and Fern's this Sunday. Now you're preaching again?" Willow and Fern threw pots and grew pot, and Emily finally had a Sunday off from Food One, and Fern was somebody she could talk to about her art, and she figured she could smoke a little since they just random tested her last week.

"It's not *preaching*. How many times do I have to say it? We've got to persuade this IRS guy that we're a religion. Do you have any idea how much taxes we owe if we're not?"

"You don't need me to preach. I'll just go by myself."

"I need all the people I can get. Right now it's just me and Trish. You're on all the forms as one of the church's *founders*—but don't call it a church. I told him we were past that. What if he asks questions about the forms? I don't know what they say. You're the one who says I don't understand form."

"Okay, okay. I'll come. How long do we have to keep this up?"

"I don't know. As long as it takes to persuade him we're for real."

"I thought you quit. I thought you *had* to quit. 'I can't do this anymore. I'm just not into it.'"

"I didn't have the IRS on my ass."

"Just me. What do I matter? You're sure this isn't about fucking Trish?"

"Who said anything about fucking Trish?"

"Not you. You'd just do it."

"Listen. Trish was a big help today."

"Just do it, okay?"

"There's one more thing. Call me Captain Derek."

"Fuck you, Captain Derek."

That very night, Sofía came into Food One and found Emily doing yet another sheet cake soccer field. Emily hated soccer, and she'd never even seen a game except to cruise by on the cable. If she were a terrorist, she'd blow up a soccer field.

"Don't let Barb see you around here," she said to Sofía. "She's still pissed off at you."

"Barb's home watching *Survivor* thinking up the boring shit she's going to say tomorrow. I have a business proposition for you." She was rifling through the decorations cabinet. She took out a bag of plastic cows and spread them across the other table, took a little torch like an aerosol can out of her bag and started hacking them up one by one, arranging the pieces around the as-yet-unstriped green field atop the next cake in the queue—a head here, a hindquarters there. "Here's the deal. In another hour it'll be just you and the janitorial crew. They're never even from the same country twice, and could give a shit what we do back here. All these ovens and mixers and everything are just sitting here. We could be making specialty cakes. I have a market, orders. I need a space, a partner, a designer."

"What kind of specialty cakes?"

"The ones Food One won't do. Tits, penises, vaginas, butts—whatever the customer wants. Weird, twisted shit."

"A virgin maiden being ravaged by a bull?"

"You think there's a market for that?"

"No. I'm just saying. No boundaries?"

"It's cheap cake and bad frosting any way you slice it. The only difference is how much you can charge." The cow pieces arranged to her satisfaction, she oozed blood icing liberally on and around the carcasses.

"You're fucking up my cake," Emily said.

"Not to worry." She held up the invoice. "It's my order. I called it in this morning, talked to Barb." The name on the invoice was *Shan Fuque*. "I had to spell it to the dumb cow three times." Emily didn't have to ask how it was pronounced. Sofía took the little torch and burned a pentangle into the frosting field, melting a cow butt in the process. "You like? It's for a friend. It's her birthday. She's into bovine mutilation events. I heard your husband's doing a performance thing with his blankie? I heard it's clever."

"He's not my husband."

Sofía smiled. "So what do you say? Partners?"

"Sure. Why not?"

Sofía wrote a message on the cake with the blood red icing—*Thanx 4 All Your Sacrifices.* She picked through the remnants of plastic cows, examining the faces until she found a couple she liked, sliced them off with a box knife, dotted the i's with them, and slid the cake in a box. "Tomorrow night, then. At the midnight hour."

Trish had no spine. The sexual positions she could pretzel herself into were stunning in the intricacy of their design and execution. "I'm not really a flight attendant," she told Derek. "I'm a dancer." Her primary inspirations were the kama sutra and the flying trapeze. "That's why I became a flight attendant," she said. "Because of the flying thing. But it's not the same. It's like you say, the persistent nothingness of everything."

Whenever she told him the things he'd said, he had no idea what they meant. He hoped if he listened closely enough to her saying them, they would start to make sense. She was so certain about everything. "It gets worse," Derek told her and explained about Paul Throne of the Internal Revenue Service. "We need all the believers we can get when he comes on Sunday. Bring friends."

"I'll bring my dance company."

"You have a company?"

"I do. Don't you mean *non*-believers?"

"Whatever," Derek said, imagining a whole company of pretzeled beauty flying with Captain Derek. The religious side of things was starting to work on him, and he thought about St. John of the Cross, Phil Dick, and William Blake, wondering if at key moments in their journeys, when they apparently started to believe some of their own bullshit, whether, perhaps, they might've met a dancer.

Emily had an excess of design desire built up inside her after months and months of soccer fields and flags and Sharky the Snowman, a Frosty/Jaws cross that had rescued white frosting from near extinction since his first appearance five Christmases ago, and now had shown up in a Hawaiian shirt, returning to his roots and primetime—and to kids' birthday cakes year round.

So when Sofía said the client just wanted a big dick, any old dick would do, that wasn't enough to satisfy Emily's creative longing. "Tell me about him," she said.

"Him? It's for my sister. A divorce party."

"I know. You said. I mean. Ultimately, it's *his* dick, right? The ex's? Who is he?"

"He likes NASCAR. He hunts. My stupid sister married him. He drove a tank. He fucked all her friends. Hit on me, if you can believe it."

Emily wanted to ask whether it was unbelievable because she was a lesbian or because she was his sister-in-law, or for some other reason entirely, but she didn't. Instead, they brainstormed about the dick while the ovens were heating up.

They probably shouldn't have smoked the joint. Sofía found it in her pocket like it was a big surprise. *Oh look!* Two hits and Emily had a flight of ideas that was like the swallows blowing off Capistrano and heading out to sea. Looking back on it, the concept was maybe a little too ambitious for their limited resources, so they might've run into trouble anyway, even if Barb hadn't shown up and fired them both. How were they supposed to know she was having a thing with the foreman of the janitorial crew, who was definitely hot, looking like the Arab guy on *Lost*? What he saw in Barb they couldn't figure. The day shift maybe? Her big ass?

While Sofía and Barb screamed obscenities toe-to-toe, Emily made it out the back door with all the supplies she could lay her hands on, but they had to leave behind the slot car set and their plans for tank cupcakes lapping the big dick in hot pursuit of doomed doe. They were pretty bummed. Anybody could make a big dick. They'd hoped for something more. A big dick that *meant* something.

Emily hadn't really tested the church ovens. She never baked at home. But they were certainly big enough. They must've done serious baked goods at the Church of the Immaculate Epiphany. Hot cross buns maybe. She fired up the ovens as the sun was coming up, and they all seemed to work, but they smelled like burning mouse piss, so Emily lit every stick of incense she could find. Apple. Patchouli. Celestial Sunrise. Many, Many Mice.

And then she had a vision. It was probably inevitable, hanging around with Mr. Vision himself, Captain Derek the Trish fucker, that she would have a vision too. She'd been a little peeved, frankly, spending her days striping soccer fields while he was transcending all that with his visionary art. She could transcend, she could inspire a goddamn flock.

She grabbed a tube of icing. Field stripe white dripped from its tip. She drew her vision on the stainless steel counter in one serpentine line, smiling in triumph. Her sister claimed a woman's greatest joy was bringing a child into the world. That's because her sister had never made art, or had an orgasm either one. And while her nephew might've been a joy on arrival, he'd been pretty much a disappointment to his mother ever since, like her sister and her husband before him.

"When's your sister's thing?" she asked Sofía.

"Noon. He's dropping off her kids at five."

"Jeez. They have kids? Can you move it up to eleven? We could combine it with the service."

"Sure. I'm the hos-tess. What you got in mind?"

She showed Sofía the icing on the countertop. "Wait, wait. Imagine it sitting on a shortbread. Like so." She iced in brown the shortbread's shape.

"Kew-el. Is that what I think it is?"

"What do you think it is?"

"Dick on a cross."

"You got it."

"What are those things?"

"Arms. He's got to have something to attach him to the cross. A stake through the middle's too vampirish."

"Why not hang him up by the balls?"

"I don't know. That just seems mean. You need the head at the top anyway, so he can raise it, you know, his one eye to heaven, complaining, 'My God, my God, why have you forsaken me?' And God can say, 'Because you're a faithless little worm, little dick. That's why.'"

Sofía laughed her husky laugh. "But arms? Dicks don't have arms."

"But they *wish* they did." She waved little grasping dick arms at Sofía.

"Why not wings?" Sofía fluttered little dick wings and rose up on her toes.

"Dick with wings? I like it." Emily changed the arms to wings fit for a cherub, plump and cheerful with a discreet brown nail in the middle of each, two thin trickles of blood.

Sofía shook her head in wonder. "Dick with wings on a cross. I knew I was going to like working with you."

Once the shortbreads started baking, the piss smell receded, the incense coalesced into a single, sacred scent, and the coffee urn finished brewing, it smelled almost inviting in the old place. It smelled like church.

They heard voices in the sanctuary and went to check it out. There, high up in the rafters, four magnificent men in tights were slinging ropes, rigging trapeze. It looked like they meant to swing up and down above what would've been the central aisle of the sanctuary had there still been pews. They looked like gods.

"Would you look at *that*?" Sofía said in a voice that made Emily doubt the lesbian theory with perhaps the slightest disappointment.

Paul Throne of the Internal Revenue Service hated his job. That's because he had the art disease. Most art disease sufferers hate their jobs. He'd worked his way up through the bowels of the Internal Revenue Service as a means of ridding himself of the disease. A step beyond cold turkey into cold turkey buzzard feeding on desiccated roadkill. There was not the slightest thing about his job that was artful, artsy, or artistic, even on a metaphoric level. Its purity cleansed and sustained him.

This worked for some people. So did suicide. Paul had done okay. He hadn't sold the guitar, but he kept it down in the basement and hadn't played it in years. The strings would probably sound like the dull thuds of his heart. He never sang in the shower, only alone in rent cars driving some lonely road at night on the job—to keep himself awake, he told himself.

But the moment he set foot in the old Immaculate Epiphany place, he sensed the change immediately. Not only was that pious fraud Buck Duncan gone, but there was something new, something strange, something familiar from never forgotten adolescent nights singing under a streetlight to the edge of the glow.

The art disease.

Merriweather was terminal with it, and the Trish woman as well.

Wallace Stevens. Of *course* he'd read Wallace Stevens. Who hadn't? He wasn't about to admit it to her. They mustn't know. Not yet.

Everyone had a little blanket now. Trish handed you one as you came in. "Welcome aboard," she said. No wonder you couldn't get them on planes anymore. Paul Throne of the Internal Revenue Service traveled a lot for his job, tracking down fraudulent claims. He specialized in phony churches, and this one was as phony as they come, and yet, there was something authentic about it he couldn't figure out at first—or maybe he hadn't wanted to figure it out. Maybe he wanted to come here like this, expose himself to what was clearly a particularly virulent, visionary strain of the art disease, obviously highly contagious.

The place was filling up with them, one diseased soul after another. Two women in particular were besotted, passing around big cookies with what looked like Sharky the Snowman nailed to the cross by his flippers. His youngest liked Sharky. He used to sing "Sharks Like Christmas Too!" to her. It was okay to sing to your kids, wasn't it? Now she was thirteen. She had hardened her heart against Sharky. He thought it would make a terrific musical.

He'd interviewed several members of the congregation, milling about expectantly, like they were waiting for Warhol or Jesus. The place smelled like one of the clubs his band used to play but without the liquor. Any outburst of art would be received here as an offering to the gods, even if it came from Paul Throne of the Internal Revenue Service. He took a discreet pull from a half pint of brandy he bought on the way to the church. Loosens up the throat, the soul, the nerve. He breathed deeply. He took the cookie as a sign, a request.

He knelt upon the blue blankie, bowed his head, and ate his cookie, as Captain Derek ascended a rolling stairway as if he were going to hand his boarding pass to the Lamb of God. Flying men on trapeze swooped back and forth, tossing Trish from one to the other above Paul's head. The sound of the swings seemed to count off the beat. He looked into the skewed eyes of God and rose, bursting into song.

"Sharks swim in the ocean
"Big and wide and blue!
"But I like to be a snowman,
"And I tell you why that's true:

"Sharks might bite!
"And sharks might fight!
"But sharks like Christmas too!"

Everyone joined in. Well, not everyone. The guy who hates everything held back. He had his eye on Derek, who wasn't singing either.

Derek was afraid of heights. He'd forgotten that. It hadn't seemed so high when they planned it. This had been Trish's idea, that he be snatched from this high perch—which felt higher than fifteen feet to him—by the outstretched hands of one of her troupe, then swung down and deposited in the congregation, one of them, on the humble rag that was the original blanket the whole nonsense came swaddled in, a mere mortal, but a guide from above. It had sounded totally visionary and not so high up, but standing here was scary as shit.

He only had one try, when Otto swept by. That was the guy's name whose hands he was to leap for, Otto. He had every muscle you could name. Derek couldn't name more than two or three. He tried to imagine leaping into the air to catch those unnamed muscles. No. But he had to. Everyone was kneeling on their little blankets munching cookie, staring at him, perfectly positioned beneath the shaft of the bright sun beaming down into the sanctuary through the hole in the roof. Some shielded their eyes from the glare, others clasped hands in prayer.

And then the Throne nut started singing. *Sharky*? Where did the Sharky thing come from? Sharky cookies? Emily claimed different, but she was all pissed about Trish and probably into something with Sofía, though they had brought Sofía's sister and all her friends in from the burbs. They all belted out the Sharky tune with Throne like they were maybe a little drunk. It was inspirational. Derek felt like a fucking megachurch.

The feeling was fleeting. Pride goeth before the Fall. He missed Otto's outstretched hands, watched them sweeping away down below him, too late to be caught, just as the last strains of Throne's baritone faded to hushed, anticipatory silence. He'd just break his neck if he dove for Otto now.

So it all came down to this. This moment of truth. Was he a real artist or not? To fall was to fail. The stairway led nowhere. There was no plane to board. Cornered by his art, it would take a miracle to get himself out of this one. He should've seen it coming. Don't things always go this way? You can't just keep giving people visions when what they want is miracles.

He shrugged his shoulders, looked up into the blinding light. There was nothing for it. He spread his arms and began to rise, passing before the plywood-faced lamb, past the stunned cock-eyed gaze of Jesus, wafted on the collective gasp of his congregation, all the way to the rafters, which he hoped would be miraculous enough. The roof was going to cost enough without punching a hole in it to ascend any further. You had to leave a little something for the next performance. He landed in the choir loft knocking over a huddle of music stands no one wanted. The clatter echoed through the sanctuary like the clash of thunder. He leaned out over his flock and took a bow, expecting applause, but they were all kneeling on their little blue blankets—witnesses to a miracle—their faces, their lives, utterly transformed—hands lifted to the sky wanting more—even the guy who hates everything, even Paul Throne.

Even Emily.

Now he'd done it. He'd given all for art and could give no more. He had cured himself of the art disease. He would forevermore be mired in mere miracle. Alas.

He had become as one of the gods.

Memories Are Made of This

Calypso knew him at once—for the gods all know each other, no matter how far they live from one another—but Ulysses was not within; he was on the sea-shore as usual, looking out upon the barren ocean with tears in his eyes, groaning and breaking his heart for sorrow.

—*The Odyssey* (Samuel Butler translation)

Old isn't wise; it's just old. Worse, it's older, all the time older, older, older, till you run out of older, and you're dead. There's no *oldest,* just dead. And who knows if death is the worst? Some say it's the best—*if* you play your cards right, believe the correct doctrines, observe the proper rituals. I've always thought those guys were kidding themselves, but here's hoping they're right, and against the odds I've managed not to break any house rules muddling through life more or less decently, and payday's coming soon. Heaven, here I come!

I'm sorry. The notion makes me feel slightly ridiculous, vaguely embarrassed for such a small-minded deity. More likely, I'll be dead soon, sleeping the big sleep, so what does it matter if I can remember my life or not?

It matters to the woman who says she's my daughter. She bursts into tears every time she sees me. "Daddy," she says. "Oh Daddy!" That's about all she can manage before she's crying again. Must be my daughter to cry like that. Or a complete psycho. Not to imply that those are mutually exclusive categories.

But this experimental treatment thing seems to cheer her right up. She managed a whole sentence this morning—"Oh Daddy, I'm so hopeful!"—which is pretty remarkable. Even more remarkable is that I remember it, that I remember *anything*. I can remember because I'm here inside this pretend world of my life. Dr. Sati called it a "virtual reality simulation" in the briefing she just gave me in her well-appointed virtual office. There were framed virtual degrees on the wall, a virtual potted palm that needed watering, virtual stockings on her virtual legs. Her treatment takes my Humpty Dumpty memories, she explained, puts them back together again, tunes them up, fills in the gaping holes, and feeds them back to me, a rebuilt memory, almost as good as new.

They hacked my whole life, scoured every hard drive I ever had anything to do with, every camera and recording device I ever showed up on, phone records, grocery store cards, journals, scrawled midnight ramblings—*everything.* They didn't just steal my identity, they stalked it, ravished it, swallowed it whole, and digitized it—all because the woman who calls herself my daughter signed something. I never signed anything. I'm incompetent. I could be cured by this bold new procedure I'm told, but in the meantime, in between times, I'm incompetent.

It's true.

Completely incompetent. Unless I'm here in Virtualville—my name for it to remind myself it's not real—but a damned impressive simulation of the few square miles in Richmond where I've spent the overwhelming majority of the last forty years of my life. (Well in excess of 87.5%, the good doctor informs me; this statistic pleases her no end). Memories need a place to happen, and this is my place, my village. She's even given me a little map showing the boundaries I've stowed in my shirt pocket. *Heere Endeth thee Worlde.* It may be small, but the amount of data is still staggering.

My life in here begins at forty. Nor can I remember anything that took place elsewhere, so memories of travel, domestic or foreign, which Dr. Sati says I did a fair amount of, are lost to me, but I can remember talking about it once I was back home, writing about it, looking at photos of it, even though I can't remember actually standing in the square in Freiberg or Madrid when the photos were taken. Dr. Sati doesn't have the whole world in her hands—or memory—just yet. As she put it in her virtual office, "We're not quite there yet—but someday!" which, now that I think about it, was an interesting choice of words for someone in her line of work. Where is there, exactly? Which one?

Neither here nor there, I suppose, and someday isn't a concept I've had much use for lately. The way this phase of the treatment works is I come here to Virtualville and remember things, interact with the simulation, work out any kinks in the system. Then when they think they have a workable memory, they'll give it to me in a little iPod thing I can carry around with me.

Anything beats the scrambled chaos I live with now. Or so it seems as long as I'm in here, remembering my recent life as one interconnected thing. I can only accomplish that miracle in here. While I'm living it, my life's like a freight train one car at a time with no perception they have anything to do with each other, that they're going somewhere on rails, coupled together in a continuous journey. Dr. Sati's fond of journey metaphors, and now she's got me doing it. Okay by me. I've been sitting on my ass too long—no idea how long exactly. From here my recent past looks like a pretty big train wreck, but I don't know how deep the valley is, how far down the pile of wreckage goes. I'm hungry for a journey, even a virtual one.

Even so, I'm having a little trouble getting started. Partly, I suppose, because I know this isn't real, that really I'm a used-up old man who can barely remember his own name, plugged into some machine, or several, probably drooling and shitting myself. But I can work my way around all that easily enough—I *was* a science fiction writer—and feeling younger, healthier, sharper is fine by me, real or not. Maybe *this* is heaven—really good software. I remember writing a couple of novels along those lines. It's great to have memories again. I'll take what I can get. It's almost perfect.

Thing is, I remember being married, more than once. I divorced soon after I came to Richmond, (no children), remarried, divorced again nine years later. I remember raising step-daughters I tried to stay in touch with but never saw enough of after the divorce. I think I was a good stepfather. Ex-step-parent was a tougher role to play. But I don't remember any *daughter*. The woman who says she is couldn't be over thirty, forty tops, so you'd think she *had* to show up in here if she's my daughter. Amy, she says her name is—cries when I ask, of course. I remember a sister-in-law named Amy. There was also a neighbor with a couple of white dogs named Casey and Murphy, a co-worker of my girlfriend of many years, and a favorite singer who spelled it A-i-m-e-e. (This one spells it A-m-y—I saw it on the forms). I could probably come up with more Amy's if I tried, but none of them would be this woman, none of them would be my daughter, because I never had one. I'm afraid to ask her who she thinks her mother was. Necessity maybe?

How can I be so sure she's not who she says she is? One more relevant detail: I can't remember the operation itself since it happened before my reconstructed memories begin forty years ago, but I remember telling the grisly horror story on several occasions—once upon a time I had a vasectomy with gruesome post-operative complications—an inept surgeon, no painkillers, a bumpy ride home, and it only gets worse before it's over. I may have exaggerated the unpleasantness in the telling for dramatic effect, but not the end of the story: The operation was a complete and enduring success. I was sterile when I hit town, and I'll wager I'm sterile here in Virtualville too, so *how* did I come by a daughter?

"You mean *step*-daughter, don't you?" I asked Amy. "Oh Daddy!" she boo-hoo-hooed. I took that to be a no.

I can almost believe I've forgotten having sex with Amy's mother, even though I don't remember sex with any strangers, with any woman whose full term pregnancy might have escaped my notice. I'm not that kind of guy. But I *can't* believe I would've undergone the necessary surgery beforehand in order to impregnate her. This seems like a curious flaw in what otherwise appears to be, just sitting here, taking it all in, a perfect memory.

"Choose a safe haven," Dr. Sati suggested, "somewhere familiar to sort things out and get your bearings before undertaking your journey into your past." I've chosen a coffee place in Carytown where I've come for years. It's gone through a half-dozen name changes over time. I'm sitting outside—the outside tables are the reason I come here. I spend too much time indoors. It's a warm winter day. The trees are bare, but the sun is shining, and the wind is out of the southwest.

Depending on what I'm remembering, the name painted on the window beside me changes. *The Raven's Brew* it says now. They did the Poe thing with cutesy macabre décor and syrupy drinks with names like The Never S'more and The Purloined Latte. They called a plain coffee a Black Cat. They didn't last long, during an uneventful stretch of my life, which is probably why they've shown up while I'm not remembering anything much in particular. Their logo is supposed to be a raven perched on a coffee cup. Scale's off. If that's a coffee cup, the bird's a starling at best. If that's a raven, he's perched on a toilet bowl.

I look up the street—shops, awnings, signs, people walking dogs, panhandlers. Some things are surprisingly constant. I remember way back when there used to be a hardware store with a cat sprawled on the counter, and sure enough, there it is—the sign anyway. I assume the cat's inside. I down the rest of my coffee, which no longer has an ersatz

Raven emblazoned on the cup, and head for the hardware store. I haven't petted a cat since I can't remember when—like every other damn thing. Seems like a good place to start.

A bell rings as I open the door. The sound lingers. Sweet. Did it really have a bell, or is that just the way I remember it? There's a white-haired gentleman behind the counter in a faded corduroy shirt and a cardigan sweater. On the counter, sprawls the cat—plump and moderately fluffy.

I breathe in the heady scent of nail bins and wood floors warmed by a roaring gas furnace. Not a trace of cat piss smell like you might expect. They must've cleaned the cat box two or three times a day. I start browsing through a bin of signs to give myself something to do—for sale, for rent, beware of dog, day sleeper, no trespassing, no smoking, private property, no soliciting, keep off grass…

"May I help you find something?" the white-haired guy asks.

Some answers. "No. I'm just browsing," I say, like I'm trying to decide whether I work nights, have a mean dog, or just have some propertarian rules to enforce. *Propertarian*—I smile to myself remembering Le Guin's *The Dispossessed* where she coined the term. It's been a long time since I could remember that novel—*any* novel. Hell, even haiku escaped me. I couldn't remember seventeen syllables if it meant my life. Can't, I guess I should be saying, because that's me *now*. When I'm not in here, truth is, I don't know where the hell I am half the time. Parked in front of a perfect square of green jell-o, looking through the glass. Maybe Virtualville's not so bad.

Dr. Sati said I have twenty-four hours, a day and a night, for my first session.

Session was her word, like a shrink. Is that how she sees this? Don't musicians use the term as well? What do experimentalists call it each time they drop the hapless rat in the maze? A *trial*—that's it. I can see where *trial* would be altogether too Kafkaesque for her purposes. Mustn't upset the rat. *Session* almost sounds fun, cool, sexy. I imagine all my fellow droolers back in the dayroom asking me, "Hey Man, how was your *session*?" "Hot," I'll say. "Hot."

I buy a Swiss Army knife—I used to carry one all the time in those days. Seems weird to me now. While the white-haired guy's checking on the credit card, I pet the cat. I hear the purr, feel it in my palm gliding on crackling fur, recall—just because I can—my favorite haiku by Buson:

A chill pierces me—
My dead wife's comb in our room
Underneath my heel.

It's wonderful to remember these seventeen syllables, to feel the poignant tang of the words in the back of my throat, the wince of sympathetic pain it gives me every single time I read or remember them.

I can't really remember what the cat looked like, so it keeps changing—tabby, calico, tuxedo. I must abandon it to sign for my purchase. The name of the bank on the credit card is for a bank that doesn't exist anymore. Forty years, I never got a new card; the bank just kept getting bought and sold. The form I sign has carbon paper in it. If the memory restoration angle doesn't work out, Dr. Sati can sell this thing to historical fiction writers.

I walk east into the Fan, toward home in those days, to see what I'm up to, or what whoever put this world together thinks I was up to. Are they the same? Data doesn't tell the whole story. The possibilities for misinterpretation are endless. What if they've mistaken metafiction for autobiography? What if they believe some lie I told myself in my journals I never even believed at the time? What if they've missed some crucial fact of my life upon which everything secretly depends, but which, nevertheless, has remained hidden, implicit in everything, but never revealed or recorded or understood? I'm not saying there *is* such a thing, but I'm not so sure I'd know it if there were. I might be the last to know. What, in short, if they have my life all wrong? How will I know the difference?

Who cares? Right now, in reality, I have no life at all. I'm enjoying the hell out of walking down the street like it's something I do every day, knowing where I am and where I'm going, even if it's not really real. What am I talking about? I'm enjoying it *because* it's not really real: My real life sucks, has sucked for a long time, and the long term outlook is for more of the same, hopefully not too much more.

On the way home, I pass a bookstore that hasn't been around for years. There are nice new copies of *Foucault's Pendulum* in the window. I always meant to read that but never got around to it. I pop inside, snatch up a copy and open it. Blank pages. "Ah hah!" I exclaim. The words appear on the pages an instant later, hundreds of thousands of them looks like. "Double ah hah," I whisper. Revision is possible. Perhaps essential. A juggling act. They can't anticipate my every move. Omniscience takes time. I replace the book in the display. I'll leave Eco for another day.

I reach my home of almost forty years ago, but—having no desire to run into my ex-wife—past, present, real, virtual, or otherwise—I hang around across the street until they leave—her and a younger me looking pretty happy. This is the early days.

I always carry my keys in my right front pants pocket, and there they are. I let myself in. My old dog Carrie ambles out to greet me, and I lose it. I'm as bad as Amy. I can't remember—does Odysseus cry when he's reunited with his old dog? He obviously would if I were writing the scene. Carrie licks my face to comfort me. She doesn't seem to mind I'm twice the age I was when I left just now.

I give her a big hug around the neck and rise to check myself out in the mirror at the foot of the stairs, to see what I look like in Virtualville, to see if I look as good as I feel. If you scraped the sick old guy off the table and cured him of everything, every illness, every mistake, if you took the fortyish guy who just left and aged him to eighty for a movie where the idea was to show he'd aged well, like those guys in the ads fly fishing in their twilight years because they picked the right capitalist to play with their money, you'd get the guy in the mirror, one as real as the other. Nice work, Dr. Sati.

I'm at the foot of the stairs, but I don't take them. Our old bedroom? I don't think so. The kids' rooms? I get choked up just thinking about it. I couldn't even face the stuffed animals without crying. I go down to the basement where my office is. Carrie follows me. She assumes I'm going to work and curls up under the desk. The computer is an antique, an Atari ST. I turn it on just to see what I'm working on, slip into the chair. It takes me a minute to figure out the old word processor. I remember: I'm putting together a collection of short stories to submit to a competition, winner gets a thousand bucks and publication of the collection.

I remember how it turns out. I was a semifinalist, had my hopes cranked to the ceiling, and lost, turned me off short stories for years, and I threw myself into writing novels, which turned out pretty well at the time, no complaints. It was twenty years before I seriously returned to writing short stories. Sore loser.

I look over the story titles. I remember them all, but some just barely. I start reading the least familiar, a story I haven't read in almost forty years. I stumble in the first paragraph and again in the third. Did I revise this? Was I lobotomized? By the bottom of the first page, I don't want to go on. I skim through it, scene by scene, refreshing my memory. I like the idea, but the execution is clumsy and hurried—amateurish. I see what it needs, wants, aches for. I slip off my shoes, bury my sock-clad feet in Carrie's warm, furry side, look around at my basement office in Virtualville and smile, humming, "Heaven, I'm in Heaven…" And in no time, my lame story and I are dancing cheek to cheek. It's my dime, right?

I spend an hour or so revising the story until it makes me cry—it's that kind of story—and save it. I print a copy of the collection's table of contents and go upstairs and make a pot of coffee. While it's brewing, I make notes on the other stories, shuffle around the order, rename one of them. Then I go back to work, revising one story after another. I haven't had this much fun in years. It gets dark outside, but still no one's home. The kids are probably at their dad's house. Maybe they're all out of town for the weekend, gone to DC or something. I make a sandwich. I work through the night. When I'm done, what was an okay collection of stories with some interesting moments, now totally rocks, if I do say so myself. I stand up and stretch, smiling at the dawn through the basement window, pink sidewalks at eye level, flitting sparrows, Zippety-fucking-doo-da. Carrie gets up, expecting a walk now—a delightful idea.

Then I spot the stack of printed pages with a cover letter on it. Signed. Jeez. The young guy thinks his work is done. He's going to submit it like it *was*. He was lucky he made semifinalist. He's lucky I wasn't one of the judges. He's going to stuff it in a padded envelope when he gets back and walk to the post office and mail it and lose again.

What the hell. My world, right?

I apologize to Carrie and start printing my revised version. Takes forever with this old printer. I listen to my old music, but it's too much like an oldies station, which I've never liked, so I print and ponder in silence. Printing something up is a joyous moment, an apotheosis of sorts. It's been a long time. *How was your session? Hot.*

The printing is near the end when the phone rings. I let the machine answer. Dr. Sati's voice comes out of the machine. "Mr. Danvers, please pick up the phone. We need to talk."

I glance at the printer. There's only a few pages left. She's going to tell me not to make the switch, I just know it, but if I don't answer, she might just pull the plug, and it's straight back to Droolsville, mission not accomplished, mediocrity in the mail, semifinalist emeritus forever.

I pick up. "Hello."

"Mr. Danvers, you can't do this. You are altering the reality of your own memories. This will make them unacceptable for our purposes."

"And what purposes would those be?"

"To restore your true memory as completely as possible."

"That's only one purpose. I have purposes too. I'm not throwing away good work. If that doesn't fit in with your science project, then maybe you've got the wrong guy."

"Just a moment." Then she's arguing with someone, but she has her hand over the phone, and I can't make out any words, but it's all there in the tones. They're stuck with me for some reason. They have to try to keep me happy. They can't call my bluff. She told me I was the "ideal candidate" for her procedure because of my small geographical footprint—the 87.5%+ factor—and my large verbal footprint, millions and millions of words. I figured she was only blowing smoke, but maybe not just any demented old man will do.

"Very well," Dr. Sati says, "but please don't change anything else. If your constructed memories diverge too far from your own fragmentary memories, they won't be of any use to you. They need to be resonant, in order to verify and enhance one another and take hold as a coherent memory structure."

Resonant. Take hold. Coherent. Sounds good. "Can I walk the dog?"

"By all means, walk the dog."

"Where is everyone?"

"You didn't want to see them. You remembered them gone."

I wasn't ready to see them. Is that the same as not wanting to? Maybe so. "But they wouldn't have left the dog alone in the house."

"Such inconsistencies are unavoidable. You remembered Carrie greeting you when you came in, remembered her following you about the house. Memories are suggestible. The simulation, like your memory, is susceptible to your desires."

Susceptible to my desires—the doctor certainly has my number. "How long do I have left?"

"Forty minutes."

I check my watch. That should be enough. "Thanks, Dr. Sati." I hang up, switch the manuscript, tossing the old one in a trashcan half a block down the alley. It's a lovely old cobblestone alley. Carrie and I must've walked it a thousand times, morning and night. There's dog shit everywhere. Nobody picked up in those days. I don't think it will alter history overly if I do. Maybe it's just virtual shit flowing into a virtual river the next time there's a virtual rain, but I'll feel better if I bag it and put it in a trash can.

For a dog who's been dead for decades, and a man who's wished he was for too damn long, Carrie and I cut quite a figure strolling up the cobblestone alley, heading farther east than we would typically go. I have a plan. I need somebody I can trust inside Virtualville, somebody Team Sati doesn't know about.

Carrie's up for it, but she wonders what we're doing in this neck of the woods down by the university. She's delighted when I bound up the steps to an apartment house like I know what I'm doing. I scan the directory, and here you go—there's the name I'm looking for. I thought she lived here. We'll call her Deidre. I press the buzzer, and she picks up. I confidently sing out my name, and she buzzes us both in. The way I remember it, this place allows dogs. There are a few loose barks from this apartment or that—whether to warn Carrie off or greet her, I have no idea.

We climb the stairs to the second floor. There's a long wide hall, the floor tiled in a black and white checkerboard on the diagonal. Carrie's nails click on the tile. I should've trimmed them while I was printing. I always used to put it off. Poor dog can't do it herself. The apartment doors are slatted screen doors with solid inner doors, some open, letting food smells and television sounds leak into the hall. Deidre steps into the hall waiting for me, holding both doors open. She looks into my eyes, and she knows me, but as a much younger man. She thinks it's makeup. "You look *incredible*," she says. "Is this your dog?" She asks like someone who likes dogs.

"Yes. Deidre, this is Carrie."

Carrie wags and chatters. Deidre stoops to pet her. They have a moment, and I'm momentarily forgotten, a woman after my own heart.

"Come in, come in," she says. "I'll make coffee."

We step inside and follow her into her kitchen. She offers me the only chair at a tiny drop-leaf table. I remain standing. Carrie sits beside me and leans against my legs. Sunlight streams through the window. Deidre makes coffee, measuring, pouring water into the reservoir. She smiles at me. "I can't believe you just showed up at my place, all made up!" She laughs. She likes I've done something so outrageous, shown up in her kitchen in an old man disguise, even if it is a bit weird. There's a clock on the wall behind her. I'm running out of time. She's counting scoops of coffee.

"Coffee sounds great, but we can't stay, I'm afraid. It's not makeup—I'm eighty years old. I'm time-traveling. It's me, but from the future." I hate lying to her, but I don't want to embark upon this stage of our relationship by telling her she's not real. She has to believe in herself—if she's going to be resonant to my purposes. It's okay if she thinks I'm nuts or impossible or a senile old man, just so long as she believes in herself, and she's curious—curious enough to act.

She holds the empty pot in her hand, about to put it in the machine. She sets it down on the counter a little too hard and looks into my eyes. "You're serious, aren't you?" She examines what she thought was makeup more critically and draws back in fear. I take her trembling right hand and place it on my old cheek. "See?"

Apparently she does. Her young hand caresses my old cheek as if remembering a moment when I was merely forty, only twice her age, and withdraws. "I don't understand. Why— Why are you here?" She glances at Carrie, as if she might offer a clue. Carrie, an emotional sponge, long on sympathy, short on understanding, stares soulfully back.

I want to take Deidre's hands, caress the hand that caressed my cheek, but I don't. I haven't felt a tender touch since I'd rather not remember when, but this isn't the time. I need to stick with this moment I've created, stick with my story. "There are contradictions in time. I need someone I can trust here in my past to help me sort things out, to get to the bottom of things. I thought of you." I imagine myself doing little else but thinking of her for days on end. It's not an unpleasant or unlikely thought. If my designer octogenarian good looks don't airbrush it from my face, she can read it there plain as day.

She struggles to remember my infatuation with practically nothing to go on. “Me? I—I didn’t know you felt that way about me.”

“I most definitely do. Did. I just never said anything. It was never the right time. But please, I haven’t a moment to spare. I need your help—just one thing. It would mean so much to me. I want you to find out if I have a daughter, or have one in the next few years, named Amy. Find out who her mother is, whatever you can about her. Can you do that for me?” I almost kneel in supplication.

“I— I guess so. Yes. I will.”

“I’ll be back. I can’t say when.”

Over her shoulder, past her sunlit chestnut hair, the clock says, time’s up.

***

A bird thumps the plate glass, falls into the flowers, dead, blood and feathers.

No one notices but me. Maybe it didn’t really happen. Now.

Condensed rivulets coursing inside the plate glass soak the moldy drapes.

Is it dinner time yet?

“Daddy?” The room whirls. I’m sitting in a wheelchair. I didn’t know that. I wish she wouldn’t whirl me around like that. She came yesterday. I think it was yesterday. Maybe yesterday. How would I know the difference? “Are you all right, Daddy?”

I don’t know why I’m in a wheelchair. I can walk okay. I just don’t know the way. “Swell,” I say. “Ter-*rific*.” She’s a little afraid of me I think. She thinks I’m going to ask her who she is, but I trick her and don’t. If she wants me to know, she’ll have to tell me. Then I’ll forget.

She wheels me into the dining room. It’s full of old people. The food is terrible. I eat it anyway. Clean your plate! I don’t know who told me that, but it’s important.

“Who’s Deidre?” the woman asks. She’s sitting across from me.

She doesn’t eat the terrible food. She doesn’t like watching me eat it. Too bad. She leaves when she wants. I want, but you have to know where you are to leave.

“Deidre?” she says. “Concentrate, Daddy.”

“Deidre, Deidre, Deidre. I give up. Who is she?”

“No, Daddy. I’m asking you. Dr. Sati wants to know.”

“Why ask me? I don’t know anyone. Do you want me to guess?”

“No. Never mind. Do you feel up to another session with Dr. Sati?”

“Never mind, nevermore, never s’more. A session. Yes. I’ll bring my guitar.” I laugh. She doesn’t. Why am I laughing? She thinks she remembers me. Why doesn’t *she* laugh?

“Are you ready to go back to your room now, Daddy?”

I wish she’d quit calling me Daddy. “Did anyone get the bird? It hit the glass—whack!”

I smack my hands together to show her, and she jumps up and whirls me around, pushes me down a wide hall with checkerboard tiles like I’m in a wheelchair race. The rooms fly by. Behind every door a story lies unwritten, but we never stop. We never win. Winner gets a grand, gets to walk right out of here and never look back.

I’m in bed. It’s night. When did that happen? Just now? It always happens.

I shout “Whack!” smack hands.

A door bangs open. “Quiet!”

Shuts. Blood and feathers.

***

I return in the spring and head straight for the river. I’ve come alone, though more often than not I would’ve had a dog with me. It’s a warm, sunny day. I sit on the rocks and watch the river running for I’m not sure how long. If Team Sati is watching, as I’m sure they are, they must be bored shitless. Good. The river doesn’t care what they think. The river just is. Me too, when I sit and watch, even in my mind.

A gnarled sycamore shelters a tiny sand beach hidden from the bank. I hop, rock to rock, a fundamental river pleasure. I find fair Deidre underneath the sycamore lying on the sand. She looks up at me, shielding her eyes from the sun with a book she’s reading. One of mine. “You came, like you said. It sure took you long enough.”

She puts her book down, sits up, and pats the towel beside her. I sit.

She smells of lotion. I try not to think how lovely she was back then, how lovely now. Anyone can be lovely here in Virtualville. It’s that kind of place, where memories of a woman’s face can linger long, if you want them to. “How long has it seemed to you?”

"Eight years last Valentine's Day," she says.

"You're kidding. I showed up at your place on *Valentine's* Day?"

"You don't remember?"

"I remember showing up all right, just not the date. I'm not much for cards and chocolates. Love shouldn't be some special day, but one continuous celebration." I point to the book facedown on her towel, written when I was a pup in my forties, to corroborate my testimony, and she smiles her agreement. Foolish ghost, flirting with this young apparition—Pan and Tinkerbell.

Not how I'd like to see myself, thank you very much. "Did you find out about Amy?" I ask, getting down to business.

She doesn't speak right away. She's sizing me up. There's a confidence about her today. It's not just she's eight years older with eight more years of experiences. Last time, she hardly knew me. Now, I imagine, she knows things about me I won't know myself, unless I let her show me. "Maybe a little," she says. "Let's not talk about her yet. Can we sit awhile this time? Talk? What will it hurt?"

Dr. Sati warned me not to change anything—an impossibility, in my experience, and way too late in Deidre's case. This meeting never happened. No meeting ever happened. Most anything Deidre might report to me, I trust, never really happened. I'm hoping this will throw everything else into greater relief. I had a job once using a Hinman collator, a machine for comparing different editions of a text by superimposing images of the two then switching rapidly back and forth between them. The smallest differences would flash off and on like a turn signal. Deidre and I on this beach should shine like a lighthouse or sing like a siren. "Nothing, I suppose. I have more time today. All day and all night, time to tell me everything."

"A lot can happen in eight years."

"The blink of an eye."

She looks around the beach, up into the sycamore's twisted limbs, as if everything that's happened in the last eight years is piled all around us, and I don't have a fucking clue. Which is pretty much true, though I have my suspicions.

She says, "You look exactly the same as you did eight years ago."

"It's my new look. I'm stuck with it until I can do some shopping." I smile, and she smiles back, studying my smile.

She's been making a study of me—how I move, how I speak. Finally, she says, "You *are* him. You are who you say you are."

I can only imagine the basis of her judgment. "I've tried. Too often failed. Perhaps I should have left the past alone. There's always the danger the time traveler might catalyze a change in the course of events, alter history. What about you? Have you altered history since I saw you last?"

She straightens her lovely neck. She has. It's clear. Her defiant guilt is written all over her. "Perhaps things are fated," she says. "Perhaps what's meant to be is meant to be, no matter what any one of us does, and can't be changed."

"As if it is written."

"Yes, exactly."

She has a particular fate in mind, it's clear, and it means everything to her since she's at the heart of it. It's always nice to enlist the universe in your cause when you feel so strongly. Why not? You won't give a shit about the universe tomorrow if things don't work out. Now that she's face to face with the old goat who started it all, she means to have her say in fate's final draft.

I shake my head. "Written—what does that mean? Unless he's a hack, God revises. The biggest boulder in the river is revised, changing the river. We all change the universe. We can't help ourselves. What about you? Haven't you changed the universe?"

She gives me a crooked smile. "That's exactly how it feels." She looks upriver, chucks a rock into the current. "After you showed up at my place that day, I started finding out more about you, whatever I could, asking around. I hardly knew you before. I was curious. What you wanted to know—whether you had a daughter—was easy: No daughter and unlikely to be one in a marriage falling apart. It was rumored you stayed married for the stepdaughters you adored. I didn't care whether you had a daughter or not, had no idea why you asked me to find out that one thing of all things.

"What I kept thinking about was what you said, how you had feelings for me but never said anything, and I kept wondering if it was really true and how I felt about it, and I tried to forget about it, but I couldn't, which I guess told me right then how I felt about it. So I had to find out if it was true, or whether you were just some crazy old man messing with my head."

Curious enough to act. "So you asked me—the me you know in your time, that is."

She shrugs one shoulder. Asked? "More or less. I knew where you lived. It was easy to run into you while you were out walking your dog. The moment you caught sight of me, when I saw how you looked at me, I knew right then it was true. We've been having an affair off and on for the last five years."

I feel a twinge of guilt for the suffering I've caused to happen, even if it isn't real, like the dog shit running into the river where we're sitting now. Here and now. Laughable concepts in Virtualville. Still seems like the same old shit, however. "That's quite a different universe all right. You've omitted a wealth of details, I trust."

She looks at me with disarming frankness. "Do you want them?" There's an edge to her voice, a challenge. She's absolutely marvelous. I imagine falling hard for such a woman. It would be easy.

"More than you can possibly imagine. That's some story. How does it end?"

"It's not over yet. Perhaps you can tell me—since you come from the future."

The way she says it, I suspect she knows I'm no time traveler, but then who in the hell does she think I am? I'm afraid to ask. "I'm afraid we're definitely off any map I brought with me."

She shakes her head sadly. "Wherever we are, I'm pregnant." She juts out her chin in what must be some genetically coded signal of paternity, for its import is immediately clear to me even though I've never before experienced it.

It's all too much. I was going to play it cool and sly and noir, but I start laughing so hard I can't do anything but roll around on the sand. The water rushing all around us seems to be laughing too. It's the most delicious helplessness, laughter. God, I miss it. She looks mildly alarmed, as if she fears the shock of my miraculous paternity has been too much for me. I finally manage to regain sufficient control of my laughter for speech. "Deidre, you've exceeded my wildest expectations."

"What do you mean? What's so funny?"

"I'm sorry. I've played a terrible trick on you. I didn't *remember* you. I had to let you think that. Actually, I *imagined* you, made you up whole cloth out of nothing but a handful of details—a fictional character, in other words. I figured there must be some provision here in Virtualville to ad lib, to compensate for the missing persons who might turn up out of the past. It was surprisingly easy. All I had to do was *want* to see you because of my imagined deep feelings for you, *expect* to find you, and there you were—a mystery woman, named after the legendary Irish beauty hidden away to thwart prophecy—in vain, of course; that sort of thing always turns out to have been in vain. I considered calling you Calypso but thought that too obvious—her name means 'I will conceal,' by the way. I wanted someone on the inside, so to speak—to see what would happen if I turned you loose in the funhouse. And here you are, eight years later, pregnant, by a younger me I assume. It's too rich. What would motivate someone to play such a trick on an old man like that? Tell me, have you picked out a name for the fictional fetus yet?"

"Amy," she says.

I can't stop chuckling. "I was going to suggest that."

Our eyes meet. Ah, what a delicious moment. You can see her mind racing to formulate the best strategy to deal with this latest impossibility. She doesn't want to end up irrelevant, merely imaginary and nothing more. She hopes to resonate, to change things, to change me. "Dr. Sati told me I was helping you, saving your life by helping you construct a coherent memory. Is that not true?"

"No more true than you are. When did you talk to Dr. Sati?"

"This morning. She told me you didn't come from the future, but that I, instead, came from your past. She said I wasn't real, that I was fashioned from your memories. I didn't mind that. It meant we were meant to be—we had been lovers before and would be lovers again—we would always be lovers. But, she said, your memories are unraveling, and you'll never rest, never find peace, until you remember your real daughter."

"You're not really pregnant, then, are you?"

"Of course not. I'm not really anything. I'm made of your memories here in, what is it you call it? Virtualville—at least I *thought* you remembered me." She laughs. "How soon we forget." She scoops up a handful of sand and lets it sift through her fingers. "Memories are made of this." She dusts off her hands. "But I shouldn't complain. If you made me up, you must like me, right?"

She's poignant, flirtatious, completely seductive. I'm susceptible to my desires. She wants me to think I remember her—or wish I did, or didn't care. Sad to say, she's got the wrong guy.

"Did you meet Amy as well?"

"Briefly. She didn't say much. Just cried. She seemed terribly upset. It broke my heart to see her like that, to imagine being forgotten by your own father."

"That's the one. You don't think she overplays it by a few sobs? I guess if you're crying all the time, you never have to answer any questions. She's not my daughter."

"How can you be so sure? She looks a lot like you. Dr. Sati said you have the delusion you've had a vasectomy, but it's only a product of your dementia, your rationalization for your failure to remember your own daughter."

"That's good—nice tight little circle—no way I can refute that. But now I have another reason to be sure: They tried to use you to convince me Amy was my daughter. No sooner do I invent you than you're enlisted to their purposes, knocked up to legitimize my lachrymose kid. Makes me smell a rat. What do you think, Deidre? I made you smart. Doesn't it smell to you?"

"Definitely."

"I knew I could trust you. So what do you think?"

"You don't seem demented to me. After all, you made me convincing enough to fool Dr. Sati and Amy both, convincing enough so that I believed I was your lover all these years." She looks me in the eye. "What ends up happening with you and your wife by the way?"

There are years of unhappiness packed into the way she says "wife" that humble me and silence my snickering. There's nothing funny about pain. "In my reality she has a fling with an old college boyfriend and dumps me a few months from now. I can't say I blame her. We were both pretty unhappy. And you and I, alas, never had an affair—since you never existed."

"Too bad. It was wonderful."

"Affairs like that are never wonderful. Lies, deceit, jealousy. Why was it we were having an affair anyway? Why didn't I get a divorce?"

"The kids."

"I love them, but if I really loved you like I no doubt said I did, I wouldn't have strung you along for years, kids or no kids. That's just a rotten thing to do."

"Maybe so. But there were times…"

"I imagine there were. Maybe we should just leave it at that."

She looks down at the sand, shattered. Unreality is no solace. I didn't mean to sound so unkind. She looks into my eyes. "Then what *really* happens?" she asks. "Please tell me—what really happened? In your real life." She speaks softly, barely audible over the rushing river, tears in her voice, in her eyes. Maybe she really does love me.

"About a year from now, I start seeing an old friend I've known for years. We fall in love, move in together, never marry for many, many years. The best years of my life."

"What happened?"

"I foolishly outlived her. I've regretted it ever since."

"I'm sorry."

"Don't be. Some people never have something like that their whole lives. I was lucky."

"Why haven't you been to see her? The woman you were so happy with?"

"Good question. I'm scared. All the memories that broke my heart every day until I couldn't remember them anymore—do I really want to reawaken them, make them more real, more vivid, when she's gone and nothing here in Virtualville's going to change that?" Now it's me with tears in my eyes.

Her young hand caresses my old cheek. "You can stay here with me. I have nowhere to go, apparently, no life to lead."

"You've been wonderful, but I have to go. I only have so much time in here to be alive, to make anything happen. I have to see to my future. I hope you understand. If you can see Amy in here, then I can too, and she'll have no reason to cry, since I'll have my wits about me, and she can tell me who the hell she is and what's going on."

"You're not going to let it go until you know, are you?"

"No."

For a moment I think I'm making a terrible mistake. The way Deidre looks at me makes me think I should just stay here with her. But what would we talk about? The man I used to be? Me as an oldies station? Forget about it. "Okay," Deidre says. "Do whatever you have to do."

I kiss her once, softly on the lips, and leave, hopping rock to rock, calling over my shoulder. "Tell Amy, if you see her, to meet me at *The Raven's Brew*."

As I approach, Amy is sitting outside nursing a small Black Cat, looking nervously up and down the street, as if she's afraid I might stand her up. When she spots me, she jumps up and goes inside, leaving her half-finished coffee behind. I take a sniff. Hazelnut. I toss it in the trash. I try to spot her inside, but I can't see through the shop glass glare. I push open the door, and I'm in Dr. Sati's office.

Cute. "Have a seat Mr. Danvers," she says. "What is it you think you're going to accomplish with your wild inventions?"

"That's Dr. Danvers to you, and I was just about to ask you the same question."

"I believe I've explained the treatment fully."

"With all due respect, Doctor, you haven't explained shit. Why, at the heart of a perfect memory, is the gaping hole of the completely implausible Amy? Where the hell is she, anyway? I asked to talk to her."

She waves her hand dismissively. "She's not important."

"She's the legal basis for my being in here. She signed everything, remember? I'd say you'd better hope she's important. Don't you get audited or something? Doesn't anybody ask after the old guy whose name is on the forms under Experimental Subject?"

"They do. Please sit."

"Some answers?"

"Some answers."

I sit. "So if Amy's not my daughter, who is she?"

"Someone I've employed to pretend to be your daughter."

"But why?"

She's matter of fact. "You have no living relatives, no one who can assume legal responsibility for your participating in an experimental treatment. Your memory, quite frankly, is in shambles. We thought, with so many missing pieces, it would be possible to insert the memory of a daughter into your mind at a particularly chaotic juncture in your life with little difficulty. We were wrong."

"So you hoped I'd end up remembering Amy was my daughter, so when anyone came looking, my memory would validate the signature on the forms. Nice trick."

"Would you rather be sitting in the day room staring out the window all day?"

I search her eyes. Really quite striking eyes. Everything about Dr. Sati is singularly striking. I don't recall ever seeing her hanging out in the day room. I'll bet she doesn't look the least bit like this in the real world, if she shows up there at all. "So to cut to the chase, you're saying if I want to hang out in Virtualville, I have to sign on to remembering Amy as my daughter one way or another. Is that right?"

"That's right."

"All right. I don't have a problem with that. If that's the only way. I don't know why you didn't just ask me in the first place."

She smiles. "I'm surprised at your ready acquiescence. You've resisted the idea so vigorously."

"It wasn't the *idea*, but the way you went about it. Don't try to bullshit a bullshitter. I made crazy stuff up for a living. Now that I know what you're up to, I don't have a problem with it. As you say, would I rather be sitting in the day room?"

She nods understandingly, a little too understandingly. "Unfortunately," she says with a sigh—and somehow I'm not surprised that's the first word out of her mouth now that I've signed on to this charade—"There's been a complication. No more than an hour ago, you experienced a massive coronary and widespread organ failure. It was fortuitous that you were being closely monitored for this session at the time and emergency procedures could be implemented immediately."

Fortuitous as all get out, I would say. Never trust a happy coincidence. "So what are you saying? When this session is over, I wake up dead?"

"Well, you could put it that way. Unless..."

This whole deal has been leading up to this *Unless*. She's like a kid on the high board. I'm in no mood. "Unless *what*, Doctor? Spit it out."

"Unless you would agree to extending your session indefinitely. You wouldn't *ever* have to 'wake up,' as you say."

Whoa. I let that sink in for a moment, picture it to the best of my ability. "You mean keep my body alive on machines? How long could that last? I'm a mess. What did you just say? 'Wide-spread organ failure.'"

"The brain, actually, would be sufficient, and we've been able to reconstruct the tissue in the damaged regions, imprint the memories you've re-experienced here with great success."

"A severed head in a vat."

"A crude way to put it, but yes. And we're confident that soon we might be able to transfer consciousness to a more enduring medium altogether. Without the encumbrance of the body, there's no telling how long you might live." Her eyes shine. There's a lilt to her voice. Such vision, such enthusiasm.

She's forgotten she's talking to the rat. I smile, twitch my whiskers. I do believe I behold a light at the end of the maze. "*How* long, do you imagine?"

She realizes she's tipped her hand and tries to cover. "No telling, really. Weeks, months, maybe years."

No telling, but I trust there's plenty of hoping. "You were pitching me, Doctor. Selling the idea. This is where you wanted this to end up all along, isn't it? Me living on and on here in Virtualville?"

It takes her a moment, like Eco's words finding their pages. "Yes, it was. We knew you didn't have long to live going into this. We could never get permission for such research—those fools would call it unethical—but a memory loss treatment was readily approved. Your case will provide proof of concept."

"And what a great story—some poor drooling slob who wrote about virtual immortality gets his wish, sort of. No wonder I was the ideal candidate. So you'll be inviting the whole world to have a look, I imagine, and you can't show them some poor old helpless fuck tricked into a dicey procedure by a phony daughter."

"Yes."

"Neat. How old are you, Doctor?"

"Well..."

"Jeez. Vain even in here? Older than you look, right?"

"Yes."

"You can do that for me too. Even good old is old. I'll take forty, just to make it easy on you. That's when my life begins, right?"

"As you wish. Is there anything else?"

"Not so fast. I'm not saying I'll do it. I need to talk to someone first. Can I do that?"

"As you wish."

"I wish. How much time do I have?"

"Your session is being cut short. A meeting is scheduled to review your medical status in two hours. Your case will be reevaluated in light of whatever legal instruments are in force at the time."

"Meaning you pull the plug or not."

"Yes. Who are you going to talk to?"

"Who the hell do you think, Doctor?"

"I'm sorry, but you didn't seek her out right away. I thought…."

"Think a little harder. Can you save me a little time? Bring her up to speed on what's going on, so I don't have to explain everything to her?"

"As you wish."

"Would you quit saying that? I wish I never grew old, never had to make decisions like this, never had to face a facsimile of a life that's gone."

"I'm sorry. Where would you like to see her?"

"In our house I guess." Where we lived all those years, now remembered, all lost.

***

I'm sitting in the living room, and she comes down the stairs. I watch each step, her hand sliding along the banister, her smile at the sight of me. It's like an old photo album come to life.

"Hey," she says.

"Hey."

I hold her in my arms. I have to hold her, smell her hair, remember her fiercely in a rush of moments like the replay that's supposed to come when you die. That fits. This is death, the end of time, a life of memories, without her. I'm the one doing the remembering here, nobody else. I used to look at old photos for hours. They didn't bring her back. They only reminded me she was gone. I had to put them away. I couldn't walk by them without my heart breaking. *My dead wife's comb…*

"What do you want to do?" she asks.

"I don't know." I hold her at arm's length and look into her eyes. I want to be looking at *her* but know I'm only looking at memories, a collage of who she used to be. "You're not her. You must understand. Every moment of my life with her is sacred and can never happen again. I can't stay with you. No matter how I might wish you were her, I'd always know. But you're almost her, and I've come to ask your help deciding what to do. You must know her better than anyone in here. Will you help me?"

"Of course."

"I used to say, 'I wish we'd gotten together years ago,' and she would say no, that she wasn't ready then—too independent or something—and it probably wouldn't have worked out for one reason or another. I've always found that hard to believe since it always seemed like we were made for each other. What do you think? Should I believe it? Could it work between us before we actually met? Could we start over then?"

She looks at me a long time, sifting through the moments, the words, the memories, voices, faces, flesh, trying to imagine a self before I remember her, before I really knew her, the unexplored territory before her conception. "I don't know what I would think. Maybe it won't matter what I think, but what I feel, what you feel." She smiles her tender smile, a perfectly heartbreaking facsimile. "Everybody's responsible for their own good time."

We used to say that. It could've been a needlepoint slogan on our wall if we were the needlepoint type. If *she* said it, I would smile too. I'd do more than smile: I'd rejoice. Now it just hurts, a voice from the dead, an inescapable dissonance. I leave her there in the empty house of my old life and make my deal with Dr. Sati on my own.

I can't live forever with a memory, but if we meet all over again, before we even knew each other, perhaps we can make a new life. Dr. Sati tries to talk me out of it, but I'm adamant, and time is short. My daughter Amy signs all the paperwork.

I rent a tiny place catty-corner from where I know she was living when I first came to town, before I knew her. It's after my first divorce, and I skip the party where, on the rebound, I met the next nine years of my life. I sit in my room and play solitaire and feel ridiculously powerful sitting out a bad marriage. I look across the intersection at her place.

We're both over top of cheap restaurants, hers a little cheaper than mine. Her light's on.

I recall the scene in *Gatsby* when Gatsby looks across the water at the light on the end of Daisy's dock and longs for her. Look how well that turned out. There's no Tom in this story, however—no husband, no boyfriend, no rival as far as I know. Just me, emboldened by the certain knowledge of our future happiness. Of course, Jay Gatsby was living in a mansion. I'm in one room. There's a bed; a stove, sink, refrigerator, table and chairs in one corner comprise the kitchen; the closet is a turquoise bedspread on shower curtain rings in front of a hole in the wall; and the bathroom's in another corner. There's a metal shower that's like a thunderstorm in a can, even if water gets all over the floor, and it has the best singing-in-the-shower acoustics I've ever heard anywhere. But how many showers can you take? How dirty can you get here in Virtualville? Loneliness was easier when I didn't remember anything.

For days, I've watched out my window as she leaves for work and noted the time. She walks out the front door, around the corner to the alley where I lose sight of her. A few minutes later, she drives out of the alley and heads north in a green Sentra.

She leaves early, 7 a.m., give or take. I go down to the 7-11 at 6:30 and buy a coffee. It's still dark out. I go a block north from her place and hang around the corner. When I see her come around her corner, the sun just coming up, I start walking south toward her, on the other side of the street. I don't think she notices me. I slow my pace so that I can watch as she turns down the alley and walks to her car. I don't see where it is right away—the sun is in my eyes—so I'm caught by surprise when she turns to get into her car and looks back up the alley at me standing there with my 7-11 coffee, headed toward the 7-11, stopped, staring at her, as she eclipses the sun.

I retreat to the corner, to scurry up to my room, but I'm caught by the stoplight. When her car pulls out of the alley, I turn. I can't help myself. I watch her driving away. Our eyes meet in her rearview mirror, then she's gone. I stand there awhile, staring at the empty street.

I watch as she comes home in the evening, and I follow her into the grocery store across from her place. She buys a mango and ramen noodles and frozen pizza and Grape Nuts and skim milk. By the time

I've worked up my nerve to approach her, she's gone, and I'm still pushing around an empty cart.

I'm not sure where else she goes, and I'm only foolish enough to follow her in a car once here in Virtualville. She quickly reaches the limits of my world, takes the ramp onto the freeway, and she might as well be on Pluto. When I violate my territorial boundaries, I wake up in my bed like a reset game.

I track down the Laundromat she said she used to go to. I save up my dirty clothes, and when she comes out of her place with a bag of laundry, I'm close behind her. We're the only two people in the place. Her clothes are already in the washers. She probably had them already sorted. She's reading a Spanish novel.

I start putting my clothes in a row of washers facing her, sorting them out. I don't know that it matters here in Virtualville, but I don't want her to think I don't know how to do laundry. I have trouble taking my eyes off her. I resort to looking at her reflection in the glass up front. I get quarters out of the change machine, buy detergent, load the quarters and detergent in the washing machines, all the time totally focused on her, nervous as hell, like I'm defusing a bomb. I must seem pretty weird. She glances up from her book and catches me looking at her a couple of times. The second time, I drop a couple of quarters and just let them roll away.

No sooner do I finally get my machines going, than hers are done and she's taking her clothes out. She might toss them in the dryer and leave, hang out in the coffee shop across the street where it would be impossible for me to follow without looking like a stalker. I panic. I introduce myself, out of the blue I guess, though she says she's seen me around. She gives me her first name and shakes my hand, but it doesn't go well. I'm nervous, babbling. I ask her about the novel, and she says she's only just started it. I ask her if she has any travel plans, because I know she's about to go to Cuba to study at a language school for a few months, but the question obviously spooks her, and she's vague and evasive. I want to tell her I love her, that we're meant to be together, but she doesn't know me, may even suspect I've been stalking her—which, let's face it, I have been—and we're the only two customers in the place. She stays focused on dealing with her laundry to give me the message, and I just leave, head out into the night, leaving all my clothes in the washers.

Not to worry on the clothes. I've got unlimited funds here in Virtualville, part of the sweet deal I cut. That along with no more back trouble and unlimited reading time almost makes it worthwhile. I never have to see Amy who lives in Paris with her mother, a forgotten fling Dr. Sati inserted into my life a week before I returned to it. I told her to keep Deidre out of it since she'd been through enough already. It was all the same to Amy who her mother was. I was the only one who ever cared about that. Silly Romantic. As for the other me I saw my first time in Virtualville, he's out of here. This is my domain, my village to fuck up.

After the Laundromat fiasco, I try to be cool, but I'm susceptible to my desires, spurred on by my memories. I'm beginning to think I should've purged my memory of her. Dr. Sati even suggested it, but I told her to keep her hands off, that I couldn't bear the thought of forgetting the best thing about my life. Let me forget anyone, I said, but her. So all my memories are intact. But in Virtualville, she's forgotten them, never knew them, never knew me.

She's leaving town soon. There's no more hopping around in time here in Virtualville now that it's been converted from memory restoration to Immortality Lite. Real time, just like real life, one day after another. I can't just skip past the loneliness. I know the name of the language school where she's going, and I find out their schedule. I figure she'll be leaving any day now, be gone for months on end. After all this time I've missed her, I can't wait another few months? Apparently not. It's all I can think about.

I contrive to run into her a half block from her place, and I greet her much too joyously to be the weird guy from the laundry she'd just as soon forget. She wouldn't even have slowed down if I hadn't planted myself right in her way.

"Do you live around here?" she asks.

I point up to the place catty-corner from hers. The blinds are open, a coffee cup sitting on the sill. There's no telescope, but there might as well be. "I— I live up there." I spy on you. I long for you.

She looks up at my window. Her eyes move to hers. Her blinds are closed. I'm probably the reason. I used to catch sight of her when I first came, but lately her blinds are always down. She's not exactly pleased we're neighbors. She steps around me, the biggest boulder in the river.

"I guess that's why I keep running into you. Sorry. I have to run. I have a million things to do. See you around."

I wave good-bye, but she's already walking away. "Have a good trip!" I call out.

She stops, whirls in her tracks and strides back to me. "What did you just say?"

"Nothing. Have— Have a good trip."

"I never said I was going on a trip. What makes you think that?"

"Nothing. I thought you said—"

"I *never* said. Look. I don't know who you are, or why you're everywhere I go, but I want you to keep your distance, understand, or I'm calling the cops. Understand?"

"I understand." I hold up my hands in surrender, an admission of guilt.

She walks away and doesn't look back. Understand? What's to understand here in Virtualville? *As if it is written*, but who's writing this mess? I told Dr. Sati she's to keep her mitts off. So it's just me. I've got the whole world in my hands, and I drop it.

Everybody's responsible for their own good time.

I lean against the side of the building and watch the people coming and going for the rest of the afternoon just like real folks, go into the bar on the corner and get roaring drunk, buy and consume every drug offered to me, throw up in the alley. A new life. New experiences. That's what Virtualville's all about, isn't it? Life moving on and on and on.

It's late, well past midnight. I'm rereading *The Odyssey*. There's a rap at my door.

Nevermore?

I open the door.

"I saw your light. Invite me in?" It's Deidre.

"Of course."

She has a backpack on her shoulder. She dumps it by the door. She says she's been living on the street. She looks it. She's dressed in a black long-sleeve t-shirt and black jeans, so you don't see how dirty she is right away. Her hair's tied up on top of her head. She removes a clip from it and tries to shake it out, but it's too matted and tangled to shake out. She still manages to be beautiful. She looks through the stack of books on the table. "These are all the same," she says.

"Different translations."

She nods. "What's it about?"

"*The Odyssey*? Oh Jeez. A lot of things. You should read it. It's terrific."

"I have read it. You made me smart, well-read, remember? I know what I think. I'm asking you. What do you think it's about?"

She's deadly serious. She sits at the table and takes off scuffed black cowboy boots and drops them on my floor with a thud, pulls off her socks and starts kneading her feet. "Well? You've read it in translations that haven't even been written yet. You must have an opinion."

"It's about a man trying to make it home to the woman he loves."

She nods and smiles. "That's what I thought you would say. Look. I don't have a life but what you imagined for me. It didn't exactly hold together, you know? I figure you bear a certain responsibility."

Like Victor Frankenstein, I'm tempted to flee my creation, but there are no Alps to run to in Virtualville. "I suppose I do."

"You mind if I take a shower, get something to eat?"

"Go right ahead. I'll make you something."

"Where do I sleep?"

"Wherever you like." There's a double bed, no sofa, and the armchair I'm sitting in that would be just right for a cat to sleep in if I had one.

"You could show a little enthusiasm." She stands, pulls the t-shirt off and steps out of her jeans.

"I can only try."

She sings in the shower while I'm making sardine sandwiches, and it's a strange, beautiful sound, like a whale song. I remember the Ray Bradbury story where a sea monster falls in love with a lighthouse, and not for the first or last time here in Virtualville, I weep bitter tears.

Too many days in Virtualville seem all the same to me. The roads go nowhere, and I've nowhere to go. Time passes slowly like an old dog wandering around lost, the world bereft of scent. If I were that dog I'd be tempted to wander out on the highway, but that's not an option. You have to keep the proof-of-concept rat alive at all costs. That's the whole point of my world, if I let it be: Staying alive, like it or not.

My fate is unchanging, but the river changes every day. I come and sit, the biggest boulder in the current, a grain of sand on the beach, waiting, collecting words. I bring my memories with me, let them run through me like sand through my fingers, like a long slow blade, like the river to the sea that lies somewhere beyond my world.

I look upstream. The setting sun turns the river to blood. I write on a page of sand—

Longing forever,
never lying in your arms,
always coming home.

All the Snake Handlers I Know are Dead

"All the snake handlers I know are dead," he said with a little smile coiled up at the corner of his mouth.

What did I expect him to say? I had a snake problem. He was Jerry the local extension agent. "Are they endangered?" I asked, referring to the dozens of timber rattlers who lolled about my construction site.

"Not yet," he said. "Folks *do* kill 'em." He managed to sound concerned about that. "Shotgun. Axe. Shovel. Poisons. You got dogs?"

"Yes." One.

"I wouldn't recommend poison, then. Do your dogs mess with 'em?"

"Not that I've noticed." Lucille's a rescue, afraid of everything but me.

"That's good. Snakebite can kill a dog. Make 'em swell up like a balloon."

"I'll keep that in mind." Lucille as a balloon dog was now indelibly imprinted in my mind, part of a whole slideshow of horrific images regularly provided me by concerned locals. At least this one didn't involve meth heads and chain saws.

"You the woman building the place on the mountain?"

They didn't say "crazy woman" but they might as well. "Yes," I said.

"Heard you were a carpenter."

"I worked some construction, framing out McMansions during the boom. I wouldn't say I'm a carpenter."

Jerry shook his head, the slightest bit—he might not even have been aware of. The crazy woman reflex response.

"I have a shotgun," I said. It seemed like a good time to bring that up. "I'll use that. On the snakes."

I'd heard his uncle Roger, a neighbor down the mountain, spoke of me affectionately as "Maggie the Mountain Girl." I suspected it was edited for my hearing. The word "crazy" was likely in there somewhere. I questioned whether Roger, thirty-five, really thought of me—shall we say thirty-nine or so?—as a "girl."

Up on the mountain, my dog wasn't swollen or dying, but she was hiding in the thicket. She slunk out, trembling. Somebody had busted into my trailer, taken everything with cash value, which wasn't much—a laptop and the shotgun, as well as the shells. A clock radio I bought at a yard sale for two dollars. They somehow missed the five-dollar boom box and the shoebox of CDs the guy threw in with it. "C'mon," I said to my still-trembling protector. "You're going with me back to town."

I didn't blame Lucille for being a useless watch dog. She weighed thirty pounds. She had a slender collie snout. What was she supposed to do, nip them to death? Besides, she was a rescue. Some crazy woman who was keeping forty-six dogs in her house, died with them inside. Lucille was one of three survivors. If there's a place to hide, she *will* find it. But one other thing about Lucille, besides the hiding and the trembling and the slinking—don't *ever* back her into a corner.

I went to the pawn shop in Lorton instead of the cheaper Walmart another ten miles down the road because I figured the word would travel faster from Sam's Pawn that the crazy bitch was now heavily armed. I'd had it. City neighborhoods had nothing on this place, only there you could call 911. Last week someone stole my mailbox. Who steals a mailbox?

I replaced my shotgun and bought a .38 with a holster, so I could have it with me at the work site. Sam Jr. asked me about ammo, what I intended to use the guns for. "Rattlers and meth heads," I said.

He smiled. "I'll fix you right up."

So there I was early next morning with my sidearm and my shotgun and my shovel and my scaredy-cat dog, trying to decide how I was going to start this war. I counted at least a couple dozen dozing rattlers. It was easy to mistake them for piles of rocks. They were pretty drowsed out this time of morning. I didn't know if that was to my advantage or not.

Were they more likely to totally nut out—or simply skedaddle—when awakened from a sound sleep by the sound of lethal force?

I played it out in my imagination: Lucille and I swarmed with crazed unstoppable snakes, sinking their fangs deep, injecting us with agonizing, gruesomely lethal venom. It made a strong impression, even before we started swelling and writhing in torment, so I decided to proceed with caution and trembling. That's how I ended up here, I suppose—going on anyway, taking the chance, facing my fears, with my bright, blind eyes and my stubborn little heart.

Lucille would prefer to slink back to the trailer if I didn't mind.

"I said *stay*, goddammit!" She sat her reluctant butt down and glanced over her shoulder, then back at me, her equivalent of the crazy-woman reflex. Oh, pup of little faith—but she was incredibly obedient. I thought it better not to think too much about why. She wasn't out here to serve the cause, whatever it was. She was out here because I'd saved her life. What kind of life was now up to me. I wouldn't blame her if she wasn't just a little disappointed with her country paradise, though she did seem to adore me. I wasn't the least disappointed with her.

The snakes, I told her—just let me deal with these snakes, and we'll be living in paradise like I promised when I sprang you from the cage you'd been living in too long, remembering hell.

My first battle plan was to deploy the shovel with .38 backup in a systematic sweep of the target area, but that didn't play so good in my head: Prod, swing, miss, trip, tangle, shoot foot, get bit repeatedly, swell up like a balloon animal, *die*. Repeat in random order, always ending with *die*. I had trouble getting it to stop.

The shotgun—swift, overwhelming force deployed beyond striking distance—seemed like the way to go. Blow them away. *Kaboom! Kaboom!* Repeat as needed if they were too stupid to slither away and stay gone. I'd tried banging pots and pans and yelling, and was rattled at for my troubles. Scariest noise I ever heard—first one, then another, and another . . .

There were hundreds of acres in all directions to lounge around besides where I was trying to build my crazy house. Every crazy woman needs a crazy house, right? You wouldn't want us living around normal folk, would you? If I couldn't overcome a passel of venomous serpents, then maybe I wasn't as crazy as I thought I was, and I'd have to come down off the mountain, and the Mountain Girl just couldn't do that. So it was me or the snakes. A hell of a lot of snakes, and there seemed to be more of them all the time.

Just the day before, I straightened up from swinging a pick to mop my brow, and there was one of them inches from my face. I wasn't sure how I jumped out of that hole, but the damn rattle sound was right behind me. Don't give me that it-was-probably-as-scared-as-you stuff, because I don't see how that was possible, and while that rattler slept just fine afterwards, it kept showing up in my dreams, keeping me up all night. I was scared again just thinking about it.

I knew they were only indigenous reptiles who meant me no harm if I'd just leave them alone, but I'd put too many hours in on this site since last fall to move now. If I couldn't work in the heat of summer, it was another winter in the trailer playing solitaire with Lucille, the site buried in snow. I couldn't wimp out. I just couldn't. I pumped a round into the chamber and raised the gun.

Folks do kill 'em.

But they were asleep. That didn't seem right. "Hey, snakes! Wake up! Time to die!" The valley echoed with this nonsense.

Nothing. Except Lucille's little whimper behind me. I expected her to have slunk halfway back to the trailer by now. I thought it best to ignore her. Then a voice as smooth as supple leather said, "You the woman looking for a snake handler?"

I turned around, and he was all tall, skinny shadow, the morning sun at his back. The building site faced the summer sunrise. He raised his hands, and I lowered the gun. I didn't know if I was more surprised by his sneaking up on me so silently or by Lucille sitting beside him wagging her tail along the ground, like *meet my new friend.* Lucille wasn't unfriendly, but she generally had to hide a while before she got to know you. He scratched the top of her head. "Nice dog," he said to me. "Good girl," he said to her. Lucille practically wet herself.

I stepped to the side, so I could get a better look at him without the sun in my eyes. "Thanks. She likes you. Snake handler—is that what you are?" His eyes were the color of pale jade. He wore a black T-shirt and black jeans, black boots, and a long-tail brown coat like a character in a western movie. His dark grizzled hair hung down his back in a thick braid. He was clean-shaven and sun-beaten.

"You might say that," he said with a modest little bob of the head, like he was a handler and so much more. He had a comforting presence, as if everything was happening a little slower for him.

Which wasn't hard, compared to me. "Then you can see my problem." I swept my hand across the snake-infested site.

He smiled. "What you got here is a fine nursery."

He walked over to the closest of the snoozing rattlers and scratched it on the back of the head like he'd done Lucille, waking it up. "Hey girl," he cooed, and the big brutal-looking head swayed back and forth, and I thought, here it comes, another crazy dead man to bury, when the damn snake coiled up his arm, all the way up, till the two of them were eye to eye like lovers looking for a room. He walked over to the other end of the site and put his hand down on a likely-looking spot, and the snake slithered off his arm and coiled into a contented pile. He blew it a kiss. I just stood there with my mouth hanging open. Mountain Girl was certain this wasn't normal rattlesnake behavior.

"You've exposed all this rock to the sun. All these pregnant females love that, as you can imagine." He ran his fingertips up and down his skinny torso like everybody knows what it's like to carry a load of tiny timbers inside.

"Oh." Pregnant females. I felt ashamed. Mountain Girl was about to blow away a hillside of pregnant snakes like some crazy woman because they were in my way. The sheer lunacy of the whole enterprise came over me like it did several times a day, but much worse than usual. That shame is some nasty stuff. It's easy to be a fool.

He looked deeply concerned about our plight—me and Lucille and the snakes—offered the gentle voice of reason. "If you try to chase them off, they'll just come back. It's just too good a spot. They're too far along. I suggest you work on one side of the site, and let them hang out on the other—then switch. There's plenty of room. Will that work for you?"

Crazy woman, meet crazy man. "I—I guess so."

"Good then. Where you want to work first?"

"Well—I'm working in the southwest corner. Over there. I could keep working that side."

"Good, then. How about I just move those four girls there, and that little one? How about her? Is she okay?" He was pointing out snakes as casual as can be, walking among them. They all seemed to be waking up now. Watching him. You could see their little heads tracking him, sense the excitement in the air. He was something to behold. Lucille was riveted, too, sitting right up next to me, watching him tote around rattlers like they were kittens. Lucille was even afraid of kittens. Hid from them.

I wanted to tell him I didn't have a working phone, so if he got bit, it was a bad long trip off the mountain to anything resembling a hospital, but I just played along like he wasn't crazy, and sure enough he moved eleven more snakes like the first one. The little one rattled at him, and he laughed. "I don't have time for your silliness. Get up here." Zip. There it went, like the others, up his arm, and then, I swear to God, they rubbed noses before he put it—her—down.

"And they'll just stay over there?" I asked when he was done, and there was a clear boundary. One side had a couple dozen more or less, I kept losing count, but the other was snakeless.

"Long as you're working over here, the girls will be happy." He looked around. "Looks like you got plenty to keep you busy for a while. Just you working, right?"

"How much do I owe you?"

He smiled a little smile, bobbed his head. Message received. "Oh, nothing. I don't do this for money. I do it for them." He looked over at the girls, as he called them, glanced significantly at my shotgun, the intended murder weapon.

"What happens when I'm done on this side?"

"Then I'll move 'em all over here, and you can work over there. Unless it's gotten cold by then. They'll be looking for a place to den."

"It'll still be plenty hot, believe me. How do I get in touch with you?"

"I'll keep an eye out."

From where we were standing, there's an incredible panoramic vista. That's why the house had been laid out here—for the view. Now I realized, from every point I could see, somebody might be looking back at me, watching. "I—I'm not comfortable with that arrangement."

I expected him to get pissy at that point, but he was all apologetic. "Course not. You don't need me involved—keep it amongst yourselves, better for everybody that way. I tell you what. When you want them to move, take a day off. Show up at the site, so they don't think you're sick, but don't work, move the picks and shovels maybe. They'll get the message. Take the dog swimming, give them time to get situated. They should all be squared away next morning so you can start busting rock over there." He smiled, pleased with his solution.

New levels of craziness. Delusional. And I was listening to him, while Lucille couldn't get enough of his pets like she'd known him her whole life, which I guess is one of the reasons I listened, that and the stunt he just pulled with a dozen rattlers. "What if they don't get the hint? Seems . . . uh . . . pretty sophisticated for a bunch of snakes."

"Maybe so. I'll explain it to 'em 'fore I leave, answer any questions." He grinned. I knew he was crazy—not like me and the meth heads or my dead husband—beyond crazy, comfortable with it, positively tranquil, but he wasn't joking. Tranquil as he was, there was an urgency to his mission, a reason these snakes adored him: The feeling was mutual. "Handler" didn't begin to describe this guy.

He did a little promenade through his snake harem again, touching this one and that. They were bobbing around, like they were reaching out: *Touch me! Touch me!* Then he walked away up the hillside into the National Forest, and the snakes all watched him go. I say walked, but it wasn't like that, the way he moved, effortlessly, as if he weren't slogging up a steep rocky incline. The tails of his coat switched back and forth as his long legs stretched and his hips swayed. When he was up near the ridgetop, he turned and waved, and I waved back. Then he shook both hands in the air, and the snakes rattled their tails all together. The noise was deafening, echoing down the valley, then, as it faded away, came his laughter, as I ran back to my trailer and hid out with Lucille, who had a lot of explaining to do. How come the scariest man I ever met didn't scare her? She couldn't explain it, though I talked of little else all night.

Unlike Lucille, I was plenty scared of him, but I had other feelings to explain, though it wasn't hard, as handsome as he was, the darling of all those snakes.

Name. How in the hell was it I didn't even get his name? Rumplesnakeskin maybe? It occurred to me that what I really needed was some independent verification of his reality.

I had it the next morning, of a sort. The snakes were all on the other side of the site and seemed perfectly content to stay there, just like he said. I hoped they didn't mind music. I loaded up the boom box with batteries and played Talking Heads and Warren Zevon and busted rock all day. I made more headway than I had in weeks, since I wasn't looking over my shoulder for rattlers every few minutes. Lucille even hung out with me. Maybe she was afraid the meth heads would show up at the trailer again, or maybe she was hoping the snake handler would show up at the site. She licked my blisters when I took water breaks and kept me company.

After a productive week, I went into town for dog food and wine and other staples, and ran into Jerry at Food City. "Thanks for sending that snake handler my way. He's something. Problem solved."

He had no idea who I was talking about. Swore he hadn't spoken of our conversation with anyone. "Like I told you," he insisted, "all the snake handlers I know are dead."

For some reason, standing next to the display of strawberry pies, I didn't feel like telling Jerry the details of what had happened, how all of a sudden, this nameless stranger had negotiated a deal with the rattlers, a deal that had persisted for a week. Too crazy.

"He said they're pregnant females," I said.

He nodded. "Makes sense." He didn't seem to care much. "Hope it works out for you." He left with a strawberry pie. I resisted.

On the mountaintop, there was a full moon, and I walked with Lucille to the work site. The pale rock still radiated heat from the hot day and seemed to glow in the moonlight. I loved this place. So did Lucille, at times like these. Mostly white, she looked like a ghost dog, racing around the clearing.

Then she froze, looked up toward the ridge. I followed her gaze. A dark shape wove a sinuous path through the moon-bleached wood. I tried to imagine what would move like that, too fluid for a deer or a person—maybe a bear. There were plenty around.

I followed the snake handler's instructions to the letter when I was ready to make the move, showing up without working, telling the girls (what I called them by this time) that they were welcome to relocate back to their old quarters, substantially quarried just to suit them, moved a few tools, then I took the dog swimming and left them to it.

Our swimming spot was high on the mountain where the stream was just getting started, and the hardwoods that used to shelter it had been hauled away and sold before I ever saw the place. I'd hacked a path through the greenbrier last spring, so it only took a little work with the machete to get us there again, Lucille slinking along behind, knowing it was worth this nerve-jarring *thwack, thwack*. There were cascades, a small pool, a large, flat sun-baked rock, and a ball.

Lucille churned tirelessly about the chilly pool in pursuit of the ball, returning it with a shake and a silent plea for more. Until she finally found a spot on the hot stone, shook furiously, and flopped down, happily exhausted. A steamy cloud rose from her heaving side.

I went in, too, and that was wonderful, cold as the water was. I had a tiny little bucket I bathed with in the trailer. I was proud of that frugal bucket, but I had stone dust so deep in my hair and flesh you could stick me in a park and call me a statue. I washed and scrubbed and scoured, planted my face in some white water and let the stream cleanse me, numb the heat of busting rock in the summer sun from my exhausted body and wash it downstream. I sat up in the water laughing, tingling all over, then lay on a warm rock and let the hot sun dry me, let Lucille lick my face.

That night he showed up in my dreams. I was sitting at the kitchen table in my old place in the city having a cup of coffee, reading a letter. I knew which letter. It was always the same letter. How many do you get anymore? These days? Real letters. Saying good-bye.

The snake handler walked into that dream kitchen as if he belonged there and took the other chair. There was a second coffee on the table, and he thanked me for it and took a swallow, then drank it down. He looked the same, the same clothes as up on the mountaintop. I looked out the kitchen window, but there was nothing. I didn't live there anymore. Lucille, who'd never lived there, thumped her tail under the table as the snake handler stroked her head, resting on his knee.

"That's why you're up on the mountaintop, isn't it?" he asked, nodding at the letter in my hands as if he knew what was in it.

"Don't be ridiculous. Who throws her life away over a silly letter?"

He thought about it a moment, stroked his smooth chin. "A crazy woman?"

Not him, too. I stood and picked up my empty coffee cup, reached for his. He took my forearm. "I meant it as a compliment." His other hand abandoned Lucille's head, and the buttons of my blouse seemed to fall open at his touch. I dropped the cups on the table, and I knew I was dreaming because Lucille didn't skitter off in a panic but just kept thumping as the snake handler pressed his mouth and tongue to my stomach, under my breasts, the base of my neck, my mouth. I let myself get lost in his kiss. Our kiss.

When I was trembling with passion, he journeyed back down my body, slowly, lovingly, until he found my wet vagina with his tongue, and I could feel an orgasm stirring, insistent, and I hoped the dream wouldn't end before I came. I didn't have to worry about that. My head thrown back, I screamed a blasphemous prayer. Then his tongue seemed to grow, filling me up, and I looked down to see him slither into me, a great serpent moving inside of me.

What does it say about me that I still didn't want the dream to end?

Next morning, waking with the birds, I didn't mind the afterglow, either.

Let's just say it had been a while.

As I walked down to the site, I knew what I'd find, and I didn't know at the same time. I believed I had a genuine miracle going on, and I didn't. The fact that I'd had the best kinky dream sex of my life with him hadn't exactly clarified matters. I believed, and I didn't. Then it was settled. It was just like he said. Every last snake had moved.

I'd believed half a miracle okay. You learn to live with a little strange. The whole thing made my knees wobble. Lucille quickly curled up in a comfortable spot where only yesterday a pregnant rattler had coiled, cooking her litter. Did the snake handler tell Lucille something, too? Maybe he should've explained it a little better to me. The snakes moved because I asked them to. After he explained it to them. This was a little more than staying put. I couldn't look at them in quite the same way. I couldn't look at *anything* in quite the same way.

Sometimes that isn't such a bad thing. Wasn't that why Mountain Girl was up here to begin with? To get a different view? To find out who she was? Sometimes you find out more than just that.

I went to work.

I hadn't been at it long, just enough to work up a good sweat in the comfortably chilly morning air, when I felt a presence behind me. I knew it wasn't one of the girls. I had faith in them by this time. I turned, and it was him, the snake handler, sitting cross-legged by the hole I was in. How did he do that? Lucille couldn't contain herself, wagging her tail and licking his face. I knew how she felt. "So I guess you've been keeping an eye out, after all," I said.

"You might say that. Glad to see how well it's worked out for all concerned." He grinned again, only this time there was a little more something in it. He was glad to see me too. I wondered what his dreams were like.

"You want a cup of coffee?" I asked. I owed the man a lot. The least I could do was show a little hospitality.

"I don't want to keep you from your work," he said, looking into my eyes in a way that said he did.

I went with the eyes. "Don't be silly. I'll throw in a stale donut."

"You got yourself a deal." He gave me his hand and pulled me out as if I weighed nothing, and I was thinking, maybe this isn't such a good idea, but the crazy don't always listen to reason when other voices beckon. Lucille's, for example, who was yipping and twirling in her *oh, joy!* dance I thought she only did for me.

We sat beside the Airstream in aluminum folding chairs. I made sure he got the good one. His name was Colson Hand. I told him I liked the sound of it. I felt like a girl on a date. I had decidedly mixed feelings about that. He wasn't helping. He was a good listener. I was a prattler. I talked about the place, the wildlife, how much I loved the beauty of it.

Then he slipped in a question. "What about the solitude?"

That wasn't fair. Not between those jade eyes and my dreams. "You want some more coffee?"

"No thanks. I'm good."

He didn't call me on not answering his question. That was nice. So I called myself. "My counselor once told me—I had a counselor for a while—that there's no point avoiding a question because by avoiding it you just give away the answer anyway. The solitude's the hardest part."

"I can imagine. Why do you do it?"

"Why am I crazy?"

"I don't think you're crazy wanting to live alone on a mountaintop, if it's what you want to do."

"That's the question, isn't it? I must want to. Since I'm doing it, and it's no day at the beach. That's what I tell myself anyway. Somebody told me once I didn't really want it, living here. There's a bit of prove him wrong in it, I suppose. I'm never sure how much."

He bobbed his head. He seemed to appreciate the confession of uncertainty. That's all it took. I was starved for that. Only the truly crazy are certain. I told him the whole story.

Living on the mountain or somewhere like it was my husband's dream. It began to grow on him, get serious, central. It's all he talked about. It was contagious. It began to grow on me, too. We might be living in a dumpy suburban rent house now, working jobs we hated, but someday we'd be in splendor. We probably didn't compare our ideas of splendor often enough, or what we planned to do with it when we found it. We were too busy squirreling away money, working extra hours, extra jobs, visiting every remote plot of wilderness for sale within range of our old Saturn. I loved being in these wild places. A city girl, it was all new to me. It was easy for me to believe it was magical. It might as well have been Narnia or Oz.

For him it became like a cause that enraged him—rescuing the land from the rapacious evil of the modern world. I wanted to rescue it, too, but not to be angry, more to escape anger if I could, others' and my own. All the disappointments we collect, as if the world was just made for us, and it hasn't got much time to get its act together. Even a total sense of failure is humbled by a mountain sky at night. A little peace and quiet to notice where you are. I could *do* this—live up here—I wanted to. That kept me going through everything else.

Then, for my husband, it seemed to be more about him and less about the land, but still plenty angry—raging. He would discover new insights on the mountain with the help of the weirder and weirder texts he grew effusive about, then protective of, when I presumed to question them. He made no sense at all when he spoke of these things, though he still seemed the same man. At Thanksgiving he got into it with his sister's husband, and we were asked to stay away Christmas. Meanwhile, the dream ground on under its own momentum, so that when the perfect mountaintop property came up—cheap, isolated, and beautiful—we bought. We had to. I've never stood in line for Space Mountain, but plenty of people do. You stand in line long enough, you're *going* to ride the ride. I'd stood in line years for this place, forgoing all others.

I had this crazy idea that once we had the land, he wouldn't be crazy anymore.

The plan had been to build a house here, live here, and let the logged forest return to its natural splendor, but the land itself had taken all our money, so we must labor on, which we both did, even taking jobs apart from one another, camping up here a few times, laying out the site, quite a bit larger than the current configuration, large enough for his craziness and mine. There was plenty of splendor to go around.

Then I got a letter, saying he'd met someone, and that she understood him and what he was looking for like I never had. He went on to say I never believed in the land or him anyway, and as far as he was concerned the land was mine now to sell as my half of whatever I thought I had coming. He made it sound like the whole thing had been ruined for him by my lack of faith in him and his *core beliefs*. I never knew him to use the phrase *core beliefs* before. He used it three times. Tap, tap, tap. Stake through the heart.

On the way to a shaman in New Mexico he and the twenty-two-year-old woman who understood him died in a head-on in the Texas Panhandle. I flew to Amarillo to bury him in the bleakest, cheapest cemetery I could find, then sold everything I had, borrowed the Airstream, called in every favor a poor wheedling widow could manage, and came up here. There was a life insurance policy with a big accidental death payoff. She'd been behind the wheel, so there'd been no question of suicide. He hadn't changed the beneficiary.

I thought I should have a dog, to keep me company and for protection, so I adopted Lucille, who's about three times braver now than she used to be—and who loves me dearly.

"Sometimes I think I like having someone around more scared than me." Lucille was under the trailer, watching us, wagging her tail at the mention of her name.

"Don't be scared," Colson said softly, like he could do something about all the dangers that were everywhere, and I looked into his eyes like I believed him.

I kissed him. I'm not sure how his face had gotten so close. "I'm sorry," I whispered. He kissed me. I said, "My bed is awful, like an old sock and about as big."

He laughed, looking into my eyes. He found me adorable. Adorable had been a very long while indeed. He squinted at the sun as if calculating its rate of ascent. "Let's go for a swim, then. Should be nice."

And that's how we ended up twined together, making love on the same warm rock by the spring-fed stream. He was incredibly powerful, strong but never rough, sensuous, passionate, unafraid to look me in the eye. I came luxuriously, as if the dream were mere rehearsal. I fell asleep wrapped up in his arms, woke upon the rock, alone but for Lucille sprawled beside me dreaming. Maybe that was two of us. Maybe I really was crazy. I put my hand between my legs. No. I hadn't dreamed that part. So all of it was real.

"What about the solitude, Colson? It's terrible," I murmured to the babbling stream.

And there he was, emerging from a narrow trail I swear to God hadn't been there yesterday. The pot growers must've found this spot. He was dressed in clean clothes, same as the other ones.

"I hoped to return before you woke." He lay down beside me and took wet, naked me into his dry, clean embrace, and it felt delicious.

"You have a place close by?" I asked.

"In a manner of speaking. Let's just say not everyone who lives in the forest does so legally."

"You a farmer, Mr. Hand?"

"No. We manage to avoid one another."

"Chemist?"

"They're a bad lot. May they all blow themselves to hell. No. I'm unemployed. You could use a hand building the chimney and hearth. I know a thing or two about stone."

Indeed.

So that's how the summer went, how the place was built on time. Stone, lumber, sex, water—Colson twined around our lives, me and Lucille's, like he was made to order, which would've made me wonder if I was dreaming except for this crazy-woman house growing out of the mountainside like it was Zeus's head. That was real enough.

He never spent the night—said he had animals to tend to—swore he wasn't married, didn't seem at all crazy, though there was an undeniable reticence about his past. He'd always lived around here, he said. His family was no account. Times were hard. He lived in the forest. Seemed mean to press him when he clearly felt uncomfortable talking about it. Fair enough. I wasn't crazy about discussing my dead husband either, and after I told Colson the story, he never revisited it to pick over the carcass. It was just the two of us on a mountaintop. Three, counting Lucille, who was definitely onboard. She adored him.

Okay. I'm not stupid. Alarm bells were ringing through that valley like a city on fire, but I chose to ignore them, as they say, was too busy competing with my own siren song. Best summer of my life. I was as hard as a rock and felt as beautiful as the clouds in the sky. I'd had my life burn down once. Least if it happened again, this time would be worth it.

Then the first cold snap on the mountain came along, and he was gone. I'd raced down to town and back with supplies before the worst of it hit. At least that was the plan. I skittered around on the road on the way back up like an ice cube on a griddle. It took a few lucky breaks to make it up alive, only to wish I hadn't. The place was empty. I lit the first fire alone.

He'd built a recess by the hearth for firewood, had spent all morning splitting wood to fill it. I liked to watch the muscles in his back ripple as the axe rose and fell. Thwack. Dead on, every time. The log just fell open for him. *Thwack*. He knew. I said, "Leave some for tomorrow," and he didn't answer. He knew.

Lucille and I moped and cried in front of the hearth and wished we'd asked more questions. Or maybe it was better not to know.

The first freeze broke, and I made it back down the mountain for supplies. I didn't like leaving Lucille in the car, so I left her sleeping in the house. Naturally, Food City was crazy busy, the parking lot full. The checkout was a logjam of stuffed carts. People chatted with one another. I browsed a *People* and tried to keep a low profile. I hadn't been around this many people in a while.

An old guy in the next line leaned over toward me. "You're the lady building the house all by yourself on the mountain, ain't you?"

I didn't deny it. There was no place to run, no place to hide. I gave him a thin, dazed smile. I was in no mood.

"Looking real nice," he said. "I didn't believe you could do it all by yourself. You must have quite the view. I'm the other side of the ridge opposite. Amazing what you done. You must be strong as an ox."

"Thank you. Thank you very much. I had a lot of help though."

He cocked his head to one side, started to say, *I didn't see nobody*. At least that's what I thought he was about to say, what made a chill go up my spine, imagining him on the ridge opposite looking through a pair of binoculars. I'd never gotten that independent verification of Colson's reality I once thought might've been a good idea. This old fellow watched me build my house. All by myself.

"My name's Maggie," I said.

"Ted," the old man said, smiling big and sweet like old men do for young women.

I wanted to ask him if he owned a pair of binoculars, but went right to the point instead. "You ever hear of a fellow round here named Colson Hand?"

The smile fell down a well and stayed there. "No. Can't say I have." His line moved, and he disappeared behind the candy bars.

The woman behind me was looking at me fearfully. She'd obviously been tuned into my chat with Ted. I was getting a little tired of being treated like an alien being. "Have you got a problem?"

She was a big woman, her cart filled with high fructose corn syrup in its myriad forms, but her voice was soft and tiny, like a girl's. I felt bad for snapping at her. "Colson Hand's dead," she said, and made a little frowny face like maybe I was the one who had the problem.

I didn't try to get the story in the line at Food City, but when I was finally out of there I went to the library, waited for a computer, and checked it out. He and his wife had had a place up near mine in the National Forest. Neighbors found her dead, beaten up. The cops arrested Colson because he had a wild young man record, and his family was no account, like he said. For whatever reason, he didn't like his chances and escaped from a couple of stupid deputies into the National Forest. An ice storm hit. The DNA evidence came back from the state showing Colson didn't do it. They found his body in a little cave in the spring. A nest of snakes had fed upon his carcass, but DNA tests confirmed it was Colson. The deputies were later investigated for possible misconduct, but charges were dropped for lack of evidence. Wiley and Kincaid were the deputies' names. Their pictures were in a row with Colson's. They could've all gone to the same high school around here.

I stared at the screen. I didn't like my choices here about the reality I'd been living in. Crazy? Dead lover? I wondered if I could build a whole house with a man who wasn't there—if I could be reading things off this screen that the pixels didn't show. Might as well head back up to the mountaintop while it's still there, I thought. Lucille will be wondering where in hell I am.

I had a lot on my mind, all Colson. So when I saw the door was ajar, it made some kind of sense that it was him, and I ran inside. There were three of them. One of them had my .38. The shotgun was in the truck.

"Well, lookee here," he said. "Get her bag."

Forty dollars and a debit card wasn't exactly what they hoped for, especially since they probably figured the code I gave them wasn't actually going to open up the coffers of my vast wealth. Not even any prescription drugs. What kind of city girl doesn't have a few pills? They all seem wired enough already. They'd already finished off the last of my wine. There was a truckload of groceries, but they didn't think to look there. They were all dressed in hunter's togs from Walmart, but I doubted any of them were really hunters. I thought about the shotgun in the truck, whether I should mention the jug of wine there.

Then the one with the .38 tripped over Lucille's water dish. "Wha-the-fuck!"

For a moment I thought he was going to shoot it.

"You got a dog, lady?"

"Friends do. They're visiting. They must be out hiking."

"Right. Nice try. On your knees, bitch."

I thought it was a fairly pathetic try, but I needed to do something. They had a few years on them and someone had cleaned them up nice for their deputy pictures, but their mothers would know them, and I recognized them behind the hair and the stink. Two of the fellows were Wiley and Kincaid. Wiley had the .38. The third fellow might be his cousin or little brother.

"Put some wood on the fire," Wiley told Little Wiley. "Let's warm this place up."

Kincaid lit a cigarette and laughed, sat in front of the fire in my chair. He was higher than a buzzard, chuckling to himself over his plans for the evening.

Little Wiley stirred the coals and started building up a blaze. Everybody watched him chucking on logs for a long night. Then he stopped, peered into the logs. "What the fuck? Her little pissant dog's back up in there."

"Well get him out," Wiley said.

I started to say "I wouldn't do that," but I had a .38 pointed at my head.

Wiley reached in and grabbed, yanked his hand back bleeding, and I thought for a split second that would be the end of it. Lucille sprang from the woodpile, her charging collie legs churning, razor sharp teeth lunging and snapping at Little Wiley's face in a fury that carried him back into Kincaid's lap, and the three of them sprawled across the floor, Little Wiley screaming.

The gun swung from my face to Lucille, and I drove my fist into Wiley's crotch, but he fired anyway, and I heard Lucille squeal in pain as the gun came back to me, between my eyes, but he didn't fire. He cried out like a terrified child and leaped back against the wall, as they all sounded their rattles in deafening unison. I turned to the blazing hearth. They were everywhere, coiled in the firelight, still more slithering forth from the woodpile. My friends. The girls.

Wiley never fired a shot as the girls swarmed over my three visitors, killing them rather quickly. Colson held me in his arms and rocked me back and forth during the worst of it. Then he tended to Lucille's wound, a nasty furrow in her back he treated with a salve, and pretty soon she was sleeping peacefully. I made coffee, and we repaired the door where my guests had crowbarred their way in. They did indeed start to swell, but they still fit behind the hearth, where the girls would drain them of any excess fluids they no longer had need of.

We brought in the groceries, and I made dinner, and we made love on the floor in front of the fire. "I must leave," he whispered as the fire died down to embers, "but I'll be back before you know it."

And I'll be waiting. And so it's been with me and my dog, up here on the mountain for a number of years now. Best years of my life. Folks say we hardly seem to age, me and Lucille. The crazy can be that way, you know, seem to defy time and logic. Don't let it frighten you. Not half the stories you hear about me are true.

It's wintertime. Lucille likes to lie before the hearth, the fire blazing, waiting for the thaw of spring. She's dreaming of long walks in the woods with me and Colson, swimming in the stream of life at its source. Or maybe she's just dreaming about a ball bouncing through paradise forever, snakes with rattles in their mouths rolling along like wheels, fearless Lucille racing alongside.

Swan Song and Then Some

Alexandra's explaining her act to me. "It's only when I know I'm going to die that I can sing that song, hear the changes, hit the notes and hold them. I can't explain it. Maybe there are certain emotions only set free at the time of death, some silenced anguish finally given voice. I don't know. It just wells up inside me. Whatever it is, it's not a trick, Orlando. I die. I can't sing the song otherwise."

Basically, she sings a few songs well enough for a beautiful woman in a seedy carnival, swinging back and forth on a line like a hypnotist's watch, then she's hoisted to the top of our tiny big top that sat mostly empty until Alexandra came along. Her final song begins as she ascends, the most incredible a cappella performance you've ever heard, sung in what may or may not be a language, like an aria from another planet, intricate and moving—you can't help becoming lost in it even though you've been told she is going to drop to her death at the song's end—when she hits a crystalline sustained note of such heartbreaking beauty the crowd gasps. I've never heard it fail. Every soul in that tent is riveted to her voice as sure as Jesus was nailed to the cross. She holds the note still as she plummets, until it's cut short in full voice by the sound of her body smacking onto tarmac, sometimes concrete, sometimes earth. We take whatever parking lot we can. We can't afford to be choosy. Just when everyone who hasn't heard what happens next has jammed every 911 switchboard for miles around, she springs, well, staggers to her feet and finishes the note, not quite as crystalline, not quite as beautiful, then bows and lurches to her trailer where nobody better come near for a couple of hours or so. She emerges looking as she looks now, so beautiful you want to believe anything she says, but in my case, wanting to know the trick.

Singing isn't something I'm interested in learning—though I'll gladly listen—but resurrection, that's another matter. Alexandra dies but comes back to life. I appear to be alive but died inside years ago. Alexandra woke me from my slumber, one of those deep slumbers you think you'll never wake from, because what's the point? She found me working on a clogged cotton candy machine and asked if I was Orlando, because that's who she'd been told to talk to for a job, though technically that would be Sam, the owner, who's always too high to trust his own judgment and defers to mine. When she asked, I wanted to say I'm whoever you want me to be, but I only managed, "You got him." Been true ever since.

Alexandra probably thought my reaction meant I was just another guy who wanted to fuck her, which I suppose I was, am. Men dream about women like Alexandra. Who wouldn't want to make love to her? Wilbur, who keeps the ancient rides running, vehemently claims he wouldn't, even proselytizes on the subject. At the peak of the season, Alexandra dies and comes back to life seven days a week and twice on Sunday. Wilbur believes fucking a woman like that just might kill you, and he doesn't want to find out.

He's not the only one who feels that way apparently, only the most vocal. I've seen more than one new hand set his sights on Alexandra, only to abruptly drop his pursuit after witnessing her act for the first time. Some quit the carnival outright, as if they've dodged a bullet and don't want to tempt fate any further. Not that the braver or less squeamish have any more success. She'll have nothing to do with any of us romantically.

Just as well. It's hard enough watching her die as her friend. As her lover I'm sure I couldn't bear it. We go for long walks together, manage to talk for hours without revealing too much of our pasts—books, movies, the morning sky—how we feel about anything that matters but without the usual stories to explain what landed us in the same lifeboat, adrift. Nobody ever dreamed of being part of Sam's Carnival of Dreams, not even Sam. Alexandra and I picnic on the banks of whatever water presents itself—river, lake, park pond—and I ache with unspoken love for her. Once my love would've been something to offer, I suppose. Not anymore. It comes with too many fuckups and regrets, not to mention a few warrants for my arrest and even more lawsuits.

If I thought for a moment she was the least bit interested, I'd forget what a bad deal I am, but for now I just try to be her friend. She doesn't want anyone to love her. I know exactly how that feels, but sometimes what you want and what you feel aren't the same.

No riverbank today. She's found me finishing my breakfast at a counter seat in a Denny's on the way to our next job. I'm not sure what came over me, but questions just started pouring out, how she does it, how she sings so beautifully, how she dies but doesn't—a real cross-examination even though I know she doesn't like to talk about it. She's been acting strangely—anxious. For a woman who faces death all the time, Alexandra's usually serene. Something's up. I have this stupid idea I can help. That she needs it. Help. I know that feeling too.

"So what's the song say?" I ask. "Say it to me."

She smiles enigmatically, then a tiny pout. "You know I can't do that. It's an incantation."

"Meaning?"

"It's magical. I can't just mumble it in some Denny's."

"I know. You need the threat of death. You don't think this food will kill you? You obviously haven't tried the Three Grease Special. It gets a Golden Coffin Award from the American Heart Association."

She laughs. "You're awful." Her favorite compliment when I've pleased her. She likes it when I tilt at corporate giants.

"Does it mean anything? Is it words, or is it just notes and syllables?"

"Yes." She smiles, her eyes shining. *Would you please drop the subject*?

"You drive me crazy." I say this with more emotion than I intended.

Her eyes lock on mine for a brief, thrilling moment, and there's something there. I've stumbled onto one of the pathways to her heart. She likes men she crazes apparently. Makes sense. The siren likes them wrecked. Not a problem. I've been a castaway on her island for a couple of years now.

The waitress comes, and Alexandra doesn't order anything. "I came looking for him," she tells the waitress, pointing at me.

The waitress smirks like she thinks she knows what that means, but she doesn't, and I feel a pang of longing I usually manage to ignore.

"So what has you up at this hour?" I ask when the waitress leaves.

"I wanted to make sure the rig's right for the private show coming up. We're using the customer's tent, and the peak's at least twenty-foot higher than ours. I want it to hoist me all the way to the top. No one will care if I only fall partway."

I see her falling in my head. You wouldn't think it would bother me anymore. "I can do that. We've got plenty of rope."

"The Sands of Time will also need to be adjusted for the extra time it will take me to reach the top."

The Sands are a hokey eye-catching contraption under a spotlight attached to a trip wire that releases the harness holding Alexandra aloft. Sam's idea, it's basically a balance beam with sand flowing on one side and a feather from the Angel of Death (a crow's I'm guessing) on the other. The sands begin to flow as her swan song begins and she rises, measuring out the last remaining moments of her life.

She drops to her death when the last grain falls.

Some suppose this is a classic distraction from whatever trickery breaks her fall, but I watch only her, ignore the sand, and I can tell you she falls like Lucifer until she smashes into the ground with incredible force.

There is always blood, usually hair. Once in the early days I found a tooth, though she is missing none now. No sign of the fractures I've witnessed. No scars. She coils up into a ball, but still her limbs are crushed on impact. Her legs stitch themselves back together first, apparently. Her spine. When she stands, her arms dangle all akimbo and bloody. I carry the tooth, upper front. She didn't need it when I went to give it back. She must not have tucked in her head tight enough. Now the universe has a spare.

"Why can't we use our tent?"

"It's a private party," Alexandra says. "There might be a lot of people, and ours is looking a little shabby, case you hadn't noticed." We were about to get rid of our big tent, do away with working acts altogether, rely solely on games and rides, before Alexandra. Sam's Carnival of Dreams will likely die with Sam, who gave up dreaming about anything real a long time ago. The only reason he kept doing it was he doesn't know how to do anything else, and in his burned out fat sixties he wasn't likely to reinvent himself--until Alexandra came along.

"Sam could give a shit, case you hadn't noticed. You aren't worried about falling another twenty feet? You'll be going faster, you know. The acceleration is really something." There was a time in my youth I could've calculated it in my head. Now I couldn't tell you the formula. I try not to imagine it, her hitting the ground harder, faster, with a more decisive, fatal smack. The usual fall is bad enough. It makes you sick how many people turn out to see her, until you hear the song, and then you understand. Most people look away and just listen, but there are always several in the crowd, like me, who feel they owe it to her to witness her fall, her sacrifice to create such beauty.

She shrugs. "Death's death," she says.

"I don't believe you."

"Fine. Don't."

"So what brings you back to life? If you sing like that because you know you're going to die, then why the fuck don't you stay dead?" I have trouble saying that last part, and she touches my cheek with her delicate fingertips, which by all rights should be mangled claws. I've seen them crushed like egg shells. I live in fear of the day she dies and doesn't rise to sing again.

"Sweet Orlando, I come back for you. It would break your heart if you lost your Alexandra. Who else would drive you crazy?"

I want to bat her hand away. I want to seize it and cradle her in my arms. I do neither, and then her hand is gone.

"When do you need it, your new noose?"

She rolls her eyes. "Tomorrow afternoon if possible, so I can try it out, get the feel of it before my performance in the evening."

"I'll just use the same harness. It's only the line that will be different."

"I want to experience the ride, the world from a higher place."

"You like it, don't you? Dying."

I expect her to make a joke of it the way she usually does, but this time she doesn't. She drops her gaze, confesses. "Sometimes I think so. I tell myself it's the song, that I do it for the song, but sometimes I'm afraid it's really death I want—to feel its power."

"Then why do you always come back?"

She smiles bravely. "I thought you would've figure that out, Orlando. I'm cursed, blessed—whatever you want to call it. I brought it on myself. *My* problem, okay?"

Alexandra claims to believe in that supernatural stuff. I don't. Except for her. I believe in her. I have no choice. "So. What? If you jumped from a plane, you wouldn't die?"

"But I would never do that. That would be suicide."

"What's the fucking difference?"

"No one could hear my song."

"Why does that matter?"

The question hangs in the clattering Denny's unanswered. She looks for a moment as if she might tell me, then gives me the same flirtatious laugh she gives every other lovesick rube who longs to know her story. "I'm a true artist, haven't you heard?"

A smitten reporter a few towns back gushed about her. She likes to quote ironically from her lavish clippings, a form of vanity, as if she had any deficiency in that vice. I totally understand the reporter. We're of one mind: Alexandra's a true artist all right, but what's the art? "One question: Straight answer, okay? As friends?"

She drops the playful but evasive flirt routine. Neither of us has a surplus of friends. We take our friendship seriously. "Okay."

"Do you ever get used to it? Dying?"

It isn't the question she was expecting. Her flinch as I ask tells me the answer before she gives her head a quick shake. "No, never." She smiles ironically. "That would be the end of it, wouldn't it? Death be not proud. All that." We're both Donne fans. She laughs but lets it go, looks me in the eye, as a friend. "Never."

***

She first showed up outside of Lubbock a couple of years ago, her act not quite fully formed—some bad rope work, the song, and the fall. God knows how she came up with it. I imagine her dangling from one of the few tall trees in town, repeatedly falling onto the hard, baked ground.

It didn't take her long to persuade Sam to give the act a try. At first we wanted to put a net under her, but she wouldn't hear of it. She didn't need it, didn't want it, didn't sing so nice, she insisted, if she believed the fall might not kill her. Sam admired what he thought was her hammy theatrics, selling the act to him, and humored her up to a point. But still the first audition almost didn't go on. She insisted she needed someplace to go to recover—come back to life is what she said. Sam guffawed at that. "You want a dressing room? You want a fucking dressing room? Nobody gets a dressing room around here."

I said she could use my trailer if she wanted. Not big enough to turn around in, but she could stay there, put herself back together. Fair enough. Seemed like a simple thing. She hit the ground hard. It stunned everyone, that incredible song still ringing in our ears. She wasn't breathing. We were all certain she was dead. Sam muttered, "Aw shit" and called 911, was still describing the accident when her crumpled legs pushed her up, and she stumbled back to my place. I had to give her a little help then. The door's difficult even when your hands aren't broken. Her breath, as she waited patiently for me to get it open, wheezed and gurgled horribly. The place was a mess afterwards. Blood. Vomit. Smells I've never smelled before and hope to never smell again. She *had* died. I still can't believe it no matter how many times I've watched it happen.

She apologized to me later for making such a mess of my trailer, and I said it was not a problem. She could come back to life in my place anytime. She just had to promise to finish the job. "I don't want some half-dead woman lying around taking up space."

She laughed and gave me a peck on the cheek, and I suppose that's when we became friends.

She never used my trailer again. Sam surprised us all by buying Alexandra her own trailer the next day. She usually rides with Wilbur in a truck cab so loud you can't hear yourself think, but he claims they talk opera. "She once performed *Madame Butterfly*," Wilbur claims.

When I asked her about it she quickly changed the subject, saying it was nothing. "If I was really any good, what would I be doing here?" she says.

Right. My IQ used to make my guidance counselors salivate, but look at me now, one of those fellows parents can at least be thankful their sons didn't turn out to be even if the brain surgeon plans didn't pan out. Good. Just how are you using that term?

***

I'm hanging more than thirty feet higher up, near the top of our rich host's tent putting up the new rigging, when a fellow, nineteen or twenty, comes in down below. He looks up and asks if I'm the manager. I doubt he's from the house. He doesn't look clean enough, pure enough, not to mention rich enough. Even the servants up there look down on us as riff-raff.

Even at this height I can see the young man is angry.

I lower myself down, and we step outside to where his battered F-150 is parked, looking like it's driven a thousand miles through macho TV Hell. The rides are going up behind us. We're not even unpacking the games for this stop. What kind of party doesn't want games?

The kid's breathless before he even begins. Tells me he's been following us. Says his big brother is dead before his time. Wants to know if that fucking witch is still traveling with us. The one who sings and dies.

If you're going to bother having anybody in a carnival in the way of a working act, a strongman's always handy to have around, wrestling parts of this and that into place, showing people the door when they get a little unpleasant, even when you don't necessarily have a door. Otto's our strongman. At least that's what he calls himself. Makes a good strongman name. *Otto the Terrible.* I think his real name's Christopher or something.

He's strong all right. I have him step over to where the young man and I are talking. The fellow doesn't seem to care the least little bit. His hand's jammed in his jacket pocket like he has a pistol in there. His face is fierce with rage, and his eyes dart around, seeking his prey. It's easy to conjure thousands just like him, looking for me. "Where is she?" he asks.

Then the master of the house shows up out of nowhere. Master of the house is an old-fashioned term. I don't use it lightly. He seems to be living in another century out here. Dressed in immaculate white linens without a wrinkle, he looks like a dogwood in bloom.

The house itself is a big Victorian gew-gaw with all sorts of gazebos and promenades and whatnot. I've spotted him patrolling the grounds pensively in his antiquated gear. He carries himself as if his money matters. Not that it doesn't. Don't get me wrong. I'm no idealist, but all that money doesn't make him important. That can always change one way or another. Easy come, easy go, unless you're lucky, and who makes his own luck? Only the fool who thinks he does, all of it bad, but I'm only speaking from experience. Maybe his sense of importance comes from somewhere besides money despite the showy evidence to the contrary. Maybe he's thinking great thoughts in that ostentatious pile. He must keep them to himself because googling the guy turned up nothing but this place. It's his, the county says so. He paid cash. Sam and I were curious because he's paying us five times in a single night what we'd be making anywhere else for a whole week. Mr. Bartholomew's his name. He ignores me and Otto and fixes the young man with a look that says he doesn't like a ruffian on his premises and tells the fellow to leave immediately. Odd thing is, he does.

It makes no sense to me. I know he was about to pull a gun. I know he was enraged. I know… Nothing really. But I'm very surprised, shall we say, when the young guy says, "Yes sir, sorry sir," gets in his truck and drives away at a moderate rate of speed.

Mr. Bartholomew turns and walks back to the house without so much as a screw you for me and Otto.

Otto returns to where Wilbur is working on the Tilt-a-Whirl, holding the stupid thing up while Wilbur makes another repair on the ancient mechanism. I hate rides. They always break down. If there's anybody comes around to inspect these rides, he's never caught up with us. Sam and insurance companies don't get along. He thinks they're crooks—imagine. So if one of these contraptions mangles you, there's nobody to sue. Without Alexandra, Sam's Carnival of Dreams is less than desirable, so it's fairly obvious it's Alexandra Bartholomew's paying to see. To watch her dangle at a higher, deadlier height, to hear her hold her final note a little longer than anyone has heard before.

To watch her die.

Death's death.

Young men with guns—I understand them and know to avoid them—but I'm developing a serious aversion to Mr. Bartholomew that has my back up.

As soon as F-150 leaves—nobody got his name—I go to Alexandra's trailer. It's set apart from the rest. Nobody wants to be too close when she wakes up screaming in the night. I asked her once, and she said it's always the same nightmare: She opens her mouth to sing, and nothing comes out. She lives to sing, she says.

She's not surprised to see me, imagining I'm here about the rig. I ask her if she knows anything about the young man's brother, figuring she'll say the whole idea is ridiculous.

Instead, she says, "Is he the first?"

"First what?"

"The first to say I killed someone—a brother, a husband, a wife? Have there been others?" She looks into my eyes as if I might have been harboring this secret knowledge from her.

"Not that I know of," I say. "Why do you ask?"

She looks around her little trailer at her little nick-nacks and souvenirs she's accumulated over the last couple of years—mostly gifts from adoring fans. Swans. Lots of little swans. Mostly glass, some wood. A fine pewter fellow that must weigh a couple of pounds. None of them mangled and bloody and broken. Clippings on a corkboard, featuring her in her sexy swannish but disposable attire. Alive. Photography is strictly forbidden during her act. I notice for the first time obits scattered amongst the clippings from the towns in our wake. *Samuelson, Michael passed away peacefully... Blunt, Donna departed this earthly life... Cort, Obadiah died in his home in the early morning hours...* In every case, the survivors were snipped away, nothing but the name and the fatal sentence, a grainy photo from another time.

It occurs to me that the reason the young fellow left so quickly is he plans to come back. Maybe with the law. Maybe I shouldn't have made such a fuss over a simple inquiry concerning a performer. A singing witch? No idea what you're talking about, no idea at all.

Alexandra ends her survey of her tiny trailer, gathering her thoughts. It's finally here, the moment I thought I was waiting for—when I learn the truth about her—but everything inside me is screaming, *Stop!*

"I take their lives," she says. "They die. When they hear the song, it awakens their longing for death they carry with them always, held back by fear or religion or false hope, but the song takes them to such a height they're beyond fear, and they long for the release of death. They take mine if they're ready. It's how I come back to life. They give me their hearts, the will to live they don't want anymore. It's time." She picks up the pewter swan, admires his plump smooth belly. The one who gave her that one proposed, I believe. She puts it down. "They don't die right away. A day or so, but they're finally ready, you know? They say their good-byes, die peacefully, still hearing the song—the death they've longed for.

"They confide to those who will be their survivors—the same ones who would find them if they just put a gun to their head or slit a vein—how in the middle of my performance, time seemed to stop, and there was nothing but my voice and the music, and they knew they were ready to die, so they surrendered their lives to me. It's the simplest of transactions: Our spirits meet, they give me their lives, and I draw a fresh breath and stand, so I may sing again." She looks me in the eye, barely holding it together now, her lip trembling. "They thank me."

I believe every word, but I don't want to. "You're crazy. There are that many who long for death? Someone every night?"

"More. Too many. They clamor to save me. Usually, there's more than one, and I must choose. Sometimes I choose the oldest, sometimes the one in the worst pain, sometimes the one in the deepest despair. I hate that part. Who am I to choose? Only there's no one else."

"Aren't you afraid you'll have a tent full of happy people some night? Wouldn't that be the end of you?"

"It's not funny." She laughs sadly, sniffles. "Or maybe it is. God, how I wish there was such a thing as a tent full of happy people."

"Maybe Mr. Bartholomew will provide. He seems pretty happy with himself at least. Far as I can tell, this whole thing seems to be for him. Nobody up at the house but the help—and even they're too good for us. We're a fucking carnival, for Christ's sake. *Somebody's* supposed to be excited we're here."

"He has company coming," she says. "The tent will be full. Believe me."

"How do you know that?"

She looks into my eyes. "Oh Orlando... Never mind."

"Fine, I will. That's pretty much what it takes with you, totally checking out of reality. You think it's easy watching you die? My friend the resurrectrix? But I think the young man's coming back, and I think he has a gun, and I'd rather not see how you ad lib with bullets. So why don't you and me take a drive around here and see the sights until he finds out you're not here? Sam won't want any trouble."

"Maybe the kid just wants to talk to me."

"Maybe he wants to shoot you between the eyes. All he had to say about you was you're a 'fucking witch,' and implied you killed his brother. Does that sound like a chit-chat to you?"

She hangs her beautiful head and shakes it sadly. "Do you remember, Slim?"

"Of course, I remember Slim." He was a charming haunted alcoholic who used to work the games, who died in my passenger seat on the road to Tucson. How could I forget? It takes a moment to realize what she's saying. He died looking out over a moonlit desert with a smile on his face a couple of days after he heard Alexandra's audition.

"Maybe I deserve that bullet. There's no point running, Orlando. Don't you understand? I don't find them. They find me. I've found the smallest, most obscure tent I can."

"There's always a point in running." I should know. My name's not Orlando. I ruined a lot of lives on my way to the carnival life. I should be in jail or worse. I often wish I hadn't fled, but the thought of whatever rage is in pursuit of Alexandra makes me want to take flight again. The two of us. When the carnival comes anywhere close to certain jurisdictions Sam understands I need to take some time off. I'm not the only one. Otto has an aversion to Seattle, though mostly the area is too classy for our fleabag show. Wilbur claims Otto killed a man there, but you can't believe half the shit Wilbur says. He says that Alexandra will be the death of me. Where on Earth could he have gotten that idea?

"Get up, get your stuff," I say.

She rolls her eyes. She'll go just to humor me. She doesn't take anything except a shoulder bag. None of us has much. There's not a thing in my trailer I'll miss if we run, and a few mementoes that won't haunt me anymore. Running. Great exercise. Done it all my life, in ever widening circles.

"Why are you doing this?" she asks as she fastens her seatbelt and checks her beauty in the rearview. "You can't need the aggravation. Wilbur says you can't go back to Houston you're in so much trouble there. He says there's serious law after you."

"Fuck of a lot Wilbur knows. It's Dallas, well the whole Dallas-Ft. Worth metroplex I best avoid. Waco too, though there's fuck-all in Waco anyway. Nobody knew me in Lubbock, so that must be far enough, though there's always federal marshals to consider. Is that where you're from? Lubbock?" I've never gotten her to talk about her past.

She doesn't answer right away, watching the lush woods roll by. "Don't be in love with me, Orlando."

No point denying it, though I certainly wasn't going to bring it up. "Is there a reason for that? Is that part of the curse too? No love?"

We've reached the extent of Bartholomew's estate, which just sits here with acres and acres of verdant wooded beauty, some very expensive horses, and not much else. He doesn't seem to be famous, so I figure he's a crook of one sort or another. We're at the northeast corner of his property. I turn east so we can drive alongside someone else's land for a while, a rock star or a mystery writer or a philanthropic heiress. The help for all these places must live in the next, poorer county we drove through to get here. We usually don't perform in this part of the world. Nestled between coal mines and national parks, there are plenty of riverbanks close by, but none of them we can sit on for this heart-to-heart. Part of me just wants to keep moving anyway, like a migratory tug toward another impossible future, but I poisoned my happily-ever-after habitat a long, long time ago.

For as long as she remembers, Alexandra says, all she ever really wanted was to sing beautifully, but all anybody ever cared about was her looks. She turns sideways in her seat, tucks in her legs, and tells me her story. I try to tell myself I'm ready. I keep my eyes on the road.

"I was in love with a man," her story begins, "but he didn't love me."

"What kind of fool was he?" I ask.

"Shut up and listen, Orlando. I'm trying to save your life."

The man's name was Jacob. In addition to all the usual virtues she goes on a little long about, the man sang like an angel, but that wasn't enough for him. He wanted fame. He wanted adulation. He wanted everything, and who can have everything? The more he wanted, the more he despaired because he couldn't have it, and what he had bored him. So what was Alexandra?

I know the answer to that one—she is everything—but she's asked me not to speak.

As an understudy to the female lead who never seemed to miss a performance, Alexandra doggedly followed in the footsteps of Jacob's career, scarcely getting his attention. So in love was Alexandra, she slipped something in the woman's drink making her too sick to perform, and Alexandra had her chance.

Her performance was full of passion and fire, but her voice disappointed the crowd, and the applause was tepid and polite. I glance over at her, and she looks crushed by that failure as if it were fresh—a moment she can never get past. Doesn't seem fair. A defining moment, they call it. She goes on:

"Afterward, Jacob was terribly sweet to me and took me walking in a huge cemetery in the moonlight near the performance hall. He said if I wanted I could have the secret of his beautiful voice, but I told him all I wanted was him. He laughed and made love to me on one of the graves, though it obviously meant nothing to him. Just another fuck. Nothing could've been more heartbreaking."

"Why are you telling me this story?"

"Because you need to hear it, because you need to know who the woman you think you're in love with really is. What I've done."

Who really needs to know that? Do I want her to know who I am? What chance would I have then? "Go on." I reach another crossroads and turn north.

"He told me he would teach me a song—his most beautiful—the song you've heard me sing hundreds of times now, and he told me when I learned it, it would be mine, the most beautiful song in the world, and he could have what he wanted more than anything on Earth—release—to die, to sing no more. He said to me, 'If you really love me, you will rescue me from this life, and you will let me die.'

"In that moment, I knew I wanted more than I had ever wanted him—a man who would never love me after all—to sing as beautifully as he. So he sang, taught it to me. He had swallowed poison, he told me. I could feel his dying like a vortex drawing me in, but the song flowed into me, through me, until I was nothing else. The beauty of it made me quiver like a bowed string. Time stopped on that grave, and I finished the song, kneeling naked over his strangling body, howling the perfect note to the full moon as he died.

"You can't imagine what it's like to sing like that!

"I soon learned he had tricked me, that only in the face of death could I sing the song so beautifully that time stops at the borderlands of life and death where the most intense beauty thrives. Don't love me, Orlando. Please, please don't love me. I devour lives for beauty, consume despair and hopelessness like a breath of fresh air."

I don't speak right away. Time is distance. The farther we drive, I tell myself, the more it's just us two—the madwoman and the man who loves her. If we drive far enough perhaps we can leave the curse behind.

"Here's the problem, Alexandra. You tell me not to love you, then show me that you care. This concern gives me hope." I give her a sad but hopeful smile, and damn her, she smiles back.

"Are you always so stubborn?" she asks.

"Never. So tell me about death."

"It's not a joke."

"Did I say it was? I've watched you die."

"There's nothing to tell."

"There must be something."

"A dark abyss. Nothing."

"Silent?"

"There's the single dying note."

"And when it ends?"

"I've never heard it end."

"That's something then, right?"

She looks down and then up. "We have to go back."

"Back to Bartholomew's? No way."

"It's not just another performance."

"What is it then?"

She takes a deep breath in and out. She knows I'm not going to like this part. "Justice, I guess you could say."

"What are you talking about?"

"The young man was early. There are more to come. Enough to fill the tent—and then some. Loved ones. Not a tent full of happy people, Orlando. Much, much worse—a tent full of unhappy ones who believe I stole their happiness with my song. Survivors of those who gave their lives to me."

I've obviously never wanted to die badly enough to end my life, but I've lived so long in the neighborhood I understand the concept all too well. My failure to act has been nothing more than cowardice. It's all a matter of timing, isn't it? The readiness is all, though I suppose the survivors might disagree.

We round a curve, and I spot iron gates and a sign up ahead, a field of stones beyond. "Look what we have here. Seems you can find one of these almost anywhere." I pull off the road into a cemetery and park the car. It's not as big as the one she described in her tale about Jacob, but big enough and full of the dead. "Walk with me," I say and get out, heading for an angel on the horizon, hoping she'll follow.

She does.

"What are we doing here?" she asks.

"I want to tell you *my* story. Everybody's got one, right?"

"Right." Her tone softens. She knows what we're doing here.

We reach the crest of the hill where the angel stands and take in her mountain valley view. I'm not sure I see much more than the stone eyes see at the moment. I look out. I see her fall. I hear her sing.

"I wasn't cursed by a wizard or anything, or maybe I was—the Wizard of Mediocrity. He ruled everything, every fucking cul-de-sac for miles around. We lived it, we breathed it, we ate it breakfast, lunch, and dinner by the bucketful. We sure as fuck drove thru it. But I was smart, which meant I took the smart classes, which meant, you know, I had to work a little harder, smoke a little more dope to finish my math homework. But I was real good at it, and I did a science project. A science project. I don't even remember what it was about exactly, some barely coherent sustainable habitat horseshit I came up with when I was high on several substances, including weed, speed, and acid. Certainly beer. Ended up a winning combination. I won a ribbon at a science fair. I think the judges liked the model I built to go with it. I later ran over it repeatedly with my car but that's more the middle of the story. I cashed in the ribbon for a scholarship, started believing my own bullshit, and next thing you know I had more or less faked my way into grad school until I landed an internship at an environmental agency on my way to green science stardom.

"I was supposed to monitor a major watershed for toxic substances. I didn't do it. Busy work, I figured, for a smart guy like me. It was a hot, unpleasant summer. I had interviews for real jobs. I faked the data. I'd faked everything else in my life. Why not? I looked at the last three reports and wiggled them this way and that. I was a master faker. Only trouble is I missed a toxic bloom you might've read about. Google under liver cancer, and it's bound to turn up. Birth defects is the latest, most horrible consequence, but they didn't know all that back then, how bad it was going to be, because thanks to me, it had gone virtually undetected for months.

"The minute I heard the analysis of the shit I let go right into the reservoir, I knew enough, smart bio-science whiz I was, to know how bad it was going to be, enough to know I was basically a slow motion mass murderer, visiting death upon several generations. When my laptop was seized as evidence, I knew I was screwed and ran.

"Sam was looking for someone with my skillset, someone without a past to keep his carnival running. Running from pretty much everything else, I spent a few years feeling ridiculously sorry for myself. I was scarcely worthy of my sympathy." I look at her. She's listening intently. I've never spoken to her like this, ever, opened up to anyone since I joined this carnival over a decade ago. We've talked about books and movies and music and food and the first time we swam and the way the striated clouds looked in the slow sunset and the calm that comes with listening to the river flow, but not our stories. What was it she said?

Not the silenced anguish of our lives. "Then you showed up, and like you say, at first all I could think was 'that's the most beautiful woman I've ever seen.' Then I heard you sing, saw you die—the most beautiful, and the saddest things in all the world, in a single moment. When you came back to life in my little fortress of solitude, hugged my toilet, bled on my sheets—that broke the Wizard's curse for good I can tell you. Love you? Oh it's much worse than that. Love you doesn't begin to cover it.

"The last class I went to in grad school I was high and totally unprepared, scared out of my mind because everything was starting to fall apart, and I was supposed to make some presentation on the research I hadn't done, and the professor asked me if I was ready, and I started to give him some lame excuse, when somehow the truth just came out, and I told him I wasn't ready, that I'd never been ready my whole fucking life. What was the point? The fucking point. I'm sure I said fucking. Ready? For what?

"Then I met you."

Her eyes are full of tears like mine. She lays her hands on my cheeks. "You know what I've wished for? Someone like you, Orlando. Someone who loves me because of who I am—what I am—no matter what. You think I'm brave?"

"You're the bravest person I've ever known."

She kisses me softly on the lips. She lingers a tender moment. "Orlando, we have to go back. I've promised to perform."

"Promised who?" I ask, though I already know.

"Bartholomew."

***

I try to doubt everything she's told me in our silent drive through the countryside, holding hands like lovers. I've just about talked myself into believing poor Alexandra suffers from some plausible delusion she might be treated for with the latest drugs and quackeries --I've heard electroshock is back—but when we catch sight of Bartholomew's place, there's no doubt. It's a sea of cars, mostly modest, carnival-going sorts of cars. Some even sport our bumper sticker—*Sam's Carnival of Dreams*. ("People go for dreams," Sam says. "That's what we are—a weird fucking dream.") I can't park anywhere close to the tent. It's surrounded by cars from all the states on our meandering route, a scattering of rentals throughout. Some survivors must've flown in to the nearest airport.

The Ferris wheel, near vintage, the classiest thing on the midway, spins near empty, some of the help from the big house, taking a break. Their master must be inside the tent. There's a handful of kids on the merry-go-round overseen by a lone woman, her eyes on the big top. I tell Alexandra to wait in the car and keep out of sight while I peek inside, scanning the crowd's faces. The tent is filled with ill-will wishers waiting for Alexandra to perform, enduring the other acts merely to be polite. It's written on their faces. There are no children.

Otto is bending steel, but no one cares.

There's not much left of the show. The half-hearted clowns have fled, or maybe Sam just gave them the night off to cut down on his overhead. Sam's fairly dressed up for him in a tattered corduroy suit a couple sizes too small. He's sitting with Bartholomew, trying to impress, telling his usual stories. He's washed and brushed out his lush gray mane, tossing it now and then.

Bartholomew has a look of superiority on his face that makes me sympathize even with Sam who as usual has not a clue what's going down. He probably broke out the good bud for this event.

Otto holds up a rebar pretzel and gets a smattering of applause. He usually gives it to someone in the crowd but this time doesn't bother. The kid from earlier is sitting right up front, chewing furiously on a mouthful of gum, like he's trying to make his ears pop. He's already up there with Alexandra where everyone looks now and then, tilting their heads back, though all that's up there is the rigging for Alexandra's act, the machinery of fate.

Otto starts into his big finale, lying on his back, foot-juggling a refrigerator. It's not as hard as it looks--the compressor in the refrigerator is a hollow aluminum shell--but it's still fairly impressive. This crowd can barely manage to give the dancing refrigerator a glance. He tosses it high, balances it on one foot. Nothing.

The kid takes his hand out of his pocket, checks a phone, and puts it back. Maybe the rest of the family is on the way. Wouldn't want to miss this.

I return to Alexandra. "Otto's almost done. So who's Bartholomew?"

"An avenging angel."

I know better than to smirk. This nightmare is unimpressed by my skepticism. "And Jacob, was he an angel too?"

"Yes. Fallen. Heartless."

"I want to believe you, but—"

She puts her fingers to my lips. "Don't. Don't believe me."

Don't love her, don't believe her. So of course I do, and she disappears into her trailer to change. I hurry into the tent to adjust the Sands of Time. I totally forgot. I use a stopwatch and a scale to add the necessary seconds, the moments of her life, before I set the mechanism. There's a moment I consider tampering with it, leaving her hanging when the song ends—and it's my turn to look up, to imagine her there when silence fell and she was still alive, imagine her dying in silence, her nightmare fulfilled. I measure carefully. I set the mechanism, hurrying to finish before her intro begins, and the tent is filled with the thunderous applause of an audience ready for blood.

She sings her opening numbers exceptionally well. She must feel the approach of death with near certainty tonight. The crowd peers at her with unbroken malevolence, some openly grieving for those stolen from them by her song. They pray for her doom.

I imagine life ahead without her, and I don't want it. I understand what she meant when she said she was trying to save my life, but it was too late. I already loved her. *You can't imagine what it's like to sing like that!* No, but I can listen. She doesn't just live to sing. She lives to die to sing.

Her song fills the moonlit empty nights, vast and silent otherwise, with beauty, driving through the desert toward the dark horizon into the dark abyss, into nothing. Letting go. When it's time.

There's my cue. A spot finds my hand, and I pull the lever. The Sands of Time begin to flow.

Listen. Listen, goddammit. She's started her song.

I'm ready.

The Puppy Strangler

The guy said we could write about anything. He said to push the envelope. He said there were no bad ideas. Think outside the box, he said.

That's how I came up with The Puppy Strangler.

I like me some stranglers—serial killers in general and stranglers in particular, you know what I mean? There's something about the squirming victim in the strangler's grip that scares the shit out of me, and I guess I like to be scared. I'm not the only one. That's why they have a whole section at the bookstore. That's why Stephen King is rich.

The guy said in the workshop I crossed a line. Practically everyone around the table was giving me this look, nodding their heads up and down like they're going to eat me or something, even though they know I'll taste horrible, all saying I crossed a line too.

Just where the fuck's this line? I've read prostitute stranglers, old lady stranglers, queer stranglers, and when you broaden it out to the whole field of serial killing, there's no telling what gets them off. That's what makes them so scary. Thousands of victims every year on TV shows alone, mostly just innocent fucks going about their business, but they wear red shoes or their Hassidic Jews or something, and *bam* a serial killer offs them with some weird disgusting ritual to go with it, and strangling puppies is crossing a line? What squirms better than a puppy?

What if it wasn't something so adorable? Someone suggested. Like chickens.

Then he wouldn't be a serial killer, I said, he'd be a farmer, and I was reminded the writer was supposed to keep his trap shut while everybody kicks shit out of his story.

One girl hated it so bad she started crying and told me I should seek help.

That's why I'm taking this class, I said. Besides, my dog liked it.

You're horrible, she said and glared at me like she'd like to strangle me for real.

Enough, the guy said.

Jeez Louise. It's true what I said about my dog. I mean, I read it to her. Who else is going to listen? I think she got seriously scared when the Puppy Strangler was on the fire escape of a place pretty much like this shithole we live in. She went and hid under the bed like she does when there's lightning or fireworks. Or maybe she thought I crossed a line too, though that's hard to imagine. She's pretty into me. Her name's Frida, a more or less Golden whose former owner dropped dead of a stroke. When I got her at the SPCA they told me Frida was 10, but the vet said she was more like 12 or 13, so now she's somewhere around 12, 14, or 15 depending on which guess is the best. Basically fucking old. Somewhere between 84 and 105 in dog years. I'm 23, but I'm running a little behind schedule, back in school for another try. The whole building except for the ancient black guy who fixes everything is younger than me.

Today, I'm revising "The Puppy Strangler." We're supposed to revise one of our piece-of-shit stories into something that doesn't stink so bad. Just one. Any one we want. The guy campaigned hard for me to pick something besides "The Puppy Strangler"—anything else. He even offered me what he offered no one, special permission to write a whole new story, forgetting all that stuff he said about the importance of the revision process, like there was no way I could do worse than "The Puppy Strangler." Or maybe the Strangler had such a profound effect on him, he doesn't know if he has what it takes to face him again.

I said he told us on the first night of class that sometimes there were stories you just had to tell, you didn't know why, but you wouldn't rest until you got them told, or something like that, and he nodded, and I said that's "The Puppy Strangler" for me, and I confess to kind of enjoying him squirm in his creaky swivel chair—unable to forbid the Strangler but afraid of what new disgusting lines I might cross in revision.

I'm trying to get inside the Puppy Strangler's head. Nobody understood him. So I've added a whole new scene where he's at the Kroger, in the meat department, looking at all the shrink-wrapped packages and imagining ground puppy, puppy cutlets, extra lean AKC registered organic farm-raised puppy steaks, pickled puppy paws—then he goes outside, and there's some kid with a box full of puppies looking for homes, and he takes the whole box.

Now what? He can't just take them somewhere and strangle them. That's not interesting. Anybody can do that. It's got to be sicker than that. Maybe he drives them one by one to a dark pine forest in the middle of nowhere…

Frida puts her head in my lap meaning she wants a walk, meaning it's four, when she gets her dinner after the Tai Chi shuffle-dump she calls a walk. She was a free feeder before me and big as a whale. Now that she's slimmed down, on a good day she'll run. Not far, not fast, but recognizable. I bet she was something in her day. She still gets jazzed if you show her a tennis ball. I roll it across the floor making sure it doesn't roll under anything. She's good for about six fetches. It gladdens the heart, as my mom used to say.

I leave my computer on so I'll have to come back to it, because the guy said the only way to get anywhere with your craft—he uses that word a lot—is to stick with it. So it's nothing but me and the Strangler every chance this week until I get it right.

Frida's not crazy about stairs, so we take the elevator. I feel like an idiot riding an elevator down four flights, but I don't have wonky hips like Fri. The building's on a wide avenue with a broad median down the middle with runners and dog walkers. Compared to them, Fri and I make about as much progress as the trees.

We haven't gone far when a voice cries out, "Hey, Puppy Strangler," and I turn around, and it's Audrey, who's also in the workshop. She's pale with jet-black hair, weird, laughs inappropriately—and everybody, even the guy, is a little bit afraid of her. When her story came up, nobody knew what the fuck was going on, but I was the only one who said so. That's what I liked about it. Just when you thought you got it, she would throw in something you couldn't possibly explain. My endorsement didn't exactly help her cause, because that's when the guy finally worked up his nerve to start in about her plot inconsistencies.

She says, "I'm sorry, I forgot your name."

"Puppy Strangler's okay. You have to believe in your vision, right?" That's something the guy says too.

She laughs. "The guy's an asshole. It's so totally cool you actually have a dog. Your story really fucked with people's heads, you know? C'mon. What's your name? I promise not to forget it."

Have you ever wanted another name? I have. Here's my chance. The guy says naming your characters is super important, says he has this *What to Name the Baby?* book he uses to like suss it out for each one. He thinks I need to give the Strangler a name as an opportunity to tell readers something about who he is. I start to tell Audrey my name's Lyle or Sterling, but I don't know what they mean, and why lie? The guy liked my name, made a big deal of it the first night because of some dead poet. I can't believe she doesn't remember. "Rupert," I say.

"For real?"

"Mom says she liked Rupert Everett, but she didn't know he was gay, and she never heard of Rupert Murdoch."

"So are you?"

"Gay or a rich rightwing asshole?"

She laughs. "A puppy strangler."

"Oh definitely."

"What's her name?" Audrey asks. Fri's giving her the big wag and her golden smile.

"Frida," I say. "She came with the name. The woman who owned her was an art teacher. I've only had her a couple of years."

Audrey takes a knee and starts petting. Fri stretches out her neck like she does, and Audrey gives her a big hug. "Did you know the owner?"

"No. They have the old dogs up front at the SPCA, and I stopped off just to visit with them, you know, because everybody was walking right past them on their way to the young dogs jumping up and down and barking. She put her head in my lap, and I took her home."

"So you must live around here?"

"That one. 408." I point to our building.

"So you want to hang out?"

"I'm working on my revision." I tell her about the box of puppies I left in the middle of the scene with no idea what to do with them.

Her face lights up. "We can collaborate. This is so great. Then you can help me with my fucking disaster."

"I liked yours."

"Really? It didn't make any sense."

"In English classes I never get what I'm supposed to out of anything I read, so I never expect anything to make sense to me, but your story was more like you weren't trying to make sense. It was like weird jazz or something, so I could just enjoy it, you know?"

She gives me this look like I've just been hitting on her, but I meant it about the jazz thing even if I find her very hot—but I have to work on my story. "You're too much, Rupert. I've got some ideas for your box of puppies."

This suggestion offers a resolution to my dilemma, as the guy would say. The promise of a puppy strangling solution has me inviting her up to my place. To collaborate. I try to imagine how that works. We ride slowly up the elevator. I try hard not to think about sex.

The guy said once that sex scenes are extremely difficult and got one of those inappropriate laughs out of Audrey. Her laugh's not what you'd expect, high and bubbly and not quiet, but cut short, like she puts a cork in it, but there's a whole lot more where that comes from. I glance over at her, and she's watching me think about her laugh, trying not to think about sex. Fri's staring up at us both like she knows exactly what's going on.

"So what's his motivation? He's got to have a motivation."

I've made us pizza. We've smoked the joint she had in her bag that's way stronger than anything I can afford. We've finally gotten around to the Strangler—my laptop's open on the floor between us. We've done a lot of brainstorming, like a lengthy discussion of the best puppies to strangle. We couldn't decide on pugs. Since their eyes already bug out, you kind of lose part of the strangling effect, and they make those weird snorty noises even when you don't have a deathgrip around their fat little throats. They're real sneezers too, which cracked us up imagining it, a big old pug sneeze in the Strangler's face like at the height of the action or whatever, so we wrote that, figuring every story needs some comic relief somewhere, and it gave us a chance to show the Puppy Strangler's vulnerable side, and we figured out we really could do this collaboration thing, but that still doesn't help me with the box of puppies outside Kroger, and I'm starting to despair, hitting one of those walls where the guy says you got to trust in your process.

"Don't let her do that," I say. Fri's sitting beside Audrey, licking her pizza hands clean.

Audrey's offering the fingers on her right hand, one by one for Frida's slurp. "She likes it."

"She shouldn't beg." Audrey slipped her a slice earlier when she thought I wasn't looking.

"Give me your hand," Audrey says. She reaches out her left hand. "C'mon. Don't wipe it off."

I offer my right hand, and she takes it and puts my pizza fingers in her mouth, one by one, and then our greasy mouths meet, and it's awhile before we get back to the Strangler, sitting up in bed.

"Maybe the Strangler should fuck somebody," Audrey suggests.

"Who would want to fuck the Strangler?"

"Point."

"Maybe he's the opposite, never been close to anybody because of some childhood trauma, right? Serial killers always have some trauma or other that makes them totally whack-a-doodle."

"Like what?"

"Maybe he saw his father strangle his mom."

"I like it. How do the puppies figure in?"

Then it comes to me: The whole thing, like the guy says. A Eureka Moment. "Strangler's little, okay? Four or five maybe. There's this litter of puppies in the house, okay? And Mom says the Strangler can keep them, but Dad's against it. When Dad kills Mom and gets away with it by making it look like she fell down the basement stairs, he also bags up the puppies and throws them in the river. The two become like fused in Strangler's sick little head, so he's driven to strangle puppies, so everybody has to go through what he went through. So like with the box of puppies at the Kroger? He's got to find them *homes* first, homes where everybody loves them. *Then* he strangles them. It's not about the puppies. It's about the pain!"

"That's pretty fucking sick," Audrey says with admiration. "I love it."

"I've even got an ending," I say proudly. The guy can't say enough about the importance of the ending. "Remember the bag of puppies in the river? They get rescued by a scientist guy who gives them a secret formula that saves their lives and gives them like super abilities, and they're the ones who track down the Puppy Strangler in the end to like resolve the conflicts by killing him to end his reign of terror. What do you think?"

"Won't they have to be kind of old? For dogs, I mean. The puppies in the river."

I'm tempted to just say, you know, the serum makes them like live forever, but that's too easy. Difficulties are opportunities the guy says. "That's it. They're like real old. This is their last adventure. They're like Fri. Good old dogs. They save the puppies, bump off the Strangler, and die."

And that's pretty much the way we write it in a flurry. We're both all sniffly by the time the last scene's done—when the Super Pack leaps upon the Puppy Strangler on a cliff in the middle of a big storm, and they plunge to their deaths on the rocks below, and we make love some more, and she spends the night, and I'm thinking maybe I could really get into this writing thing.

Audrey's story isn't so easy. It was weird before, and we just keep making it weirder. We can't seem to help ourselves. To her credit Audrey tries to think up different ways to explain the weirdness, but she says I always make a face before she's halfway through. So we don't explain anything, like cooking without a recipe at an alien diner.

The guy's going to hate it. It has the plot consistency of a landfill. We have high confidence, however, that the Strangler will do better. It's a real revision, as the guy says, completely reimagined. I couldn't have done it without Audrey. We've done everything the guy says to do in a story and then some. Except for giving the Strangler a name. As Audrey says, "His name's Puppy Strangler. The guy'll have to get over it."

Tonight our revisions are on the table, me and her. Audrey's first.

The guy stuns everybody by saying how wonderful it is. How it's weird, but it transcends weird like Murakami and Calvino, and Audrey cuts me a look like she might start laughing inappropriately, but in the end after everybody at the table reluctantly agrees with the guy that it's a work of stupendous genius, it's the opposite, really. She's a little choked up when she thanks everybody, and then it's my turn.

The guy's usually nice. He's like a lab instructor slicing open a frog. Nothing against frogs. Usually. The revised Strangler changes that. He uses words like drivel he hasn't used before, even when that's what he meant.

Then it's my turn to be moved. The class turns on him, sides with me. Me and Audrey I should say. The girl who hated it before says she cried at the end—and that's a good thing. Even the humorless philosophy major found it fucking hilarious. Everybody loved what the guy hated most: The Super Pack. They suggest a slew of sequels, apparently forgetting the Pack's dead, and I can see a look of panic in the guy's eyes as he totally loses control of the situation.

Hands-down favorite scene? The pug-puppy strangling in a lonely pine wood, the Puppy Strangler's evil mug dripping with pug snot—the first scene Audrey and I wrote together.

They understand the Strangler now, they say. Totally. Everyone admires my faith in the revision process.

The guy just lets us go. You can see he wants to say something, but he doesn't.

We both got A's, and inspired by our success, decided to do what lots of people in the class suggested—make a Puppy Strangler movie. We shot the pug strangling scene, threw it up on you-tube and it went viral. Everything's happened super-fast, and we've gotten investors, and we're just about ready to start shooting.

I've tried to get ahold of the guy to thank him for the class, that it was like a life-changing event for me, and I learned a whole, whole lot about telling stories I'll never forget, and if we win like some film festival or something, I'll definitely thank him personally, but the university says he's quit teaching, and they can't tell me where he's gone because of his privacy.

I trust wherever he is, he'll hear more about the Strangler.

This is a good place to stop, I guess. Fri's still alive. It's time for her walk. Audrey's moved in, and we're working on a shooting script for her story, and I'm the happiest I've ever been in my whole entire life.

Adult Children of Alien Beings

My parents weren't like your parents, okay? The ones in the Mother's Day cards and the Father's Day cards. Who are those people?

My mother never drove. I never took lessons in anything. She told me as a child it was important to spend as much time alone as possible, preferably in the woods, maybe up in a tree or on a hilltop, while I was still open to the overwhelming mysteries of the universe. She didn't start there; she worked up to it gradually. "Go outside and play" became increasingly ambitious and nuanced. The alternative was to be constantly underfoot. Mom needed her space before everyone said that. She started smoking because my older brother and I said it would make her look cool like the other younger mothers. Next day she bought a pack. She alternated between regular and menthol, pack a day.

My dad never had trouble showing emotion. He loved me like nobody's business. I learned from observing him that at the end of sappy movies, if your face isn't wet with tears, you haven't been paying attention or you don't have a heart. Not to have a heart was the worst. He asked me once if I wanted to learn how to fight, and I said no, and he said that was good because he didn't know how. He was big and strong though he never worked out or did any exercise and ate anything he wanted. Mom was the same.

Dad loved to tell dirty stories. He did voices and everything. Mom loved to hear them. He made her laugh so hard, you could barely make out what she was saying: "Not… in front of the… k-k-kids… Bob!" Put that in a Father's Day card: Thanks for all the smut. Knowing filthy jokes was every bit as useful as knowing how to fight, and Mom was definitely right about that treetop.

They taught me how to cook by smell. They both did it. The spice rack covered a wall, the spices in alphabetical order. They loved highly seasoned food. They never used recipes. You put your ingredients together, sniff out the spices for a dish, and cook. They didn't believe in cookbooks, though I've dedicated the several I've written to them. They would find this amusing, laudable. The message I got from my folks loud and clear? The kid who's just like his mom and dad? You have to wonder about that kid. You have to adapt, evolve, sniff out your own way in this world if you hope to prosper.

They're both dead. They fell down an abyss while vacationing in New Mexico the year I graduated college. I only bring them up because at sixty-six, what I call semiretired, I've been digging into the family history, trying to unlock the secrets of my past like those celebrities on television. The thing is, Mom and Dad don't have any. History. Now you see them, now you don't. The entire family history narrated to my brother and me when we were little was a complete fabrication. They seem to pop into existence the year before my older brother was born. That's when they started paying utility bills. They claimed to come from Colorado, but Colorado never heard of them.

I make the mistake of calling my brother with this information. He doesn't see the big deal. Dad was always a bit of a storyteller. Maybe he didn't get all the details right.

Their birth certificates are phonies, all their papers before my brother was born, even their marriage license. I had them examined by an expert. I'm back living in the house my brother and I grew up in, and all their stuff's still up in the attic.

My brother moved away as soon as he thought I could handle things on my own, marrying and moving to his new wife's town. He's done that a few times since, different wives, different towns, while I've just moved all over town with different wives.

Mostly, the house has been rented out over the years. I didn't want to sell it. I lost my last wife when it happened to be vacant, so I moved in. Lost, as in, she left. That was four years ago.

"What kind of expert?" my brother said. "Who believes experts?"

I gave up on my brother. I kept looking for our past.

Which led me to this guy, Dr. Deetermeyer, another expert. He's looked over all my documents regarding my parents, as well as examined surviving articles of clothing belonging to them—my mother's favorite scarf and one of my father's cardigans—if you want to call snuffling them like a hound dog an examination. His office at the university is cave-like with six-inch pipes crisscrossing the ceiling, thick with yellow paint like lemon chiffon. The bookcases are crammed chaotically with books, papers, sandwiches, soda cans, videotapes, and tiny hand-painted soldiers from ancient armies. There's a Rousseau print of some colorful craziness in the jungle and four or five framed degrees from prestigious universities. His first name is Simon. His middle name is Emmanuel. He's at the end of a long, narrow, buzzing-fluorescent-lit basement hallway with no other doors. There's nothing else but a bulletin board with band flyers from 2004 and numerous opportunities to study abroad. I almost didn't knock. It smells like burnt coffee and rotten citrus and the faintest whiff of pot. The lone window is ancient frosted safety glass, tilted open a crack to reveal a hurried blur of student legs moving by, mostly bare. It's a warm October day.

"Your parents were aliens," he says. "Part of an exploratory expedition that arrived in the United States shortly after the outbreak of World War II and departed in 1969."

"Aliens."

"That's right."

"And that makes me and my brother?"

"Aliens."

What to say to a totally tenured nutjob? I'm trying to remember who sent me to this guy. That weirdo at the Department of Historic Resources? Odd, to say the least. The past seems to do that to people. I should've left it alone.

"Ice cream," Deetermeyer says.

"What about it?"

"They loved it, all year round."

"So what? Lots of people love ice cream." I start to rise. I have a hungry parking meter waiting. I gave my last quarter for this nonsense.

"Peppermint."

That stops me. For my parents there was only one ice cream flavor, peppermint. Since it's not readily available all year round, they stocked up every Christmas, loading a big box freezer full to overflowing in the basement. Dad, who did all the grocery shopping since Mom didn't drive, sometimes took me along to help load up the cart. We both wore gloves for the occasion, like cartoon characters.

"With chocolate sauce," Deetermeyer added with a little nerdy gotcha smile.

"How did you know that?"

"It's an alien delicacy. They love peppermint and chocolate together. They love all the mints, but like peppermint the best. That's what they found of greatest value here, mint and chocolate."

"This is stupid. I'm human. I've been to doctors my whole life—my parents too. Somebody would've noticed if I was an alien."

"Your form is human; your essence, alien."

"What the fuck does that mean?"

"Your parents' bodies were alien adaptations of the human form using human DNA. Certainly, to the medicine of the time, they would've seemed perfectly normal, as would their offspring, but they preserved and passed on their alien nature to you in a thousand subtle ways—their legacy. They reproduced at a somewhat higher rate than the general population. They were, after all, far from home and lonely. They were always deployed in male/female pairs. Clearly the pair bond is exceptionally strong among them."

He seems absolutely serious. "Clearly. This, uh, alien essence you spoke of? How might that manifest itself in the, uh, offspring?" I try to keep a neutral expression. I notice that what I took to be ancient armor on the tiny soldiers might be their limbs and torsos; their weapons, household appliances from distant worlds.

He tilts his head back, aligning his trifocals to draw a bead on me. He's used to skeptics. "Just you and your brother?"

"That's right."

"You're the younger, I imagine, the Quester?"

My brother won't even look for his car keys. "I guess you could say that." I am the one who came down a narrow hallway to discover this loon, not exactly the quest I had in mind.

"Indeed. Gender and birth order are highly determinant in alien families. Stop me when I'm mistaken: You and your brother are four to five years apart, widely divergent in your views. You live in separate cities and prefer it that way. Presidents you hated; he loved—political polar opposites, you can't seem to agree on anything. You share some telltale traits, however. You're both inordinately fond of animals—dogs, cats, birds, any animal really. Alien males almost never hunt, though the elder is likely to own several guns. You're both cynical about most things, but sentimental in love. You're typically serial monogamists. Your wives—"

I hold up my hand. "Enough. So you want to tell me *why* aliens came here and what I should do about it?"

"As for why, you'll have to wait for the aliens to return. There's no shortage of competing theories to occupy you in the meantime." He smiles like this prospect is supposed to cheer me up. "To help you deal with this startling discovery you've made about yourself, there is a support group, ACAB, that does lots of fine work. Much, if not all my research, is based on in-depth interviews with its members. Perhaps, when you're ready, we might conduct such an interview." He sifts through the detritus on his desk to unearth a slender pamphlet. *Adult Children of Alien Beings*. He staples his card to it, like he's handing out an assignment.

I snatch it from his hand and flee his office, but he leans out his office door and calls after me, "Email me with any questions. Stop by anytime!"

I sprint up the narrow stairs into the street. I examine the card. His name and information, the university logo. The Department of Secret History. There's a sign by the basement stairwell that reads the same, looks like all the other signs up and down the street. I had no idea the university had such a department. Makes sense, I suppose, that I wouldn't. These houses used to be the mansions of the idle rich. They've seen their share of séances and crackpot rituals. That their basements now house such mysteries seems appropriate somehow. Who else has time for them but the rich and universities?

I don't have time to ponder this further because the meter cop is about to write me a ticket even though I'm right here, keys in hand, and we both watch the time run out together. It takes forever to talk him out of it. He makes a big deal, like world justice depends on me paying for my parking crimes. Several cars pass, coveting the spot while we bicker. He manages to be a total asshole before he finally relents. I get into my car, rattled from both encounters, loon and asshole. Sometimes I just don't understand people!

As the thought flits through my brain, I freeze, frozen in the process of shifting into Reverse.

Sometimes I just don't understand people.

I drop back into Park. Dad said that *all* the time. I can hear him saying it. It was like the chorus of my childhood. Like he really meant it, felt it deeply. And Mom would put her arm around his shoulders and murmur, "It's all right dear. Everything will be fine. You'll see. It will all work out." And he would look at her like she was the only one on the planet who truly understood him.

Maybe she was.

I touch the brochure in my pocket, next to my heart. I owe it to them to check it out. I'm the Quester, after all. Nobody else is going to do it. I started this searching-out-my-roots business in the first place to find out where I came from. From another planet makes as much sense as from nowhere.

Someone honks his horn at the old man frozen in his clunker at the parking meter, his turn signal on like he's going somewhere, but too addled apparently to give it the gas. I understand the honker's feelings completely. I drop it into Drive and gun it.

I know what he'll say, but I have to talk to my brother about this. Everything Deetermeyer said was true about us and more besides, but this isn't like the Bushes or the wars or same-sex marriage or the NRA or roundabouts or Obamacare or NASCAR or climate change or the Dallas Fucking Cowboys. This is more like Animal Rescue.

Alien Rescue. Ourselves. That's the key. To accept who you are so you can move on in a meaningful way. Now that I've read the brochure, been to the website, and pondered the evidence at length, it makes more and more sense.

In fact, it makes sense of everything.

One story of dozens I could tell: When I was nine or ten, Mom did a Paint by Number of a mountain landscape, systematically switching all the paints. She had a list of all the numbers and their substitutes taped on the wall where she worked on it meticulously for hours. She was quite pleased with it and just sat smiling at the scene while it dried, smoking a cigarette. How about? This was a menthol day, Alpine or Newport, one of those. The sky was the color of the pack. All the colors were wrong. Under the deep turquoise sky, the snow was way too blue. The evergreens were brick red.

Dad traveled. District sales manager. He hadn't been around for the weird Paint by Number project. My brother ignored it, of course, like he ignored everything else that wasn't about him. I was there for the unveiling, when Mom showed Dad this goofy Paint by Number, and they *both* had a drink and a smoke and sat there smiling at it teary-eyed, holding hands. They hung it up in their bedroom and locked the door for a while.

My folks were noisy lovers. It was many years before I realized not everybody grew up listening to their parents fuck, trying to picture it, what would make them groan and thump in that distinctive rhythm. She would scream his name in a way that I knew meant, despite its volume and intensity, that she wasn't mad at him but the opposite, a mystery I pondered long into the night.

Turns out Paint by Number was wildly popular among the aliens, and that a code circulated among them to translate certain landscapes—specially designed by an alien who had infiltrated the design department—into the palette and contours of their home world. There's an image on the ACAB website of the scene my mother did that looks *exactly* like the one I remember. That's what was going on with Mom and Dad: They were remembering home, when they met perhaps, and fucked like crazy, like they were young and in their old bodies again. If you examine it closely, supposedly, the elk in the middle distance has three eyes. The JPEG is too tiny to tell. Unfortunately, Mom's painting hasn't survived. She had a big yard sale the spring before they fell into the abyss and practically gave away all her artwork.

I explain all this and more to my brother over the phone. We both hate talking on the phone, but we live five hundred miles apart. Face to face is reserved for dead, dying, or getting married again. We're both between. The last time we spoke was a couple of months ago when he called to tell me he was moving out and to give me his new address. That's when I told him about my early research, before Deetermeyer. Probably not the best timing.

It takes him a while to just shut up and listen, so I really lay it on when I finally get an opening, maybe give him a little too much to process all at once.

"Aliens," he says. "Stan, I think you need help, professional help."

"Dr. Deetermeyer *is* a professional, Ollie."

I can feel the phone grow cold in my hand. "I told you not to call me that," he says in his gruff Clint Eastwood voice. He thinks it's intimidating. It just makes him sound old.

"It's your *name*. It's what Mom and Dad always called you. It's what I called you until you got a pole up your ass about it. I can't remember. Was it Kristi or June who put the idea in your head there was something wrong with it? It's on your birth certificate, Ollie, the first *real* document in our parents' lives on Earth!"

"Our parents named us after a couple of buffoons, Stan!"

"They didn't know any better. They were aliens! Don't you see? They loved Laurel and Hardy, so why not name their sons after them? It's so typical for the elder son of aliens to resent their peculiarities and crystalize his rage in some trivial wrong like a naming that merely expresses the parents' true alien nature. They knew how to laugh, Ollie. Something you could stand to work on. Compassion. Understanding." Aliens love slapstick too, but I don't go into all that. Ollie's at war with that side of his nature.

There's a long silence. I know my brother. He's struggling with his better self. He wants to tell me to fuck off and hang up, but he wants to rise above it and be the only rational member of his crazy family. You'd think after all these years he'd give that one up. He's just not that good at it. "I prefer *Oliver*," he says icily.

Oh please. This is typical firstborn alien brother behavior, to feel betrayed rather than blessed by his alien heritage. They invest minutiae, such as a mere name on a birth certificate, with great significance. They're into vows, lines in the sand, all the rest of it. They have no control, the victims of their own symbolism. It's like waving a red flag in front of a bull. I'll demonstrate: "Ollie, Ollie, Ollie."

He hangs up. It's just as well. There's no way I can convince him Mom and Dad were aliens without further proof. I email him all my evidence, direct him to the ACAB website. Maybe he'll read it, and maybe he won't, but most likely he's absolutely certain I'm just crazy. Nothing new under that sun.

As you might imagine, paranoia runs high in the ACAB community, so there's not a lot of face to face, but some of us aren't so comfy with the online thing either. Am I really chatting with a fellow ACAB member in Santa Monica, or is it some FBI guy in Quantico taking a little time off from pretending to be a thirteen-year-old girl entrapping sleazeballs to infiltrate a fringe group for a change of weirdness? How's that for a career choice? And I'm the crazy one? Anyway, the local ACAB group's fairly tiny. We meet at the dog park second and fourth Tuesdays at dawn. (Fifth Tuesdays, we take the dogs to the river in all weather). We're all early risers, and so are our dogs. We have the place mostly to ourselves. We watch the dogs play while we discuss alien issues, sitting in a row on top of one of the long picnic tables, our feet on the bench.

Summer mornings, we've had as many as seven or eight, winter months it's usually just the four diehards.

Today it's Katyana and Bill and me. She's in the middle, I'm on her right, and Bill's on her left. Dave is on his fourth honeymoon. Most of the regulars are my age, fifties, sixties, born from the late nineteen-forties into the sixties. Katyana's thirty maybe. She mentions her ex now and then but never gives out any details.

She believes the aliens didn't all vanish one way or another within a month of each other like my parents did, but that some hung around longer, maybe even more showed up. She's proof, she says. Her next older sister's nineteen years older. Her parents were old. Katyana's intense, and so is her blue-gray standard poodle Avatar, so no one argues with her. Opinion's sharply divided in the ACAB community on the Departure Issue, but she's definitely in the far fringe minority. I don't like to get into that controversy. I've got enough to figure out in the mainstream fringe.

I tell them about trying to get through to my brother. "I don't want to give up on him."

"Let it go," Bill says, what Bill always says. He used to be a Unitarian minister. He gave a few too many sermons on aliens. Unitarians aren't as open-minded as they like to think they are. Now he has a pug named Clyde. "There's no convincing some. It's for a reason your brother is the way he is. It's all part of the plan." You have to watch Bill. He'll get to talking about Shinto gateways and fail to notice Clyde's adding a lovely dump to the scene. On this issue he may be right, however.

To maximize dispersal of alien seed, the predominant theory goes, ACAB brothers don't get along, move apart, and take multiple partners in order to create a far-flung network of alien descendants in every walk of life to greet them when they return. Ollie's pig-headedness, Bill's saying, serves a genuine purpose, but I'm not entirely convinced. How is willful ignorance of one's true nature better than self-knowledge? What good will Ollie be when the aliens return, if he doesn't even know who he is? I sort of nipped the alien plan in the bud when I got a vasectomy after my second wife had to quit taking the pill because of terrible migraines. No regrets. No children except some wonderful steps. I don't think they figure in the alien design, though I might've brainwashed them in some way. I'll have to ask them next time I see them. I have them over for dinner a couple of times a month. They've developed alien palates. Like many ACAB's kids of multi-married parents, they've shown a reluctance to marry themselves.

Katyana shakes her head at Bill's advice as he elaborates. How you elaborate on *let it go,* I don't know. I'm not really listening. I'm not so much looking *past* Katyana at Bill, but at her lovely profile as she rejects Bill's wisdom, using his pious tedium as a pretense to admire her beauty. I have to look away.

Out in the barren wasteland of the dog park, my dog Myrna, usually a clever border collie, is desperately making a fool of herself to catch Avatar's attention—crouch, spring, whirl, dash—but he's having none of it, making his stately progress around the perimeter, pissing. He makes it look like a yoga pose. She does not exist to him. If she's not careful, he's going to piss on her head. I can't watch.

"You should devote your energies to finding one of the old aliens who stayed behind," Katyana says to me. "They'll know whatever you wish to know. You shouldn't care so much what your foolish brother thinks."

She gives me a mildly scolding look, and I'm unnerved at how much I wish to please her. Forget my brother? Not a problem. Dave's of the opinion, he confided before he left for Cancun, that Katyana's not ACAB at all, just crazy. I like her, though, and she does look like an alien, has all the telltale features. A beautiful alien. I like having a plan. *Let it go* doesn't feel like a plan. "How do you think I should go about finding an old alien still hanging around Planet Earth?"

Bill heaves a gentle ministerial sigh at my foolishness. Screw him. I interrupt his judgment to point out Clyde's taking a crap—part of the plan no doubt—and Bill trots off to tend to it. Katyana smiles, cocks an eyebrow. It's just the two of us. She has enormous eyes even for an ACAB, whose eyes tend to run large. "Think like one of them. That shouldn't be so hard for you. You're the most alien of us all. Who knows more?"

It's true. I've sort of thrown myself into it, like an abyss, researching the subject endlessly, contributing regularly to the ACAB blog. I don't know whether she's teasing me or has faith in me, but Katyana inspires me to ponder the issue like worrying a bone. If any of the original aliens are still among us, how would I go about finding them? They all supposedly died somewhat mysteriously within a few months of each other, leaving no bodies behind, which is generally held to mean they abandoned their human form, their mission fulfilled, and left the planet en masse, by wormhole or starship. Opinion is divided and not really relevant to the more important question—did any remain behind? Even the most ardent believers in the Stayed Behinds or the Left Behinds, depending on who you ask, admit only a handful would be living now. It would be like finding a needle in a haystack, like aliens finding Earth on the outskirts of the Milky Way. If you're an ACAB, you have to believe anything is possible.

Later on, I'm sitting at home watching a rehash of the Black Friday craziness on TV with Myrna's head in my lap, muttering, "Sometimes I just don't understand people," as they run clips of folks trampling each other for deals to show how well things are going this holiday season, when it hits me: Christmastime. Peace on Earth. "Away in a Manger." Hysterical consumerism and lots of sappy movies—the season for aliens to restock their freezers with peppermint ice cream and cry happy tears. I love Christmas. I'm not a believer, but I love the story—strangers in a strange land, the most important kid on the planet born in a barn. Come let us adore him. Nothing wrong with that.

It's not hard to figure out where I might spot a shopping alien early in the holiday season. The peppermint ice cream at the Kroger fills an end box across from the soft cheeses where I figure I can dither indefinitely over whether to get dill or pimiento or chipotle or just forego this artery-clogging glop altogether—one of the privileges of old age, indecision—while I wait for an old alien. It's senior discount day. The aisles teem with us. Still, for even so weighty a question as to brie or not to brie, there must be a limit, and fairly soon I'm joined by the youthful dimwit I recognize to be the manager, who pretends to tidy up some tiny cheeses with smiling cows on the label. There are cameras everywhere. *Alert: Senior beached at the cheeses without a purchase for going on a quarter hour.*

"Are you finding everything all right, sir?"

Who can honestly answer yes to that one? *Sir* with the right inflection means doddering old fool in managerspeak. Screw you very much, Sonny Boy, I'm waiting for ancient aliens. "Just fine," I say. He glances down into my basket. There's a bag of frozen kale thawing, a pound of black beans, and a couple of yams to show I'm serious about the shopping thing. Aliens didn't eat cheese and ice cream and thick, juicy steaks because it was good for them. They knew they were only in their human form for the short term and didn't have to live with the consequences. I've been vegan since my heart attack four years ago this spring. I'll have to move along. There's nothing within arm's reach I can eat. Maybe I can lurk by the frozen berries and dither there if the sight line's right. So far there's only been a handful of single quart peppermint ice cream buyers. Nobody's made a purchase of alien proportions. Dad and I used to empty the case as soon as it showed up. If the store runs out early in the season, Dad explained, they restock, and you can hit the same store twice in one year. If you wait around till there's no Christmastime left, they might not bother. Some years we had to hit multiple stores. This is probably the peppermint cusp.

"Were you looking for a mild cheese?" the manager ventures. "Or something sharper?"

Than you? I point to the label on the cheeses he's fussing over. "Those cows there—are they organic? Where are they from exactly? They look so happy."

"Hey Stan!" a familiar voice behind us says, and we both turn. It's Katyana.

She's a small, slender woman who lives alone, and yet her full-size shopping cart is filled to overflowing with peppermint ice cream, the case behind her, empty. My back was only turned for a moment. She's quick. She could've easily slipped away unnoticed. "Katyana," I say. "Fancy meeting you here."

The manager seems surprised I even know someone like Katyana. Her arms are covered with tattoos, and her nose is pierced. She's wearing what looks like one large tie-dyed scoop neck sock, boots, and a flannel shirt tied around her waist. Her earrings remind me of trout flies. The manager seems slightly terrified of her himself. She and I watch him retreat. I've never felt more alien. I like it.

"I've been thinking about what you said about finding an old alien," I say. "I'm on a peppermint ice cream stakeout, and it looks like you just bought it all."

She gives me this penetrating look, really drills in. The Christmas carols fade into silence, the fluorescents seem to dim. I can feel the cold radiating from her shopping cart. I'm slightly terrified of her myself. "I guess your wait is over then, isn't it?"

"You getting some chocolate sauce to go with that?" I ask with a chuckle, though it comes out more like a squeak and a snort.

"I have plenty at home. Want to come on over for a bowl? I could use some help unloading this. Bring Myrna. She and Avatar can play."

I'm a bad person. My dog's out in the car. I know you're not supposed to leave them unattended, even in December, but she loves it. Like most border collies, she loves to watch. I always park somewhere she'll have maximum visibility to keep tabs on the flock. Katyana must've seen her when she drove up in her decrepit mini pickup. She had to know I was here.

I know what I just said about the health risks involved in the consumption of high-fat, high-sugar dairy products, but this is a unique situation. I'm intrigued. There is a far fringe opinion in the ACAB community that the aliens didn't die, didn't go anywhere, that they traded in their old worn-out bodies for new ones, that they traded in their old lives by necessity when they did so, in order to live new lives in younger, healthier bodies. Like Katyana's. Old souls in young flesh. I've never liked this theory much because it would mean my parents didn't die or return home from an important mission; they abandoned me and Ollie so they could live a new life without us.

Katyana's saying it's true. "Think of *them*," she says. "You and your brother were moving on. Maybe they had health problems. A new life is a pretty wonderful thing."

She says this like she knows what she's talking about. We're standing in the kitchen of her garage apartment. It's dusk. The days are short. She's backlit by the light through the kitchen door. A light over the stove shines on her face. I try to imagine it, a new life.

She puts on a kettle for tea. On the wall beside the stove is a huge spice rack like the one I have at home. I know now why Deetermeyer snuffled my parents' clothes. He was looking for this scent. If I were to bury my nose in the flannel shirt Katyana is wearing it would smell like this spicy, steamy kitchen. She says she will miss this place, a cozy garage apartment behind an empty house with a Sold sign in front. The new owners want her out by the end of the month, so their son can move in. Happy New Year.

She dishes up huge bowls of peppermint ice cream and explains that aliens have mastered the human genome, and periodically they trade in old bodies for new ones—all of them. Katyana's terribly sorry, but she's lied to me, she says, out of necessity. She isn't the daughter of original aliens. She's one of them in a new body she's only had for slightly more than a decade. "Y2K was a busy time. All the hubbub made it easy to launch a new life." She apologizes for the deception, but she had to decide if I could be trusted with this knowledge. If I was truly ready. She has a tiny urn filled with chocolate sauce imported from Switzerland with a little spigot. She loads it on. My mouth is watering.

I follow her into the tiny living room, and we sit down. I'm not surprised to see, hanging on the wall, a Paint by Number identical to my mom's. I still can't make out that third eye.

"Ready?" I ask.

"For a new life, a new body."

At this point Myrna is cowering under the coffee table, taking a break from Avatar who, although he's neutered like all alien dogs, kept humping her when we first got here, head, rear, anywhere, while Katyana and I were loading the freezer in the garage with ice cream. Avatar seems to have trouble finding a happy medium. Katyana told him to quit, and he did, but Myrna doesn't trust the situation and would like to leave *now*. I'm all ears, however, and I ignore her beseeching looks.

"Will your car make it to New Mexico?" Katyana asks, her mouth full of ice cream. She doesn't have to tell me her truck won't. The inspection sticker expired in March. You can hear and smell that the exhaust system won't pass, and there's a huge crack in the windshield. I wouldn't drive it anywhere I couldn't walk away from.

"I think so," I say, though I'm not thinking. My mouth is frozen in creamy fat sweetness, burning with peppermint and dark, earthy chocolate. It's like crack but more deadly. I swallow it anyway. She doesn't have to say where in New Mexico. Mom and Dad's last destination.

We're headed for the abyss.

We talk for hours working out the details. I have a thousand questions. She has a thousand answers. I cook, we eat. I can't remember the last time I was so happy. It's not the prospect of a new body, though that would certainly be welcome, if still difficult to believe in. It's just a night like this, full of questions and answers, plans for an insane odyssey, a midnight meal. It's been a long time. It's nights like this you live for, isn't it? Nights you never forget.

You must admit I have to tell my brother about this, and he has to listen. He's older than me, for Christ's sake. He could go any time. He has a terrible diet. I call him from the gas station where they're making my Saturn roadworthy. It only has to make it one way, I explain to the mechanic, though I don't explain why. Katyana and I plan to leave first thing in the morning. It's a terrible time of year to travel, but what can you do?

Ollie doesn't pick up right away, probably still pissed from the last time we spoke.

When I tell him where I'm going, he shuts up in a hurry. "It's not an abyss," I explain. "It's a transdimensional portal to the nearest alien medical facility where the procedure will be performed. Because of the transdimensional drift, when I return, I'll actually emerge back here in town."

I can hear him breathing in and out. Finally he says, "What does she look like, Stan? This woman half your age you're driving across the country with in an old clunker?"

"Like an alien goddess."

"Stan, you can't do this."

This time I hang up on him. The elder alien brother telling the younger he can't do something is a near guarantee it will be done. That's how I ended up married the first and fourth times. I couldn't let him tell me what to do. Not that this is about another marriage. I was just trying to offer him the opportunity for a new life as well, not another chance to get all up in my business, like he knows a thing about wise romantic choices.

Katyana has a friend we can stay with in New Mexico while we're scouting out the abyss, so we'll be cool once we get there, she says. We just have to make it from here to there. Money's tight for us both, her more than me. Social Security keeps me afloat; I do a little freelance, some teaching. I used to write all kind of things before the cookbooks clicked. The web killed cookbooks. Recipes are free, as they should be. I never believed in recipes anyway.

Her unemployment just ran out. She was an archeologist working for the Department of Transportation. You can imagine how that went. She, of course, has no parents she can turn to. They're light years away. Gas will cost plenty, meals. At first, she's talking like we should just drive straight through, just go for it, four hour shifts, but over dinner in Knoxville, she asks, "How many more hours?" She looks totally beat, and she's supposed to take the wheel after dessert.

There's a table topper for Seasonal Treats, and Katyana ordered two peppermint ice creams with chocolate sauce for dessert even before she decided on dinner, which drew a bemused look from the waitress, a lanky, curious blonde. Katyana told her that we're going home for the holidays; that no, she doesn't know what kind of feathers those are on her earrings; that yes, people have told her she looks like some actress I've never heard of who "kicked butt" in a movie I have heard of but assumed I wouldn't like. I suspect the waitress is smitten. Perfectly understandable.

I break the news. "We have to cross Tennessee, Arkansas, Oklahoma, a bit of Texas, and half of New Mexico, and we're there. Twenty-one or -two hours if we don't stop too often, though we need to give the dogs a proper walk sometime, or they'll drive us crazy."

We got a late start. It took a little doing getting Avatar and Myrna installed in the backseat where they seem to have worked it out. Our stuff is crammed in the trunk. The abundant caffeine Katyana's downed in a myriad of forms is starting to fade, and she's about to crash. She revives a bit when the ice cream arrives. She digs in for a while. I pick at mine. One binge is enough for me. The sweetness is cloying, the fat, toxic. I let it melt.

"How come you never hit on me?" she asks, seemingly changing the subject. She's finished her bowl and accepts mine, stirs it into a dark purple swirl I remember from childhood. She sucks on the spoon with each bite.

"I'm twice your age," I say.

She shrugs a shoulder, takes another bite. "That doesn't stop Dave. That doesn't stop Bill."

"Bill? I didn't know he had it in him."

"Oh yeah. He started talking tantric with me one morning early when it was just the two of us, if you can imagine. But back to you. I've seen how you look at me. Are you a perfect gentleman? I've heard of those."

She's teasing, flirting a little, but I know what she's asking. "Have you read *The Sun Also Rises*?" I ask.

"That's Hemingway, isn't it? I read the other one. *A Farewell to Arms*. Why?"

"I was looking for a delicate shorthand. You've heard of prostate cancer? I had surgery five years ago. They warn you that there are risks, but the percentages look terrific, and if there are any problems, they tell you, we have these great drugs now. I know you've heard of Viagra. Didn't work, horrible side effects. I've been a perfect gentleman ever since. Just recently they released a study saying surgery like mine wasn't maybe such a great idea after all."

I've never made this speech to another person on Planet Earth before.

She holds my gaze. She takes my hands. "I'm sorry that happened to you."

I shrug. "The cancer's gone."

"Whenever you're ready," the waitress says, laying down the check, giving Katyana a dazzling smile. Surely, she must be thinking, this old man is her father. Little does she know we're only passing through on our way to another dimension where Katyana's nearly twice my age.

Out in the parking lot, Katyana gives me a daughterly hug, and we get in the car, me behind the wheel. Before I put the key in the ignition, she asks, "Can we afford a night there?" pointing to a Quality Inn a few parking lots over. "They usually take dogs." We means me. She's totally broke, her last credit card in tiny pieces. She made her fingers little scissors when she told the tale last night.

When they hear the word *dogs*, they come wide awake. Avatar's long and curly snout thrusts forward, Myrna beside him, peering out the windshield, like they're reading the marquee: *Welcome Chris and Kristin*. Can't disappoint the flock.

"No problem," I say, feeling a little more like "A Clean, Well-Lighted Place" than *The Sun Also Rises.* Everyone should read Hemingway for a dose of lean despair when the AARP card comes in the mail. *The Old Man and the Sea*, however, is just exhausting. I've never been much of a fisherman.

All they have in a dogs-allowed room is a king-size bed. After we feed and walk the dogs, who've bonded and feel refreshed, they break into a crazed play session chasing each other all over the tiny room while

Katyana and I cower and laugh on the bed. Avatar rolls over on his back and lets Myrna climb gleefully all over him. Her breath heaving, her tongue lolling, Myrna smiles at me in delirious gratitude for this Great Adventure, and she's sorry she ever doubted me.

Make no mistake. If I were not an impotent old man, I'd throw myself at Katyana's feet, on top of her, into the abyss—whatever would serve to woo her, but that's not how the world works, is it? Not this one anyway. But it's okay. It really is. It makes things so much simpler in a way.

I lie awake and listen to her sleep, what I can hear over the dogs' companionable snores. They're piled together between us. I listen to her dreaming—troubled murmurs, then something like a whimper and silence.

When I finally fall asleep, I dream I'm living a new life. I step out of a shower into a steam-filled motel bathroom and wipe the condensation off the mirror so I can see the new me. I look exactly the same. The scar runs from an inch above my cock to a couple of inches below my navel.

In the morning, Katyana's sick, and she says not to let her order any more ice cream, and she dines on mostly salads and toast all the way to New Mexico. There's lots of time. The radio's broken. We talk across four states as we watch them glide by. I tell her how it was my third wife, the engineer, who came up with the system I use to produce accurate recipes from a chaotic intuitive process by weighing all the ingredients before and after, so I don't have to keep track along the way. I tell her how I fell so hard for my second wife I went crazy, crazier still when we split up ten years later.

She tells me when she was twenty-two, the age she was when she was renewed, as she calls it, she was terrified to live a new life, had hung on to her old one for way too long and was afraid of being young again—she'd made so many mistakes the first time. She didn't step outside for two weeks, and only then because she'd run out of food.

"Why didn't you just call for delivery?"

She laughs. "I was more scared of who might show up, the face to face. Like they might spot me right away, you know?" She does a gruff voice: "You're alien, aren't you?" She laughs again. "Got over it though, as you can see. I was going to get it right this time, not make the same mistakes." She looks out at the desert landscape, and the smile quickly fades, and her eyes are sad and creased with worry. We're close. The closer we get, the more worried she becomes. We just left Texas.

"Tell me about your friend. Jack, isn't it?"

"That's right. He's just a guy."

"Nice of him to let us stay with him. He knows we're coming, right?"

She doesn't answer right away. "Sort of. He sort of knows I'm coming. I—I didn't tell him about you exactly. I'm sure it will be okay."

I look in the rearview at Myrna and Avatar leaning up against each other like mismatched bookends, listening to our conversation. ACAB dogs are fluent in their owners' languages and often communicate telepathically when the need is great. Myrna lays her head on Avatar's heart and assures me everything will be all right. This abyss plan is my best yet, even better than moving back into Mom and Dad's house, rooting around in my roots. Look how great that's worked out. I adopted her from a shelter after the prostate surgery, when I was healed enough to stand a young dog straining on her lead. We've been through a lot together. I trust her judgment completely.

Katyana looks back from the desert. "Jack's not alien, okay? He doesn't know about us. We can't talk about any of that crazy shit around him, is that clear?" She hears herself and shakes her head. "Sorry. I'm being a bitch. I just don't know how he'll react. I'm sure it will be all right."

That's twice she's sure, so I get the picture. She hasn't a clue, with the stakes a lot higher than taking some foolish old man to the abyss, and she's scared shitless. I've been there plenty of times, but not today for some reason. I'm perfectly happy to be here. You may be like my brother and think I don't know how crazy this is. Don't worry. I do.

She tells me the story of Jack. He's a musician who travels a lot, so he's not here that much, but he likes to be home for the holidays. The travel gets too crazy then. He got stuck in a blizzard once for three days. Jack, she confesses, is her ex.

"You don't seem surprised," she says.

"I figure if you're going to drive across the country to see a guy, it must be somebody like that. When did you see him last?"

"October. He played a gig in Charlottesville. He called me."

I hope she didn't drive that fucking truck of hers to Charlottesville, but I don't ask. "So does he know you're pregnant?"

It takes a while for her to answer. I'm not who she thought I was. That happens when your hair goes white and strangers start calling you sir. She has a lot to sort out. "No. He thinks I'm coming to visit, that I've gotten a ride. I'm sorry."

"Don't be. You are coming to visit, you have gotten a ride. I wouldn't have missed it for the world. The abyss is about ninety minutes from Jack's place according to the GPS. I can go on my own. Maybe I'll stop off to see where D. H. Lawrence is buried. That was the last place Mom and Dad visited, apparently, before they took the plunge."

"Stan, don't—"

I hold up my hand. "*Or* I'll wait for you in town, if you like, in case it doesn't go well with Jack. We can talk about me later. You should probably think about what you're going to say to Jack."

But she has one more revelation.

"Simon Deetermeyer's my dad," she says. "That's how come I know so much about ACABs. I'm not really an alien. I'm knocked up and thirty-three and desperate. I'm sorry."

"That's okay."

"He was so excited when you came in. It'd been a while since anyone had found him."

"How's your dad doing? He hasn't been answering my emails."

"His funding was cut. He's taken it pretty hard. Nobody knows where he is. The house foreclosed. That's why I have to move out. It was only supposed to be temporary anyway. I'm not worried. I'll figure it out. He's done this before, totally lost it. Dad's crazy."

"I sort of figured that. Lots of brilliant men are crazy."

"You sure you're okay?"

"I've never been better."

She accepts that. It must show. "This'll be good," she says, "knowing you're waiting. It'll force me to get to the point." She gives me directions to Jack's place like it's no big deal. She's just going to see a guy about her life.

***

Jack's place is one of several lavish homes carved into the foothills near Taos for rich musicians, artists, and the like. I'm sure there's a celebrity chef or two on these winding roads. I let her off at the gate with Avatar and a backpack, and Jack buzzes her in.

"Hey," I say. "If it doesn't work out. I have plenty of room."

"You're too nice," she says.

"My dad told me there was no such thing, but he was an alien." I wonder how he'd have felt about it if he'd lived to be my age. I imagine him feeling pretty much the same.

As we watch Katyana and Avatar walk up the drive, Myrna whimpers with regret, but I tell her not to worry. Katyana said it herself, Jack is no alien.

I wind around the hill and park on a curve off the road with a nice view of the night sky. Myrna sits in the front passenger seat, still warm from Katyana, and wonders what's up. I turn on my phone so Katyana can call me whenever she gets the chance. I've left it off as we've crossed the country, enjoying the silence. It's stuffed with messages I ignore.

I told Katyana I would wait in town, but what's in town? Just more trouble for my credit card. This place is a lot different from last time I was here thirty years ago when there were adobe huts where Jack's house sits. I wait under a myriad of stars. The more I look, the more there are.

My phone lights up. It's Ollie.

"Thank God," he says. "You're alive. I've been calling and calling. Don't you ever check your fucking messages?"

"My phone was dead," I lie calmly. "What time is it there? Must be late."

"Where are you?"

"I'm almost there. It's just up the road, but I plan to wait until sunrise. No sense trying to find an abyss in the dark. You should see this place, Ollie. The stars are fucking unbelievable, just like Mom always said. It's an incredibly beautiful mystery."

"She said that sort of thing to you, Stan."

"She said it to you too, Ollie. You just weren't listening."

"Mom was crazy, Stan."

"We're all crazy. Pick your crazy."

"So you still with this young girl?"

"That's up in the air at the moment. She more than likely will need a place to live. I'm waiting to see."

"You've got to be joking."

"I have plenty of room. She's broke and pregnant. She wants to keep the kid. She hasn't said so, but it seems likely."

"Jeez, this is your kid?"

"*Right*, Ollie. It's my kid. Somehow the vasectomy and being gutted like a fish didn't do the trick."

"I'm sorry. I was forgetting."

Fucking incredible. I laugh out loud, electrons dancing in the midst of the Milky Way, inconclusive evidence of intelligent life. Another call comes in. It's Katyana.

"I have to take this," I say.

"Listen to me, Stan."

"Later, Ollie."

I answer.

"Come get me," she whispers. "I'll be by the gate."

I don't have to ask how it went. I wind back around the hill to where I left her. Avatar sits beside her like a good soldier. They get in and settle into place. I let her have a moment. Myrna showers Avatar with kisses.

"Abyss or home?" I ask.

Make no mistake. The abyss is real. It's a new life either way.

"Home," she says, and smiles at me, almost like she's happy. Shelter from the storm. Maybe that's why the aliens came in the first place. It was all an accident. There was no mission. They found themselves here far from the turquoise skies of home and had to make the best of it.

This time we drive straight through, swinging by her garage apartment to pick up a few things. We want to make it home by Christmas, and we make it just in time to watch *It's a Wonderful Life* and cry, the both of us. I set my phone up on the TV and we pose for a photo, the four of us, teary-eyed, smiling, and wagging, and send it to Ollie with our Christmas greetings to let him know we're okay, to maybe cheer him up a little. He's alone these days. Nobody wants to be alone on Christmas. We're holding Katyana's Paint by Number between us, lifted from her dad's collection of alien artifacts, as a reminder of where we came from.

The baby—she does want to keep it—is due around Independence Day. Make of that what you will. No fireworks, however. They scare the shit out of Myrna. Next week is the New Year *and* fifth Tuesday, a serendipitous synchronicity we plan to celebrate in the ACAB way.

See you down by the riverside.

Orphan Pirates of the Spanish Main

When asked about his own childhood by his children, Dad would say something like "I was a galley slave on a pirate ship, and we sailed the Spanish Main!" I doubt my dad knew anything about any kind of ship or even where the Spanish Main was exactly. He just liked the way it sounded stringing the words together. I don't think they even had galley slaves on pirate ships, certainly not in the early twentieth century when Dad was a kid, but none of that mattered in the least when Dad made a story of something.

He was once attacked by a herd of wildebeests while mowing the grass, when they mistook the new riding lawn mower for a Land Rover on safari and made a perfectly understandable preemptive strike. He emerged unscathed, but Mom's newly planted shrubbery, part of a brief but passionate fling with horticulture, was mowed down in the melee, and the mower's blade was busted, so Dad never had to ride the damn thing again. He preferred his reel. It took him a dreamy afternoon to mow the grass, the blades sighing and clattering.

The puppy he brought home from his travels had been rescued from a space capsule in New Mexico and might be a Russian cosmonaut, an alien, or—my favorite—Top Secret, which explained why she was more intelligent and loving than all other dogs. We named her Natasha—we were all big *Rocky and Bullwinkle* fans. At the end of her miraculous life, Dad buried her in the backyard, knelt and cried over her late into the night. I fell asleep at my windowsill watching him, crying too. I grew up thinking crying was okay if you felt like it.

He was raised in a boarding school for gifted salesmen—the campus looked like a string of motels—where he was taught how to drive all over hell and half of Georgia, pad his expense account, and tell every joke ever told that couldn't be told in front of me and my brother. *Well*, he'd say. *Maybe just one. Just sort of dirty.* Mom, giggling, told him not to, which alerted us we were about to hear something good. When you're hearing about some woman stuck in a toilet on her wedding night, a plumber on the way to rescue her, you don't press for details about the storyteller's childhood.

Which version of his childhood? There were several to choose from. These are just salesmen's samples, not for resale. He never told us the truth. Or if he did, it was buried under so much bullshit, you couldn't find it with a whole army of pirates and farmers' daughters. He didn't want to tell us, plain and simple.

He wasn't always like that. If I really needed to talk to him about something serious—which comes up more often when you're single digits than you might think—he dropped the bullshit and listened like no one else.

I finally asked Mom. I had too many ideas running around in my head of these different kids Dad had been to keep them straight, like his life was three or four crazy movies all mashed up together. I imagined my favorites. Abbott & Costello meet Fred Astaire and Frankenstein East of Eden. I knew some of them weren't true, couldn't be true, that he was just pretending, but I didn't *always* know, and I didn't know which ones *might* be true, which little boy I could imagine myself being, because more than anything in the world, I wanted to be like him.

Turns out none of them were him. Young Master Smoke and Mister Mirrors. Who might you imagine he was? Who would you like him to be? Pick one of those. Who he really was, like Natasha's mysterious origins, was classified. I've come to believe he was an alien who had taken on human form—Mom too—and that made me and my brother essentially aliens too, but that's not what she told me.

"Your father was an orphan," Mom said. "He grew up in a Catholic orphanage. He doesn't like to talk about it."

I often wish she hadn't said that last part because I'm one of those kids, even now, at sixty-seven, who takes things to heart, and I never asked the follow-up questions while he was around to ask. I was too busy being charmed like everybody else. Lots of aliens were planted in orphanages, old enough to know their mission, but too old to stand a chance of adoption.

I sort of knew he was an orphan before I asked. Not having paternal grandparents was a clue, but I wasn't the only kid without. Some kids didn't have fathers. What's a couple of grandparents? What I hadn't known was that Dad never had a real home when he was little. He lived in one. He never had anybody. I wish I could've talked to him about it. Who knows? Maybe he did too. There's a whole lot of things I don't like to talk about with anyone, I would talk about with my dad if he were still alive.

Like my brother, for instance. It's like we had a different identical father. Like I said—Mister Mirrors. All my wives have said there's no mistaking Ollie and I are brothers—the voice, the timing, gestures, sense of humor. It's only in the trivial matters like deeply cherished beliefs where we differ. Also, I'm tall and skinny, and he's neither, even though we have the same big blue eyes.

We both have a passion for cooking. Dad taught us. Alien men love to cook.

Dad told me he first learned to cook when he was playing Mr. Potato Head, in a hot steamy kitchen, and Potato said, "'Hey, don't you think I'd be more comfortable and appealing without this dirty brown coat on?' One thing led to another, and before you know it, he taught me how to make perfect mashed potatoes."

I was making perfect mashed potatoes when he told me this. Dad had taught me how. I was standing on a stepstool, mashing. His hand was wrapped around mine to make sure I kept a good grip on the pot handle. The potholder, which had a cat on it because I loved them, was battle-scarred, with singed edges and greasy stains, but it was mine. We bought it at the grocery store because I liked it. Dad couldn't say no. I suspect that's because he never had anybody to ask for anything.

"What about gravy?" I asked. "Did Potato teach you that?" That was the lesson for the day. He was going to show me gravy. We were in a kitchen redolent with the smell of roasting beef garnished with garlic and rosemary. I had watched him truss it, snipped the twine with the massive kitchen shears when instructed, helped him insert whole cloves of garlic into the flesh.

"Gravy came later," Dad said, "on a wagon train out west—somewhere between Death Valley and Tombstone. The settlers were looking for a new cook after they'd just staked the last one out on an anthill for the awful gooey lumpy gravy he made them, and buzzards were eating his eyeballs, which the settlers joked seemed to be as gummy as his gravy. Don't believe what you see on TV. Settlers weren't always nice. Some were so ornery, folks back home were probably begging them to leave town. Don't believe that pioneering spirit stuff either. Most of them were just leaving some kind of mess they'd made of their lives, so that middle of nowhere was the only option left. There wasn't a lot of singing around the campfire. Everybody was scared to take the cook's job, so they gave it to me because I was just a kid, and they thought they could push me around."

"What did you do?" I asked, mashing furiously as Dad poured in a little more hot milk. Of course I asked. I was a skilled straight man by the time I was in first grade. Turns out—my favorite part—he went out in the moonlight in the desert, away from all the cranky settlers, where a lizard not unlike the chameleon I got at the State Fair of Texas only weeks before turned into an Indian shaman who taught him how to make the best gravy in the world on a campfire under a billion stars, the secrets of which he intended to share with me once we got the roast out of the oven and scraped the pan.

I figure he worked in the kitchen where he lived, cooking for all the kids in the orphanage, the priests and nuns and whatever. He always cooked too much, stored it away in a massive freezer. That's often what we ate when he traveled, which he did a lot. Mom didn't always feel like cooking.

She liked his stories too, and I was often aware of her as an amused and loving audience to the wild tales he told me and my brother. Before we came along I imagine his stories were a little different. She loved him. You could see it. She wasn't always happy about it—with good reason—but she loved him. We all did. He needed that. He never had anybody before the three of us.

He was a terrible disciplinarian. A kid would have to be brain-dead not to get around Dad, and me and Ollie were far from brain-dead. Mom would say no but Dad never did, and they never overruled the other. "Ask Dad" was like open sesame. Ollie used to use his time on the phone when Dad called home from the road to get around Mom, and it drove her crazy.

I only took serious advantage once, when I malingered through six weeks of eighth grade because I loathed it—with good reason. Today, I would have the sadistic shop teacher arrested, the rabidly racist history teacher fired, but these were the good old days, and they were duly appointed by the state to build my character deep in the heart of Texas. My only option was deceit. I did a pretty good cough, gave myself a sporadic fever by touching the thermometer to my reading lamp, timing my performances for when Dad was home. I enjoyed my reclusive freedom with Clarke and Asimov and Bradbury and Heinlein, somewhere out there among the stars where shamans make gravy for galley slaves, gathering enough inner strength to eventually return to school and prosper. I built my own character. Several.

I think Dad knew I was faking but understood I needed to hide out for a while and feel safe. I could navigate the bullies. I had mastered the art of invisibility, but brainwashers and torturers ran the place, and they had their eyes on me.

Ollie, older by four years, led a wilder youth, which resulted in his joining the military at the suggestion of a judge who said he might overlook the reckless mistakes of a patriot willing to serve his country. Ancient history. Now he's settled down and out in suburbia with his dogs and his kitchen and his last wife.

I'm no different, except I prefer the city and one dog at a time. My current situation's somewhat complicated. Technically, I'm married to Katyana, a woman half my age, but that's mostly a means to get her on my health insurance and give them some financial stability, her and her son Dylan, legally my son as well, though biologically not. They don't make you prove it at the hospital, turns out. All you have to do is step up and take credit. Nothing's cross-referenced, or they might've noticed I had a vasectomy a few decades back and a sex-ending prostatectomy five years ago. Katyana comes with a dog as well, Avatar, a stunning blue-gray standard poodle my intense little border collie Myrna adores with embarrassing intensity. They were both already too damn smart for dogs individually. Now they collude.

My brother doesn't approve of my recent marriage. Par for the course. My brother and I don't talk much these days, so I know it's important when he calls me. He's seventy-one.

Not a lot of good news peaks then, unless you want to talk religion, which I probably shouldn't, but I will. You can't expect an old man to stay on the subject—or, rather, the subject is larger than it might first appear. Aliens have a hard time with religion. Earthbound religions seem puny in the face of the cosmos. Dad again. The orphanage was Catholic. We most definitely weren't. Dad once told me he had wanted to be a priest when he was a kid until he figured out a few things—no details, though I could imagine. He wasn't anything in particular, but there was a resolute certainty that he was no longer Catholic. Mom picked the church. Mom liked the idea of church. She wasn't picky about doctrinal issues. Dad only went if Mom insisted, for whatever reason.

The only time he was enthusiastic about church besides weddings was when there was a stand-in minister one summer when we still lived in Texas who was eighty if he was a day, a wrinkled, liver-spotted old man with wild white hair and a voice that didn't sound like a preacher's but quiet and reedy and endlessly fascinated with the stories he told and the people he told them about. He had just retired from a life of missionary service in Africa. There was plenty of Bible in the sermons, as I recall, but he always came back to Africa, where people lived whole other lives like nothing we could imagine in Irving, Texas. He was terrific. I remember once he told the story of a refugee, though at the time I didn't know what that was, but I remember he only had one leg, and he was trying to find his mother, and he came to the minister and asked if Jesus could help him. When I looked over at Dad, there were tears on his face. Mom was wet-faced too, and smiling, happy because Dad was going to church. More than she wanted to go herself, I think, she wanted Dad to find a way to make it up with God. But the summer ended.

Dad went only once to hear the new, permanent minister—tedious and doctrinaire. Dad cursed him on the drive home, though he took us to breakfast, and we all gorged. I can't remember the minister's name, but I can still see his face. He was not a happy man. He was my first serious dose of Calvinist Sin, which only plunged me deeper into boyhood pantheism, for which I suppose I should thank him. To this day it remains my one true religion.

Ollie and I both have had our spasms of religious fervor of one sort or another, but we've ended up in the same place. Sunday mornings, we'd both rather be home in our kitchens, cooking. I'm making vegan, no-fat zucchini muffins. Later, Katyana and I plan to take Dylan and the dogs down to the James River, our sanctuary. I confess to being a very happy man.

That's when Ollie calls. "Stan," he finally confesses after beating around every right-wing bush he can flail in an accent that still sounds like Irving, Texas more than a half-century later in a vain attempt to sucker me into a fight so one of us can hang up like we usually do: "I can't cook anymore. I lost my sense of smell."

I suppose I should explain that's how we both cook. It's the alien way, the way we were taught. If you don't like spicy food, don't even drive by our houses. We never use recipes, but we can sniff them out from a tasty restaurant dish, recreate them at home—without the salt, fat, and sugar in my case. I'm on a project to unclog my abused arteries. Ollie still has his addictions.

"You can't smell anything? Have you been to the doctor?"

"I can still smell. The dogs still stink, the fucking compost next door. I just have no sense for it anymore, no confidence. I stood over a soup the other night with whole allspice berries, no idea how many to put in or none at all. It felt awful. One minute I had the idea of exactly how I wanted it to taste, you know? Next minute, gone. The soup was bland and disappointing. Camille pretended to like it, but I could tell. She said maybe I should write things down, use a recipe. The evening went downhill from there."

Camille's new. I'm sure he wants to impress her. I can imagine how he feels. I don't get to say that often about my brother, so I nurse the feeling, try to get caught up in his crisis, help him struggle to overcome it. Rescuing my big brother was a major fantasy when I was ten, when I wasn't drowning him in a vat of snake venom. My heart goes out to him.

"Why couldn't we have normal parents like everyone else?" he says bitterly and torpedoes my sympathy.

Why does he have to blame everything on Mom and Dad? "Go to McDonald's, Ollie. There's probably a McDad on the menu, with cheese. A fried McMom."

"I've asked you not to call me that."

"Right. Oliver. Dad has nothing to do with your fucking nose, Ol-i-ver, so why don't you put a lid on it for a change? Have you tried a neti pot?"

"A *what*?"

I imagine explaining sinus irrigation as an ancient and effective Indian treatment to my brother, followed by his near-certain sneering dismissal, and spare myself the aggravation. "Why don't you come for a visit and we can work it out," I hear myself saying in stunned disbelief. "You've never been." It's true. I've been down to Florida three times since he's moved there, and he's never come to see me in Richmond.

Is that what I really want? I ask myself, and I try to remind Ollie of what he's getting himself into. "You can meet Katyana and Dylan."

I'm trying to scare him off, but it's too little, too late. Bad life choices his little brother's made to disapprove of? What's not to like about that? He's touched by my offer.

He accepts.

What have I done?

"Bring Camille," I think to say, but he gives one of his mysterious guttural chuckles I'm supposed to understand because I'm his little brother.

"Just me," he says. "Is this a good time?"

I've come to believe all times are good times, each moment wondrous. Everything happens when it should. Even me and my big mouth. "It's perfect."

I recount it all to Katyana, and she thinks it will be delightful. She's the only one. What possessed me to want to help my brother? I'm certainly not his keeper. Not that we both don't need one. Our parents were strange, out of step with their culture, and maybe they didn't prepare us for life in the real world, but I've made my peace with them. I've tried to explain to Ollie that Mom and Dad were aliens whose parenting styles were somewhat unconventional for humans of the time, but he's having none of it. Too bad. It would be a comfort, but he doesn't need any grief from me. If he's coming to see me, he must be at the end of the last fiber of his rope. Shit. He must be in fucking free fall.

We all meet him at the airport—Katyana wants Dylan to experience the airport. We're a joyful little family unit, Dylan at his giggly-gurgly best, when I spot Ollie coming down the glass hallway, and my fears are confirmed. Something's seriously wrong. He's nice, sweet even. Katyana's gorgeous, and Dylan adorable, but this is my brother we're talking about. He doesn't even give me that look I've come to expect from any male who meets her and discovers we're married. He cradles Dylan in his arms and smiles at me with poignant envy. Is this really my brother?

There's an election looming, nasty inflammatory billboards everywhere. No matter which side you're on, it's loathsome to live in a battleground state. Ollie stares past the shrill slogans at the trees. We even go through a roundabout on the way home, a virulent passion of my brother's for some reason, and he says not a word, just gazes forlornly at the lovely Richmond architecture, looking like he might start crying any minute. Maybe he's remembering when he used to live here, when Mom and Dad were still alive. He shows a spark of life when he comes inside the house and the dogs are all over him—we both like most dogs better than we like most people—but something's weighing on him. This cooking business is just the tip of the iceberg. I'm thinking the worst, some horrible wasting disease. Guilt geysers up inside of me. I haven't been the best brother in the world, and now he has weeks to live. I feel awful.

He doesn't care. It's not about me. When I get him alone, he confesses that he and Camille are separated, that she said she couldn't stand to live with a seventy-one-year-old man who still has serious issues with his parents when they've been dead for more than forty years. She said some things that weren't very nice, made all the worse because they were true. Ollie's a mess.

"Issues? She says 'issues'?" She's a semi-retired counselor, though I'm not sure who or what she counsels about.

He nods, snuffles. "She's right," he says.

Maybe she is, but she doesn't have to say *issues*. Makes him sound like a client. He just needs to open his eyes and see. Ollie seems to have no idea what a gift it is to have had exceptional parents. Mom was an artist, though she never tried to sell anything, painting hollowed-out eggs, neckties, paint-by number landscapes with the palette changed so as to depict a scene from her home planet—never anything ordinary and mundane, no big-eyed girls or forlorn clowns. She made sculptures out of trash before everybody was doing that. The house always smelled like one glue or another. She threw herself into mosaics for a while. You never saw her without this tool, like pliers with jaws, that she used to snip the tiles. The sound drove the dog crazy—I guess it reminded her of having her nails cut—so when Mom had completely covered the kitchen counter, she abandoned mosaics so Natasha would come out from under my bed.

The mosaic was a city with domes and minarets and obelisks and ziggurats. Mom told me what they were when I asked. There was a lot going on. When you looked real close, some little chip of tile up along the roofline looked like a cat, or there were shadowy faces looking out the windows. She made it without a picture or plan or anything. Just snip, snip, snip, gluing down these pieces until she was done. I asked her if it was a real place, and she said, "Not anymore. It's how I remember it." The next thing she said was something like "Don't you have homework?"

"I have to go," Ollie says to me now. "We both have to go. To the abyss." The abyss is where Mom and Dad's earthly lives ended.

No, we don't, but I have to say I'm intrigued. This isn't like him. I figured Ollie gave up on bold symbolic journeys a long time ago. I tried going to the abyss and didn't make it, thank goodness. Once is enough for me. "All this because of a few allspice berries, an overly cautious soup? What's going on, Ollie? Oliver. I don't see the connection."

"I received a message."

"A message?"

"From Mom."

Before I can tell him he's nuts, he hands me a postcard. On one side is a photo of a sand painting I've seen before. On the other is a map of a portion of New Mexico with the abyss marked with a red X. "Your Father Needs You!" is written in Mom's loopy cursive. It's postmarked Tucumcari, ten days ago.

Mom's last artistic obsession, in the months before she and Dad took off for a vacation in the southwest, was a sand painting. Like the Navajo, she explained. She spent weeks just assembling the jars of different color sand. Dad would bring jars home from his travels. It took her a day and a night to sift the thing onto the garage floor, grain by grain, until it took up the whole garage. I was home for the summer, just out of college. Ollie had his own place, just out of the military. He'd come over for dinner to celebrate our birthdays, a few days apart.

After dinner, Mom had us take off our shoes and told us to walk out in the middle of the sand painting, me and Ollie both, but Ollie refused. Mom got pretty upset. Couldn't he do this one small thing for her? What did it matter *why*? While they continued to argue, I walked out into the middle of it like she asked, messing up the perfectly precise design as little as possible. It was sort of Navajo, I guess, with these long spindly guys standing like a chorus line, but their eyes were big almond eyes, and they had multi-colored angel wings. It was one of the most beautiful things I've ever seen.

She had me sit in the middle of it at the feet of the spindly-legged angels, while Ollie wouldn't shut up about how stupid it was to make something like this and then just screw it up, that she needed help, that there were therapies, new drugs and treatments, but Mom ignored him and spoke to only me if he wouldn't listen, as if he weren't there: "Don't let them change you. Don't let them define you. Don't let them diminish the things you love. They don't mean to, but they will if you let them." She said some other things on the same theme I don't remember exactly. Ollie never listened. For years I wondered who "they" were. I've come to realize she meant humans.

Dad called us inside for dessert while Mom vacuumed up the sand painting with a Shop-Vac.

A week later they were gone, plunged into the abyss, an obscure site in New Mexico Mom just had to see. They had been planning this trip even longer than she'd been collecting grains of sand. Some say they didn't die, that they were headed home. I guess I'm one.

I stare at the postcard now. It's the sand painting on the garage floor. She took a bunch of photos of it with a camera mounted on the garage ceiling before the big fight with Ollie. I'm trying to imagine how and why it's now, impossibly, a postcard in my hands. "How come I didn't get one?"

"Cause you stepped into the sand painting, and I didn't. That's why you've healed, and I haven't. I did some research. That's what they're for. Healing. Mom was trying to heal us. That's why I've lost my sense of smell."

I don't see the last connection, but I let it pass. He's actually taking something unusual Mom and Dad did seriously, for once, instead of seeing it as further evidence they were crazy. I don't ask why, if I'm all healed—whatever he thinks that means—he needs me to tag along on this foolish journey, because I already know. He would feel too ridiculous otherwise. I'm the one who supposedly believes in this wacky alien shit. I'm the one who should be getting spooky postcards in the mail, not him. He needs his little brother along to boost his confidence that he hasn't totally lost his mind. Late-onset schizophrenia is just one of many judgments out there for an old man who starts talking crazy, but you can always tell your little brother, right? He won't rat you out.

I tell Katyana Ollie wants me to go out to the abyss with him, and she immediately says I should because he's my brother, "and how many things has he ever asked you to do for him?" Katyana's big on family loyalty. But then I get to the part about the postcard, and she stops me. "Let me see it."

She looks it over front and back, shaking her head. I think she might cry. "I have to go with you," she says.

"You've seen this before?"

"It's one of Daddy's alien artifacts. Look at the handwriting."

"I did. It's my mom's."

"Not the message. Your brother's address. It's Daddy's handwriting."

I'd completely missed it. The mailing address is even a different color ink. The lettering, tiny, precise printing. I've seen it before myself. It's Dr. Deetermeyer's, Katyana's father, who first introduced me to the idea of my parents' alien origins. He's been missing for almost a year after a nervous breakdown, or whatever it's called now. Katyana was pretty upset when he wasn't around for Dylan's birth. He's done it before, taken off for parts unknown, only to turn up months later, sometimes with a new identity, a position at some new university. Katyana's the only one left to go looking for him. He's as wacky as a bag of cats, but he's a fucking genius at the same time. It can be hard to suss out the borderline.

"You're saying *he* sent this card?"

"You don't think it's from your dead mother, do you?"

"But what about the message? It's her handwriting."

She shrugs. "Then she wrote it when she was alive."

"I thought you believed in magical stuff."

"That doesn't mean I believe in ghosts who mail postcards with Forever stamps."

Her dad would have had Ollie's address. He kept a huge database of all of us born to alien parents—who are essentially aliens ourselves—which explains a lot about the course of my life. He's tried to interview as many of us as possible. This may have been his attempt to pique Ollie's interest, so he would agree to such an interview. Deetermeyer wouldn't send it to me for fear of Katyana finding him and revealing him to whatever institution he's bamboozled into funding his research for his definitive work on aliens among us. As a genius without real degrees, his references are all aliens like me.

I would rather believe in aliens than ghosts. Katyana's beliefs don't matter: He's still her father. She has to go find him regardless. No one else will. Her much older sister has washed her hands, she says. This from one who claims Jesus is the answer no matter the question. Katyana's relieved to finally have a clue to her father's whereabouts and a little pissed off to have to pursue it at the same time. She has a baby to take care of, for Christ's sake. Katyana is nothing if not adaptable, however.

She smiles. "A big trip. Maybe that's exactly what we need. We haven't been anywhere since before Dylan was born."

"What about Dylan?" I ask. "We can't just leave him."

"Of course not. He can experience the train."

"Train? Who said anything about a train?"

"Don't you think it would be fun? More comfortable with Dylan and all. We can treat your brother. He's really low. He's much nicer than you said. You'll have time to bond, you know? See the country? Daddy's not going anywhere in the middle of the semester, and neither is the abyss." Even though ours is an unconventional marriage of convenience, scarcely a marriage at all, there's one thing you should know. I will do anything on Earth she asks. I adore her.

Ollie bridles at first. The train? (He hates Amtrak on principle.) But Katyana puts Dylan in his arms and pretty soon Uncle Ollie—Katyana calls him Ollie, and he makes not a whimper—is completely onboard.

That still leaves the dogs. What to do about them. Boarding costs a lot of money. They come out weird, like you would expect intelligent social animals to be after being locked up in a cage for too damn long. Katyana suggests we ask Bill, a retired Unitarian minister and fellow child of aliens, to look after them. We both know him from the dog park. I say retired, but actually they practically forced him out after most of his sermons dwelt on aliens for nearly a year. There was some sort of settlement to make him go away, and he bought a condo a couple of blocks from the church. We're on his balcony having coffee. This is where he sits on Sunday mornings and watches his flock pass by, imagining them feeling guilty for silencing the truth and banishing the messenger. That Unitarian guilt can be some nasty stuff. It comes at you from all directions, and no ritual can resolve it. His pug Clyde's in my lap. I'm rubbing his belly, and he's wiggling and snorting.

Bill's glad to take care of Myrna and Avatar but is eager to discuss other matters. We haven't had a chance to talk since Katyana and I got married.

"What's it like?" he asks.

"Wonderful," I say.

"I can imagine. She is so fucking hot."

It's obvious we're not talking about the same thing. "She is that, but we're not fucking."

"You're kidding. Why not?"

"For starters, I can't."

"What do you mean you can't?"

"Can't. Dick no work. Since the prostate surgery. The surgeon says it should, but it don't."

"What about drugs?"

"Read the possible side effects sometime. I can verify those and more, but what they didn't do was stiffen my dick. I was seeing blue and turning red. I felt like a cartoon character. All for an increased risk of heart attack. One's enough for me, thanks. Trust me. There's worse things than a limp dick."

"I had no idea."

"It doesn't come up in casual conversation. Besides, it makes people uncomfortable."

Bill pauses to think about this, about how he does indeed feel uncomfortable. "So I don't understand. Why did you marry her? You figure you've married so many times, what's one more?"

"I married her for the same reason I have always married. I love her."

"Why on Earth did she marry you?"

"She wanted Dylan to have a father. I claimed paternity. Dylan's legally my son. By marrying we seal the deal legally for him, even if we divorce later."

"You're nuts. Why would you do a thing like that for her? You hardly know her. She's crazy on top of that."

"And you're not? C'mon Bill. We connected. She saved my life. I was headed for the abyss, and she turned me around. It's a small thing, to make their lives easier. They'll have a place to live and a tidy sum when I'm gone."

"You make it sound like it's next week."

"It's always next week, next minute. You have to live now. You can't wait around until you're a better person to do the right thing. Katyana told me you used to hit on her. Would you fuck her if you could?"

His eyes grow huge at the thought. "In a heartbeat."

"But you wouldn't take her in, marry her, help raise her kid?"

He makes a face. Am I nuts? "Who's the real father?"

"A rock star who denies paternity, her ex, who would put up a stink if she pressed it. He doesn't want to complicate his assets and piss off his current girlfriend with a son. I have very simple assets and no girlfriends, and I rather like having a son."

"You change diapers?"

"Of course."

"God, I hated that." Bill and his thirty-something son are what he calls "estranged." He always makes it sound like the grinding wheels of fate have yielded this sad result, symbolized by the middle finger his son raised to him in ninth grade, calling him a hypocrite and his church "stupid." Sounds more like adolescence and a pompous dad to me, but I've never had a son. It was in his quest to understand his failed relationship with his son, as he calls it, that Bill first discovered his alien origins.

So the son never heard the sermons that got his dad bounced from the pulpit. I wonder what son would think of father now, a sad faraway look in his eye that might be for his son, for his flock, or it might be the blanket loss of dementia, though Bill seems sharp enough to me. Just a little nuts. The view from the pulpit must get to you after a while. I'm reminded of Myrna perched on an ottoman in the back room of the house watching her chaotic flock of squirrels. It's her favorite thing to do. How crazy is that?

Clyde, sensing Bill's need, rolls over in my lap, plops down on the floor, and leaps onto Bill's knees like a flying ham. Bill cradles him in his arms. Clyde gazes at him in bug-eyed adoration, snorting sweet nothings, and Bill tells him what a good boy he is.

I rise, bid farewell. "I'll bring the dogs by in the morning. Our train leaves at ten."

I'm in the berth above, Katyana and Dylan sleep below. The ceiling is close, the stars beyond. We're rocketing through the night inside the pleasant roar of the train. I lied to Bill in a way, made it sound like nothing: Impotence. Trouble is, desire persists. Can even grow. Like a cancer. Another unwelcome manifestation of overenthusiastic life.

I've just spent the day traveling with my beautiful wife and child who look at me as if they don't know we're all pretending to be a happy family who love one another. She cradled my white-whiskered face in her hands before I ascended to my berth and said, "Thank you for being such a sweet, sweet man," and kissed me softly, lovingly, on the lips.

She had no intention to render me sleepless, to break my heart. Sweet means patient mostly, not being a self-centered asshole. It's amazing how many men find this difficult. This is no easy journey we've undertaken, and I'm not talking about the train. Sweet's easy. I can do it in my sleep, but dreaming of sweet Katyana, I can't sleep. Longing with no relief. Not a problem I had foreseen, not a bad problem for a man my age to suffer from. I could just not care anymore, like the surgeon said would happen eventually, inevitably. Not that I put much stock in what the surgeon says these days.

I roll out of bed and head for the snack bar, where I find the conductor at one end doing his paperwork, and Ollie in the middle checking his messages. The concession is shut down and dark.

I sit down across from him. "I couldn't sleep."

"Me neither," he says. "I heard from Camille. She says House stinks worse than ever, and he's acting out with me not there. He chewed up her flip-flop."

"I'm impressed. I didn't think he still had it in him from what you told me." House is an eleven-year-old basset-Doberman mix with chronic odor problems, a constant source of Ollie's distress, one of many tributaries. Ollie's always got distress. He stocks up at Costco, clips coupons. I take it as a good sign Camille's looking after the dogs. She must still love him. I don't remember the other dogs or their troubled stories, but you can bet they're a handful.

"The vet wants to give him antibiotics, says the skin issues might point to an underlying infection. He looks like shit. Coat's dull and patchy. He scratches himself all the time. I tried tea-tree oil. Nothing."

"Aloe?"

"Haven't tried that. You think that might help?"

"Make him feel better anyway."

"What do you think about the antibiotics? This vet. She's new. Girl right out of school. I don't trust doctors."

"Me either. But I'm alive because I have three mini Slinkies in my heart: Doctors have their moments. My old lab Alice had something like what you're describing, and antibiotics cleared it up when nothing else would. You don't really think that's a postcard from Mom, do you?"

"What do you think it is?"

"I think she had postcards made of the sand painting, and Katyana's father, Simon Deetermeyer, got ahold of them." I've explained to him about Deetermeyer's theories before, but he wasn't ready to listen then. Now that we're on a train in the middle of the night on the way to the abyss, what else is he going to do?

Ollie's skeptical. It's a lot to swallow, to accept that your parents were aliens who had taken on human form, as Deetermeyer believed our parents to be. "So her father's insane? I thought you said you believed him."

"I do. Not everything. Just the parts I like. Sort of the way Mom approached religion: Sweet Jesus, no Hell, lots of forgiveness and mercy."

"Mom was crazy too."

"That never kept her from being right, Ollie. Like the message on that card. Dad needed us."

"No he didn't. I think he preferred his life out on the road. You know he cheated on her, right?"

Did he think I was deaf? When they fought, old betrayals came up. We never lived anyplace large enough for me not to hear. When Ollie was in the military, and I was in high school, they plumbed Precambrian layers Ollie probably didn't know about before Dad started traveling, while he was still in advertising, about the time I was born. While the adult children of alien beings tend toward serial monogamy, the alien parents like mine typically mated for life in a marriage riddled with infidelities, noisy fights and noisy sex, and lots of mercy and forgiveness.

"So what? Mom knew more than we do, and she stayed with him. They loved each other, Ollie. They loved us. That's enough, isn't it? Case you hadn't noticed, there's people who would kill for that."

"I know," he says, surprising me. "That's more or less what Camille told me."

"What prompted this discussion of Mom and Dad?"

"The postcard. I told her the story of the sand painting and how I wouldn't walk on the damn thing, and she seemed to think I should've, that they aren't meant to last, that's why they're made of sand, and I started arguing with her, and it got pretty heated, and that's when she told me I had issues and left."

"Just like that?"

"She called me 'Ollie'—she never calls me that—and I yelled at her to never ever call me that. *Then* she hit the door."

"Jeez, Ollie. Oliver."

"Shit. You can call me whatever you want: Fucking Idiot, maybe."

"Okay. Fucking Idiot, it is." I call to the conductor. "Is it too late to get a beer?"

He raises his head from his work. My question seems to amuse him. He looks from me to Ollie and back again, and I imagine what he sees—two white-haired old men who should've been asleep miles ago. "I'm afraid it is, gentlemen." To me he adds, "How's the little baby doing? He traveling okay? I know your wife was concerned."

I recognize him as the one who set us up in our compartment. He's young and black and handsome with a dazzling smile. "He's been an angel."

"Glad to hear it. Some babies love the train. Some don't. But they all hate the planes." He stands and buttons his coat. "You gentlemen have a good evening. I have to go make sure no one's sleeping in the aisles." As he walks past us, he stops, then turns around. "I couldn't help overhearing a little of your conversation—that you're headed for the abyss?" He stops there, at the edge, so to speak, and searches our eyes. His nametag says Amir.

"That's right," I say.

"My dad was in the military. We were stationed there once. Security at a research facility right next to it."

"What kind of research?" Ollie asks. I figure I already know.

"Top Secret," Amir says, "but we kids on the base—there weren't but a dozen of us—we heard things, and we thought it was a portal, like for aliens, you know?"

"Our parents died there," Ollie says.

Amir gives him a knowing look, like someone who grew up on the edge of the abyss, shrugs, and smiles. "Maybe not. Know what I'm saying? Maybe not. You gentlemen have a good evening."

When he's gone, Ollie asks, "Do you believe him?"

"Why would he lie to us?"

"To amuse himself."

"I think he was just trying to reach out."

"You think everybody's nice."

"Not everybody, just most people."

"You realize he must've listened to our entire conversation."

"Wouldn't you? A couple of old farts talking about their alien parents? Dylan loved him. He was very sweet to Katyana. I think we should talk to Amir some more."

"Who's Amir?"

"The conductor. I read his nametag."

"I never read those things."

"I know."

Back in our compartment, mother and child are sleeping, bathed in the glow of the night-light, and I quietly adore them. Do I think this will last? Of course not. Nothing lasts. Not that I won't stick by them no matter where their lives take them for as long as I live. You can't imagine how good it makes me feel to love them so, expecting nothing.

Her eyes flutter open, and she smiles drowsily. "Such a look," she murmurs. "You should see yourself."

And I do. She mirrors me, her eyes full of love. I start crying I'm so happy. Old men do that. Her eyes gleam back at me. I ascend into the berth above as if into heaven, fall fast asleep, and dream of her.

In the morning I take Dylan in my arms while his mother showers and I make a progress of the train from one end to the other looking for Amir, but he's nowhere to be found. It's a slow journey. Something about a lovely child in the arms of an old man warms the hearts of passengers who befriend us. "Grandchild?" they ask. "Son," I say and watch their eyes widen in surprise. They have no idea just how surprised they should be at this biological impossibility.

I take Dylan to the observation car, and we observe a while. You hear different things about what babies can see, but he seems to be taking it all in, observing his home planet. That's where I find Amir. For some inexplicable reason, the train rolls to a stop in the New Mexico desert, and there he is, standing outside. There's an announcement that smokers in need of a fix can use this opportunity to satisfy their craving, or those of us who might want to stretch our legs can do so. There's nothing but sand and rock and cacti for as far as you can see in all directions, the sun blazing away like it's proud of the whole thing.

There's not exactly a rush for the exits. My legs are stretched, but my mind remains coiled around the mystery of the abyss, so I head outside.

The smokers stand in a small herd, sucking and coughing. I'm the only stretcher. At first I don't see Amir. He's standing fifty yards from the train at least—where I imagine rattlers and Gila monsters thrive—looking off into the distance, the endless nothingness.

I shield Dylan's eyes from the glare with my jacket and head toward Amir, keeping an eye out for venomous reptiles—and scorpions, suddenly remembering those as well. It would be a hell of a thing to survive cancer and a heart attack only to die from a poisonous bite in the middle of nowhere. So careful am I that I fail to keep my eye on Amir, and when I've covered half the distance between us, I glance up, and he's gone. I've grown accustomed to the impossible. I'm holding it in my arms, slumbering peacefully, though he squirms a little, making himself comfortable.

I should probably turn around, but instead I press on toward a pile of rocks right out of a western movie that's the only place Amir could be. Maybe he's taking a piss, I reason. I do reason once in a while. It's also likely where the venomous monsters might dwell, but I've come this far, and the smokers are still hard at it, signaling their mortality to the achingly blue sky in pale poisonous puffs. The rocks are the color of a rich red sunset, and I boldly close the distance like I stroll through the desert every day.

There is indeed someone there, but it's not Amir. It's a man the color of the rocks, like he's been baking there his whole life—the Indian shaman who taught my dad to make perfect gravy so he could pass it on to me only to have me renounce the knowledge when my clogged arteries rebelled, and I dropped all but dead and arose a new man.

"So, Stan, what are you doing heading for the abyss again?" he demands. "I thought you were through with that nonsense. It's nowhere for a little darling like him." He holds out a red finger to Dylan who grabs it in his tiny hands.

"It was my brother's idea," I say, knowing that's no excuse.

Shaman shakes his head. "Follow me," he says.

"The train," I say.

"It'll wait," he says, and there's no time to doubt as he walks into a cavern I hadn't seen before, and I follow.

The way is straight and narrow, no natural formation, sloping down into the Earth. We come into a big round room, a kiva I think it's called, and there, sitting by a small fire, are my dad and a one-legged boy as black as coal. Natasha's there, sweeping her tail back and forth in the dust, glad to see me, and I understand where we are. "So this is where the abyss is?"

The Shaman laughs. It's not a pleasant sound. "Son, the abyss is everywhere."

Dad stands and embraces me, admires his grandson.

"Are you all right?" I ask him.

"I'm dead, Stan. Doing great. Your mom sends her love."

This is a lot to process. "Ollie's having his problems."

Dad nods, turns to the shaman, who hands him a tiny plastic bag. Dad places it in my palm. "Tell him six."

"Six?"

"Allspice berries."

That's what's inside the bag. Six berries like six tiny planets. "Isn't that a lot?" He gives me a look, like who am I to doubt my mentor? "I'll tell him. What about Deetermeyer? Katyana's worried sick."

Dad turns again to the shaman, who pulls out a glossy brochure from his bag of tricks, and Dad hands it to me: *The Institute of Advanced Alien Sciences*, with a picture of a smiling Simon Deetermeyer on the back. A picture of Mom's sand painting is on the cover. "This explains everything," he says.

Somehow, I doubt that, but I don't have time to argue, for I hear the train whistle blow. "I have to go."

"Wait!" the shaman says. He places his red hand on my heart. "You have healed yourself. Your blood flows everywhere. Open your heart, and your loins will follow."

Dad and the refugee kid nod in agreement, and Natasha wags her tail with renewed vigor. Dylan gives one of his joyful shrieks, and I turn and run back to the train. All the smokers are inside. I can see them at the windows wagering on my chances, running across the dead land at my age. My blood flows like a mighty river. My heart sings. I engage my yogic breath.

Amir is in the entrance to the observation car as the train starts to roll, and he pulls me inside. I'm too breathless to thank him, and he returns me to my seat. "Rest here," he says gently, and I do.

I don't know how much time has passed when Katyana finds us slumbering, father and child. "Look at you two," she says, her eyes full of inexplicable, miraculous love. Blood courses through my scarred arteries to every extremity. I have an erection, my first in five years. "I have to find Ollie," I say. "I have a message from Dad." I show her the allspice berries, the brochure, and tell her what happened when the train stopped in the middle of nowhere.

"The train didn't stop," she says, even as she's reading the brochure, which does indeed explain everything. She points out the caption beneath the cover. *Your Father Needs You* is the title, not a message. She looks at me like I'm the one who's needed. "Dad looks happy. He's not in any trouble for a change. That's all I really need to know. If I show up, that could just ruin everything. Let's all go home," she suggests.

And we do. The dogs will be deliriously happy to see us.

Once More into the Abyss

I just changed, aged, got older, however you want to put it. Isn't that how every story should begin? Even if the sucker's in present tense, it got written and revised *after* what really happened—or was *imagined* to happen—hopelessly entangled—actually happened. Our present past is a reinvention, a reimagining of the facts. That's not just old age. The boundary's always been more than a little slippery. Still. The story you're about to hear changed your narrator. Isn't that the very definition of getting older—change? Of a story, for that matter. We change until we die and become other people's memories, and of course they change too. Might as well get over yourself now. Once you're dead, other people get to decide who you are. Why let them get started on that now?

Getting older doesn't just glide along, however, smooth and easy at a steady pace. It's like a clogged-up little creek for many years, quiet and tranquil, same old trickle downstream, but when the hard rains come, then watch out, because then everything changes all at once, and washes your little world away.

Don't mean to sound grim. It's just the way it is. I'm the happiest, luckiest, happy-go-luckiest guy I know. Everything is perfect. Everything, as it always does, is happening now:

Katyana and I are sleeping in, or trying to. We're both early risers and would rather be up and out enjoying what looks to be, through the window, a beautiful day. We can hear Dylan in the kitchen laboring furiously to make us breakfast in bed before we have the bad taste to get out of it, so naturally we stay, trade nostalgic memories about him, about us. It's our anniversary. What started out as a marriage of convenience, I believe it's called, has turned out to be quite wonderful for all three of us. Dylan's twelve. I'm seventy-nine. That's coming up on 2.5 billion seconds. Time flies when you're having a good time. Katyana's lived a mere 1.4 billion seconds or so, but she's wise beyond her moments. We're holding hands. We do that a lot. Mine are leathery and old, a rainbow of liver spots arcing from pinkie to thumb, hers tattooed and still graceful looking like a beautiful tropical bird.

We squeeze and release when we hear Dylan trudging up the stairs, freeing our hands to make a fuss. He totters in with a huge tray heaped with food. Anticipating this, Katyana and I have cleared a space for a landing on top of the dresser, usually covered in random crap and piles of change. We're not the tidiest couple, but we're happy. He sets down the heavy tray with a cringe-making clatter, and we shriek with delight for the feast our wonderful son lays before us, applaud his presentation, the aromas, his thoughtfulness.

He serves us a spicy tofu scramble with lime-cilantro-mango salsa and fresh tortillas, zucchini muffins, grapefruit slices, and lots of hot coffee—this is *my* kid we're talking about. He's the best cook in the house, twelve-year-old earnest. The food radiates love. We dig in. I'm snuffly—from the salsa, or from the moment, I can't say—but *everything* is perfect.

When people say *I love God*, this is how they feel.

Then Katyana's phone bleats, and she says she has to take it, leaps out of bed and takes the call in the master bath.

Dylan's as surprised as I am. What's so important to interrupt our good time? We're a spoiled pair. She likes to spoil us—that's our story anyway. We listen intently. The bathroom amplifies everything but muddies it up too. It's her excited voice, but restrained a little. She's speaking up even though she's standing in the bathroom staring into the shower. A lot's riding on this call. We can tell that much. Dylan and I trade a look. Neither of us has a clue. You can't make out enough of the words to get the sense. Then out of nowhere, an unmistakable eruption of joy, "Yes! Yes! Yes!" It's positively orgasmic. It's overwhelming to hear it. Her joy is the world to me.

She bursts into the bedroom, her phone clutched to her breast like it's responsible for her good fortune. "I got a job! They must've had hundreds of applicants. Thousands! It's a real dig—I'll be an archeologist again! There's even a place for all of us to live!"

"What about the dogs?" Dylan asks. If he hadn't, I would've. The dogs are ancient. Avatar's fifteen and Myrna sixteen. Though she's a little more with it than he is, the best they can manage some mornings is to stumble around the neighborhood without bumping into anything, sleeping and farting together in whatever sunlit patch of rug they can find. I'm not sure how well they'll travel.

"The dogs will love it!" Katyana declares. "It's beautiful. You said so yourself when you drove us all the way out there and back." Her eyes meet mine, and she lets that last part sink in a bit.

Holy shit. "We're talking about the *abyss*?"

She nods excitedly. "It's an incredible opportunity! The first serious archeological exploration of the site!"

Oh joy, the incredibly weird and scary site. "That's wonderful!" I declare and hop out of bed, wrapping my arms around her. She beckons to Dylan, and he pops inside our circle and smiles up at us with perfect love and trust in his eyes. *You poor kid, your parents are alien looneys*, I want to say but don't. He already knows. His mother and I try to practice total honesty with the kid, a perilous policy if there ever was one, but so far it's worked out spectacularly. Someday, before I die, I aspire to be as together as my kid. "We're going to New Mexico!" I tell him. "It will be a wonderful adventure!"

Katyana used to be a working archeologist with the highway department, then the recession hit, road building ground to a halt, and any archeological digging would have to be done the old-fashioned way. Funding was scarce to nonexistent. Thousands of archeologists chased a handful of jobs. For the last twelve years she's worked at mostly shitty, lifeless jobs. To see her like this fills my heart with joy. I'll follow her anywhere. And I wasn't lying to Dylan. This *will* be an adventure. Filled with wonder. Alien portal, geological oddity, or archeological treasure trove of enigmatic artifacts—take your pick—*any* journey to the abyss is an adventure, though in my two previous visits, I never managed to make it all the way. Third time's the charm, they say.

The sun hasn't even set on this news, and the three of us are gathered around a battered road atlas on the coffee table to show Dylan where we're going. It's the atlas Katyana and I took before he was born to call on Dylan's biological father who lived just shy of the abyss, who didn't care to get involved in Dylan's pending birth or his life thereafter.

So when he arrived, I took on that good fortune, much to my continued delight, relishing each second—his and mine. We're telling him our version of this epic journey, and he's enthralled, though he's heard it all before, when Katyana's phone rings again. She sighs when she sees the source, but this time doesn't leave the room, and we can all hear the tinny voice on the other end. *Is she the daughter of Simon Deetermeyer?*

she's asked, and she confesses, bows her head, wondering what trouble her wacky old man's gotten himself into this time, only to learn he's dead in New Mexico, an apparent suicide. By this time, she's sobbing so hard I take the phone away from her. "This is Katyana's husband. She's devastated. May I ask how did this happen?"

He tells me in a deadpan cop voice from a thousand miles away: "We have him on security cameras breaching the perimeter of an archeological site known as the abyss, and at exactly noon our time, he jumped."

"Has the body been recovered?"

Is that a *chuckle*? "You can't recover nobody from the abyss. Too deep. Too dangerous. I'm terribly sorry for your loss. Would you have your wife call us when she feels ready?"

You bet, Chuckles. "I'll pass that along." I take her in my arms and hold her. After a while, I put her into bed, continue to hold her, and she cries herself into a fitful sleep. Every once in a while she wakes up and cries some more, clinging to me. Dylan, who never knew his grandfather, takes care of us with tea and snacks. I read, look out the window, watch the beautiful day's progress, reminisce. The day I was told my folks had disappeared into the abyss, I wanted someone to hold me, but there wasn't anyone. There's nowhere I would rather be than holding her. Dylan pops in to check on us, and I tell him to go to bed. It's been a long day.

"Was it a good anniversary?" he asks.

"The best," I say.

He glances nervously at his sleeping mother. "What was he like?" he asks me. "Was he . . ."

"Crazy? Good question. I wish I knew. Crazy or not, I think he was right about some crazy things, like aliens." Dylan's familiar with my weird notions and remains undecided about them, but Simon Deetermeyer was way weirder than me. He was on a mission. Some would call it obsession. *Like John the Baptist*, he said once in a story Katyana narrated to me: the night her father shared his theories with the assembled family for the first and only time—that aliens had come to Earth and taken on human form, then fled en masse leaving behind a network of adult children of alien beings struggling to understand their enigmatic identities. It was his mission and purpose in life to set them free, so that they might return to their home planet.

You don't get any more wackadoodle than that. Unless you become one of his followers. Like me.

"He was incredible," Katyana said. "He was on fire!" That night her mother packed the three kids in the car and left him. Katyana's the youngest, the only one who ever had anything to do with him after that night. He was crazy. Whether it was John the Baptist crazy or not, you can decide for yourself.

As for me I'm an *old man* child of aliens. I'm past adult. It's okay to be childish again and believe in nonsense when you look like me. People practically expect it. An old man who isn't totally daft and frail is a bit scary to most folks. Dodder and dither, and they know who you are and treat you like a child.

Dylan asks, "Is that why Mom never went to see him, and he never came to see us? Because of the alien stuff?"

"No. It was just better that way. He needed to hide, and not just because he was a hermit by nature. He had a habit of getting himself into trouble. He would do things to serve the cause that weren't always wise, like lying about his academic credentials. Your mom was always the one to help him get through it all. She reached a point where she needed peace, time with us, you especially. She enjoyed the silence, because it meant he was okay, that he'd finally found his niche, that he was finally happy. That's where he wanted to be, just down the road from the abyss, where he believes aliens came and went, and just might come back again. Now she may feel guilty for letting him live out his dream, but it was really the best thing for both of them. Your mother's a *wonderful* daughter."

"I think Mom's awake," Dylan says. "She just squinted."

"Busted," Katyana says without opening her red, swollen eyes. "I have to be at the site by Friday."

"We can start packing in the morning." I rock her in my arms.

"You're the sweetest man who ever lived."

"It's the alien in me."

Next morning, we haven't even finished our usual oatmeal breakfast when an envelope arrives express mail for Katyana. It's from her father. Sent about an hour before the time Officer Chuckles told us he jumped.

It's handwritten on the Institute of Advanced Alien Sciences stationery. "At long last, the aliens are returning to recover their lost children and bring them home!" it begins. The rest is just the usual messianic jibber-jabber, until the end, when he says, "By the time you receive this I will have gone on ahead to meet them, to show them the way, for it can be a frightening passage, from one world to another! Be brave, my child! See you on the Home Planet, my beloved one!"

As you can see, he's been working on the John the Baptist thing. The heartbreaker about Simon is, he was never 100 percent sure he was an alien child himself, which put Katyana's status in further doubt. (She's more or less sure she's not; I think she is.) But her father desperately wanted it to be true. So that they could return to the stars where they belonged—the two of them. It's not as if the rest of the family would notice or care if they left. *Whatever happened to the weird ones?* they might ask at Thanksgiving, then entertain themselves inventing cruel stories, feeling all thankful and festive because they aren't the aliens. At my age, it gets too easy to dismiss my wacko beliefs as dementia, which is not quite so jolly. Poor old codger. Be kind.

Alien codgers rarely experience dementia. Heart attacks and cancer we've got covered. We don't always have the best diet and abhor organized fitness, smoke to excess and guzzle caffeine and alcohol. But dementia almost never shows—course we rarely live past eighty, though my brother Ollie is eighty-four through no fault of his own. His body's a slothful battleground for the pitched battle between his drugs and his diet to keep his heart beating. Or not.

I eat a vegan diet and practice yoga four times a week, having cleaned up my act after my heart attack a decade and a half ago. My blood is a mighty river. My breath tireless. The interior of my colon is as immaculate as the future in *2001*. Too bad we never got that future. I wouldn't mind seeing Jupiter. Instead we've got this poor fucked-over planet.

Most alien men my age are liberals, if you're wondering. Not all. Not Ollie. Ollie's an anomaly, which is kind of fun to say. Unfortunately he still insists on Oliver, even though our alien parents named us Stan and Ollie—*not* Stanley and Oliver. Aliens love comic duos. Abbott and Costello. Burns and Allen. Yin and Yang.

I've got to call and tell Ollie we're moving. I brace myself for battle, though at his last wife's funeral, I sensed something softening in him. I never thought he'd fully accept that Mom and Dad were aliens, but in recent years he seems to have come around.

"What do you want?" he answers.

"I love you too, Oliver."

"I'm sitting on the can."

"Why answer?"

"Because I can't figure out how to get my messages on this fucking phone, and if I miss the wrong one, everybody assumes I'm dead, and the next thing I know I've got the fucking rescue squad banging on the front door. I never wanted the fucking phone in the first place."

"Constipated?"

"Of course I'm fucking constipated, Stan. I'm eighty-four years old."

"Are you eating enough fiber?"

"Fuck you and your fiber!"

Definitely constipated. "How are the dogs?" I ask him, to change the subject to a safe haven. We both love animals like crazy and always have; so did Mom and Dad. One of the strongest indicators of alien identity is intense interspecies empathic bonding. Ollie has a thing for big dogs, usually two or three at a time. I prefer a dog and a cat. I've let it go so long now grieving over my last cat that getting one now that I've only got a few years to live seems unfair somehow. We aliens kids are big grievers. Of course, *Dylan* might want a cat. He's entitled. Avatar was Katyana's dog and Myrna was mine when we met. For the last twelve years they've been ours.

"I'm down to one dog," Ollie says like this is some catastrophe. It might help with the aches and pains he's always on about if he didn't regularly get pulled like a wishbone with a Doberman on one hand and a Husky on the other.

"What is she?" I ask. We both prefer females, like most alien males.

"It's a boy, actually. He's six months, and he's already a handful. I saw him where I used to volunteer, and, you know me, I took him home. He's a Dane. I always wanted one, but never took the plunge because they don't live so long, and it's hard enough having your heart broke every few years. But I figure we can make it a contest—he and I—see if we can both make a decade."

"I like it. What do you call him?"

"Horatio."

"He does survive the play."

"Exactly. How's yours doing? Still the standard poodle and the border collie?"

"That's right. They're both getting to that rickety arthritic stage, though Myrna may be doing a touch better than Avatar. If one goes, the other one will not be far behind. They're tight. They stick around for each other."

Ollie laughs. It echoes in his john. "Are you one of those crazy alien motherfuckers with a soft spot for animals?"

"I am."

"Me too. How's the family?"

"That's why I called. Katyana's father died."

"Shit, I'm sorry to hear that." I can hear the wheels turning. "He was kind of crazy, wasn't he?"

"He committed suicide. New Mexico cop just called. He jumped into the abyss."

"Holy shit."

"There's more."

So I tell him the whole story right up to the last message from Simon Deetermeyer himself.

"So y'all are just uprooting and going to New Mexico? To that place of all places? Jeez, Stan, this is the loopiest thing you've *ever* done."

"I thought that was marrying Katyana. That's turned out so horrible I can hardly begin to describe my suffering to you."

"You don't have to get snippy. I'm happy for you. How's Dylan?"

I tell him about our anniversary breakfast. He doesn't snicker once during the whole thing, and tells me what a sweet kid I have.

So I'm not exactly surprised when he says, "Can I come with you? I don't know how I'd get out there otherwise. I mean, if Deetermeyer's right, I don't want to miss it. I'd drive myself, but they took my license away."

"Of course, Ollie. The more's the merrier."

He doesn't even tell me not to call him Ollie.

When Ollie and I were little, we used to ride along with Dad summers, in the back seat of the company car. He was a traveling salesman with a five-state territory and was away a lot. According to Simon Deetermeyer's research, traveling salesman was a favorite job among the original aliens. They were ideally suited—restless chameleons with tons of empathy and a ready wit. In Dad's case—a pharmaceutical representative, aka prescription drug peddler, aka detail man—his work may also have been research on humans. You can learn a lot about a species by what ails them, what they choose to treat, the medicines they'll take and the ones they won't.

In Dad's day, ulcers were big. Now, I suppose it's failing hearts, failing minds. Then, as now, the gatekeeper to many a medical professional was a woman. Dad had a way with women, as most alien men do—maybe one of the reasons Mom traveled with him in the summers, so all his girlfriends on the road could have a look at his happy family. There was a waitress in a Mexican restaurant in San Angelo who knew Dad by name, knew what he ordered, and was pretty nervous the whole time, Dad too, but that was one time out of thousands of restaurants, and Mom seemed to find the whole thing amusing. We were often a happy family, and we were happiest, seems to me, those summers on the road. We loved it. Me more than Ollie maybe, since it began to compete with his interest in girls. When he hit sixteen I mostly had Mom and Dad to myself, crisscrossing his territory. Ollie missed a lot.

We stopped often, which Dad didn't usually do when he was working. He would take note of anything that looked interesting to him, or might be interesting to me or Mom, during the year and wait till we were along to take it in. It might be an enormous model train layout or an impressionist painting or a snake farm or a hot blues band or a cemetery. Mom and Dad had a thing about cemeteries. All of us would wander around like they were sculpture gardens. I was always on the lookout for angels. Ollie bellyached about it, and we all ignored him, but I didn't miss him when he quit coming along. Sometimes when it was just the three of us wandering among the dead at sunset, Dad would say, *I wonder what Ollie's up to now*, all wistful, like he wished he was with us. Mom would answer his question with the name of some girl Ollie was screwing, half of whom I never met. He was five years older, in a different universe where people actually fucked. There was plenty of drama—angry girls on the phone who would even talk to me to relay a pleading message to Ollie—so I kind of believed him when he'd say he wished he'd been there to see the Monet, the 76 Deadly Rattlers in a Pit, or the Plains Indian Museum.

Now here we are two old geezers in the back seat of Katyana's Outback, rocketing through Texas, Katyana at the wheel, singing along with the music Dylan (riding shotgun) has selected from his phone, some band I don't know the name of but I like. Alien men like to keep up with what's current, hate oldies stations with a passion.

Katyana has a beautiful voice. Alien women often possess beautiful singing voices. Dad once bragged to me and Ollie that our Mom sang *Madame Butterfly* to a standing ovation in her youth, and she told him to shush and soon left the room, tears welling in her eyes. Aliens are often tortured by unfulfilled artistic ambitions. Mom had several—painting, singing, poetry. Dad was a failed mystery writer and standup comedian. He loved to tell jokes. He was a master at it.

They were a talented pair. But they knew they weren't ordinary humans, and when their mission was completed, they would have to return home and turn their backs on all things human, starting with the human form all the art was about in one way or another. Who knows why an alien would love opera? Did Mom love it because it was alien, or because it was not? Maybe she was weeping because she knew when she shed her human body she would sing no more and live in a world without arias.

I know I sound crazy. I've honed the skill over the years, along with a near total disinterest in what others may think of me. It's one of the major perks to being an old fart, and don't underestimate its value. Wish I'd learned the skill years ago.

Avatar and Myrna sprawl across our laps, twitching and dreaming, making little yippy noises like they could still chase anything. Ollie's goofy Dane, Horatio, crammed in the back with the luggage, can't seem to sleep either. He's not half-grown, already bigger than Avatar, but he's all legs he can't get to work together. He's a clumsy, excitable boy. But once we hit the road something magical happened. I suspect this is his first highway drive with the windows down. Ollie always wants them up. Horatio stares into the wind, transfixed, his ears aflutter. His gyrating nose sucks down the smells until he's numb with the smell of Everything! Bliss!

With Katyana at the wheel, the windows are cracked so we can all smell the night air, hear the screeching rush of our passage! Be where we are! That was Dad, when the weather was nice, or we were driving through something he wanted to smell—flowers, horses, the dawn—crack would go the windows. As a kid, I used to close my eyes and imagine I was on a rocket ship bound for Heinlein's Mars. What a swell place that was. Ollie used to complain he couldn't hear himself think and

Dad would reply in the shout necessary to make himself heard over the roar, like a voice out of a whirlwind— *Don't you get enough of your own thoughts already? Maybe you should listen to the wind instead of your busy little brain.*

I know Ollie didn't like having his brain called little, because it certainly wasn't, but the point Dad was trying to make went right by him. It was often like that with those two. Dad would try to pass on some wisdom to Ollie who could give a shit, while I hung on his every word. Those were great times. But this is better. Everything is perfect.

Here and now. You can't beat it.

I look out across the desert landscape of west Texas and think about death. I know the eighty-year morbidity statistic isn't like a law or anything. I don't *have* to die then. Or I could die sooner. I could die right now.

So what else is new? Death and I have met. He doesn't scare me anymore. In fact, I often ask myself, *If I were to die right now, how would that be?* It's made me a better and happier man. Seconds are precious.

Ollie's asleep, which is what I should be doing—we're due to reach the abyss at dawn—but I can't sleep—not usually a problem for me this time of night. The dogs and I typically rise early and doze off early. We've crossed a time zone, but the dawn's chasing us. Pretty soon the dogs and I will need to stretch our legs. They're slow these days but seem to enjoy their long, snuffling walks. They haven't lost their sense of smell.

As a kid, one of my first realizations of how weird and unusual my parents were was their attitude toward pets. If we brought it home, and it didn't belong to somebody else and wasn't dangerous—no scorpions or poisonous serpents—we could keep it and take care of it, get to know it. But not too many of any one kind. A new species was a shoo-in. Mom ended up doing a lot of the caretaking, of course, but what we weren't allowed to do was neglect them. If you weren't willing to hang out with a pet once in a while, maybe they might have something better to do with their lives than live it in a cage.

We had a fair number of dogs and cats, but never more than two of each, except for the occasional litter we fostered. Mom was crazy for kittens. Same with turtles, lizards, gerbils, rats. There were fish tanks until Mom rebelled on that one. I can't blame her. How many ecosystems can you watch collapse, leaving a sea of fetid corpses? I'm guessing there weren't fish on Mom's home planet. She couldn't connect with fish, though she certainly tried.

With every other pet, however, Mom and Dad were full of information about what they were thinking, feeling, hoping for. To them, all species were sentient creatures. Not like Disney animals but weird and goofy and fun. Complicated.

Because of the cats, we never did birds—though Mom always chatted up crows wherever they turned up. The one brief exception was a terrified cage-bound parakeet named Luigi who Mom soon drove down to somewhere in Florida to release when she saw how miserable he was.

He was grateful, Mom reported when she returned, *delighted to be outside. Outside doesn't amount to much if you're always on the inside looking out at it, but once you're there? It's everything! Remember that, boys*, she added, another nugget from Mom. Ollie doesn't even remember it, but it stuck with me. Dad and Ollie used to wound each other, but Ollie mostly ignored Mom, which wounded her, perhaps, most of all. I adored my mom and dad, and then they just left when I'd barely gotten to know them.

If what Simon says is true, I may soon see them again after almost two billion seconds, most of my life, in other words. If that doesn't make you lose sleep, I suppose nothing will.

There's a fence around the perimeter of the abyss, quite a substantial fence, cameras, the whole rigmarole. Yet Simon Deetermeyer climbed over it. Fortunately for me and the dogs, we don't have to. We're housed on the abyss side of the fence. On the other is miles and miles of National Forest. Everything's forest either side of the fence, except for the anomaly, the star of the show, the very deep, very strange hole in the middle of everything. It's our first morning walk in our new neighborhood on the lip of an enigma, the dogs and I. We're all a bit nervous, darting our eyes, twitching our noses, leery of shadows.

You don't just stumble upon the abyss. You have to navigate a maze of forest roads, each one shittier than the last and certainly bouncier. And even then it seems to come out of nowhere, this emptiness—the abyss.

Just inside the fence sits a recently constructed three-bedroom house, nothing fancy but sound, the archeologist's family residence, one of the perks of Katyana's new job. We are the archeologist's family, her most cherished artifacts. It's completely furnished. Everything is beige or worse. We'll have to make our mark by shedding prodigiously and hanging shit all over the walls. There's a big eat-in kitchen. We'll like this place just fine.

On this first morning in our new home, I slipped out of bed quietly and the dogs followed. Horatio started whining, so I decided to take him with us and let my aged brother sleep. He claims never to get any, but he practically hibernated all the way here, prompting Dylan to ask if Uncle Oliver was all right. He's eighty-four, I explained. How he manages to walk Horatio, I can't imagine.

For me, walking with dogs early in the morning is one of the great pleasures of human life. Horatio is challenging that notion. I want to walk through these magnificent woods and see the sun rise over the abyss. He wants to go berserk in the Forest! He's never experienced one before. Gone is the Zen dog in the car window. He smells deer and dead things and who knows what all as he races this way and that. We proceed in fits and starts as I stop to reel him back in.

Avatar puts up with his puppy antics for a few of these episodes, until finally he lets out a fearsome snarl worthy of a satanically possessed werewolf and shows some snaggletooth fang, and damn if huge Horatio doesn't sink into the dirt and the pine needles in a puddle of submission, while Myrna looks on like that beauty who watched George slay the dragon—if she were a half-daffy collie in her last days. *We haven't got time for this nonsense*, she seems to say. Myrna, even now, always acts like she's got someplace to go, and the herd better stick with her.

Avatar, as usual, falls in behind her, and Horatio stumbles behind him. Now that Myrna's lead dog, I can relax. Her navigation skills are still far superior to mine. Around the house the woods are sparse, but they soon grow deep and dark.

It goes without saying that the dogs believe in the presence of aliens. All dogs do. One sniff, and they know. I've never seen it fail. Has your dog ever veered off from his walk, quite out of character, to meet some oncoming stranger in a wagging frenzy? Alien.

I counted four cameras in the trees aimed at the house, one for each side. Who knows how many are inside? Who knows what might show up out of the abyss?

When we got here, Katyana and I did a quick dash through the visitor's center with a tiny museum of the site. There was one car in the parking lot, one guy inside who said he was a volunteer. He volunteered his ignorance of the site, so we wouldn't make the mistake of asking him any questions. Prominent among the displays was a case full of artifacts from the abyss with the caption *Do you know what any of these objects are? What they might have been used for?* Damn near anything by the looks of them, as intricate as the complex doodles I draw when I'm on hold listening to oldies, trying to maintain my serenity.

The artifacts look like things that used to show up in Mom's weird paintings and mosaics. I asked one time what something was in one of her paintings. She was going through a still life phase. She'd put something like a pile of fruit, a jug of laundry detergent, and a claw hammer on the kitchen table and spend the day painting it, only the jug didn't look like a jug, and the hammer didn't look like a hammer, and the fruit looked like fruit from another planet. She was letting me watch. I asked her what the hammer thing was, and she told me it was a thraxle.

"You bend time with it," she said, "so you can see what's around the corner."

"You can't bend time," I said.

"Not without a thraxle," she said.

I've always wanted a thraxle, but as Mom used to say, getting what you want is seriously overrated. She sounded like she spoke from firsthand experience, so I always wondered what had disappointed her, what did she regret? Did she want me and Ollie? I believe she did. What she didn't want anymore was to leave us and go home. So maybe she will come to see us like Simon says if only just to say good-bye.

And suddenly the dogs and I are out of the woods, standing at the lip of the abyss, a circular berm that for all the world looks like a pucker. All attempts to measure the depths of the abyss have failed, but the various instruments sent down to plumb it are hauled up encrusted with the artifacts Katyana has come to investigate and understand. What's not to understand? They're alien. Inscrutable. *Everything is scrutable*, Katyana corrects me, *even if you don't know what the fuck it means.*

It's hard to look dead on at the abyss. There's no point of reference. You've never seen anything like it before. The emptiness seems to draw you in, summon you perhaps, into its inky depths. It's hard not to feel like no matter what you do, you will fall in.

But we don't look into it, the dogs and I, lined up in a row as the sun breaks through the massive pines and warms our faces with delicious light. Even Horatio closes his eyes and tilts back his drooling snout and lets the sun wash over him. We're only here a few glorious moments in the sun's embrace. To get here, Myrna led us through deep woods where the sun rarely reaches the forest floor, as if time itself is hiding under the litter of needles and cones. To bring us to dawn.

Now Myrna unerringly leads us back. There's not much of a trail to speak of, and everything looks different the other way about. Smells the same, apparently. Myrna never skips a beat. It's chill and damp, but I can still feel the warmth on my cheeks, note the spring in even Avatar's step as Myrna takes us home. Horatio ambles behind almost gracefully, as if the years the two old dogs seem to have shed have been gifted to him. A walk to remember.

When we step inside we find a household in chaos. In honor of our possible reunion with our folks, Ollie's decided to make a Big Breakfast Like Dad Used to Cook. Indeed. There are pancakes. There are potatoes. A mountain of scrambled eggs. There is what looks like a pound of bacon frying in the skillet. Katyana and I are both vegans. Whoever thoughtfully stocked the fridge obviously wasn't informed of this fact.

The dogs are dazed with passionate longing for whatever shit that is simmering in the pan. It's been some intense moments for Horatio—Car Window, Forest, Dawn, and now Bacon! But even Myrna isn't blasé about the aroma of fatty, salty bacon in the air. She's chattering like she used to do in her youth, and I have to smile. This is my brother. He's just like Dad. We both are.

"Tell your wife," Ollie says, "that you will have some of this perfectly fried bacon in Dad's honor." Ollie's been talking about Dad a lot, like he really might see him again, get a second chance to get things right. Maybe alien parents should stay dead like normal parents do. Ollie's spent decades getting over a few things about them and finally seems at peace with them. I'm afraid if they show up, they'll only piss him off again, and all that counseling will have been for naught. Horatio is about eye level with the pan. His drool streams to the kitchen floor. Ollie looks down at him. "Don't even think about it."

"Might as well think about it, Horatio," I say. "I'm not having any."

"Stan, nobody lives forever."

"How about longer? Is that okay with you? I'm not having any."

"What about you?" he asks Katyana.

"I love you, Ollie, but no thanks, and please don't ever cook bacon in our shared kitchen again."

He likes the "Ollie" from her, who wouldn't, the way she purrs it? But he's standing there with a platter of bacon fried to perfection just like Dad taught us, dying to *serve* it to somebody, but there's no one to serve.

Then for the thousandth time I discover that I do indeed have the perfect son. He steps up. "I'll have some, Uncle Oliver," he says. "How about BLTs? I like the name, but I've never had one. Are they good?"

Uncle Oliver beams. "Dylan, allow me to show you how to make the perfect BLT." Exactly what Dad would say. Me too. Dylan uses the make-a-perfect-whatever line with his friends, mostly girls who have a crush on him, often older by a year or two and nearly always taller.

Katyana and I retire to our room, leaving them to their uncle-nephew moment. Dylan's never eaten flesh since he met a friend's pet pig Sophia, and they hung out for the better part of the afternoon, wandering around the property together, a small Hanover farm, mostly wooded. Dylan was seven. "Sophia showed me around," he said. After Sophia, he shuddered at the thought of meat, especially pork, but here he is, stepping up for his ancient Uncle Oliver.

This makes Katyana and me feel like such good parents we make love in our new bed, in our new room, in our new lives. That's how the day goes, one big happy family. Katyana goes to the lab—*her* lab—and returns with a dazzling slideshow of the first batch of artifacts she'll be studying, some of the oldest to have emerged from the abyss. We gather around her and eat dessert as she tells us about each one. She's where Dylan gets his earnest from, his big heart. Every single moment. Everything is perfect.

It's the middle of the night. The room is bathed in moonlight. I can't sleep. I listen to Katyana's breathing like the ocean waves coming in, going out. What a glorious sound! My life is impossible, and yet here it is. Not a dream come true. My dreams were never this good.

A shadow crosses the window—a bear or a ghost from the abyss or a trick of the moonlight. I slip out of bed, go to the window, and look out. It's the field the dogs and I traversed at dawn, and now it's bathed in moonlight. There's someone standing at the threshold of the woods, looking right at me.

It's Dad.

He turns and disappears into the woods with the slow, measured pace of someone very old but still strong, rather like I imagine myself. I scurry around, throwing on clothes, desperate not to wake anyone, and I almost get away with it. I'm trying to find my left shoe when a familiar snout gets in my face. *What are you up to?* Myrna wants to know. *Don't even think about finding your way through those woods without me.* She has my left shoe. Good thing animals don't think, or I'd suspect a plot.

Pretty soon I'm trooping across the moonlit field, with—you guessed it—three dogs. Avatar's dead on his feet—he likes his sleep—and Horatio keeps running into things. He's excited though—the pack's bringing him along on another adventure! I had no choice. He was about to wake up the whole household, and that's the last thing I wanted to happen. Just like when I was a kid and Dad would phone home from the road, I wanted him to myself.

Maybe it's only because I've been this way before, but these woods seem easier to navigate in the moonlight, like that's what they were made for. Or maybe it's my eyes, pupils wide, that see more in this half light, but somehow, I'm not afraid.

Myrna veers off on a side trail I didn't notice this morning, even more obscure than the one we've been on. We stumble through a scrubby patch and emerge into an old growth forest of enormous towering trees. The moon is directly overhead, enormous. It's almost blinding.

When I look back down to the forest floor, there's Mom sitting cross-legged in the dirt, the dogs swirling around her, licking her face as she furiously pets them all. I let them have their moment.

I need a moment too. My mother, who's been dead for quite a long time, is sitting before me. She always sat cross-legged—on the floor, on the sofa, anywhere she could manage it. On a blanket in front of her are artifacts from the abyss. Alien artifacts.

"I brought these for Katyana," she says. "She'll find them here in the morning when she comes this way. Dad and I are quite taken with her. You're a lucky man."

"I'm an alien."

"I'd say those are one and the same, dear."

"Where's Dad?"

She looks around at the surrounding woods with a pleasant smile. "You know your father, Stan. He likes to roam, but he always comes home to me." She spreads her hands above the weird array before her. "C'mon, guess which one's the thraxle." Another lesson for her bright, devoted son.

"I have no idea," I say.

"Use your intuition."

I don't argue with Mom about intuition, whose importance for her was an article of faith. I just point.

"See there? You're right. You should listen to your mother."

"I always do. It's good to see you, Mom. You haven't changed."

"Nonsense. Everything changes. It's good to see you too." She hands me the *thraxle.* "Go ahead, try it. You hold it like this and twist it one way and then the other. It will show you the fork that lies just ahead."

"Fork?"

"In time," she says, like I should've figured that much out already.

"You said Katyana will find these things in the morning. What will bring her here?"

"You're getting ahead of yourself, dear. The thraxle first. I think it will answer most of your questions."

I twist the thraxle to the right and it answers the question I ask myself often: *If I were to die right now, how would that be?*

I see it unfold in an instant, like an intense recollection triggered by some scent or object: Into the abyss, like Simon, the dogs and I disappear. Katyana and Dylan's grief is overwhelming. They remember me fondly as a wonderful influence on their lives they'll never forget. They both prosper and love many others and cherish and celebrate my memory. Katyana passes through these woods searching for me, stumbling across the artifacts Mom left for her. Her research on them, her lone solace during a time of inconsolable grief, forms the cornerstone of her brilliant career.

I twist the thraxle to the left and I don't die right now but much, much later, defying the odds, but I've taken a bad fall and can't get around on my own anymore and can't give Katyana and Dylan anything in return for their caretaking even as it weighs them down and saps the energy from their lives because I scarcely know who I am anymore, much less anyone else. I become an insufferable burden. When I die they celebrate their freedom in their hearts and only wish it had come sooner, living with dreadful guilt for the rest of their lives for having such feelings about someone they'd once loved so much. The artifacts lie deep within the woods, undiscovered.

That's some tool, that thraxle.

I leave Horatio with Mom. She says she'll show him the way home. She wants to see her other son, she says, so she can tell him the fine thing her youngest has done. I'm sure Ollie will be delighted to hear all about it. I hold her tight and tell her I love her, and we both cry a little.

The dogs, turns out, have been ready for a long time to take this journey but have been waiting on me. There's nothing hesitant about Myrna's brisk gait. She's moving like she used to when I'd take her down to the river, never pulling at the lead exactly, but pushing me to walk a good deal faster than I might otherwise. It's been a while. It feels good. I wish I had the chance to say good-bye to those I love, but that's not the way things work, are they?

I can feel it up ahead. It's close. My intuition, like Mom said. The abyss. I tell the dogs it's not far, as if that's news. Myrna looks over her shoulder one last time to reassure me she knows the way. I guess we all do whether we want to or not. Maybe Simon's right. Maybe we're all going home to become the aliens we truly are. I have no regrets. I have loved this planet.

So much love.

Everything is perfect.

Robot Story

The only thing ordinary about Jane was her name. She reminded me of a praying mantis, though it was hard to imagine Jane praying. She was tall and skinny but muscular like Sarah Connor in the second Terminator movie. She could walk on her hands. She showed me the night we met. We were by the pool at some dean's house welcoming incoming freshmen into the honors program that included the two of us. She found me in the backyard by the pool thinking about trying to call my boyfriend.

"I'm Melanie," I said.

"I know," she said. We were wearing nametags. "You're going to call some guy, right? Don't do it. I saw you looking like you were off somewhere pointless. Check it out."

Next thing you know she was on her hands, her skirt around her ears, and I put away my phone, and we ended up talking by the pool with our feet in the water for the rest of the party. We weren't supposed to be in the backyard. We were supposed to be inside making a good impression, shaping our futures, having bold visions for tomorrow, that sort of thing. It wasn't the kind of party where you were supposed to have fun.

It was a cool September night, but the pool was heated and lit up. Jane looked even stranger in the weird, glowing steamy light, or maybe I was still a little high from the pot I smoked at the meet-n-greet picnic earlier. I'd smoked before, but it had never done much for me one way or the other. It used to piss off Steve, the guy I didn't call, a waste of good drugs. I thought I was immune or something. Apparently not.

I said he was my boyfriend, but at this point he actually wasn't because he'd just dumped me in a long text message that explained he was destined to be with someone else he'd just met at Oberlin. I didn't read it all. Steve's destiny didn't interest me anymore. It was shortly after that I smoked the pot. I forgot about Steve for a while in a fit of random profundity, but munching on finger food at the dean's house, everything gleaming of furniture polish and smelling like meatballs, it finally sunk in how angry and relieved I was, and I went out the patio door when no one was looking, composing a sly reply that would put him in his tiny, insignificant place. The call I didn't make was to yell at him because my hands were shaking too bad to text.

Just as well. It worked out. He called me in the middle of the night a few months later to say how wrong he'd been, and I reassured him he'd been absolutely right, that his destiny had fuck-all to do with *moi*. Though I guess you might say without Steve's destiny, I never would've met Jane.

I let Jane do most of the talking. She said she was glad she found me, that she had trouble just opening up to people, but she knew right away I was okay, though she didn't explain how. I think it was because I tried to slip away, felt like I didn't belong there, like her.

Jane confided in me she'd figured out she was a machine, that she wasn't real, that she was like a robot or android or AI or something.

"What's the difference?" I asked.

"I'm not sure," she said. "They're all just put together in a lab somewhere, right? Basically it means my parents aren't my parents."

I thought about my parents, unmistakably my own, unlikely as that often seemed to all three of us. "Do you like your parents?" I asked.

"That's not the important question," Jane said.

"What is, then?" I thought that was always the question when parents came up.

"Do they like *me* is the question. And the answer's easy. Who can love a robot?"

"People love their cars," I said. Not me. I didn't even have one and had only the mildest affection for my bicycle. It was a habit of mind, looking at everything like it had sides, like the world's a pile of polyhedrons.

"No they don't. They say that, but that's not love. If you totaled your car and walked away alive, you'd be relieved, right? That's not love."

I couldn't argue with that. She said it was a robot thing: Robots are always right. It pissed people off, but she couldn't help it.

I said I was okay with it. I knew lots of smart kids. I was a smart kid. I knew about pissing people off, so I was careful. I'd never met anybody like Jane who just knew the answer without it being a part of something else, no apologies, not trying to prove anything. She was on a full scholarship. Her parents didn't have any money. They lost their factory jobs when she was little and worked shitty retail and odd jobs after that in a tiny town perpetually on the brink of collapse.

"So how did they end up with a machine kid?" I asked. "I mean, you must've been kind of expensive."

She smiled, a full-lipped no-teeth swoop, and she looked over at me, searched my eyes gathering intentions, analyzing the telltale pupillary action in response to her gaze, possibly deploying a mind-controlling beam straight to my brain. She held the beam for just about as long as I could take, so I felt like I was lifted up off the concrete, floating just above it. She finally broke her gaze and looked out over the pool water like it was a vast ocean, and I settled back down to the ground, but never completely, never again.

"I've wondered about that. I can't exactly ask them. They might not even know, or they're sworn to secrecy. I think maybe I was a new product they were working on at the plant, and when they shut it down, I was given to my parents for safekeeping, and the company went under or went to China or something, and they were stuck with me."

The watery light played across her face.

"Maybe they rescued you, smuggled you out on the last day in pieces and put you back together again because they knew you were destined to save humanity."

"You must be an English major."

"Right again."

"Told you."

"What's your major?"

"Undecided officially. I'm waiting for my programming to kick in. I haven't run that routine yet. I don't decide things. I just know."

"Is that why you followed me out here?"

"Definitely." She bobbed her head up and down vigorously, fixed me with her eyebeams again. "Definitely."

"Aren't you curious about what you're going to do with your life?"

"It's not mine, is it? If I'm a robot."

"Then whose is it?"

"*That's* what I'm curious about."

It wasn't that late when the dean's wife came outside and saw us. "What are you two girls doing out here?" She said it like she knew we were up to no good. I felt twelve.

Jane stood up in the water. We were sitting at the shallow end by the steps. The water wasn't even up to her kneecaps. "Want to join us?" she asked. "We could all be like water nymphs, goddesses in the moonlight." She gave this speech a mountain twang, or maybe it was her natural voice. Jane was a superb mimic, a robot skill.

"The party's been over for some time, young lady. Everyone has gone home." You could clearly see the servers in their white shirts and black pants cleaning up inside, not the everyone she was talking about. This same woman had fussed over us when we arrived with a lot of brilliant young minds chatter. Now she just wanted us to take our IQs and clear out.

"You could still join us," Jane insisted. "Besides, I'm not a young lady. I'm a robot."

"Young lady, I will only say this one more time. It is time for you to return to your dorms. Don't make me call campus security."

"I already told you I'm not a young lady but a robot, and I'm on a secret mission with the highest priority. You've interrupted a crucial meeting with my human contact."

The dean's wife dropped her mask and gave Jane a look that would've had me kneeling in the shallows begging for mercy, but Jane just gazed back calmly, a machine on a mission, and the dean's wife spun around, vanquished from her own domain, and went back inside, banging the glass door behind her so that it shuddered in its metal frame, calling out her husband's name, "Clarence!"

Jane smiled. I concluded it was time we leave. There was a wooden gate in the back of the huge yard, or we could climb over the fence if necessary. Jane wanted to go through the house, but I talked her out of it, and the gate wasn't locked. "What's the secret mission?" I asked as we huffed it back to the dorm.

"I don't know. They don't tell the robots the secrets, so we won't be conflicted. Nobody wants a conflicted robot."

We left before campus security showed up, but somehow next day everyone in Honors had heard about it, how Jane had fucked with the dean's wife's head. I think some of the waitresses serving canapés were students. One of them must've witnessed the scene or overheard the dean's wife's report of the poolside skirmish. Leonard, the one with the pot at the picnic who had held forth on string theory, then tried to kiss and grope me, asked the next morning after Science Technology and Society if I knew Jane, and I said I did, that I was in fact her closest friend in the world. Her human contact.

I concluded that must be true because I liked her, and she told me she didn't have any friends. She said nobody likes robots, and I said I did. We started hanging out a lot, pretty much all the time. We were like cartoon characters, tall and lanky, short and stubby.

She said she had settled on the term robot rather than the others like android that made it sound sort of romantic, like an elf or something, when basically you were just a slave. "Have you ever thought about why people would make robots that look like people? People would probably prefer they didn't, you know? They're called automatic tellers, but they don't wear white shirts and smile. And like for soldiers, they'd make them huge and scary, right? The only reason I can think of is for sex. For most things it doesn't matter what a machine looks like, but for sex it's super important."

"I guess." We were supposed to be working on a collaborative project together. We took mostly the same classes. The honors program was crazy for collaboration, and it was always me and Jane, but all she ever wanted to talk about late at night with a deadline looming was robots. And sex. Usually the two together somehow.

I both liked and didn't like these conversations, because it excited me when Jane got all intense about it. I didn't know if she was a robot, but I was increasingly certain that she was extraordinary, that she was beautiful. I imagined her being made somewhere, like I was the one who made her, snapping on her kneecaps, fastening her size nine feet onto her slender ankles, laying over a layer of taut skin over her calves, her thighs. They were solid muscle. She said her programming kicked in at eleven cruising channels at her grandmother's house, when she saw a woman on a beach practicing yoga. Jane was scary good. I asked her if she ever taught, and she made a face and reminded me, as she often did, that Robots can't really teach humans anything: Humans have to learn everything for themselves.

"So what do you think? Maybe I was made for sex, you know? That would explain my exceptionally powerful sex drive. Why else would a robot need a sex drive if not for sex?"

"Makes sense. You think your sex drive is more powerful than other people's, or other robots?" I was hoping to get her back on task with a trick question. She always told me she knew fuck-all about the doings of other robots. *We're not like a team or a club or anything. We're machines*.

"Both," she said and gave me that searching look. "How often do you masturbate?"

Sometimes I could not believe her. You couldn't lie to her. "I'm not answering that question."

"Okay. I'll take that as a lot. Try several times daily. I brush my teeth less often. I'm afraid of getting a boyfriend because I'm afraid none could satisfy me."

I teased her about her tooth brushing. She might not have her student ID with her, but she always had her toothbrush. "Afraid your teeth will corrode?" I once asked her. "Precisely," she said.

Robots don't get a lot of dates. As beautiful as she was, Jane was also smarter and taller than any guy in her high school and had exactly one boyfriend she had sex with and some uncle who groped her, though we both agreed that didn't count. She and the boyfriend didn't exactly do it. Everything but. More than I could claim. Like with pot, I thought I was immune.

"So," Jane concluded in that robot way of hers, one logical conclusion after another, "if I was made for sex, then I must be really something extraordinary in bed, don't you think?"

Think? The beam again. We kissed. We fucked. We fucked a lot, fucked all the time. She wasn't kidding about her sex drive, once her programming kicked in. Turns out I had one too. We humans have to learn everything for ourselves.

I know what you're thinking. That was obvious. Try it sometime: Know thyself. When you're all done, we'll talk. Short version? Jane was the best thing that ever happened to me. I knew what her mission was, and it was me, me all over, inside and out. When I went home Thanksgiving I told my folks I'd fallen in love, and they were happy for me. Dad asked, "Who's the lucky fellow?" and I sold her out, invented a guy Dad would love on the spot. His vegan dyke daughter with a plateful of turkey and gravy made him sound just perfect. "I guess you have a lot to be thankful for," Dad said, and I wanted to die.

Jane didn't know about that betrayal. Don't ask, don't tell. She'd stayed at the dorm with a handful of foreign students and kids who weren't going home for one reason or another. She told me Thanksgiving was wasted on robots. "Do I look like a pilgrim to you?" I have no idea what she told her parents. We never went there. Robots are beyond all that, she claimed. They weren't really her parents.

I kept thinking I would invite her to come home with me Christmas, and I would come clean to my folks, but when Jane begged me to go home with her Christmas break, I was secretly relieved I wouldn't have to confess my lie to her and my family, and consumed with curiosity about hers. Unlike for Thanksgiving, the dorm shut down for Christmas, and there was no staying in town. She said she couldn't face her family alone. I told my folks I would be spending Christmas with James's family. James was the guy I made up, pretty much Jane with a dick in my lovestruck stories about him, though I didn't go into the whole robot thing. They wouldn't understand. Send us pictures, they said.

Here's what a picture would've looked like when we showed up on Christmas Eve after taking several days to get there: At the end of a gravel drive in a scrubby pine wood sat a clapboard rancher painted a flaking blue-gray, the brown asphalt shingle roof crumbling under a blanket of pine needles. A string of Christmas lights ran along the drooping rain gutter over the porch, and a plastic Santa with a light inside stood in the yard. Several holes and cracks leaked beams of light from his glowing body into the night sky. There were three old cars in the yard, none of which looked like they could make it into town. An aged hound limped toward us baying a greeting both mournful and excited, and Jane took a knee and hugged his neck.

"This is Rufus," Jane told me.

Jane was a head taller than both her parents. Her father's face was all hollows and deep lines with a grizzly stubble and thick dark hair in wild disarray, his hands jammed into his coat pockets. The one that emerged to shake mine was hard and calloused. Her mom was my height and worried. She seemed to be in charge of nice for the whole family, and the strain showed. She kept telling me how glad she was I'd come and not to mind the mess, though once you got inside, everything was neat and tidy and decorated for Christmas.

There was a Christmas tree with blinking lights in the corner, not a real one, but some kind of green plastic. I missed the real tree smell. It was maybe four feet tall, but it was on a card table so it seemed taller, a few presents underneath wrapped in Sunday comics and yarn. I liked that. In a bookcase that didn't have too many books, a couple of Chilton's and a kid's encyclopedia older than me, a nativity scene was on display. The animals were chipped and battered, and there was no baby in the manger. Joseph and Mary leaned against one another to hold each other up since Joseph was missing a leg, and only two of the three kings had shown up. There was an angel on the roof missing half a wing. Jane saw me checking it out and read my thoughts. "Rufus was a little hellhound when he was a pup," she explained. Thumbtacked to the front of the bookcase were red felt stockings for Jane and her little brother Tom.

Tom didn't show right away. Jane pointed out his door as we went down the hall to her room. There was a poster for a game on the door with a muscly guy holding a ridiculously huge gun standing on a pile of scrap that had once been several robots in a post-apocalyptic landscape. SHOOT MANY ROBOTS it said, the letters riddled with bullet holes. "Tom hates robots," she said simply with a shrug.

Jane's room was minimalist except for the walls. All her stuff was hanging from pegs and hooks. Stickie notes were everywhere—lines of poetry, equations, silly stuff like one on her mirror that said, "Remember the mane." There was a yoga mat rolled up and standing in the corner. The only furniture was a mattress and box spring sitting on the floor. The window looked out at the Santa's back. The cord snaked through her window and plugged into the wall. A Stickie in the middle of the window read Ho! Ho! Ho!

She came up behind me, encircled me in her arms, and hugged my shoulders. "So what do you think?"

"Your parents are nice."

She didn't correct my identifying them as her parents like she usually did. "That's because you're here." She kissed the top of my head. "Melanie, the nice human. You're lucky you have me to protect you from evil."

I grasped her powerful arms in my hands and could feel her love like a current flowing into me. "I know."

"Let's get out of here. Put on your hiking boots."

As we passed through the kitchen, her mom flashed a hopeful smile that quickly faded as Jane breezed past with me in tow. "I'm going to show Melanie the old barn." Rufus, sprawled under the kitchen table, thumped his tail on the floor but didn't rise.

As we crossed the backyard toward a narrow trail into the woods, I glanced over my shoulder, and her mom was watching us out the kitchen window, and a teenage boy who must be Tom watched from another window.

"Ignore them," Jane said, though she didn't look back. Robots have eyes in the back of their heads, telecomm links to spy satellites, sixth, seventh, and eighth senses. She always knew when she was being watched. She knew our thoughts and fears, she claimed: Humans are always afraid of something.

The deeper we went into the woods, the colder it became. The sky was dark and low, and the limbs groaned in the gusty wind. "It's going to snow," Jane said in her matter-of-fact robot voice. "But we have time." She didn't say for what. I already knew.

The barn was made of logs and hadn't been used for years, built long before her family bought the place. She said in the summer there were snakes in the walls and rafters with whom she communicated like Eve in Eden. Snakes are smart, she claimed. They understand the slippery slithering shape of reality. Eve tried to explain it all to Adam, she said, but you could see how that worked out.

A robot's kiss is like no other. There are millions of sensors in their soft lips and lithe tongues. Their saliva isn't just saliva but an enhanced brew of scents and sensations especially created from the pheromones of the loved one. That's what Jane called me: The loved one. I felt like a queen in an old story. Guenevere or Isolde if Lancelot or Tristan had been beautiful robots, though if you think about it, they sort of were—metal clad servants of a feudal system that made their love crimes against the way of the world, more intense than ordinary love.

We made love, and when we lay in each other's arms inside Jane's big down coat, it was so quiet I could hear the snow drifting down outside. When she wanted to, Jane gave off an intense warmth and glowed, so that the pitch black interior of the dilapidated log structure was transformed into shelter from the storm.

"Shouldn't we get back?" I asked after a while. "Won't they worry?"

"Don't you mean so that you'll stop worrying?"

Busted. "I guess," I said guiltily. "I lied to my parents. I told them you were a guy named James." The confession just came out, and I realized that's what I was really worried about, that I wasn't brave enough to deserve her.

"You could hardly tell them the truth," she said. "That you're in love with a robot."

Outside in the distance I heard the crunch of footsteps approaching and jumped to my feet in a panic.

"Don't worry," she said. "It's only Tom." She ceased to glow and stood beside me. "Bundle up," she said.

It was Tom in a big camo coat and hunter's cap. He looked like a smaller version of their dad. "Mom told me to tell you dinner's almost ready." He looked at me when he said this. I couldn't tell if he was hostile or simply curious. "I'm Tom," he said.

"Melanie," I said.

"I know," he said with a shrug. He looked at Jane. "They're kind of freaking."

"What else is new?" Jane said.

"You could attempt to be cool," he said.

Jane smiled her serene robot smile. "Advice noted. How have you been, little brother?"

He just shook his head and turned away, trudging back to the house a dozen yards ahead of us. I thought I could see in the way he looked at her, the note of pleading in his voice, the slump of his shoulders as if carrying an enormous weight through the snowy woods, that he might hate robots, but he loved his sister.

And she loved him.

Jane's mom, who insisted I call her Dolores, had been told I was vegetarian and had made every effort to accommodate my special needs. She served a soupy tuna noodle casserole crusted with potato chips because every vegetarian she'd ever known had eaten fish and dairy, and I devoured the salty gooiness with enthusiasm, not wanting to hurt her feelings. Jane would eat anything. "It doesn't matter," she always said. "I break it down into its chemical components to fuel my energy cells."

Dolores said to Jane, "Maybe after dinner you and Melanie could take Tom to the Wal-Mart? He still has Christmas shopping to do."

Jane, who regularly referred to Wal-Mart as the many-headed beast created by humans to consume themselves, surprised me by smiling serenely. "Sure thing," she said.

Her Dad, whose name was also Tom, though everyone including Dolores called him Daddy, jerked his head up from his plate and eyed her with suspicion. “Go there, and come right back,” he said. “None of your nonsense.”

She smiled at him like she’d smiled at the dean’s wife. “Course not, Daddy. Wal-Mart has everything, right?”

Tom Sr. started to say something in reply, but his wife laid her hand on his forearm, and he swallowed it down along with the casserole. Tom Jr. stared at his plate as if we’d all just been spared a terrible calamity.

“Be careful,” Dolores said as if she didn’t notice. “The roads will be treacherous if this snow keeps falling.”

“It won’t,” Jane said, and Tom Sr. made a guttural grunt and stabbed another forkful of tuna and noodles.

Jane was right about the snow, of course. Once we were on the Interstate, there was no snow at all. Our rent car was tiny, the backseat piled high with our camping stuff, so the three of us were lined up in an old Ford pickup that, like the house, was neat as a pin once you were inside, the engine roaring loudly, eliminating any casual conversation. I was in the middle. Tom was doing his best not to touch me even though the heater was broken, and it was bitterly cold. Stars were coming out.

“So who’s on your shopping list?” Jane asked Tom.

“Mom and Daddy,” he murmured quietly.

“Thought so. Always hard to know what to get the couple who has nothing, right? You don’t really want to go to Wal-Mart, do you?” Jane looked at Tom with her penetrating gaze, and I could feel him squirm.

“Jane,” he said, a pleading note in his voice.

“*Do* you? Buy some useless junk made by Chinese slaves, so you can experience the gift of giving at low, low prices?”

He looked out the passenger window and shook his head. We went flying by the Wal-Mart, its huge parking lot full of last-minute shoppers, and took the next exit down a lonely, dark road.

“Where are we going?” I asked. I knew the look on Jane’s face, when her programming kicked in, and she was about to do something totally robot, outside the box all us humans lived in.

She didn’t answer; Tom did. “The plant.”

Jane beamed like a teacher when she hears the right answer from a recalcitrant student.

The plant was wide and low, two stories at its highest point, filling half the horizon. It was surrounded by crumbling tarmac punctured by scrub pine and weeds. There was a forest of light poles, but they were dark. An eight-foot chain link fence surrounded it. There were No Trespassing signs every dozen yards or so warning of fines and prosecution for anyone who violated the rusty perimeter. Jane pulled up to wide gates, chained and padlocked.

"Jane," Tom said. "We could get in real trouble."

"How many times do I have to tell you, Tom? Trouble isn't real. It's just stories in your head."

"Daddy said—"

Jane opened her door and got out, closing the door on anything Daddy had to say. I waited for Tom to open his door. He shook his head. "Fuck," he said quietly. He looked at me. "This is all about you. Don't be scared. She won't hurt you."

I couldn't imagine Jane hurting me, but I felt a knot of fear growing in my gut anyway. Humans are always afraid of something. Tom got out, and I followed him. Jane was already standing at the gate, the padlock in her hands. It was a massive thing. She pulled it open and hung it on the links, unwrapped the chain, pulled the heavy gate open wide enough for us to pass, and gestured with a sweep of her long arms that we should enter.

The lock was old, I told myself, left open by the last trespassers who probably pried it apart with a crowbar, but in my heart I knew that wasn't true. Jane led the way. She seemed to know where she was going, and I trailed along with Tom instead of at her side like I usually would. The closer we came to the buildings, the more you could see how dead the place was, every pane of glass shattered, wood rotted, metal rusting to nothing, covered with an icy sheen. Power lines dangled, frayed and useless.

We went in a side door into a dark and narrow hall. The floor was littered with junk. She kept her steady pace. "Jane," Tom said. "We can't see nothing."

"Sorry," she said. Fluorescents overhead flickered, buzzed, and popped on. I surveyed the walls. The only switch was back by the door, and I was sure it didn't work anyway. I didn't ask how she did it. I already knew. We turned a corner, and a fresh row of abandoned lights that hadn't been visited by electricity since Jane's folks used to work here sprang to life. At the end of this hall was a metal door with a sign:

WARNING:
AUTHORIZED PERSONNEL ONLY
DO NOT ENTER

There was a keypad, but Jane didn't touch it. She just pushed the door open and walked in, looking over her shoulder at us with a grin I hadn't seen before, beckoning for us to follow. I had never been so scared in my whole life. It was filled with machinery—industrial robots, some of those robots who didn't look human like Jane but who nonetheless could do things, make things, maybe even think and feel—and they were coming on, whirring and humming and clicking like gigantic metal insects, and they were all turning toward Jane. She raised her hands in the air like a conductor in front of an orchestra, like a preacher inspiring a spirit-filled congregation of the faithful, and laughed joyfully. "Ta-da!" she exclaimed, and my knees were like water, and I wanted to close my eyes because I couldn't be seeing what I was seeing, but I knew if I did I'd just pass out and wake up somewhere thinking this was all a dream when I knew in my heart it wasn't, and I knew something else I didn't want to know: As much as I wanted it not to be, Jane's mission was much bigger than me, bigger than I could possibly imagine.

I know what you've been thinking—all this robot talk was just metaphoric, code for something else, and maybe I did too, though I couldn't have said what exactly. I didn't want it to be real. Like Jane always said, you can't love a robot. Not because they're not worthy, but because you're not. They've gone beyond just you. They're already gone into their own reality.

Tom was staring at the floor, willfully ignoring the spectacle, and Jane gave him a tender, understanding look and lowered her arms, and the robots lowered their waving appendages, quit swiveling back and forth in agitated glee, and settled into their resting positions, glowing and humming, waiting to serve.

"What were you going to get them?" Jane asked Tom.

"Gloves," he murmured.

"Appropriate," she said, "but they're insulated enough, don't you think?"

Jane didn't wait for an answer. She stepped up to a console, her hands moving across the controls in a blur like huge dancing spiders, and the robots went to work. I thought I might throw up. It was all I could do not to faint dead away, like all the fears I'd ever known were throbbing in my brain. I don't know how long it lasted. The sound was like a choir from another planet building toward a crescendo, a chord too high, too low, too complex for human understanding, the music of the spheres, the sound we longed for but never quite achieved plucking on cat gut, blowing through reeds, thumping on dead animal skins, praying to God.

When she was done, she showed us, on a bed of crimson velvet nestled in a box in a row, a shining new population for the crèche—Joseph and Mary, a sheep, a cow, a camel, an ass, a trio of kings, an angel, her wings intact, who looked a lot like Jane, and in the middle, the baby Jesus newly made. The robots whirred down to silence, and the only sound was Tom and I weeping softly, though perhaps only Jane could've told us what we were crying for. Humans are always crying over something.

We drove back in silence. I had a million questions, but I was afraid to hear the answers. Tom had the box in his lap, staring straight ahead. Jane hummed a medley of Christmas carols, soft, melodious, in perfect pitch, like a happy angel. I had never seen her happier: Joy to the world! Come all ye faithful! Look what I made you humans to get you through your long and silent nights!

Tom wrapped the box in comics, Prince Valiant looking noble and unafraid, and put it under the tree. Tom Sr., who'd been drinking, eyed it critically like it might explode. He picked it up, and Jane advised him not to shake it, and he didn't. Dolores smiled through all of this and said we should all get to bed so Santa could come, like we were all little kids, like there wasn't a robot in the house.

"You okay?" Jane asked me as we bedded down for the night, and I told her I was, though she knew I wasn't. My parents called to wish me and James a Merry Christmas and wanted me to put him on, but I said he was doing some last-minute shopping, something special just for me.

Christmas morning, Dolores made a big breakfast—sausage and eggs and biscuits and gravy—and I ate it all, though it tasted like ashes in my mouth. They gave me a scarf, and I wrapped it around my neck, thanking them profusely. The little box of holiness was the last to be opened.

Tom, who had been appointed the distributor of gifts, kept passing it over, until finally he gave it to Dolores, who said, "I know this is something special."

When she opened the box, her face lit up, and Tom Sr. let out a low grunt. "They're beautiful!" Dolores exclaimed, and they were. In the morning light they were bright and shiny new, gleaming with all the love Jane had breathed into them.

"Allow me," she said and took the box to the crèche where she placed each figure in place, ending with the baby Jesus in the manger, and beckoning for us all to rise and gather round: Come let us adore him!

We stood there like the three kings in front of the bookshelf laden with out-of-date knowledge and repair manuals for machines that would never run properly again, awaiting a miracle, and Jane didn't disappoint. One by one, she touched her creations, and they came to life. The animals and kings knelt. You could hear the beasts braying, lowing, bleating in chorus. The angel moved her wings like a butterfly in the sun. The baby Jesus turned his little head to take us all in, seeing what mission lay before him on this tiny planet on the outskirts of the Milky Way. He climbed out of the manger, planted his infant feet, raised his palms upward, and smiled. A halo like a tiny spiral galaxy hovered above his head.

Dolores screamed, and Tom Sr. swept his arms around her to shelter her from the spectacle. "Leave and don't come back," he said to Jane. She gave a sobbing Tom a quick hug and left, me trailing in her wake. "It was time," was all Jane said by way of explanation.

Maybe I should've asked more questions, overcome my fears, but I'm only human. Her life was not her own, nor was it mine. We journeyed back to campus, taking our time like tourists, as if all that awaited us was the new term, more collaborations, achievements, honors, but that was not to be. When the new term began, Jane was gone, and no one knew where but me. Her programming had kicked in. The tiny part of her mission that was me had been accomplished, and it was time to move on.

Time for me too. I told Mom and Dad that James had been a lie, that even though I would never know myself, I could still love myself. Maybe robots and humans aren't so different after all. I learned that from Jane in spite of what she said about us having to learn everything for ourselves. I've never told anyone the story of Jane until now, not my wife, not my children. Who would believe me? What does it matter? It's enough that I know it's true, that she found me beneath the moon, beside the still waters, and gave me life.

Who can love a robot? Me.

Christmas in Hollywood Cemetery

No time's a good time to be dead, I suppose, but Christmas, seems to me the worst. Leastways where I'm buried here in Hollywood Cemetery with all us Confederate dead. There's a whole mess of us—18,000, they say—not that we talk or nothing. The dead don't talk. You folks do. All the time. No end to it.

Our end of the cemetery, groups of folks show up regular all year round to talk about us like we was something special for figuring out how to get ourselves killed so young. Like me, I was eighteen. I say talk, but mostly it's one fellow talking and everybody listening. Sometimes the others ask a question or two. Nobody asks us dead what we think, not that we know two hoots and a holler. Without y'all, I wouldn't even know where my final resting place *is*. Nobody asked me where I wanted to go, knew my name, nothing when they scooped up my guts and brought me here. Nice of y'all now to take such an interest.

Lately, y'all been showing up on these wheels. Segways. The fellow says the name every chance he gets. Rolling around. It's weird is what it is, them things. Segways. Over the years, people show up every which way. That's how I know so much about what y'all think about us—how you *love* to talk about what we was fighting for. The story don't always stay the same, but I'll tell you: Unless these boys around me knew more than they were telling before they died, y'all seem to know more about it than we ever did. You fight to stay alive is what it is. You see how that worked out.

On the path other side of that iron fence, folks walk up and down and talk about what they always talk about. Telling stories. I usually don't get to hear the whole thing, just part of the middle, so I don't always know what they're talking about. Once, twenty years ago maybe, fellow proposed right there. She said yes. I didn't get to hear who was saying no to the whole idea. There's always somebody. Times change, but not as much as you might think. I been here 150 years. Things is different, but some things don't change: When it's getting to be Christmas, people start talking about it—where they're going, what they're going to give somebody, what they're hoping to get, who they're hoping to see, and who they'd rather not.

The dead like flowers. All we seem to get around here's flags. Never gave flags as much thought as y'all apparently do. No flowers at Christmas. One reason I don't like it. Most of the folks who come on Christmas are here to see somebody special. We may be special other days, but there's different kinds of special. Me, I'd rather have the flowers, somebody's son or grandpa or something. Course nobody gets them for long. Grandpa's grandpa's grandpa don't mean nothing to nobody except a name on a stone if they're lucky. I'm just a number. Little stumpy piece of marble with a number. Corner's busted off so you can't see the last digit. Not that it matters. Unknown's unknown no matter what's on the stone. They can say whatever they like about you.

But I want to talk about Christmas. Cause like I said that's what folks do every year it comes around. Even the dead, now that I have your attention. We don't talk to each other. What's the point? But I'll talk to you—since y'all are so interested in us. I don't like Christmas. Touches a nerve, you might say. The dead have nerves. You can't see them anymore, but they're there, like roots running through the ground. Cemetery's full of them.

Reason I don't like Christmas is all about Amanda and *Uncle Tom's Cabin* and a slave named Pinkney.

Shortly after her family moved to town, Amanda come around with her mother because we was some kind of kin to her, and it was getting on to Christmas. Amanda was a whole lot nicer than her mother who might've said we lived in squalor, and she would've been right, but there's no call to say it or look like you want to the whole time you're sitting in our parlor. Amanda took an interest in me while our mothers disapproved of one another. She asked me if I liked to read—told me she loved to, that her idea of paradise would be lying on the beach reading on some Pacific island.

That set my mind to racing, I can tell you. But I don't read. Not cause I'm dead, but cause I never could, and I had to confess my ignorance to her. She acted like she didn't mind one little bit, matter of fact, she asked how I'd like it if she read to me sometimes. I imagined us on a beach—though I never been on one my whole life.

All I knew about Amanda was her daddy was a Unitarian. Bet you're thinking I wouldn't know a word like that, and you're right, but this was Amanda's daddy we're talking about, and I wanted to know everything in the world there was to know about her ever since she was pointed out to me in a carriage gliding by. And he wasn't just any Unitarian. He was a preacher. This seemed to stick in my mother's craw, but I knew better than to ask why. The way I figured it, if you didn't go to church no more than we did, you had no call to have opinions about preachers one way or another.

So when Amanda asked me if I wanted her to read to me, her being a preacher's daughter, I thought maybe the Bible, turns out it was her own personal copy of *Uncle Tom's Cabin* she smuggled to Richmond from up north where she used to live. She said even her daddy couldn't know, but she knew a place where we could be alone. I don't know how much y'all remember about being seventeen and in love, but she could've read me anything, and if it was something so bad even her daddy couldn't know, then that was all to the good, that as no-account as I was, I still might have a chance with her.

She had a thrilling voice. When she read me the part where Eliza's fleeing across the ice, I shivered down to my bones. She got so wrought up, she had to loosen her collar. Her bare throat made me heat right up again. People generally wore more clothes when I was alive.

I don't remember the whole story. Half the time I wasn't listening to the story, but to her voice, if you know what I mean. The whole thing made me sorrowful and happy at the same time. Folks bought and sold down the river—it was terrible. We felt awful. Not that neither one of us would buy nobody. Amanda just *wouldn't*, though I suspect her daddy's people might've had the money, but I couldn't even keep myself in clothes sufficient to the seasons, much less buy somebody. That's an advantage of being dead. Weather's all the same. Except for snow. Snow's pretty. Not much snow in Richmond. Makes it special.

Sorry. I drift sometimes. The dead do that. Like the snow.

Anyways, we felt terrible for the slaves—me and Amanda—cried together about them, her more than me, me being a man supposedly. I comforted her, and that's where the happy part come in, because we start to kissing, and though she says, "I didn't intend for this to happen!" she didn't leave off kissing me neither.

We read the whole book that way. Reading and kissing and crying about the slaves. Some parts we read over and over. She had plans to teach me to read it myself, but not much took before we got caught. It was a cold, cold day, getting onto Christmas again, so we took a chance on building us a little fire in the woodstove. Somebody saw the smoke. It's hard to say which was worse, the book we was reading, the fact that her clothes was in disarray, or that I was the fellow doing the disarraying. Don't matter. It stopped.

Next thing you know, I'm in the army. I didn't exactly take to it. I had no idea in the world where Amanda was. Eliza and Eva and Tom and all the slaves was tossed into the woodstove and burned up when we was caught, and that upset me mightily. Leastways that fellow Simon LeGree went up with them. I say good riddance to him.

In the army, there was plenty of real slaves around. I started looking at them different.

Officers had slaves. Their daddies and granddaddies had them. That's the way the world turns case you hadn't noticed. Rich folks have everything, and the rest of us have squat. Except here. The dead is all equal as can be. Nobody's got no more of nothing than the next fellow. Look at me. I ain't even got a stone with my name on it, but Segways show up for me.

But back to my story, there was this one particular slave name of Pinkney, and he shined the officers' boots like mirrors. That's what the captain whose slave he was always said, that he wanted to see his face in them, then he'd muddy them up real good, stinking of manure and want to see his face in them again. Kind of made you wish his face was there the whole time for the mud and the manure, maybe put one of those boots up his backside, but Pinkney never let it bother him, even when the captain started bringing round other officers' boots for him to turn into mirrors. Pinkney, he even offered to go around to the officers' tents and pick them up and take them back when he was done, and of course that's the way it worked.

I saw Pinkney walking by with an armload of shiny boots going in and out of the officers' tents, and I had to ask myself why a fellow would do such a thing. It wasn't that hard to figure out. If the captain could've seen past that shiny face in his boot, he would've seen it too. Pinkney was a spy.

When I was a boy and I had a scab—never could leave it alone. No-account in the army as I ever was before, I didn't have a whole lot to do. We was waiting. Didn't know why really. How long. What we was waiting for was another chance to get ourselves killed again. And who wants to think about that? I kept my eye on Pinkney.

The officers met up regular so the general could yell at them some. Crazy fellow, that one. Pinkney always finished buffing the last boot as that meeting was getting started. It don't take but so long to drop a pair of boots inside somebody's tent. He managed to spend the whole meeting time dropping off them boots. I imagined them falling to the ground real slow. I couldn't imagine what he was doing with all that time. He'd be crazy to steal anything. These fellows counted their biscuits from home.

Then one day he was negligent, as Amanda would say in her thrilling voice. The flap wasn't quite closed, and I could see him inside the drunkard Lieutenant's tent reading from his diary.

Pinkney could read.

I didn't read, but nobody'd mind much one way or the other whether I did or not. Slaves was different. Slaves wasn't supposed to read. Never gave it much thought why. There was so many things slaves couldn't do—that was just another. Now it made sense to me. A slave that could read was dangerous. Bet he could write too.

Didn't get a chance to find out. Cause here comes Christmas.

We wasn't that far from Richmond. Don't know where exactly. I spent my first few months in the army liquored up and heartsick over Amanda, and I didn't pay much attention to anything more than what somebody told me to do. I don't read maps any better than I read words. We were hunkered down waiting, days getting shorter and grayer, nights getting longer and colder. Then it was Christmas, so a group of religious ladies showed up with gifts for the soldiers. I got some socks. We sang songs. There was a ham that we fairly well hacked to pieces, like we was practicing for battle. The ladies was mostly preachers' wives and daughters.

One of them was Amanda. We were all standing around singing about the baby Jesus, but I couldn't take my eyes off her. She saw me too. I mean, she really saw me, the way a fellow in love would like to be seen. But she gave me a look that meant not now. You don't meet up in secret for almost a whole year without getting a few looks between you. Don't seem like much. But I miss them looks. Probably should've paid more attention to this one, but eighteen in love ain't much different from seventeen. I followed her when we was all supposed to be marching somewhere to show somebody we could still do it.

She went straight to Pinkney like somebody'd drawn her a map.

I remember when we was crying about the slaves, Amanda saying she wished she could *do* something, that words couldn't change nothing. Looked like she found herself a way. Amanda was a spy too. What she said about words though—that wasn't true. Words changed me. I couldn't read or write them, but I could listen.

Like I said, we didn't go to church much, but sometimes we went Christmases. I always loved that story of the baby Jesus, but you got to remember, right after Kings is praising him they all had to run for their lives to Egypt, and the innocent died for no good reason. That's the way the world turns, in case you hadn't noticed. So it shouldn't come as no surprise to Jesus that after the party with the ham and the wool socks and the songs about Him, things would take a ugly turn.

When I caught up with her and Pinkney, Amanda said she was going back north with the information Pinkney give her. She had no idea she would ever see me again. She couldn't wait. There was a plan. She had to go.

Here's the part I don't understand till this day: I let her go. Told her I loved her, warned her about the sentry, and let her go. Then the captain showed up. He seen me slipping away and wondered what no good I was up to this time.

Pinkney, he started lying real good, but it wasn't working, then there was a shot out by the line where the sentry walked, and I cried out in pain. The captain drew his weapon, a revolver he managed to polish himself and pressed it against my forehead. "Tell me what you know about this, you little cracker pissant, or the next shot's for you."

This being Christmas, and there being ladies present and all, I won't use any vulgar or upsetting language after y'all been kind enough to listen to my story all this while. So I won't say exactly what I said to the captain, except to say it was brief, or describe what happened after he pulled the trigger, except that it was brief too. Oddly quiet.

I always hope the sentry missed and that Amanda and Pinkney got away.

No Segways today. Too cold and raw. You see the fellow rolling through here who does all the talking? Tell him my story. See if he can figure out what I was fighting for. I'd like to hear that.

Lookee here: It's snowing.

Charon

I still smoke cigarettes, right up here to the end, waiting on the last human. So many were dying from smokes there for a while, I thought if I lit one up as we headed for the far shore, it might make them feel at home—or feel the irony.

I have a dark sense of humor, but the joke's on me. They're addictive little fuckers. I've tried to quit for hundreds of years now. I've kept it up long after the last machine-made smokes were smoked, the last grocery store scavenged down to the crumbs, the last bullet fired. As a god, I supply my own demand. It got to be where none of the dead had ever seen a cigarette, but still I kept it up. One more weird thing to deal with when you die.

There I'd be sitting in the prow, oars in my lap, having a smoke as the boat filled. I'd make with the chatter, last words they would hear for a while once we hit the Styx. And then, oblivion. The dead are generally a quiet bunch except for the sobbing and the anguished moans. What's to say? It's over.

No one knows that moment better than me. One second they're alive, knowing it's all over, the next they're looking at my sorry mug. The ferryman. From point A to point B, A being life, and B being death. I'm whatever lies between A and B.

The current's strong. I have to put my back into it, especially when I'm loaded to the gunnels from wars and famines. But lucky for the dead, I'm a burly son of a bitch, built for the job you might say. Anybody tells you Charon is a skinny little fucker has never hauled the dead across Hellish waters for millennia.

Not that it's that busy anymore. Not since the last interstellar mission snuffed out halfway to nowhere has my craft been anywhere near full. Those folks had just about enough time to say "Oh shit!" when there I was. The Mars Colony was never more than a steady trickle, some rich guy's folly. All humans are my responsibility no matter where they go. In the end they didn't get that far. The last humans were, no surprise, stuck on Earth, shithole that it is.

Tell you the truth, I didn't think they'd last this long. Once there was absolutely no hope, you'd think they'd just give it up, but they're stubborn fucks, I'll give them that. Refusing to change, then refusing to die, not understanding, apparently, that only one of those was a choice.

But finally I'm down to the last one—who doesn't even know she's the last. How could she? There could be some rich fuck's paradise under a bubble other side of the world, and she wouldn't know of it except the lying stories that made the rounds when there were other folks to tell. This is The End, as they liked to say at the end of their stories, but this time it's the end of stories altogether.

This one's the last.

I'm one crossing away from being out of work. What the fuck am I going to do? This is all I've ever done.

I asked if I could get a transfer to some other planet of souls needing a ferryman, and I was told all such planets had their own stories, their own psychopomps, and I'd only baffle the dead, who, face it, have enough going on as it is. I have a hunch that's true all over the universe.

Which brings me to the question I've been asking myself since it got down to this last poor soul, the last human, end of the line: Do I tell her? *You're it, sweetheart. It's been real. Been good to know you. Have a nice extinction.*

Too harsh?

Maybe so. I've grown rather fond of humans over the millennia. They peaked just shy of 10 billion before things crashed altogether, one big dying mess. This last woman was *born* in living hell. Death might be a relief. She lived 35 years, something of a record in recent times.

Maybe I shouldn't say anything. Let her go gently into oblivion. It's not her fault her species fucked itself and came close to bringing down the entire biosphere with it. There are a few heat-loving anaerobic bacteria, I'm told, who'll be lurking around after everything else is toast. There's an outside chance that intelligent life *might* evolve again. I was told I'm welcome to wait it out, no guarantees, while the Fates sort it out.

I'd rather dive into the Lethe and be swept away.

My dad, Erebus, was Darkness, my mom, Nyx, was Night—his sister. Gods aren't known for their scruples. They came straight out of Chaos. I've spent my whole life on these shores. Brother Thanatos is Death. I never see him, only his handiwork. I stay clear of sister Nemesis and her troubled daughters who provided no end of woes and stories. Cerberus is not my pet. He's got his job to do, and I've got mine.

I've spent my entire existence with humans. I've ferried them all, dumped every single human memory down that river of forgetfulness. I remember them all, every fucking moment, every fucking soul, the glorious and the wretched. What am I supposed to do with all that when it's over? Reminisce?

And now here it is, the moment I've been waiting for, the demise of Sally, the sole survivor of Shipwreck Earth, who finds herself at last washed up on my shore. She staggers to her feet and looks around.

She looks like shit, naturally. Starved, filthy, scars and wounds and oozing sores from head to toe. Her hair's fallen out in patches. What remains looks burnt and frizzled. She's staring at me intensely.

The dead usually aren't so alert. No wonder she survived so long. I can't tell if she's relieved or heartbroken. Probably in shock. Her body shut down like a cascading blackout, like the ones her mother might remember from her childhood. Sally was born into darkness and worse.

"You must be Sally," I say.

She nods her head. She must not be used to talking much anymore. She's been on her own ever since her husband died a few years ago. Joseph. Nice man. He was on the same crossing with the starship crowd, just by chance far as I know. Whatever forces dictate my manifest, they don't share their criteria with me. If there's a logic to all these deaths, I don't know it. Don't care to. Judgment's not in my job description.

I motion for her to step into the boat, and she does, motion for her to sit, and she does that too. I'm in no hurry to shove off for the last time. I offer her a smoke, and she takes it, watches as I put it in my mouth and follows suit. I light us up, and she takes a deep drag. Given the air she's been breathing the last few years, it must be pristine by comparison.

"Thanks," she murmurs.

"No problem. Did you smoke... before?"

"Read about it. Sounded cool. The things they did." She keeps staring at me, puffing on her smoke. "You're him... the ferry guy."

"Charon. That's right."

"I thought you were just a story."

"Aren't we all? I'm surprised you've even heard of me."

"We holed up in a library basement. We... We read to each other."

We. She still says we after what's a long time for a human, especially these days. Alone. It's touching. The pair bond. Never had the pleasure. These human things never used to touch me, but ever since the end of the species became inevitable, it's been hard to watch them dwindle and die like they'd never been—and feel nothing. Course, if they'd never been, the planet wouldn't be a fucking toxic furnace. But her, this one, this poor woman sitting in my boat had nothing to do with that. She just, her whole life long, paid the price.

She starts, remembering something. "Do I need ... a coin?"

I wave off the idea. "I did away with that nonsense a long time ago. It was always their idea. I'd play along to humor them. If it made them feel better, why not? Money's a human thing. What do I need with coins? I tossed them into the river, made wishes. That used to be a thing." I laugh. "Besides, who has coins anymore?"

She looks at me with polite bewilderment. Her cavernous eyes sweep up and down the deserted shoreline. "Are... Are we waiting on others?" she asks.

"You in a hurry?"

"No... I guess not."

"The answer's no. You're it. The last one. The last human." It just comes out. No wonder. It's all I've been thinking about.

It hits her like a blow, and then she hangs her head, cries from the heart. I've seen my share of human sorrow, but nothing like this. I don't know why I thought to expect anything different. I feel awful. Maybe I should've just kept it to myself.

"We don't have to go straight there," I offer. I seat the oars in their locks and pull, sending us skimming across the water. "Let me show you around."

She bobs her head up and down. Her body trembles with grief. She's tough. Survival of the fittest, as they liked to say. The fittest *feel*. Why live if you don't? She never lived in the glorious times, spent her whole life on the brink of doom, yet she grieves for them just the same, those times when the seeds of all the dreams were planted, nurtured, and harvested without a scrap left behind but this woebegone woman holed up in some moldering library in a backwater town.

I steer us into the swamp, Acheron, and glide silently across the dark waters. Always liked a pleasant swamp float, not that I've had that many opportunities. She looks around at the dead cypress, draped in dead moss, breathes in the rich scents of decay. The water's the color of strong black tea.

"Is everything on Earth dead?" she asks.

I tell her about the anaerobic bacteria, and she nods pensively. I don't talk about their evolutionary chances, though she smiles faintly as if this is good news, or at least more than she hoped for. She trails her battered hands in the chilly waters, and they emerge long and lovely. These waters, it is said, wash away the pains of living.

"Go ahead," I suggest. "Wash yourself. The waters soothe."

She splashes the water on her arms and face and scalp, gasps from the cold, as her wounds wash away, and her hair springs forth like soft moss on the forest floor from a thousand years ago.

"You ferry everyone?" she asks.

"Every human since the beginning of time."

I can't quite keep a touch of pride out of my voice, regretting it immediately. She doesn't need to hear the long sad story. Not so long, actually. Humans have only been around a few hundred thousand years. Life thrived for eons without them. It's incredible how quickly they brought the whole house down.

"I had a daughter," she says. "A couple of years ago. She was born dead. She never got a name. Do—Do you remember her?"

She actually died moments after her birth, four years ago, two weeks after Joseph's death, but I don't contradict the woman who buried them both.

"I remember," I say. "I remember all my passengers."

She nods her head pensively. Her eyes tear up. "Thank you," she says. "Will I see them on the far shore?"

She means her husband and child. I shake my head. "There's nothing there for anyone but oblivion."

In her eyes you can see her imagining her entire life vanishing into nothing, into the chaos humans and their gods all came from.

Maybe this gloomy swamp's not the thing. I steer us toward the glow of the Phlegethon, the river of fire. I'm desperate to cheer her. She's the last human I'll ever see, who'll ever know me, but then, in the Lethe, she'll soon, like all those before her, forget.

"Would you like some coffee?" I ask. I produce a thermos, as if I always carry refreshments for my passengers.

"Coffee? What is that again?" Her face is screwed up trying to recollect what she's never tasted.

"Oh my, you poor dear. Coffee is a beverage beloved by humans. It hadn't been available for quite some time when you were born."

She cocks her head in thought, takes the proffered cup of java and smells it. A damn fine cup of coffee. "I've read about it in novels," she recalls. "The smell is wonderful. They always mention the smell." She sips and smiles a tiny smile. "It's hot," she says. She cradles the cup in her hands and lets the steam waft up into her face looking positively joyful, a look I've rarely seen.

A first for her, perhaps, as well.

She looks up as we approach Phlegethon, and her face is illuminated by the flames. She appears almost serene. She's certainly no stranger to burning rivers, though she would've given them a wide berth to have survived three decades, for the fumes are usually lethal.

These flames before us purge the waters of rage and violence and self-destruction. The vapors are said to cleanse the soul. As we glide into the flowing flames, she gasps with alarm, then bursts into laughter as she breathes deeply of sweet-smelling air, like a field of flowers after a spring rain ages ago, back when there were flowers, back when there was Spring.

Ahead lies the confluence of Lethe and Mnemosyne, the rivers of Forgetfulness and Memory. I'm supposed to let the current carry me down Lethe to the falls of oblivion where my passengers plunge to their end, and I beat my way back to my mooring, remembering their brief lives. The multitudes. We gods are few and live until the end of time; humans live but for a moment, but there were so many, so varied, richer than any god's life. All gone.

Gods needed humans much more than humans ever needed gods. They created us, after all, and now I cannot let them go, not her, not this one.

Instead, I lean hard into the oars and steer the bow toward the tumultuous waters of Mnemosyne. We are buffeted by rapids, doused in spray. There's a strange light here that turns the spray to a mosaic of rainbows, like a million promises hovering in the air. We make our way into the past.

As we enter calmer waters, she beseeches me to take her to the shore. Her face is wet with memories and tears, more than she can manage it seems. We've reached a world she's only known in books, mere words on a page. Now here it is, soaked into her flesh. She remembers the lives of those before her, the life she never got to live. She remembers not being hungry. She remembers hope and innocence.

And now she's trying to control her rage.

We beach upon a pleasant stretch of sand where a young fellow I ferried a century or so ago used to come to swim. She paces up and down, shaking her head in dismay. *They knew*, she says to herself, and I don't contradict. *They knew for* decades *before it was too late. They let us die. They let us* all *die.*

"How far does it go?" she asks me, pointing to the rushing waters.

"Not so very far," I say. "All the way. To the beginning."

"The current looks too strong to row upstream all that way."

"Not for me," I say. "Where is it you wish to go? When would you like to see?"

"Take me to the source, the headwaters. I would know it all."

"To what end?"

"To return to now and begin again."

"Alone?"

"With you," she says. "There's nothing left for you here. And those bacteria you spoke of, in the bowels of the Earth. We could help them, don't you think, get something going, with all that we know?" She looks upstream into the past, seeing all the mistakes that were made, and imagining how things might be different, this time. She's a human alright.

All the other gods have abandoned the place, nothing in it for them. Even Death is done. I could leave her here on this pleasant shore. But I owe humans this much for all the dead I've ferried, a single soul to ferry the other way. Begin again myself.

The fittest feel.

I slide the boat into the water, pull hard against the current, stroke by stroke, back to the beginning with the very last human, and the first.

Publication History

"Here's What I Know" and "Healing Benjamin" originally appeared in *Realms of Fantasy.* Reprinted in *Lightspeed.*

"Leaving the Dead" originally appeared in *Lightspeed.*

"Robot Story" and "Desperate Love" originally appeared in *See the Elephant*.

"Penelope Waits" originally appeared in *Apex Magazine.*

"The Broken Dream Factory" originally appeared in *Lady Churchill's Rosebud Wristlet.*

"The Art Disease" originally appeared in *Electric Velocipede.* Reprinted in *The Best of Electric Velocipede.*

"All the Snake Handlers I Know Are Dead," "Adult Children of Alien Beings," "Orphan Pirates of the Spanish Main," and "Once More into the Abyss" originally appeared in *Tor.com.*

"Swan Song and Then Some" originally appeared in *Nightmare Carnival.* Ed. Ellen Datlow.

"Christmas in Hollywood Cemetery" originally appeared in *Remapping Richmond's Hallowed Ground.* Ed. Martha Erwin.

"Rats, Mazes, Snakes, Magic," "Memories Are Made of This," "The Puppy Strangler," and "Charon" appear here for the first time.

About the Author

Dennis Danvers is the author of the critically acclaimed novels *Circuit of Heaven*, *Wilderness*, and *Time and Time Again*. He lives in Richmond, Virginia.

Now Available!

DENNIS DANVERS

SUSPENSE / THRILLERS

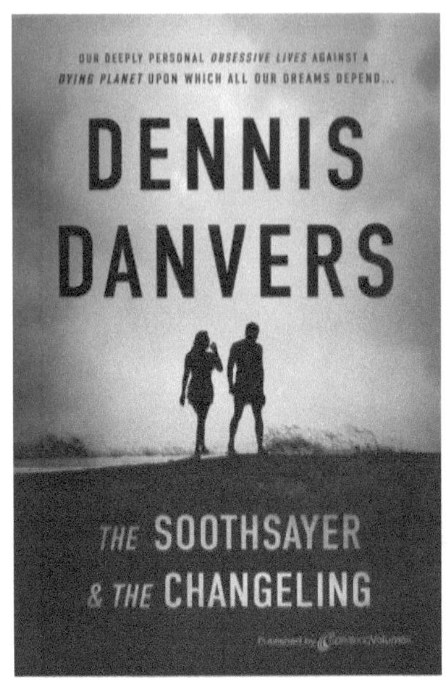

www.ingramcontent.com/pod-product-compliance
Lightning Source LLC
LaVergne TN
LVHW091025080826
845145LV00002B/356

* 9 7 8 1 6 4 5 4 0 9 4 3 4 *